The cigarette w............................e reached his truck, but he crushed it out anyway—he hated the odor of stale smoke in the cab the next day—and climbed up into the seat. Backed out so fast he almost nicked the bumper of the black Camaro behind him. Angrier than he'd realized maybe. An evening wasted that he could've spent at home with Shawn. Or—get honest—waiting by the phone in case *she* called.

He turned south out of the lot onto Sweetwater Road and headed toward South Bay Parkway, driving well over the speed limit. When he rounded a curve, he heard something banging around in the back of the truck. One of his guys must have left a tool belt back there, he figured, although his men weren't usually that careless—a loose tool belt would scrape the hell out of the metal. He slowed down to let the cars behind him pass and pulled off onto the shoulder. Taking a flashlight out of the glove compartment, he got out and walked to the back, aiming the flashlight beam into the truck bed.

And realized, with a sickening sense of disbelief, that it wasn't a tool belt making the racket.

Up till then he'd thought nothing could get his mind off Noel. He'd been wrong. The sight of Barry Bischoff's body cumpled in the back of his pickup truck wiped her clear out of his mind. . . .

Nailed
by Lucy Taylor

only half-spoiled when I

NAILED

Lucy Taylor

AN ONYX BOOK

ONYX
Published by New American Library, a division of
Penguin Putnam Inc., 375 Hudson Street,
New York, New York 10014, U.S.A.
Penguin Books Ltd, 27 Wrights Lane,
London W8 5TZ, England
Penguin Books Australia Ltd, Ringwood,
Victoria, Australia
Penguin Books Canada Ltd, 10 Alcorn Avenue,
Toronto, Ontario, Canada M4V 3B2
Penguin Books (N.Z.) Ltd, 182–190 Wairau Road,
Auckland 10, New Zealand

Penguin Books Ltd, Registered Offices:
Harmondsworth, Middlesex, England

First published by Onyx, an imprint of New American Library,
a division of Penguin Putnam Inc.

First Printing, July 2001
10 9 8 7 6 5 4 3 2 1

REGISTERED TRADEMARK—MARCA REGISTRADA

Printed in the United States of America

PUBLISHER'S NOTE
This is a work of fiction. Names, characters, places, and incidents either
are the product of the author's imagination or are used fictitiously,
and any resemblance to actual persons, living or dead, business
establishments, events, or locales is entirely coincidental.

For Don

Chapter One

Sitting at the bar of the Yellow Rose while he waited for his office manager to show up, Matt Engstrom found himself obsessing about Noel. Missing her, hating her, going over every word of her goddamn phone call and coming up with scenarios terrifying enough to drive any man to drink—chief among them the one where he never saw or heard from her again.

Hell, he thought, as he hoisted his third Diet Coke of the evening, *at least things can't get any worse.*

Then he remembered how desperate she'd sounded that night on the phone and wondered if such optimism wasn't wishful thinking on his part.

Matt? Matt, are you asleep?

The call had woke him just after one a.m. At first, he'd thought he was dreaming. It wouldn't, after all, be the first time in recent weeks that a dream about Noel had awakened him with all the subtlety of a backhoe thundering through the wall of his bedroom. Then, as his mind cleared, he had realized he was holding the phone in his hand and that it really *was* her talking. That lush voice that turned slurry and syrupy once she got a few shots of Jose Cuervo under her belt. Now fear added little serrated teeth to her consonants, and an undercurrent of dread permeated the silence between her words.

Instantly he was wide awake, sitting bolt upright in bed. "Noel, what is it? What's wrong?"

"Oh, Matt, I've been trying to call you but—I'm so afraid you're going to hate me."

"Where *are* you? Jesus, I tried calling you so many times. What the hell happened? You just gave up your apartment, quit your job! Just disappeared!"

"I know, I know. I'm sorry."

"*Sorry!* That's it, sorry?" Suddenly he didn't give a damn what she'd called to say, he just wanted to unload his anger on her, vent his rage. "How could you *do* that to me? If you needed to take some time off, you could have *asked*, dammit. You could have *explained*."

"I left you a *note*, didn't I?"

"Yeah, right. The note: 'Dear Matt, Go fuck yourself.' "

"I didn't write anything like that."

"Yeah, well, I may not be a genius, but I can read between the lines."

"Please, Matt, don't shout."

"What was it, you found another guy? A better fuck?"

She started to sob. He liked the sound. Hated himself for liking it.

"No, Matt, there wasn't another man. There isn't."

"Where are you? Are you at a bar?"

"Outside one. There's a phone booth—"

"Where? I'll come get you."

"No, that wouldn't be a good idea."

"Why not? What's wrong?"

"We've got to talk."

"Damn right we do."

"No, I mean—we've got—a situation." Her voice changed. She was still crying, but now she sounded rehearsed, stiff, like she was saying words she'd practiced earlier before a mirror, struggling to get the correct pitch, the right inflection of woe. "There's something—oh, Matt, I've been trying to get the nerve up to call you for I don't know how long, and oh, fuck, I know I've got to tell you what's wrong, but you've always been so good to me, and I don't want—"

Her words got sloppy, and he knew she was drunk. Probably high, too. *Oh, Jesus, Noel. You promised me you were going to clean up your act.*

"What is it, Noel? Talk to me!"

"Oh, God, Matt, how did things get so screwed up? I pick up the phone and dial your number, and then hang up before it can ring. Again and again. I need to tell you . . . it's something important . . . but I don't . . . I mean, it's . . ."

"*What*, Noel? Are you pregnant? Is that it?"

Her crying turned to racking, gut-wrenched sobs.

"Oh, Matt, I just want it to be like it used to be. I just want to curl up in your arms and have everything go back the way it *was*."

"Noel, please, listen to me. Calm down. I'm sorry I yelled at you. Just take a deep breath, will you do that for me? Another one, good. Close your eyes. Pretend we're on the bike, headed up into the hills. It's sunrise and there's nobody else on the road, and we're flying—we're doing a hundred miles an hour, a hundred and ten—just like you love it. You're holding on to me and we're just a blur, and the roar of the motor—it's so loud you can feel it all the way down to your bones. It's just us, Noel, you and me and the Harley all alone in creation, and you're holding on to me and I've got you, I've got you, we're never going back. Close your eyes and see it. Take a deep breath and listen to the motor. There, there, that's it. Now, slowly, calmly, talk to me, honey. Tell me where you are and what's going on."

In the past, when she was depressed or upset, he'd been able to help her out of the bad mood by getting her out on the bike. Something about the speed, the noise, the power of the Harley and the loop of erotic energy that seemed to envelop them when they were on the road transfixed them both. If she had ever loved him, he suspected it was not when they were making love, but when they were flying down the road on the Harley.

Now her crying softened into low, gasping sobs. "Oh, Matt, I don't know how to tell you this, but—"

"Please, Noel, whatever it is can't be that bad. Talk to me. *Try*."

"Oh, God, Matt. If only you were a bastard, but you're such a good guy. I *know* you don't deserve this. I don't care what anybody says I have to do, I just *know*. Fuck, I don't care—I can't do this. I'm so sorry, Matt. I just *can't*."

"Wait, Noel, what are you talking about? No, please, Noel, don't hang up!"

But she did.

Leaving him sitting there in the bed, stunned and shaken, with no way to contact her, no one to call who might know where she was, what she was doing. *I don't care what anybody says I have to do.* He'd stayed awake the rest of the night, trying to guess what she'd meant by that, praying she'd call back and growing, by turns, more angry and more despondent when morning came, and still he hadn't heard from her.

Now, over a week later, he was still playing the conversation over in his head. Wondering where the hell she was and when—if ever—she'd contact him again. Wondering what was wrong and what the hell it was she didn't think he deserved to have happen to him.

He drained the last of his diet soda, half-melted ice cubes clunking against his front teeth, and glanced toward the cherry-wood French doors with their big ovals of frosted, gray-tinted glass. Impatient for Barry to walk through them and get this meeting over with, so he could go home.

"What'sa matter, suguh, you been stood up?"

The bartender, a brunette with an inch of tattooed cleavage pressing up above the neckline of her pearl-buttoned, pink satin blouse, eyed him appreciatively.

Matt shrugged and managed a smile. "Looks like it."

The woman pursed cherry lips and made a tsk, tsk

sound. "If you was *my* fella, I wouldn't leave you sit-
tin' here, coolin' your heels. Some other gal just might
snap you up." She poured a clear stream of Smirnoff
into a blender full of some frosty concoction the color
of a Caribbean sunset.

Matt tried to feel flattered.

"Actually, I'm being stood up by a guy." He realized how that might sound to her. "A friend, I mean.
Guy who works for me. Some business to discuss."

She added rum to the mix in the blender and let
him babble away. "What business you in?"

"Construction."

"Yeah, you look like you do construction." She
made a show of sizing up his biceps and chest. "I'll
bet you work a forklift or a crane. You look like a
guy who knows how to operate heavy equipment."

"I did my share of that. Now I own my own
company."

"Now, that's a sweet deal," she purred. "Do your
own hirin' and firin', be your own boss—never have
to go home and bitch to the wife about that asshole
who's bustin' your chops."

If she was fishing to find out if he was married, Matt
didn't bite.

When he let the conversation falter, she added a
wedge of lemon to the rim of a highball glass and
slung a fresh soda in front of him. In spite of himself,
he couldn't help but notice that every time she handed
him a drink, it looked like another pearl button on
that blouse had come open.

She tilted her head, and gave him a sly glance. "All
those sodas—hitting it pretty hard tonight, aren't
you?"

"I gave up booze for Lent."

She blinked, looking as if she was trying to decide
whether to take him seriously, then laughed. "I'm not
Catholic or anything, but I do know Lent was back
last spring and this is June. What is it, you on the
wagon?"

"Something like that."

The woman tossed her mane of dark brown hair and leaned over the bar, resting her substantial breasts on the polished surface. From habit, Matt took a long look. Felt nothing. Found himself wondering if Shawn was doing his homework or glued in front of the TV watching people performing sex acts Matt hadn't known about until he was almost through high school.

"I can't imagine not drinking. How do you have fun?"

"I gave up fun," said Matt dourly.

Her dark eyes twinkled impishly. "For Lent?"

"For good."

She gave him a quizzical smile. "You're joking, aren't you?"

He shrugged. "Honey, I'm not sure if I know myself."

Her smile lost some of its wattage.

A couple of studly young guys in tight jeans, cowboy boots, and embroidered shirts that he figured were the masculine version of what the bartender had on were all but crawling onto the bar to get her attention. She didn't seem sorry to leave Matt to his diet drink and bad mood.

He glanced at his watch. At Barry's insistence, he'd agreed to meet with him here at eight. Now it was almost eight-forty. Unusual for Barry, who was unfailingly punctual. And whatever his office manager had wanted to discuss, he'd made it sound urgent over the phone. *Ten more minutes*, Matt thought, *and I'm out of here.*

He got up off the bar stool, which was immediately taken by a heavyset girl in a frilly ankle-length skirt and tooled red leather boots, and went back to the pay phone he'd used earlier, located in an alcove just past the rest rooms. At the moment it was being used by a lanky blond boy who, from the snippets Matt got of the conversation, was trying to convince someone named Flo to come give him a ride home. He stood there for several minutes, clearing his throat occasionally in case the kid didn't notice he was waiting, but the conversation dragged on, veering into more intimate territory as the boy tried to persuade Flo to let him spend the night at her place.

Matt used the rest room, checked on the phone again, then went outside to stave off the headache he could feel insinuating its way into his frontal lobe. He was glad that the sun had gone down. It was cooler now and a soft, purple-tinged darkness blurred the edges of the vehicles in the parking lot. He kept imagining Barry walking toward him, apologizing for the delay, then the two of them going inside, finding a table away from the general hubbub, where they could discuss whatever it was Barry thought was so important and so private it couldn't be dealt with at the office.

Five minutes later, when he went back inside, the kid was still jawing. Matt was ready to yank him bodily away from the phone, when he shouted, "Well, fuck you, too, Flo! I'll find somebody else!" slammed the phone down, and hauled ass for the door.

Matt figured this was Flo's lucky night.

He called Barry's apartment again, got no answer, then hung up and used the quarter to call home.

Shawn's sitter Maria answered the phone. No messages, she told him, between crunches of what sounded like popcorn. Shawn came on the upstairs extension.

"When you coming home, Dad?"

"Soon, buddy. Looks like Barry's pulled a no-show. If he's not here in ten more minutes, I'm heading home."

He dug another quarter out of his pocket and dialed his office, expecting to get the answering machine. Phil Rollins, his accountant, picked up the phone. Phil was a late sleeper who often straggled into the office in the afternoon, but made up for it by frequently working nights. He told Matt there'd been no phone calls except one from a client who had discovered a minuscule crack in his marble countertop and was demanding that the entire four-thousand-dollar slab be replaced.

"I told him that's how marble is," said Phil, "it *cracks*—ask the ancient Romans, that's what gives marble its character—but I don't think he bought it."

"I'll tell the crew to wait till he's out of the house and just flip the damn slab over," Matt said, wishing everything could be that simple.

"Hey, that's the bad news," Phil said. "The good news is I just heard on the news that Detroit beat Edmonton 3–2. Andre Vykos scored the winning goal."

"Terrific. Sounds like the Red Wings are on the way to the Stanley Cup."

"Thanks to Vykos. That guy's incredible."

With even a little encouragement, Matt knew Phil would fill him in on the game play by play. An avid ice hockey fan, Phil had Detroit picked for this year's Stanley Cup winner and had, Matt gathered, placed a hefty bet on the outcome.

In the background he heard a Betty Boop-ish voice that he recognized as Phil's girlfriend Paula. She sounded about the right age to go on a movie date with Shawn, but Phil had told him she worked for a prestigious interior design firm. Go figure.

"Hot date at the office?"

He could almost feel the heat from Phil's cheeks radiating out of the phone. "I'm just showing Paula some stuff on the computer. Hope you don't mind."

"Long as what you show her is on the computer, not on top of it."

Phil's laugh sounded forced.

Matt hung up, found an unoccupied table, and positioned his chair so he could keep an eye on the door. A scuffle broke out at the bar between two beer swillers with matching string ties and big bellies, and he watched this with a kind of grim enjoyment, feeling mildly guilty about being entertained by the sight of other men acting like jerks.

A few minutes later, when the band started to rev up for another set, he said to hell with Barry's "urgent dilemma," whatever it was, and left.

Navigating his way through the packed parking lot,

the humidity of the San Diego summer enveloped him. He could smell honeysuckle and beer and the lingering freshness of a summer shower earlier in the day.

The parking lot at the Rose was big enough to accommodate the crowd at a Super Bowl, so it took him a few minutes to locate his black 4X4, during which he counteracted any salubrious effects of the clean night air by lighting up a cigarette. Shawn wouldn't have approved, but then Shawn didn't have to know Matt had recently picked up his first smoke in almost a year and that, in his heart of hearts, he still believed in a man's God-given right to expire from lung cancer.

The cigarette was only half smoked when he reached his truck, but he crushed it out anyway—he hated the odor of stale smoke in the cab the next day—and climbed up into the seat. Backed out so fast he almost nicked the bumper of the black Camaro behind him. Angrier than he'd realized maybe. An evening wasted that he could've spent at home with Shawn. Or—get honest—waiting by the phone in case *she* called.

He turned south out of the lot onto Sweetwater Road and headed toward South Bay Parkway, driving well over the speed limit. When he rounded a curve, he heard something banging around in the back of the truck. One of his guys must have left a tool belt back there, he figured, although his men weren't usually that careless—a loose tool belt would scrape the hell out of the metal. He slowed down to let the cars behind him pass and pulled off onto the shoulder. Taking a flashlight out of the glove compartment, he got out and walked to the back, aiming the flashlight beam into the truck bed.

And realized, with a sickening sense of disbelief, that it wasn't a tool belt making the racket.

Up till then, he'd thought nothing could get his mind off Noel. He'd been wrong. The sight of Barry Bischoff's body crumpled in the back of his pickup truck wiped her clear out of his mind.

Chapter Two

You killed him, didn't you?

The words dug into his temples like fists.

Killed him in cold blood.

Matt paced to the end of the narrow, bleak little room, paused to take a deep breath, and slammed his fist into the wall. Pain launched itself from his knuckles, rocketed into his wrist, and chainsawed into his elbow. For a second he saw white, throbbing stars. When the pain receded from incapacitating to barely manageable, he started pacing again.

After he made the 9-1-1 call on his cell phone, enough squad cars had converged on his truck to deal with a riot. Two cops had interviewed him on the scene, then driven him over to the Rose so he could try to pinpoint, without much conviction, the exact place where his truck had been parked when Barry's body was placed in it.

Assuming, of course, that he was telling the truth, that he hadn't murdered Barry elsewhere and then, driven by some bizarre urge to ease the tension of having just committed murder with some good ol' foot-stomping country music, detoured to the Rose with Barry's corpse thumping around in his truck. The blood that he'd got on his hands and clothes when he turned Barry over to see if he was still alive hadn't helped convince the cops of his innocence, either. Nor had they been particularly happy when they ran his name through the computer and found out he had a record.

He hadn't been arrested yet—technically he was "being detained"—but the cops had cuffed him and brought him to the police station, where he'd called home to ask Maria if she could spend the night with Shawn. When Shawn came on the line, Matt had stretched the truth by saying he'd been a witness to a crime. He was going to have to stay at the police station to answer some questions. It might take all night. Shawn sounded scared, but Matt tried to reassure him.

Then he'd called his foreman, Coop McDonald, and asked him to swing by the house and pick Shawn up the next morning. Shawn's summer job was working with Coop at the Bledsoe-Tull job site, where Engstrom Construction was building an office complex and parking garage. Coop had sounded a little bleary, like Matt had caught him well into the second sixpack, but said he'd be happy to do it.

Lastly, he'd called his lawyer, Alex Devereaux, and left messages at his home and office.

Then there was nothing left to do—except wait.

Matt knew that most police stations had two different interview rooms—a "soft room" with nice furniture and low lighting for those suspects the cops wanted to feel somewhat at ease, a "hard" one for those they liked to watch squirm.

Not tough to guess which one he was cooling his heels in right now. It was stuffy and lit up like an operating room, the scent of Lysol competing with that of stale cigarettes and stress-induced sweat. The decor consisted of a table with a dirty black plastic ashtray in the center. And four straight-backed chairs. Cheap stucco walls that had once been painted lime green, but were now faded to the shade of old algae.

The door opened and two detectives stepped in. The younger one, trim and athletic-looking, wore a tan sport coat and an expression so bland it suggested facial muscles in a state of partial paralysis. Only one eyebrow, canted askew, hinted at pique or perplexity. His heavily lidded eyes were baby blue and viper sharp and swept over Matt like wind off a glacier. Matt thought he looked like a doctor whose golf game was just interrupted by somebody inconsiderate enough to be having a heart attack at the ninth hole.

"Detective Mulholland," he said, extending a muscular hand.

Matt returned the handshake, but his gaze kept straying to the second man, a graying tub of gelatinous flesh who grabbed a chair next to his partner, turned it around, and straddled it. He was holding a bag of peanut M&M's, which he munched with the methodical torpor of a lizard crunching beetles. When Matt's eyes met his, a disgusted smirk curled his lip.

In the nine years since Matt had last seen him, time had carved up Pete Uhlenkamp's face like a relief map of west Texas, all cracked, dried-up arroyos and flat, sand-bitten plains. What remained of his dark hair was now graying and thin and combed in greasy wisps over his bald spot. He didn't offer to shake hands, but then Matt wouldn't have expected him to.

Mulholland pulled out a spiral notebook and pen. He said in a surprisingly mellifluous voice, "Tell us again, Mr. Engstrom, where you were tonight."

"That is, *before* your buddy's dead body materialized in the back of your pickup," Uhlenkamp added.

Matt repeated his story. When he finished, the only sound was Uhlenkamp's resolute crunching.

"Was it your idea or Barry's to meet at the Yellow Rose?" Mulholland asked.

"Barry's."

"Do you go there a lot?"

"This was the first time."

"What about Barry?"

"I think he went there from time to time."

"Have much to drink?"

"I don't drink. I had diet sodas. Ask the bartender."

"We did," Mulholland said. "You told us Barry wanted to talk to you about something. What was it?"

"I don't know."

"Any ideas?"

"None whatsoever."

"But Barry was your office manager, right? So wouldn't there have been plenty of chances to talk during the day? Over lunch, at the coffee machine?"

"Some days, yes. Some days, no. We've got four different projects going right now, one of them a parking garage and office complex going up next to the Bledsoe-Tull high-rise. Lots of days, I'm out in the field at one job site, Barry might be at another. It's not unusual for a whole day to go by and the only time I talk to Barry is over my car phone."

"You and Barry socialize as a general rule?"

"Rarely ever."

"Except for last night, when you say he asks you to meet him. You didn't ask him what for?"

"I thought maybe he was having some kind of personal problem. Either that, or he'd found another job and he was going to tell me he had to move on."

"You got a temper, Matt?"

"No more than the next guy."

Uhlenkamp made a sound that was part guffaw, part disdainful snicker.

Mulholland studied him. "What happened to your hand?"

Matt looked down, saw the bruised flesh and the blood on his knuckles. Not exactly testimony to his levelheadedness. "I punched the wall, all right? Something that, given the circumstances, I think anybody might do."

Uhlenkamp's tiny bright eyes drilled him. "Anybody given to murderous rages."

If I were prone to murderous rages, I'd have my hands around your fat neck right now, Matt thought. He said, "I didn't kill Barry. I've got no idea who did or why they wanted to frame me. Maybe you should ask Barry's friends. Maybe he had enemies."

"We're checking into that," said Mulholland. "Tell

us again how you got Bischoff's blood on your hand and your shirt cuffs."

"When I saw him lying there, I jumped into the truck bed and turned him over to check for a pulse. Maybe it was a dumb thing to do in terms of incriminating myself, but I had to see if he was still alive."

Uhlenkamp poured another handful of M&M's out of the package. He picked up a blue one and stared at it. "Never cared for blue food. Had blue ice cream one time. Made me nauseous. Doesn't seem natural—blue food."

"So from a few minutes before eight until five or ten minutes after nine, you were inside the Yellow Rose," said Mulholland. "At the bar all that time. Right?"

"I got up to use the phone a couple of times."

"Bartender says you left the bar for at least fifteen minutes, and we can't find anybody says they saw you during that period."

Matt thought about the kid arguing with Flo, about his stroll outside. "I went outside for a couple of minutes, that's all."

"Just a couple?"

"Maybe more. There was a guy hogging the phone, but I didn't want to go to my truck to get my cell phone 'cause then I might have missed Barry. So I hung around outside near the door."

Mulholland folded his arms, the expression on his face suggesting he'd heard all this before and was wishing that, if the criminals of the world couldn't stop their wicked ways, they could at least come up with more creative alibis.

Uhlenkamp said, "What was it, Engstrom? Did Barry do something to piss you off? Don't tell me—maybe it was a setup. Maybe he crawled into your truck and sliced his own throat just to make you look bad?"

Mulholland's eyebrow creased slightly. "What?"

"An interesting story. Remind me to tell you 'bout it sometime." He leaned forward, eyes glinting with bemused malice. "What is it, Engstrom, you like prison so much, you can't wait to go back? C'mon, admit it. You and your buddy had a falling out, so you lost your temper and killed him. Then you decided to call the cops and act all upset that there's a corpse in the back of your pickup truck."

"I don't think I'm going to say anything else till I've talked to my lawyer," Matt said.

Mulholland looked weary. "Suit yourself," he said, "but that fifteen or twenty minutes when you weren't at the bar and nobody else seems to have seen you— that was plenty of time to meet Barry outside and kill him. And his blood *was* all over your hands."

"You know what that means, Engstrom," Uhlenkamp said with an undercurrent of glee in his voice. "We gotta arrest you."

The laws of physics changed when you were inside a cell, Matt had discovered. Time, for example, slowed to a fraction of its normal speed so that a day spent locked up passed at the pace of a week, a year equaled a decade. Nor had this principle changed, he discovered as he lay on his cot. The hours until dawn seemed to stretch into a lifetime. Sleep was impossible. He kept thinking about Shawn. What would he think when he woke up and found Matt hadn't come home last night? When he found out *why* he hadn't come home?

Vividly, he remembered the last time he'd been locked up. Having to call Calla and tell her what had happened and where he was. What he'd done. Hardest phone call he'd ever had to make. He could still hear the agonized hitch in her voice as she asked, "Oh, God, Matt, what's happened? What have you done?"

And Shawn, just a toddler then, but able to pick up on the anguish and rage in his mother's voice, screaming in the background.

"What have you done to Shawn and me?" she'd shouted into the phone. "What have you *done* to us?"

But, of course, in all his grand self-preoccupation,

he'd never thought about it as anything he'd done to
his family. About the reality that the wives and children of men who got sent away to prison went to
prison, too. About how they got sucked right into the
same system that had swallowed their men—the ap-
peals and the lawyers, the d.o.c. caseworkers funneling
too many felons toward too few halfway houses, about
the grim little rooms where, if you were up to it, you
got fifteen or twenty minutes—no contact allowed—
with your loved one every week or so.

Prison had changed him, of course, but he honestly
felt it had changed him for the better. He thought now
before he acted. Walked away from fights and avoided
the guys who were dumb enough to think they could
break the law on a regular basis and come out on top.
He no longer saw himself as the center of the universe—or if he did, at least it was only *part* of the
time.

Helluvit was, four years of prison had changed
Calla, too. She'd never promised that she'd wait for
him. That rose-tinted fantasy was something he'd
come up with on his own. Yet still the idea that she
was seeing other men was so unbearable that he
hadn't allowed himself to think it. No, blind trust
seemed better, if the alternative—imagining the sighs
and sweat and friction of rigorous and raunchy sex, of
vivid visions of Calla in all her resplendent lustful-
ness—was to sink into a pit of black despair and howl-
ing anguish from which no promises of freedom to
come could ever resurrect him.

Yet when he got out of prison, she was a different
woman, just as he was a different man. They'd made
love a few times—for old time's sake—and though
their bodies still responded, she was worlds away and
lifetimes gone. Not long after, when she said she
wanted a divorce, there was no rancor to it, no bitterness or malice, but only a strange numbness, as though
in his absence something had been cored out of her
and she was either powerless to search for it again or
simply unwilling to try.

At that point he should have realized that he'd lost her and gone on to rebuild his life, but he wasn't willing, wasn't able to let her go. Working eighteen-hour days while he tried to get his business on its feet helped keep his mind off the feelings of guilt and failure. Booze helped, too, at least for a while. When he wasn't working, he was at a bar, hoisting a few with his crew. Sometimes he combined the two. Occasionally—when his body couldn't stand it any long—he slept.

And then, when he'd actually thought things might be warming up a bit between him and Calla, he'd heard from her lawyer. The divorce papers were ready to be signed, a time and place set up to do the deed.

He remembered scribbling his name on the appropriate documents, then saying he had business to attend to, and storming out. He remembered Calla sitting between the two lawyers, wearing a dove-gray suit he'd never seen before—expensive, tailored, the kind of thing some high-powered lady real estate agent would wear to a closing—making a great show of not looking at him.

That was the last time he saw her alive. Two nights later, sometime in the wee hours of a February morning that Matt spent drinking alone, that Shawn spent sleeping over at his grandfather's, someone murdered Calla and dumped her body off on a stretch of desert road outside Borrego Springs.

After his years in prison, Matt had thought nothing could touch him again, but the pain of losing Calla had made that period of his life seem like a trip to Disneyland.

"Engstrom?"

He was awake, still sifting restlessly through the wreckage of his past, wondering how his life could have taken this new and dreadful turn, when a guard unlocked his cell and took him upstairs to a visiting area that was plush by comparison to the interview room he'd been in the night before. After a brief wait, the door opened and Alex Devereaux's hulking frame blocked the doorway. Matt hadn't seen Devereaux look this stressed and haggard since the two of them met four years ago, right after Calla's murder, at a support group for people who had lost loved ones to violent crime. Alex, new to San Diego, had just lost his younger brother back in Des Moines to a convenience-store robber with an AK-47. Although neither had found what they were looking for in the support group, the two became friends.

"How you holding up, Matt?" said Devereaux, taking a seat. He wore a gray pinstriped suit, a burgundy tie and a look of grim trepidation that Matt did not find encouraging. With his coarse features and slicked-back black hair, Matt thought that, in spite of the expensive suit and Gucci shoes, his friend still looked like a street thug dressed up for Mass.

Devereaux plopped down into a chair, took out a handkerchief, and mopped the copious sweat off his forehead. Of the two of them, Matt thought his lawyer buddy looked guiltier than he did. And probably was guiltier. Of something anyway.

"Not one of my better days, Alex."

"I looked over the police report. I just need to ask you one thing. Did you kill this guy?"

"Jesus, Alex, of course I didn't. And if you think I did, then I need to find another lawyer."

"Sorry, Matt. I'm your friend, but I'm also acting as your lawyer. I had to ask."

"I thought lawyers didn't give a shit about that guilt or innocence crap? Look, I can't stay here. I've got a son to take care of and a business to run. Can I bond out? What's gonna happen?"

"Two o'clock," said Devereaux, "you'll go before the judge for the arraignment. Just a formality. Shouldn't take more than a few minutes. The judge will set bond, and if you can pay it, you can walk out of here a free man—well, semi-free anyway—this afternoon."

"How much do you think it'll be?"

"Hard to say. Fifty, sixty—maybe more."

Matt felt the muscles in his belly spasm like he'd

just taken a punch to the liver. "Jesus, I'll never be able to come up with that kind of money."

Devereaux steepled thick fingers. "Maybe this is none of my business, but don't you have other resources?"

"Investments, you mean?"

"More personal."

"I'm not following you."

"Calla—her last name was DeGrove, wasn't it? Of the DeGrove Hotel chain? I thought maybe your father-in-law would be willing to help you out."

"Forget it, Alex. Out of the question."

"You're not on good terms?"

"Fair terms, I'd say, although he always made it clear he didn't think I was good enough for Calla. The only time I even see the old man now is when I take Shawn to visit. I'd never ask him for that kind of money. Alex, you gotta get the judge to set a lower bond."

"I'll do my best, but it won't be simple. You gotta see it the way the law does, Matt. Bischoff's body was found in your pickup truck; you had his blood on your hands."

"I explained to the police I turned him over to see if he was alive."

"I hate to say it, but—"

"I didn't kill him, Alex."

"—from the cops' point of view, you look guilty as hell."

"Thanks for the pep talk. I feel inspired. Now, can we get down to business?"

"Right, Matt. Tell me what happened."

Matt lit a cigarette and repeated the story of the previous night, trying to account minute by minute for the time he'd spent away from the bar. When he finished, Devereaux said, "We'll have to see what forensics comes up with when they autopsy the body. Find out, for one thing, if Bischoff was killed in the parking lot and dumped in your truck, or killed elsewhere and brought to the Rose."

"By someone who knew that I'd be there waiting for Barry."

"Maybe. But for all we know, Bischoff recognized your vehicle and walked over there for some reason—maybe gonna leave you a note under the windshield, maybe knew he was being pursued and was looking for help, who knows—and that was when he got whacked. Your truck just happened to be convenient for the killer."

Matt snorted his disbelief at that scenario.

"Look, forensics will come up with something—hair fiber or bits of skin under the nails that'll prove somebody else did this. Plus, maybe they'll find the murder weapon."

"The knife, you mean?"

"Not a knife."

"But there was so much blood. I thought his throat was cut."

"It was. Guy used a razor blade. Cops said it looked like he was surprised from behind. Whoever killed him was strong as hell, almost took his head off."

"Jesus. Was it robbery?"

"Not hardly. He still had his wallet on him with over a hundred in cash."

"I just don't get it. Who would do this to Barry? He was a great guy."

"Well, somebody didn't think so. Now, all we have to do is prove that somebody wasn't you."

"I've got to get out of here, Alex. Do me a favor, would you, call my office and talk to Phil, my accountant. I've called a couple of times already, but he's not in yet. Maybe he can call in some favors from a few subcontractors who might be willing to wait for their money a little longer."

Devereaux nodded. "I'll get to work on it. Anything else I can do? You got somebody to look after Shawn?"

"He's hanging out with my foreman Coop today, and the sitter agreed to come back again tonight if I'm not out by then—God, Alex, this can't be happening. I didn't have anything to do with Barry's death."

"I believe you, Matt. Except—is there something you haven't told me? That smug bastard Uhlenkamp made some remarks as I was coming in. I get the impression he knows something I don't."

Matt had figured this was coming. He'd just hoped it might not be this soon. "He does, Alex. I never told you this—I mean, hell, I never felt like there was any reason to. It's not something I talk about to anybody really, but—I was in some trouble before. Eight years ago, I did four years in Pelican Bay State Prison. A guy name of Harold Petrovsky. I killed him."

Chapter Three

Around dawn, Miranda Watley floated out of the peach-colored guest bedroom in Howie DeGrove's sprawling San Diego mansion, looking like she'd just had a week of pampering at some outrageously expensive spa. Her tanned skin glowed, her normally subdued hazel eyes danced with sparkly new shades of lapis and jade. She glided into the spacious kitchen with none of the tension and nervousness that had knit her muscles into tight little bundles the night before.

Had anyone suggested to Miranda that this ebullience was the result of exceptionally great sex, she would have rolled her eyes and laughed. To Miranda, sex was no different than nursing or real estate or any other paying position she'd held over the years—granted, you had to put a lot more time and money into upkeep, but compared to a regular job, the hours were great. And since sex as a sport wasn't something she relished, her two previous marriages all had followed a long string of *no* and *no* and *do you understand the meaning of the word no?*

Over the four months of their courtship, Howie had made a show of impatience, done the snorting stallion routine, but deep down, she knew that he respected her insistence that sex could only follow marriage. A true endangered species among his gender, Howie had a streak of the old-fashioned, a bent toward chivalry, however sexist, that might flower into something truly marvelous given a little judicious thwarting of his libido.

Last night, Miranda's virtue had paid off. Howie had offered a proposal with all the trimmings—elegant, candlelit restaurant, serenading violinists, the little velvet-lined box containing a heart-stoppingly beautiful engagement ring. Not a diamond—everyone had diamonds—but a square-cut ruby the size of a grape.

Best of all, Miranda felt she might be capable of genuinely loving Howie. What had admittedly begun as an infatuation with his status as a retired, childless multimillionaire had developed into a fondness for the man himself.

And so, thinking herself on the verge of falling in love for the first time in her life, Miranda hummed to herself, enjoying the solitude in this opulent house that one day soon would be hers.

In one of the polished cherry-wood cabinets, she discovered a selection of imported coffees and selected one of the little foil-wrapped packets with a name that sounded more like an exotic honeymoon destination than a morning caffeine fix. She emptied it into the filter, savoring the rich fragrance, then switched on the coffeemaker, and went to get a mug from the shelf above the gleaming, stainless-steel stove. A trio of arched windows next to the breakfast nook admitted the first morning light. From here, she could look down on a terrace with a Japanese garden, artfully raked stones swirling like smooth gray water around small shrubs and smooth, domed rocks. Beyond that, lay the broad expanse of the beach exposed by low tide, stringy clumps of kelp just becoming visible as darker streaks against the pale half-light of morning.

The coffee ready, she filled her mug, added milk, and turned around, intending to go back upstairs and carry it out onto the upstairs deck. The maid would be arriving soon, and Howie would be getting up. He was one of those people who carried fitness to what

Miranda thought a masochistic extreme. A five-mile run along the beach and then a two– to three-mile swim every morning. And that was on what he called a "light" day.

Oh, well, she thought, *maybe all that exercise helps him sublimate his sex drive.*

She chuckled inwardly, then turning around, almost spilled her coffee all over the brightly colored ceramic squares of the Spanish-tile floor.

A figure that had no business being there was huddled on one of the white sectional sofas in the sunken living room that extended past a central fireplace. A folded newspaper on her lap went unread. Silent, motionless, she stared into space. Miranda had the impression of a stage set seconds before the curtain rises. She knew she had only to walk into the living room and make her presence known and something would be set in motion. Something that sent a tiny tremor of dread worming up her spine.

Like a sleepwalker, still carrying the mug of coffee, she padded barefoot to within a few feet of the woman collapsed upon the couch. Taking in every detail in the instinctive sense that something vital might later hinge upon her observations. Except for her large breasts, the girl was painfully slender, thin to the point of boniness. Denim cutoffs and a T-shirt drooping off her shoulders. Frizzy red hair tossed forward over freckled skin baked to that deep bronze sheen that lifeguards get by summer's end. A small face hidden in hands whose chipped nails were painted a flamboyant fuchsia.

For some reason that she didn't really understand, Miranda felt afraid of this creature. She said, "Who are you?"

Got no response.

Cleared her throat. "Does Howie know you're here?"

The girl came slowly alive, rocked back and forth. But for her breasts spilling against the thin fabric of the T-shirt, she seemed so *young.* Childlike and lost, as though she'd somehow wandered into this big house by mistake.

"I said does Howie know—"

The girl looked up. Miranda took a step backward, felt the breath hitch in her throat. The girl's face was a tapestry of colors melting into one another. Left eye blackened, right cheekbone blooming ripely with the brown and eggplant colors of a fist-size bruise. More marks on her temple, jaw, her chin.

In a voice so soft and toneless, Miranda had to strain to hear it, she said, "He had fun doing this." She pointed to the bruises. Her eye: "This was a left hook. It hurt the most." Her cheek: "This one was a straight right to shut me up when I started to scream." Her jaw: "This one was an uppercut. I woke up on the floor. My legs were spread. Underpants off. Bra up around my neck. He was standing over me. Said that was how he liked to fuck his women. When they were tenderized."

Miranda gawked, mouth open. "You're not saying *Howie* did this to you?"

"It's that or I was skiing at Tahoe and a tree jumped in front of me."

"But that's insane."

"So's Howie."

"And you are his—his—"

"Girlfriend, paramour, mistress. What'sa matter, you didn't know he liked them young?"

Now it was Miranda who felt like she'd been punched. It wasn't possible, not when things were going so well . . .

Miranda felt like her brain had turned to gelatin. Total meltdown. "Who are you? What's your name?"

"Just say I'm your future."

"Don't bet on it. I don't know what kind of scam you're pulling, but Howie's a wonderful man." She added primly, "He and I are engaged."

The girl smirked. "Yeah, right. Sister, I *know* the man. He's a loony woman-hating prick. Soon as the knot's tied, believe me, he'll be knotting one around

your neck, bringing his buddies over to have a piece
of the new bride, making you pose for his filthy
photographs."

For someone supposedly terrified of a violent lover,
the girl's voice trembled more with rage than fear.
Her eyes, an unnaturally brilliant turquoise that had
to be tinted contacts, blazed blue fire. The anger
seemed to emanate off her body in waves, causing
ridges of clammy gooseflesh to rise along Miranda's
arms.

"He's addicted to pornography, didn't you know
that?" the girl continued, her voice rising with mali-
cious glee. "The king of kink, that's what his buddies
call him. S/M, bondage, anything and everything up
the ass—you ever fucked a guy with a strap-on, lady?
Ten inches of lifelike rubber dick. That stuff's not just
for bull dykes, didn't you know that?"

"All right, shut up!" Miranda hissed. "Enough!
You've been injured. Come here and let me look at
you. Then I'll drive you to a hospital."

"No fucking way!" The girl leaped up and pivoted
away in a quick, lithe movement that was almost
frightening in its suddenness. Miranda had the image
of a ballet dancer or, more disturbingly, an expert in
some arcane martial art exercising a cat-and-mouse
maneuver.

Maintaining a safe distance on the opposite side of
the sectional sofa, the young woman challenged,
"Don't tell me he hasn't hit you yet?"

"No. Of course not." Miranda was close to stammering. This simply couldn't *be*. Howie could be tem-
peramental, sometimes moody to the point of
surliness, but he was gentlemanly to a fault and down-
right paranoid when it came to Miranda's safety. He'd
given her a car phone in case she broke down on
the road and a can of Mace to carry in the glove
compartment. He'd insisted on having new dead-bolt
locks installed in her apartment when he deemed the
locks she already had to be a joke—"my ten-year-old
grandson could kick in that door"—and promised her

a bodyguard if she were ever forced to travel without
him after they were married. Could a man so obsessed
with guarding women from the potential violence of
other men actually inflict it?

No, she decided, *it was ridiculous, unthinkable.*

"Unfortunately, I've been with violent men," she
said, "so I have some experience in this area. There
was a time in my life when the folks at the local wom-
en's shelters knew me by name. Howie's not one of
those men. He would never hurt me or any woman."

"Oh, no?"

"I don't know why you're telling such lies, but I
intend to find out. I'm going to wake him."

She started for the stairs. The girl said quickly,
"Wait, we aren't through talking yet. How long have
you been with him?"

"Long enough to know what kind of man he is."

She laughed. "Not long at all, then. Howie and I've
been together for years. I know the *real* Howie, the
bully and the sexual sadist. You just haven't hung
around long enough to meet *that* Howie."

"No, it isn't possible," Miranda said, but her mind
was racing to come up with more evidence in Howie's
favor. "I happen to know Howie donated fifty thousand dollars last year to a battered woman's shelter.
Not to mention the fact that one of the main selling
points of DeGrove Hotels is security for women trav-
elers. It was a feature even back in the sixties, when
Howie was just starting out, when not that many
women even traveled alone and nobody thought about
providing extra security for them."

"Guilt," said the girl. "Compensation for what's
really in his heart. What'sa matter, you never took
psychology?"

"I still don't believe you."

"Then fucking don't. Go on, think up something to
make yourself feel better. Maybe she asked for it, you
could say. Maybe she provoked him. I know what
you're thinking." Her voice got high-pitched, sing-
songy. "He'd never do it to me. Never, never, never

in a million years. I said that, too. Now look at me."
The girl put her hands on her prominent hipbones.
Her shorts were so tight that the cleft between her
legs was visible. Her bruised mouth curled in a sneer.
"You're fucking him, aren't you?"

"What?"

"You didn't hear me or you didn't understand the
question?"

"It's none of your damned business. If you don't
want me to wake him, then why don't you get whatever you came for and go?"

The girl tossed her short mop of hair and came
swaggering around the coffee table. "I was going to,
but now I think I'd rather talk to you some more. I
can do you some good. Dispense sisterly advice, even
though you're obviously much older. Howie's a good
fuck, isn't he? Maybe a great fuck. Well hung, too.
Odd, isn't it, because usually it's guys with little dicks
who beat up women, not the other way—"

"Trina, what the hell are you *babbling* about?"

Howie strode into the room. For a man who stood
barely five feet four, he looked enormous. He wore a
white terry-cloth robe, white slippers, and a look of
furious consternation. His slate gray hair was wild and
spiky, his blue eyes almost demonic in their intensity.
For a moment Miranda thought she had been wrong,
that here was a man truly capable of violence toward
anybody or anything.

"How did you get in here?"

"I have my ways. Scary, isn't it? A state-of-the-art
burglar alarm system, and I can foil it every time."
She turned to Miranda. "I can't tell you how many
times he's given me a key, then gotten mad at me for
some trifling little thing and changed the locks. Maybe
he's scared I'll sneak in and shoot him in his sleep.
Or maybe he's afraid I'll bring a gentleman friend
over like I did last year, and let him catch us in—oh,
how would you describe it, Howie?—the ropes went
underneath my tits, and he was shoving the riding crop
up into my—"

"Good God, Trina, shut up! Not another word! Good Lord, what the hell have you done to your face?"

The girl—Trina—ignored the question, but spun around and marched past the sofa. Stood posed next to a floor-to-ceiling panel of a Chinese waterfall. "I was just having some girl talk here with your friend. You didn't tell me about this one. Is it serious or is she just another one of your casual affairs?"

"I mean it, Trina, this isn't funny." He lunged and snatched her by the arm. "Your face—what have you done to yourself?"

Miranda cleared her throat. "She says you beat her."

"Oh, bloody hell."

"Howie, I need an explanation."

Trina arched one delicately plucked eyebrow. "Yeah, explain this, Daddy. Looks bad to me. Looks like material for Jerry Springer. Here's a woman beaten up, sitting in your living room, now revealed to be your daughter."

Miranda's head jerked up. "I thought you told me your daughter was *dead*, Howie? That she was murdered?"

"She was," said Howie. "Calla's dead. This is my younger daughter, Trina."

"The one he *wishes* were dead."

"Trina. That's *enough*!"

She shrank away. "Don't hit me, Daddy."

Miranda said, "Let her go, Howie. I don't know what's going on here, but if you touch her, I'm calling the police."

Trina hopped up and down clapping her hands. "You tell him, girlfriend. We women gotta stick together."

"So far you're only right about one thing, Miranda," Howie said. "You don't know what's going on here. That's what she's counting on. But I've been around this block a time or two. She's pulled this kind of stunt before when I had lady friends over. How about I let you in on the joke?"

He grabbed Trina, who commenced to struggle with what appeared to be real fear. To Miranda, she looked as supple and strong as a python, muscles flexing hard and wiry. "Let go of me!"

Howie grabbed the terry-cloth belt of his robe and dragged the nubby fabric across her cheek. When he brought the cloth away, it was dark with color, and the bruises on Trina's face were smeared down to her jaw.

"Look at her bruises now, Miranda! They're only makeup."

Trina jerked free, glaring at Miranda. "Well, Daddy, one thing I can say for you, at least you're not out chasing hot young chicks. You definitely are developing a taste for women of a certain age."

"Trina, stop it! Your behavior is inexcusable. I want you to leave right *now*."

"Aw, do I have to, Daddy? I was having so much fun."

"Trina, I swear, sometimes . . ."

"—what, Daddy, you swear you want to turn me over your knee and paddle my firm little butt? Is that what you want? Or is what you *really* want for me to not be here at all? For me to be the one who got killed instead of Calla?"

Her words seemed to strike Howie like a brick to the back of the head. His heavily muscled shoulders sagged. Beneath the disheveled white brows, his blue-violet eyes blinked out tears.

"Trina, if you had any idea of the pain you cause me when you talk like that, you'd never say those things. You're going to put me in my grave, girl. Sometimes, I swear, I don't care if you do."

"All right, Daddy, I'm sorry. It was a joke, didn't you know? Really I only stopped by to have breakfast and discuss this morning's news with you—I thought it would be of interest—I didn't realize you had a girlfriend, let alone a *fiancée* here with you till I peeked in the window."

"I was going to tell you about Miranda and me, Trina, but—"

"Sure you were, Daddy. Maybe you'd even get around to telling me you were married a year or so *after* the wedding?"

Defeated-looking, drained, Howie slumped into a chair. "And maybe if you didn't pull these stupid stunts, I'd feel free to tell you more about what's going on in my life."

"You don't trust me," she said airily. "I understand. Well, it looks like an invitation to join you two for breakfast won't be forthcoming, so"—she swiped at her face, smearing makeup in big raccoonish circles around her eyes—"I'll leave you alone. Don't worry, Daddy, I won't bother you anymore. You don't tell me what you're doing, no reason why I should bore you with the details of my life. Or anyone else's life, for that matter," she added, snatching up the newspaper and heading for the door.

"Oh, Trina, good Lord, don't be angry." Howie got groaningly to his feet.

"Howie, what are you doing? Let her go," Miranda said, but he was so intent upon going after Trina that her words might as well have been spoken in Swahili.

Trina turned back, lower lip trembling, tears forming in her eyes. "I can't help being mad, Daddy. I know you hate me. I know you wish I'd been the one murdered and not Calla. That's why I do these stupid things—to get your attention."

"Dear God, girl, I don't hate you. Whatever would make you *think* something like that? Is it that over-priced Freudian-Jungian-lesbian-God-only-knows-what-kind-of-quack-she-is therapist that you go to? Does she plant these ideas in your head? You're my life, don't you know that?" Putting his arm around his daughter, he led her over to the sofa and sat with her, smoothing her hair. From a vital, athletic-looking man in his sixties, he seemed to have gotten pale and gray and dwarf-like, wearier than Miranda had ever seen him. He looked decrepit, frightened, lost.

Unconsciously, Miranda's hand went to the ruby

ring, twisting it. "Howie, don't you think we should all—"

"Miranda, please, not *now*," he said. Then, turning back to Trina, "I love you, don't you understand? You and Shawn are more important to me than anything else in the world. I'd protect both of you with my life."

"I want to believe that, Daddy."

"Well, you *can*. You say you do these things to get my attention, but if it's my attention you want, why is it you're never around? Half the time, you don't return my phone calls. I get you a cell phone so I can find you when I want to, but you don't keep it charged. You think I don't wake up in the night sometimes worrying about where you may be, what you may be doing, who in God's name you may be doing it with?"

"I don't want you to worry about me, Daddy. But I hate it when you hide things from me—important things—like the fact that you're planning to get married." Over Howie's shoulder, she fixed Miranda with an icy glare.

"You're right, Trina. I should have had you and Miranda meet a long time ago. But I was so afraid you wouldn't like each other and if you and Miranda didn't get along, then I wouldn't feel right marrying her, so I suppose I was, well, rather apprehensive."

"Wait a minute." Miranda, who had been trying to wait patiently, interrupted. "Howie, what exactly are you saying? Do you mean that you won't marry me without this girl's *approval*?"

"Please, Miranda, this isn't the time."

"Oh, no, I think it *is*. I want to know what I'm getting into. I want to know *now*."

"My God, Miranda, can't you see Trina's upset?"

"*She's* upset? After the display she put on? I'd say she's more than just upset, I'd say she's crazy!"

"She's my *daughter*, Miranda," Howie hissed. "You don't speak of her like that."

Miranda, watching him stroking Trina's hair, consoling her, realized suddenly that she was invisible, that

Howie and this wild, mad girl existed in some other level of reality, some private, cocreated universe that she would never enter, never be privy to except as a voyeur.

"I think I should leave now," she said sharply.

He looked up at her, befuddled and incurious. Surprised, apparently, to find she was still there. "Yes, maybe so, Miranda. I'm sorry, but maybe that's best."

She drew herself up, twisting at the ruby ring on her left hand as she did so, starting to remove it. Knowing she was about to wager everything. "You understand, Howie, I'm not talking about leaving for the moment? I mean for good. Forever."

"For good, Miranda?"

"I won't be party to this kind of craziness. This young woman is sick. She needs help, not a pat on the head."

He sighed and shut his eyes. "She's my *little girl*, Miranda. I'm sorry."

Trina, cuddled in her father's arms, stopped crying long enough to fix Miranda with those unnaturally bright turquoise eyes. "What'sa matter, Miranda, aren't you going to return my Daddy's ring?"

"I don't think so. I think I earned it." Miranda gave a chilly smile, shoved the ruby back onto her finger, and marched toward the door.

"Daddy, are you going to let her get away with that?" said Trina.

"Let her keep the damn ring. She's right, it's hers."

"You were really going to marry her, weren't you?"

"I wanted to, yes."

"And now I've spoiled it."

Howie sighed. "Or saved me. Who the hell knows— the way she talked about you, maybe I'm better off without her. But in the future, I don't want you pulling any more crazy theatrics, you understand? And in return, I promise to introduce you to any ladies that I start dating. Let you get your two cents' worth in before I get too involved."

She squealed and hugged him. "Oh, thank you, Daddy, you're the best!"

A few minutes later, after Trina had washed off her makeup, they had coffee and scones out on the patio, looking out at the flat metallic dazzle of the sea. The air of emotional intensity that had permeated the house earlier had dissipated like fog, as though nothing odd or untoward had ever taken place.

"Water's still today, isn't it?" said Trina.

"Don't let it fool you," Howie said. "There's riptides will swallow you down."

"Be careful when you go swimming, then." She lifted a scone to her mouth, put it down. "Why can't you just do laps in the pool like any normal person."

"Because there's no challenge in it. What's life without a challenge?"

"Longer," Trina said. She unfolded the newspaper she'd been holding, a copy of the *San Diego Union Tribune*, and handed it to her father. "I hate to be the bearer of bad tidings, Daddy, but I really did come here to show you this. Shawn called me at the crack of dawn this morning, all upset. He had a baby-sitter spend the night with him. Apparently the little bitch heard something about Matt on the news, and she told Shawn. He wanted to know if I could do anything, so I rushed over here to see you. Then I saw that woman here, prissing around like she owned the place, and I got sidetracked."

She pointed out the article, and Howie scanned it, brow furrowing more deeply as he got near the end. "Good Lord," he murmured, "what's Matt gotten himself into? A murder charge? Poor Shawn, what will this do to him?"

"Poor *Matt*," said Trina. "Looks like your former son-in-law just can't stay out of trouble. What'd'ya think, Daddy? Did he do it?"

Shaking his head, Howie said, "It's possible, I suppose.

"Matt's got a temper, doesn't he?"

"That he does."

"Still, I don't see him as some kind of cold-blooded killer," Trina said. "His bail's probably going to be out of sight, though. Are you going to help him out with it?"

"Of course not. Now that Calla's gone, it's not as though Matt's a member of our family. I don't feel I owe him anything."

"But he's Shawn's *father*."

"I'm well aware of that, and I'll do everything in my power for that boy," said Howie. "As far as Matt goes, though, I always thought Calla chose unwisely when she married him."

"You thought she could have done better?"

The question actually seemed to make Howie's skin flush a shade or two darker. "A construction worker? She married a construction worker. Need I say more?"

"But he *is* attractive," Trina said, "in a rough-hewn sort of way."

"A little too 'rough-hewn,' if you ask me," Howie said. "You know I've always tolerated Matt for Shawn's sake, but who's to say Matt's the best one to be raising him anyway? Who's to say Shawn wouldn't be better off with me?"

Trina slid her arm around his shoulder and hugged him to her. "Yeah, Daddy, who's to say?"

Chapter Four

"On your feet, Engstrom."

Pete Uhlenkamp's gravelly voice coming from outside the cell interrupted Matt's morose ruminations, all of which were adding up to one grim conclusion: *I am fucked.*

He'd been back in his cell less than an hour since he and Devereaux had appeared before the judge for his arraignment. Bond had been set at seventy-five thousand dollars—an impossible sum for him to come up with on short notice. But if he cashed in his CD's, maybe took out an equity loan on his house . . .

At the sound of the key turning in the lock of the holding cell, Matt popped to his feet so fast he bumped his head on the bottom of the overhead bunk. Didn't even feel it. All he could think was that the cops had found the guy who killed Barry and he had confessed. His hopes surged. The nightmare was over.

Uhlenkamp flung open the cell door. He was shaking his head, fleshy mouth twisted off center, nostrils flared with disgust.

"What happened?" said Matt. "Did you find the guy who killed Barry?"

"We sure as hell did, but we gotta let him go—for the moment—'cause somebody with more bucks than brains came up with his bond." Uhlenkamp stepped back, gave an exaggerated bow as Matt stepped past. "You are one lucky son of a bitch, Engstrom. But we'll nail your ass yet."

Upstairs in the booking room, a desk sergeant returned Matt's wallet and other personal belongings.

"Did my attorney bond me out?"

The desk sergeant shrugged and scribbled a signature on some forms. "I couldn't tell if the gal who paid your bail was a hooker or a lawyer, but then what's the difference these days?"

He glanced over Matt's shoulder toward the door. Some cops over by the coffee machine had stopped talking and were turning to stare.

Matt turned and saw his former sister-in-law approaching. Her heels were high, her stride brisk and no nonsense. Her short hair, arranged around her face in masses of tight curls, was dyed a shade of red so dark it looked almost black. She wore a leotard top of some shiny red material. A wispy scrap of white silk served as a skirt. Her eyes today were the stunning blue of some exotic gemstone. On other occasions, Matt had seen them olive green and the pale, milky hue of moonstones. In all the years he'd known her, he'd only seen Trina's real eye color—chocolate brown with flecks of hazel—once or twice.

"Matt, what on earth happened? What have they done to you?" She flung her arms around him, enveloping him in a musky cloud of head-turning scent— part the hundred-dollar-an-ounce kind, part simply her own natural aroma. She slipped an arm through his. "No, don't even tell me yet. Just come on. Let's get you out of here."

Matt allowed himself to be hustled outside into sunlight so bright it struck his retinas like shards of glass. He blinked, momentarily dazzled, and felt her hand grip his arm. "God, you look like shit. Did you get any sleep last night?"

"You ever try to sleep in a holding cell?"

"I knew it, sleep deprivation. A form of torture. Get you to confess to stuff you didn't do. It's police brutality. Didn't you know?" She steered him toward the curb and across the street to where a cherry-red

Jaguar sport coupe was double-parked, a parking ticket flapping beneath the wipers.

She held the car door open for him and helped him in, leaning over to display her cleavage. Snatching the ticket out from under the windshield, she tossed it onto the dash along with two or three others.

"Still collecting parking tickets, I see."

"It's a form of harassment. Expensive, sporty cars—especially expensive, sporty *red* cars—get more parking tickets, didn't you know that?"

"The trucks I drive, guess I don't have anything to worry about in that department."

She turned to face him, poppy lips parted to retort with a wisecrack, he figured. Then her face softened, and she looked at him with a strange, wistful sweetness that made Matt feel like he was Shawn's age and Mommy had just come to whisk him out of the principal's office yet again.

"No offense, pal, but you *do* look like shit. You want to swing by my place, take a shower, see if I can find some clean clothes that might fit you, before I take you home?"

"Do you think your boyfriend would appreciate your giving his clothes away to another fella?"

"For your information, at the moment, I don't *have* a boyfriend. I have friends who are male, guys I sleep with—fuckbuddies, you know—but honey, it ain't the same thing, as you're well aware. Furthermore, I like wearing mens' clothes. They're cheaper and better made than the stuff sold to women, didn't you—"

"No, guess I didn't know that. Thanks, Trina, but all I want right now is to get home and see my son."

"Yeah, that's what I figured. He was trying to sound cool when he called me, but I could tell he was shaken up."

"Shawn called you?"

"He saw the paper, Matt—or rather the little bitch who's babysitting for him saw the article this morning before Coop came by to pick him up, and she freaked out and showed it to Shawn."

"*Shit.*"

"Yeah, well, Shawn was pretty upset. He didn't out-right ask me to bail you out, but I knew that's what he wanted. And I can't let my favorite nephew down, now, can I—even if his father *is* a menace to society?"

"I didn't *do* it, Trina."

"Only joking, Matt. God, aren't we testy this morning?"

"I thought Alex Devereaux must have called you."

"Devereaux? Isn't he the one who lost that class action suit for those homeless guys who claimed the city was violating their civil right to loiter? Hell, with Devereaux representing me, I could probably wind up in maximum security for a speeding ticket."

She whipped through a caution light, accelerating to fifty in a thirty-mile zone. "The way you drive, you may yet," observed Matt.

"Hey, I'm just your average, almost solid citizen who commits the occasional misdemeanor. I'm not the one who got picked up on a murder charge last night. Speaking of which, I'd ask if you did it, but I figure no way would you be dumb enough to throw a dead body into your own truck and then call the cops to report it. I've known you to be self-destructive, but not outright suicidal." She steered wide around a curve, the centrifugal force pinning Matt against the passenger door. "I'm right, aren't I? You aren't drink-ing again, are you?"

"I'm not drinking. And even if I did go on a bender and got hammered out of my mind, I'm still not going to go around killing people."

She shot him a look, one eyebrow raised in the start of a challenge, but Matt eyed her right back, silently daring her to throw the past in his face. Knowing Trina, he figured her tongue must have teeth marks.

"So what *did* happen, Matt? The paper said it was some guy who worked for Engstrom Construction?"

"Barry Bischoff. Helluva nice guy. I can't imagine he'd have any enemies. Not the murderous kind anyway."

"Sometimes the nicest-looking people have the wickedest playmates."

"Yeah, but it's hard to imagine Barry generating the level of hate necessary to kill."

"Not to touch on a sensitive subject, Matt, but this Bischoff guy wouldn't happen to be somebody you met in the can?"

"As a matter of fact, Trina"—he heard the edge in his voice and reminded himself this was a woman who'd just put seventy-five thousand bucks down on his behalf—"no, I met Barry somewhere else. As far as I know, his biggest run-in with the law was getting busted for pot possession in the seventies."

"Sorry, but I know one of your weaknesses is a fondness for hiring ex-cons."

"I don't consider it a weakness, Trina. And not to be harsh, but you're starting to sound like Howie. I admire the old man—he created an empire from the ground up and sometimes I'm goddamned envious—but he can also be a little narrow-minded."

"You mean, as in a little to the right of Attila the Hun?"

"Shit, how do I tell him?"

"Oh, don't worry. He already knows."

"What? I thought Howie said he refuses to read the paper or watch the news on TV?"

"He won't," said Trina. "He says it upsets him too much to know the world's going to hell in a hand-basket and the prisons are just country clubs that coddle cons with a little barbed wire thrown up for appearances' sake."

"Hell, yeah, I still miss the polo matches and rack of lamb."

"Anyway, I happened to be in his neighborhood this morning, so I stopped by his place with the paper. A good thing I did—caught him being a naughty daddy again. Some woman old enough to be my mother was waltzing around like she had her name tattooed on his dick, so I played one of Trina's little practical jokes. Seems the bitch didn't have a sense of humor. I don't think she'll be sniffing around Daddy anymore."

"Jesus, Trina, what did Howie ever do to deserve *you*?"

"Oh, come on, Matt, every great man has his cross to bear. Besides, Daddy doesn't need some floozy in his life. He should be grateful to me for keeping an eye on him. Anyway, I showed him the story about Barry's murder."

"You did *what*?"

"What was I supposed to do? He's Shawn's grandfather. He needs to know."

"He'll be worried sick."

"He's concerned about Shawn. I don't know if this is going to generate much media attention, but you might want to consider letting him stay with Daddy or me for the time being."

"Yeah, maybe. With your dad, I mean. I'll think about it."

"Anyway, Daddy's holding up okay. He got pretty upset at first, but by the time I left, he was headed out for his daily swim and run. I told him to train hard. The Olympics are only a couple years away."

"So he hasn't changed?"

"He's gotten worse! Fitness is his religion. Right now, he's training for the Iron Man Triathlon in Hawaii next fall—he's a contender for first place in the sixty-and-over division."

"I have to hand it to Howie. He *is* amazing. Sixty-three and doing triathlons."

Trina grinned. "Sixty-four. I call him Iron Dad."

They were approaching the on-ramp for I5. "Can I ask another favor," Matt said. "My truck's been impounded as evidence. I'm going to need something to drive. Instead of going to my house, how about running me by the office so I can pick up another vehicle?"

"Sure, Matt."

"Thanks, Trina. For everything, I mean. I know that's a helluva lot of money—even for you."

"Don't worry about it." She reached over and gave his knee an affectionate squeeze. "I can trust you, can't I? Not to skip town? That seventy-five thousand dollars—I had it earmarked for this great little black BMW convertible I saw the other day."

"Just what you need, Trina. Another sports car. At least it's not red."

She grinned. "Oh, hon, Trina *has* to have red. I'll get it painted." They pulled up in front of Engstrom Construction, a ten-minute drive from Matt's house in Chula Vista. Before he could get out, she leaned over and kissed him quickly on the mouth. Her lips tasted of cinnamon.

A couple of framers who had stopped by to pick up their checks gaped with sensory overload—gorgeous girl, gorgeous car, wondering no doubt how their less-than-gorgeous boss figured in this picture.

"Want me to wait for you?"

"No need. You've done enough."

He started to get out of the car, then turned back. "Can I ask one more favor?" Trina's blindingly turquoise eyes met him, and he was almost forced to look away. Her eyes, Matt realized, looked much older when her feelings weren't masked with a smile, as though she'd been seeing things, too many things maybe, for many years more than her age.

"I've never understood why you wear those crazy-colored contact lenses," he blurted out. "You have beautiful eyes."

"*That's* the favor? You want me to stop wearing contact lenses?"

"No. No, I don't even know why I said that. God, I'm so tired I'm not thinking straight. What I wanted to ask is that you play this down as much as possible to your dad. Let him know I'm okay, and it's all a mistake that's going to be resolved soon. He took it hard enough when Calla died. Iron Dad or not, I don't want him to go through any more than he has to. Assuming, of course, you *do* believe me? That I didn't have anything to do with Barry's death."

"Stop, Matt." Trina angled herself around so that her long, satiny legs were displayed to advantage. "I know you didn't kill Barry. And even if some people think you did, so what? Remember what Daddy says, 'what other people think about me is none of my business'—even if it makes the front page."

"The *front* page? Jesus, you're kidding."

"Hey, but not the headline or anything." Then she grinned. "Just kidding. It was buried on the inside. Don't worry, Matt, you're still a nobody."

She started the engine and was already turning the corner, accelerating through a caution light before Matt even got up the steps to the door.

As he walked up the hallway, which was decorated with framed floor plans of homes and buildings that Engstrom Construction had built or renovated, a bizarre thought—one so inappropriate that he could barely acknowledge it—insinuated itself into the turmoil of his thoughts. So Barry's murder had made the paper this morning? Well, hell, maybe that was a kind of sick plus to this nightmare. Maybe Noel would read the article and find out he'd been arrested. Maybe she'd call to help or offer comfort. Maybe this whole ordeal was going to bring her back to him.

C'mon, Noel, he thought, *go out and buy a goddamn paper for once in your life. Turn on the news. And then call me, Noel. Call!*

Chapter Five

Noel Juliette Smith liked to watch videos. Sometimes she rented three or four at a time and watched them all in one cinematic binge before returning to the store for another batch. If a particular scene in a movie struck a chord, she would watch it again and again, obsessively, until the scene and dialogue were so burned into her mind they felt real, like her very own experience.

She was watching the ending of the movie *Body Heat* now for the fifth or sixth time. The part where Kathleen Turner lounges on a chaise in a tropical land, drink in one hand, sexy suitor hovering at her side.

Noel had the drink part down, all right, Smirnoff neat with a twist, but the only male presence in the bungalow she'd rented in the hills outside the small town of Ramona was a photo of Matt stuck in one corner of a wall mirror—he was straddling the Harley, wearing chaps, a leather vest, and a red bandanna she'd given him. And the only hint of the tropics in her surroundings were the half dozen pythons snoozing inside their cages, a few others languidly lounging on furniture with much the same attitude of sensuous torpor as that of Turner's character.

The movie faded to credits. Noel hit rewind on the remote for a few seconds and began the ending again.

This time, though, she didn't watch the TV, but stared at the cordless phone that lay on the floor next to a bowl of uneaten cherry-vanilla ice cream, now melted to pink-flecked white sludge. To call or not to call? And if she *did* call, what kind of response could she expect?

The movie played itself out. This time, Noel didn't rewind it, but got up off the sofa and went over to one of the snake cages, where a four-foot python named Simba was still dawdling with his dinner.

Noel cooed to the snake, tried to coax him to eat, feeling slightly sick as she did so. This was the only aspect of her pets that she *didn't* like and could never completely get used to. The snakes had to be fed live mice. Dead ones? Forget it—the pythons didn't even recognize the tiny corpses as food. So every few days she drove to a pet supply store in Ramona to buy mice. She hated doing it. The mice were cute and sweet and trusting, with the round shoe-button eyes of Disney cartoon characters and winsome, twitchy pink noses. They had no idea of the fate in store for them—being swallowed alive and asphyxiated in the reptiles' dark depths. But her snakes had to eat, they had to *survive*, so what else could she do?

"Hey, Lola. What's up, Monique?" She squatted before another of the cages, admiring the way the light that filtered through the partially open drapes gleamed on the bronze and black coils. No mice in sight.

She unlatched the cage door and lifted the snakes out, letting them undulate up her arms, over her shoulders and down her back. They thudded softly to the floor and slithered off in opposite directions.

Noel felt a queasiness in her stomach and closed her eyes a moment, grimacing. At thirty-two, she was a small, curvaceous woman with jet hair, ripe-looking lips, and saucy, almond-shaped eyes. Her only physical flaws, if they could be called that, were that little color remained in her face and that her ribs, visible below the yellow halter top she wore with a pair of khaki shorts, were starting to show. Any more weight gone, and she'd be in danger of losing the stripper lushness that was essential to her popularity onstage.

She turned back to the first cage. "Come on, Simba, *eat.*"

Just food, she told herself, that's all the trapped mouse was. *Food.*

The python was not impressed by her pleas. He eyed her balefully.

The mouse cowered in a corner of the cage. Simba flicked his tongue out. Didn't budge.

Noel moved to another cage. Later, after all the snakes had eaten, she'd let the rest out to slither around the bungalow. She had to be careful none got away, though, because people didn't understand her snakes were harmless. Most folks either associated large snakes with horror movies where people met agonizing deaths in the embrace of a huge serpent or, like the men who came to watch her dance, they ascribed to the snakes some mystical eroticism, a dark and decadent sexuality.

Noel hadn't danced in public recently. That would be too risky. If Matt were looking for her—and she was sure he *was*—he'd search the clubs and topless bars first. She had, however, put the word out to a couple of low-end motels that she was available to dance privately for clients.

So far, she hadn't done too badly, but it wasn't enough. Money never seemed to last her very long. Her expenses were exorbitant—and getting more so.

Her stomach was still bothering her, so she went into the bathroom, took a bottle of pills down from the collection on the shelf, palmed a few, and gulped them dry. Saw there were only a dozen or so left in the bottle.

Money, I'm gonna need more money.

She went back into the living room and squatted before Simba's cage. "C'mon, big fella, stop dicking around. You know you're hungry. Do what you gotta do."

Do what you gotta do.

Noel was good at that—doing what had to be done

before emotions and scruples had a chance to get in the way, cloud the issue.

She picked up the phone, dialed the number of a private office a few miles away, crossed her fingers.

"Good afternoon, Brandon here." The familiar voice, with its clipped, precise syllables that implied the call was being received in a boardroom where a multimillion dollar deal had just been closed, irritated her immediately. Sophistication and ennui, with just enough pretentiousness thrown in to make her want to puke more than she already did.

"Is it afternoon already?" she said, making her voice sound drowsy, languid. "I just got up."

"Oh. It's you."

"Gee, don't get so excited, Brandon, I'll think you care."

There was a pause, followed by what sounded like a door being closed. God forbid anyone should hear them sounding less than lovey-dovey on the phone. Then: "I *do* care, Noel. That's always been the problem—that I care. Now, what can I do for you? Or should I rephrase that, how much do you need?"

"Why do you always assume I want money?"

"Why do I assume the sun's coming up tomorrow morning? How much?"

"You're in a good mood today, aren't you? Well, since you asked, a thousand would help. To tide me over till I get a job at another club."

"Dancing, you mean?"

"No, washing dishes."

"Look, Noel, there are other things you can do besides dance that still pay good money. I offered to help you go back to school, but—"

"Oh, c'mon, I'll pay you back."

"Noel, you *never* pay me back."

"I *need* money, Brandon. I've got a lot of expenses."

"Drugs, you mean?"

"Yeah, but not the kind you think. I don't do that kind anymore. I mean prescription stuff. You know

those headaches I get? Over-the-counter stuff just isn't
doing any good. And I'm having a hard time keeping
food down."

"Ever heard of medical insurance? The kind that
comes with legitimate employment?"

"Oh, you mean like *your* job? Yeah, I see what
your job does for you. Let's see, you get to sell your
soul, live a lie, develop an ulcer—"

"All right, Noel, touché."

"Look, I really will pay you back. I've got a lot of
money coming for some work I did, but it's taking
longer than I thought to get paid all of it. The guy's an
asshole—he's waiting to make sure I finish the job."

"I don't suppose you're going to tell me what kind
of 'job' it is you have to finish?"

"No, I don't suppose I am."

She heard him take a deep breath and release it
gradually, buying time. He was thinking about her request, mulling it over, probably mentally referring to
some self-help book or the latest *Oprah* show. Not a
good sign. With Brandon, her best chance was to goad
him into making a quick decision in her favor, then
using guilt to keep him from reversing it.

"I can't this time. I'd like to, but I can't. I've got
expenses of my own."

"Like what? Your cats need fancier kitty litter? Are
they eating higher quality tuna these days—or do they
still eat *cat* food at all?"

He chuckled. "A strange choice of sarcasms given
the way you pamper those snakes of yours."

"They're how I earn my *living*, Brandon."

"Well, that's the whole point of this conversation,
now, isn't it? You're *not* earning your living."

"Oh, fuck you. What expenses have *you* got?"

"I might be moving."

"What?"

"I'm serious. After all, I'm alone now. And what
you said about my work, you're right. I hate my fucking job. These rich jerks I have to deal with are all

assholes. I might just fulfill my life's ambition and say fuck it all and go."

"Where?"

"I'm not sure. I'm considering several places."

"You can't do that!"

"Why not?"

"What if I need you?"

"Now that your friend Matt's out of the picture, you mean? I didn't get too many calls while you were seeing *him*, did I? Not even when I practically begged you to go to that party with me." He was trying to sound nonchalant, but the not-quite-mastered anger gave his voice an unbecoming shrillness. "You never *did* tell me why you dumped Matt."

"It just wasn't working out. I needed to move on."

"Well, there you have it, Noel, because that's exactly how I feel. I need to move on."

"But not right away. Not *immediately*."

"No, Noel, I'm not like you. I wouldn't just slink away in the night. I'd have to give my notice at work. Line up some movers, get organized. But moving does cost money."

"Look, a thousand's nothing for you. I only need it for a little while."

"I'm sorry, but I just don't believe you anymore. You've lied to me too many times. I love you, but I've come to realize the best way I can help you is by *not* helping you at all."

"Oh, great, and which self-help book gave you *that* pearl of wisdom?"

"Take care, Noel. Try to stay out of trouble."

"Brandon, wait—" But she was talking to the dial tone.

Now it was *her* turn to be angry. So Brandon wouldn't give her money—all right, she knew someone who wouldn't have a choice. And he'd not only give her what they'd agreed upon, but more besides. A *lot* more.

She thought she had the number memorized, but nervousness blanked out her memory. She had to look

the number up again in her address book by the bed
and, even then, she misdialed twice. When he finally
answered, sounding annoyed, like she was just another
flunky, she said, "I want the rest of my money, and I
want it now. Otherwise, I'll call Matt, just like you
want me to, but I'm going to tell him *everything*."

She recited Brandon's address. "You can have
someone drop the money off there. Punch airholes in
the package, and tell the guy who lives there it's a
snake. Believe me, he won't open it." She reached up
with one hand and repositioned Monique, who had
slithered across her shoulders and was now running
down her back like water, trying to tuck into the waist-
band of her shorts. "No, I won't be there when you
drop off the money. I'm staying someplace else. You
don't need to know any more."

From the other end, a grudging assent before the
connection ended.

There. Done.

Glancing over at the python cages, she noticed
Simba had eaten his meal. The mouse was gone. The
tip of the white tail protruded limply from between
the snake's tightly clamped jaws. A shudder traveled
throughout Noel's sleek body.

Not a mouse, she reminded herself.

Food.

Chapter Six

Phil Rollins was on the phone in his cubicle when Matt walked in. A stocky, dark-haired man in his late twenties, Phil normally had the meticulously well-groomed, expensively suited look of the rising young entrepreneur and investor he aspired to be. Today, however, there was a sallow cast to his salon-tanned skin and dark pouches under his deep-set eyes that suggested a sleepless night or a serious hangover.

On the way to his own office, Matt glanced over at Phil's desk and saw a spreadsheet of figures for the Ryder project on his computer screen. As Phil finished his phone conversation, he reached over and struck some keys. A different screen appeared, this one showing columns of figures Matt was preparing for a bid on an office remodeling in Pacific Beach. Matt had forgotten the project entirely, but now he remembered the deadline to get the bid to the architect was in two days. Normally, he and Barry would have stayed late crunching numbers, but now . . . his stomach muscles clenched around what felt like a ball of barbed wire lodged in his gut.

"Hey, Matt." Phil put the phone down and keyed a few more strokes in on the computer. "That was Bill Travis from Best Floors. They're backed up at another project, so he's not going to be able to get a crew over to the Ryder house to put in that pine floor until Friday. I thought I'd try to get a plumbing crew in there tomorrow, so when the Ryders get back from

Bermuda next week, everybody won't be descending on them at once."

"Sure, fine."

"Bill was worried you'd be upset about the delay. He knows what a pain Jack Ryder can be. I told him if there was any problem, Barry would handle it. Take the Ryders out to dinner or something. Mellow them out."

Matt stared at him. "Phil, don't tell me you—when did you get in the office?"

"Well, to tell you the truth, Matt, I owe you an apology. Paula and I tied one on pretty good last night. I overslept and just got in about an hour ago."

"Then"—he found himself unable to go on and sat down heavily in the leather swivel chair across from Phil's desk—"you mean nobody told you? The police haven't talked to you yet?"

"About what?"

"Oh, Christ. I don't know how to say this. Barry was murdered last night."

"What? Jesus Christ, no way!"

Phil just kept shaking his head and looking down at the floor as Matt recounted the events of the night before, skimming over as much as possible the fact that the cops considered him the prime suspect. When he finished, Phil fumbled in his pocket and pulled out an object that Matt had occasionally seen him roll between his fingers, like worry beads or a rosary, in moments of stress—a bronze medallion embossed with the Chinese character for good fortune. Considering the wins he'd told Matt about after his weekend trips to Vegas, maybe there was more to it than just superstition.

"Barry—dead? I can't believe it."

"Neither can I."

"Jesus, who'd do such a thing?"

"That's what the police are trying to find out."

"Was it quick, at least? I mean, did it happen so fast that Barry didn't know what hit him or did he suffer?"

"I think it was quick," Matt said, more for Phil's sake than because he believed it.

"Good God, poor Barry. I mean, shit, the guy was still in his thirties—he was just starting to get ahead. What a world, huh?"

Matt went over to the coffee machine, more for something to do than anything else, and filled two styrofoam cups, one of which he set on the desk in front of Phil.

"He had wanted to talk to me about something last night, but I don't know what it was. Did he mention anything to you?"

"Not a thing. Barry was in the field most of last week. I hardly saw him." He picked up the coffee cup, but his hand was unsteady, and he set it back down before it could slosh.

"Look, Phil, why don't you go home?"

"I just got here."

"Yeah, but you're not going to be able to focus on work today. Neither am I. I just got dropped off here to pick up a vehicle and go home."

Phil looked surprised. "What happened to your truck?"

"It needed some work done," Matt said quickly. "Anyway, screw work. Go on home."

"You're sure?"

"Go."

"Yeah, I guess you're right." He lifted the styrofoam cup again, took a sip, put it down. "What I need right now is a real drink."

"I know the feeling."

"Want to join me? I mean, for a soft drink or something?"

"Not today, Phil. I gotta get home and see Shawn. You go on home, too."

"I will. Just give me a minute. I think I just need to sit here for a second, take this in. Jesus, poor Barry."

As Matt pulled the door shut behind him, Phil was still sitting there, staring out the window while his hands moved almost imperceptibly, passing the Chi-

nese lucky piece from one hand to the other, back
and forth.

Of the three trucks owned by Engstrom Construction, the only one not in use at the moment was the
brown Ford, oldest of the bunch, a gas guzzler with a
clutch that had seen better days. It took Matt a few
minutes to find the right key on his key ring. By the
time he located it and was ready to leave, Phil still
hadn't come out of the office. Matt thought about
going back inside to make sure he was all right, then
discounted the impulse. What mattered now was that
he get home and take care of his son.

When Matt had looked for a place for his home
and office four years ago, after Calla's death, he'd put
practical considerations first. Prices in Chula Vista
were closer to reasonable than in most of Southern
California, the junior high Shawn attended was five
minutes from their house, and a strip mall with an
inexpensive ice-cream parlor, video arcade, pizza joint,
and Mexican restaurant a few blocks away provided
dinner and entertainment on those nights Matt didn't
have time or energy to cook. He'd built his house on
a small corner lot, a stone's throw from the Nature
Estuary and the Mexican border. A mixed blessing—
he got to see a lot of egrets and herons and a lot more
besides. Often, late at night, he'd hear shouting and
see the lights playing across the flat, marshy expanse
of the estuary as immigration authorities closed in on
the illegals making their way north. And sometimes
there were no lights and no voices, but only the faint,
spectral shadows of those making the crossing without
being detected and the soft splat of their feet on the
spongy, waterlogged earth.

Matt still remembered one night a few months after
Calla's death. The long gray numbness of depression
and grief hadn't yet started to dissipate—he was wondering if it ever would—and he was sitting on the
front porch, shrouded in the soft purplish black of the
November twilight, when he heard a birdcall that
wasn't birdlike enough. In fact, it reminded him of the

beat of a rap song that the teenager's stereo next door had been spewing forth at all hours.

The call came again and was answered, this time by a low, muffled voice speaking Spanish. He put out his cigarette and sat very still, his eyes on the broad expanse of the estuary, where the darkness was not yet absolute, but permeated with the pale light of stars. Presently he could make out their shadows. Three of them hunkered low, holding hands as they made their way through the cold, knee-deep water. They stayed in the water, paralleling the fence and the street beyond it, unwilling perhaps to move into the populated area until it was completely dark, or maybe planning to rendezvous with someone in a car who waited for them somewhere beyond.

He had stood up then and walked to the edge of his yard, staring after them, listening for their whispered voices, for the strange, almost comical birdcall. Who were they? Where were they going? What were they running away from? Running toward? He had experienced an almost unbearable sensation of longing, a visceral urge for migration so intense it brought tears to his eyes. *Let me go with you*, he wanted to cry out. *Whoever you are and wherever you're going, let me go, too.* Into the unknown, the unchartered, into the night with all its dangers and promises.

Let me go with you.

Then he had walked back into his house, closed the door, and read to Shawn for a half hour before the boy fell asleep. But the memory of the aliens and that strange, fluttery hunger deep in his gut and his soul had stayed with him—*let me go, too*—tempting and beckoning.

To his enormous relief, there were no reporters waiting when he got home, and the only familiar vehicle was Coop McDonald's Jeep Wrangler parked in the drive. He was barely out of the truck when Shawn rushed out of the house.

"Dad, you're home!" The boy flung his arms around

Matt, held on tight. "They let you out! I knew they
would. Aunt Trina paid your bond, didn't she?"

"She sure did."

"I knew she'd come through." He looked up at
Matt. "You're not mad 'cause I called her, are you?"

"No, of course not. Trina's family. I'm just sorry
any of this had to happen."

They walked toward the house. "A bunch of people
have called. I think some of them were reporters.
Coop wouldn't let me answer the phone, but I
watched the news. Have the cops figured out who
killed Barry yet?"

"Not yet, but it's just a matter of time," he said
carefully.

With Matt's arm around his son's shoulders, they
went inside. The TV was on and an HBO movie, the
same one Matt had watched several nights—and what
felt like several lifetimes ago—was playing. Coop Mc-
Donald, his chief foreman, was ignoring the TV and
paging through Matt's coffeetable book of the history
of Harley-Davidson motorcycles. He wore a plaid
work shirt with the cuffs rolled up over meaty forearms covered with some of the intricate scrollwork
tattoos he'd acquired while serving a five-year stretch
for drug dealing.

"Hey, man, good to see you!" Coop jumped to his
feet and grabbed Matt's hand, clutching it with such
vigor that Matt wondered if he'd been given up for
dead. "I wasn't sure what was happening, if you were
gonna be stuck there another night or what."

In that brief moment when they pumped hands,
Coop's breath hit Matt's face, and he caught a whiff,
faint but unmistakable, of bourbon.

"Thanks for staying with Shawn, Coop. I appreciate it."

"We didn't just goof off today, Dad," Shawn said
quickly. "We worked over at the Bledsoe-Tull project
all morning. I helped Coop take measurements for
the walls."

"That's great."

Matt went into the kitchen, got a Coke from the fridge, and carried it back into the living room.

"You guys eat yet?"

"We were waiting for you. I told Shawn we'd send out for pizza if you didn't show up pretty soon."

"That sounds like a good idea. I'm not hungry, but you guys go ahead."

"If it's all the same to you, Matt," Coop said, "now that you're here, I'm gonna take off. Shawn worked me too hard today. I'm beat."

"Sure, Coop. Thanks."

"Oh, about the phone calls. One you might want to attend to is Jonas Grey. Didn't say what the problem was, but he sounded shaken up."

"Probably heard about Barry."

"One other thing, Matt. Could I ask a favor?" He lowered his voice so Shawn couldn't hear as the two men walked toward the front door. "If my wife calls later on, could you tell her I just this minute left your house? I thought I'd stop by the bar on my way home, have a couple of shots to settle my nerves. You know how Eloise can be, she don't understand."

"I'm not gonna lie to your wife for you," Matt said, "but I don't plan on taking any calls, either. How about I just don't pick up the phone?"

Coop shrugged as though he understood, but an undercurrent of resentment permeated his voice as he said, "You do what you have to do. I'd just rather she didn't know I was at the bar."

Following Coop out onto the porch, Matt reached for the pack of cigarettes in his pocket. Then, remembering Shawn was in the house, he changed his mind. Pulling a couple of hard candies out of his shirt pocket instead, he offered one to Coop while he unwrapped the other and popped it into his cheek.

"Those A.A. meetings I told you about," he said, "they have 'em every day. I'd be happy to take you to one."

"For drunks, you mean?"

"Or people who think they might have a problem with alcohol."

"No, thanks, Matt. I don't have a problem. Or, if I do, the name of the problem is Eloise, not alcohol."

"Suit yourself, Coop." He started to say more, decided to hell with it. They were both upset about Barry. If Coop had an alcohol problem—and in the construction business alcoholism and drug abuse were rampant—this wasn't the time to confront him about it.

After Coop left, Matt ordered a sausage-and-mushroom pizza and cannoli, Shawn's favorite, for dessert. It was his habit, if he got home in time, to catch the six o'clock news, but tonight he cut the TV off. He figured if he wanted to hear what was being said about Barry's murder, he could catch the late news after Shawn went to bed.

When the dinner came, they sat on the sofa and ate. The phone rang a few times, but it wasn't Noel, who was the only person Matt would have talked to right now, so he let the answering machine take the calls.

"I'm glad you're home, Dad," said Shawn, pushing the last half of the cannoli around on his plate.

"Me, too, son. Me, too."

"Did they put you in a cell?"

"They call them modules these days, but yeah, it was a cell."

"It sucks that Barry's dead."

"It sure does. He was a good man."

Shawn sipped his Coke and stared at the TV screen as though the picture were still playing. He didn't look at Matt as he said, "When you called last night, I was so scared. I thought maybe, I thought you might have—"

The question was almost too painful for Matt to get out, but he forced himself to ask it. "You thought maybe I actually did it?"

"Oh, no, Dad." Shawn looked genuinely horrified at the idea. "I know you'd never hurt Barry. But if the cops think you did, then—I was afraid maybe if they let you out, you wouldn't come back. I was afraid you'd have to run away. Leave town."

The pizza Matt was chewing turned to cardboard.

"Shawn, I'd never do that. I'd never run out on you no matter what. Never. Haven't I told you that?"

"Yeah, I know. About a zillion times. I was just scared, that's all. Things happen so fast sometimes. Like when Mom died. One day she was right there, telling me to brush my teeth or go to bed, acting like she'd be around forever, then the next day I wake up and Granddad's there telling me she's dead. And I didn't know where you were, and I thought—Dad, I never told you this, but—" His features bunched together with concentration.

"What, Shawn?"

"After Granddad told me Mom had been murdered, I remembered how mad you got when Mom said she wasn't going to come back to you. I thought maybe you'd gotten really, really mad and maybe you killed her, and you'd go back to prison and I'd never see you again, either."

The last words were spoken in a furious rush, without benefit of breath or punctuation, and ended with a great, sobbing inhalation. Matt tried to speak, but a combination of sorrow, grief, and anger jammed his throat.

"It's okay, Dad, I know you didn't kill Mom. I knew that a long time ago. It was just in the very beginning, when you didn't come home that I got so scared."

"But I explained that, didn't I, Shawn? I was drunk that night. Your Mom and I had quarreled earlier, it's true, and then we got together with the lawyers to sign the divorce papers. That was the last time I saw her, and I drank that night, and it was the last time I had a drink of alcohol."

"I know. You went to Aunt Trina's house looking for Mom, and you got drunk and passed out on her sofa."

Matt didn't say anything.

Shawn said, "I don't ever want you to have to go back to prison, Dad. When you were in Pelican Bay, Mom would never let me go with her to visit you. She said I was too young."

"I didn't want you to come there, Shawn. I was dying to see you, but you were just a little kid. I couldn't stand the thought of your coming to that place. Maybe it was my pride, but I didn't want you to see me like that. I didn't want you to have memories of your father that way."

"But sometimes, after you'd been away for so long, I couldn't remember what you looked like. I'd have to look at your pictures so I could remember."

"You were so young then."

His voice broke. "I was afraid when you *did* come home that I wouldn't recognize you."

"That's over now, Shawn. And it was different, because I did do something very bad, and I deserved to be punished. I turned myself in. We've talked about that. You do something bad in this life, you have to pay the consequences. Sometimes that means going to prison, sometimes it means just having to live with yourself and knowing about whatever you did. One way or another, whether you get caught or not, you always have to pay, because God knows, and you know, even if no one else does. But this is different. I didn't do anything."

"I know that, Dad. Why don't the cops know it?"

"They will. It just takes some time."

The phone rang. Jonas Grey's voice, infused with a west Texas twang, came on the answering machine. "Hey, Matt? Goddammit, where are you? Pick up, will you? We got a problem."

Matt reached over and turned down the volume on the machine. "Sorry, Jonas, not now. I've got enough problems for one night."

Later, he and Shawn took their plates and silverware back to the kitchen and washed them, and Matt went upstairs to his bedroom. He'd intended to read, but his exhaustion was overwhelming, and sleep closed over his head like deep, soothing water.

He dreamed he was an illegal wading through the black water, following the sound of a birdcall that floated up out of the darkness, leading him on.

Chapter Seven

Howie was swimming a half mile off shore, his mind roiling with worries about his daughter, his grandson, and his former son-in-law, when a powerful current took him and started dragging him farther out to sea. It was brutally strong and prodded him onward like a mugger with an AK47 to his head. Shocked by the suddenness with which it seized him, for the first few minutes he fought furiously, treating the water as if it were a human enemy—as something to be overpowered and destroyed.

Very soon it became apparent, however, that he didn't stand a chance. He found himself thinking back to the article in the paper Trina had brought him the day before, wondering if this sense of rage and helplessness was what that poor bastard that Matt was accused of murdering had felt during the last seconds of his life. If so, at least, it must have been over quickly.

He stopped struggling, trying to gather his wits, and let the current take him, while the shoreline receded with a speed that anyone half invested in staying alive would have found terrifying.

Strangely, however, a great calm settled over him, and the idea that he might indeed be facing death started to exert a grim appeal. Despite all his physical activity, in the years since Calla died, he'd grown so very tired. Just keeping the tormenting thoughts out of his head took so much willpower and energy. He hated quitters and weaklings and cowards—couldn't stand the thought that, deep down, he might be one of them—but still, he got so damned exhausted. Life felt like some kind of infernal triathlon that asked its contestants to keep going interminably. A never-ending ordeal that never proclaimed a winner and never permitted rest.

Never allowed him to cease plotting and planning and trying to predict what might come next.

He lay back now, almost floating, staring up into the radiant blue sky while the water tossed him along.

For all his wealth, Howie's troubles had started long before Calla's murder and the advent of Trina's bizarre mood swings. There was his wife, Abbey, who had walked out on him when his daughters were still small. He'd tried to be a good husband to her, but she claimed he was controlling, emotionally inaccessible, shut down. Needed to go pound drums in the wilderness, let his anger out, get in touch with his anima, for God's sake. All of it poppycock—fancy New Age speak for the fact that he didn't fuck her, that was what it amounted to. He knew that. He wasn't an idiot. He understood that his wife—any woman—required a decent amount of servicing. It was just that so often he couldn't do it or maybe his dick wanted to, but his head didn't or his head wanted to, but then his dick said *don't even think about it, fella.*

Last he'd heard from Abbey, she was married to a professor of economics and teaching English in some private school in Tokyo, of all places. And Calla dead now, and Trina so strange and unstable that sometimes he wondered if her sister's death had actually unhinged her. And, of course, the nasty situation with Matt.

Who could blame him if he wasn't sure how much he wanted to live? If the water sweeping him along might be as much a mercy killer as an enemy?

Whatsa matter, tough guy? You don't like it? Whatcha gonna do about it?

The bullying sea smacked him from side to side.

Smashed him in the nose, the mouth. Slapped him with a face full of brine while whipping coldly at his groin.

Sadistic and capricious.

Maybe I've earned this, he thought grimly. *Maybe this is what I deserve.*

And a part of him believed he *did* deserve it. Not so much for the things he *had* done over recent years as for what he'd been unable to do long ago.

Come on, come on, give it up. You know you ain't got the balls to do anything about it. You know . . .

His head went under. He came up sputtering, disoriented. Started swimming halfheartedly against the waves.

The sea laughed at him. Small, churlish waves broke mockingly over his face, salt scalded his throat. He was nothing. He was less than nothing. He deserved to die.

Stop me, tough guy. Come on, come on, see if you can stop me.

The strength seeped out of his muscles, deflating his powerful biceps and quads into small, saggy balloons. Coming in fast and low, like a below-the-belt blow, a small wave sucker-punched him. Forced choking water into his slack mouth.

He did a weak sidestroke, watching the distance between himself and the land open up and the stately houses along Bay Shore Avenue shrink to specks and then disappear.

I'm going to die, he thought in the detached way that he might observe he was getting ready to sneeze.

The sea was confident now. It slapped him and toyed with him, seeped under his goggles, burning his eyes, sat on his head with its heavy, wet weight, crushing the air from his lungs.

And still the idea of death didn't faze him. Death was an option, not the most attractive experience on the menu of life, but certainly the ultimate one. Exotic in a way that both intrigued and repelled. Like the fried locusts he'd encountered at a feast in Zaire or that odd Scottish delicacy, haggis, that he'd once dined on in the spirit of culinary adventure at a castle near Loch Ness, but which had left him nauseated for days.

Like the locusts and haggis, he could gulp down the sea, swallow death, and be done with it all.

I can do it, he thought. *I can get off the bus. I can let go and the world will go on, and there won't be much I'll miss either, except . . . except . . .*

But what about *her*? Suddenly it was as though the dark water turned translucent, clear as gin. He could see down and down and down. What he saw was the person he loved most in the world, only like the God of his childhood, she took three forms, three identities.

Trina and Calla and his mother Yvonne.

Three women.

Two of them gone.

Which left only Trina, so strange and quirky, her moods so mercurial they verged on deranged. What would she do when she found out he hadn't come back from his swim? And later on, as the years passed, what if she needed him? What if some dark night, she called out for her father and he wasn't there, because he'd let Death lead him around by the dick. Like a chump, he'd gone and let himself die, and now she was in trouble, menaced by a man or a monster-in-man's-clothing or some accident or fatal disease. What if his younger daughter, his *only* daughter, needed her daddy and Daddy had lain down and submitted to the sea and gotten fucked by the fishes.

He could see her so clearly now, this most wondrous of creatures—Trina/Calla/Yvonne. Hair fanning out in gorgeous rivulets of russet and black and dark blond, skin filmy and translucent as the sea that submerged her.

Calla and Yvonne, daughter and mother, shimmered and faded, their colors diluted and finally absorbed by the cold, carnivorous sea.

What if she needs me?

And what of Shawn? Only a little boy and already he'd seen his father sent to prison, his mother murdered. What would happen to him now, with Matt's life falling apart?

He had such plans for his grandson. The boy was bright, spirited, sensitive. More like his mother than Matt. Which pleased Howie, of course, but frightened him, too. The world wasn't kind to boys who were too sensitive, to boys who didn't like to fight back, the kind of boy who'd rather mend a wound than open one, who'd rather learn to paint a picture of a deer than sling a rifle across his shoulder and go kill one. Boys like that needed extra guidance and careful molding, or the world would eat them alive. Beat them down into pathetic parodies of maleness or, worse, break them so badly that they retaliated by becoming monsters, icemen whose range of emotion extended no farther than violence and vengeance.

Shawn might not realize it yet—and certainly Matt didn't—but he would need his grandfather in the coming years. He would need his grandfather's strength and experience, his fierce sense of protectiveness and commitment to putting family above all. To putting *survival*, his own and his family's, above everything else in the world.

He was starting to shiver as the current muscled him along into colder, deeper water. His goggles came off and were swept away before he could grab them. He could barely see now, the shoreline was a distant muddy blur through his salt-swollen eyes.

And in his head, the voices, the terrible voices: *You wanna stop me? Go ahead, try and stop me. What'sa matter, you scared?*

Hateful, evil voices mocking his weakness, his smallness, his helplessness.

He put his face in the water, eyes scrunched shut, holding his breath for as long as he could while he felt the strength trickle out of his muscles and the waves, like cold, sodden blankets, fold over him.

You gonna stop me? Go ahead and try.

There was a hole in his chest, gaping and black, and now the voice from his past burned it deeper, gouging open his heart. What about Calla, the *memory* of Calla? The memory of his mother? Didn't he still owe something to *them*, too?

He shut his eyes and, when he did so, realized he could see down and down, to the very bottom of the sea, where his mother Yvonne gazed up at him from a radiant chasm. She wore red lipstick and sapphire earrings, and in her dark mahogany hair gleamed a tortoiseshell comb. Her long, fragile-looking fingers clasped and unclasped. He could see the blue veins on the backs of her hands. She was crying and pleading, imploring.

So many times, he'd seen her like that in that terrible dream, when sleep shattered around him like glass breaking, and he was left sitting up in the bed, gasping and shaking, his face scalded with shame and with tears. *Please*, she was whimpering, *please . . .*

For the first time since his boyhood, his heart opened to permit the possibility that perhaps there was still something he *could* do, that his pride had prevented him from doing all these years. He couldn't go back and make things turn out differently for his mother, but he could beg her forgiveness. And he could fight to survive, so he could protect Trina and Shawn. That much he could do.

A wave thundered on top of him, smashing him under the surface, punching his mouth full of brine. He came up blinking and sputtering. Realized he was a few swallows away from drowning and that the land was hopelessly far away.

Gathering himself, he challenged the current with a series of powerful strokes. The water retaliated with a cold, heart-numbing surge. He gritted his teeth and began to swim in earnest, repeating in his mind with every stroke, *I'm so sorry, Mother. So very, very sorry.* It became a kind of mantra, hypnotic and lulling at the same time, spurring him to uncover new reserves of stamina and strength.

He swam and floated, floated and swam, until gradually, with excruciating slowness, he was able to edge his way out of the current and start to swim back toward the land. It wasn't his day to die, after all. Not yet.

Almost an hour later, he crawled out of the surf up onto the beach miles away from his house and collapsed on the sand. Lay there panting and shivering, his mind for once as empty and calm as the seamless sky overhead.

A couple of kids not much older than Shawn approached, heading into the water with boogie boards under their arms. They stared at the gasping old man half covered in sand, and then one of them, tentatively, asked if he wanted them to get help.

"I look worse than I am. I'll be okay." He forced himself to his feet, knees creaking, weakness and dizziness making him reel. "You kids be careful out there. There's a current." He knew the boys would ignore him, but couldn't stop himself from warning them anyway.

After walking a mile or so, he eased into a jog. The sun was up now, baking his tanned, freckled shoulders and muscular back. He ran past a few familiar faces—the woman who walked her two Llasa apsos every morning, the stoop-shouldered guy with the metal detector—but didn't pause to exchange pleasantries as he usually did.

On the terraced balcony at the back of the house, he saw a woman staring up the beach, shielding her eyes from the sun, and for a moment, he thought it was Trina, looking for him, worrying because he was so late. Then he realized, of course, that it was only the maid.

By the time he reached the house, she'd had time to prepare a tray with coffee and croissants and was carrying it out onto the balcony. A plump Hispanic woman with intricately braided locks and multiple ear piercings, she greeted him with a warmth he was certain she didn't feel, but which he appreciated nonetheless.

"Good morning, Mr. DeGrove. Your swim took you a long way this morning."

"Yes, a very long way."

He declined the breakfast tray, but asked her to bring him a phone. She scurried to comply, returned moments later with a cell phone. Howie dialed Trina's number. She answered, sounding sleepy and cross, then instantly brightened when she realized it was her father.

"Daddy, you called me! I thought after yesterday you'd be too mad to talk to me for a while."

"Oh, nonsense, forget about that. I had an idea while I was swimming this morning! An inspiration! I want us to fly somewhere!"

There was silence—Howie could imagine her shooing some man out of her bed, so they could talk in private—then she started to giggle the way she had as a little girl when confronted with one of her father's outlandish pronouncements. "God, Daddy, you caught me by surprise. I'd love to fly off with you into the unknown. When do we leave?"

"Today! Right now! I'll call the airport and make sure the plane's ready to go."

"But *where?*"

"It's a surprise!"

"Why? What for? It's not my birthday, is it? I know it's not yours. My God, it isn't even nine o'clock yet. Can't it wait till tomorrow?"

"No, it's got to be today!"

"But why?"

"Because I *say* so," he bellowed good-naturedly. "And I'm your father and old as hell and richer than sin, and you have to indulge me once in a while."

"My God, you're in*sane*," laughed Trina, though clearly she was delighted. "You've got to tell me where we're going? Rio? Is it Rio? What about Guadalajara, Guadalajara's nice this time of year?"

"I'll tell you this, it's in the U.S., but that's all I'm going to say. And you don't need to bring anything. Dress for warm weather. We'll be back by tonight."

"Tonight? You mean we won't even get to stay in one of your hotels and get fussed over and treated like royalty?"

"Where we're going, honey, they've never *heard* of a DeGrove Hotel."

A few hours later, they both arrived at the San Diego Airport, where Howie's Cessna 182 sat fueled and waiting to go. Trina wore shorts and sandals, a San Diego Chargers T-shirt, and a white windbreaker emblazoned with the logo of *Club Med* in BoraBora. She sat in the plane and waited while Howie hurried through the preflight checks, then climbed into the cockpit and radioed the tower that they were ready to take off.

They headed northeast, climbing briefly over the mountains, then leveling out as they headed toward the empty, frying-pan flat deserts of southern Utah and Nevada. Trina kept her face pressed against the window, gazing down raptly, peppering her father with questions about the towns she saw below, the rivers and highways and lakes, and of course, their destination, which he continued to keep secret.

"Oh, Daddy, this is so exciting," she gushed.

Sometimes, thought Howie ruefully, his thirty-one-year-old daughter sounded like she was ten years old.

Sometimes, he thought wistfully, he wished she was.

Chapter Eight

The same morning that Howie had almost drowned, Matt woke up with the worst headache he'd ever had that didn't involve an evening spent with one of his former buddies, Jack Daniel's or Jim Beam. He'd forgotten to set the alarm, but jerked upright at seven sharp just the same. Outside in the driveway he heard skateboard wheels and knew Shawn was already up and making the most of the early morning coolness.

He put on a pot of coffee and was scraping marmalade onto an under-toasted slab of sourdough when the phone rang and the answering machine picked up. Jonas Grey, sounding like a man sorely in need of a good night's sleep, said, "Engstrom, stop dicking me around and answer the goddamn phone."

Matt picked it up.

"Well, it's about time you quit dodging my calls."

"I haven't been dodging anybody, Jonas."

"Yeah? I was beginning to think you might be on a plane headed for some banana republic that don't have an extradition treaty with the U.S."

"My office manager was *murdered*, Jonas. Sorry if that's made returning your phone calls kind of low priority."

"Yeah, well, I'm sorry about Barry. I only met him a couple times, but I liked the guy. He seemed like a straight-shooter. Cops got any idea who killed him?"

Matt hesitated. "A few ideas, nothing definite."

"When they find the son of a bitch, I hope he fries.

Far as I'm concerned, we *need* the death penalty. Fear, that's what keeps civilization running, good old-fashioned fear of retribution. We don't have enough fear of the law, and this is the result of it. Hang 'em, zap 'em, shove a stick of dynamite up their ass and light it for all I care, just get the hell *rid* of 'em."

Matt had been holding the phone away from his ear as Jonas's voice grew sharper and more strident, fueled by the passion of righteous wraith. He let the rant continue for a while, before interrupting, "I hear you, Jonas. It's a damn shame they aren't juicing more crooks. Now, what can I do for you?"

"Oh, yeah. Guess my wife's right, I do get carried away. I know you got your hands full right now, but you and me, we gotta talk about some serious business."

"Look, Jonas, I'm on my way down to the police station right now to talk to the detectives again. See if they got hold of anybody who was at the Rose the other night who might have seen something."

"You don't understand. This can't wait."

Matt exploded, "Is this about Jack Ryder's god-damn marble countertop with the crack the size of an eyelash on the top? Are all former NFL stars such a pain in the ass? If he's doing his prima donna routine, then—"

"It's not Ryder making me go through a pack of antacids in two days—it's Engstrom Construction. You got some pretty creative ways of doing business, Matt."

"What are you talking about?"

"Just you come by my office. Otherwise, I don't like to say this, but you won't be the only one goes to talk to the cops this morning."

Suppressing the urge to tell his subcontractor to shove it, Matt gobbled a few bites of toast, swigged down some industrial strength coffee, and drove over to Jonas's Pacific Heights office.

Thick-waisted and balding with a cigar poking out between yellow-stained teeth, Jonas Grey had fought some of the top amateur junior middleweights in his youth and battled prostate cancer in middle-age and had managed to survive all of it more or less unscathed. Only his bulbous nose, with more twists than a corkscrew, bore testimony to his boxing days. As far as the prostate cancer, if it was slowing him down any, his third wife, fifteen years his junior, didn't seem to find anything to complain about.

Over the phone, Jonas had sounded even more abrasive than usual, but now his mood seemed to have mellowed to the point Matt wondered if there was something else in his mug besides coffee.

"You know, I didn't mean to bust your balls just now, going on like that about frying the bad guys," Jonas said, offering Matt coffee, which he declined. "I didn't know—I mean, I *did* know about Barry, of course, but not that the cops got you figured for the killer. I guess when Coop was telling me about it, he forgot to mention that part."

"What, you saw something in the paper?"

"No, but my wife did and she called to—well, to—"

"To warn you that you might be working for a dangerous lunatic?"

"Oh, hell, Matt, I already knew *that*. But I don't think you murdered Barry. Nothin' else, good office managers are too hard to come by. I told my wife everybody knows what you read in the paper don't mean squat."

"So what's up then?"

"Well, that's what I want to know. We got a big problem, Matt. For starters, you know my men and I still haven't seen a dime for this Ryder renovation."

"No, I didn't know that. I thought you'd been paid, but I'll talk to Phil and make sure he cuts you a check today. You know how I operate, Jonas. Phil does the accounting, takes care of the payroll. It must have been some kind of oversight on his part."

"Maybe so, but that's not what I'm steamed about."

"What, then?"

Jonas gnawed on the cigar, then exhaled a thick,

toxic cloud. "Had a conversation with Jack Ryder a few days ago, and I haven't had a decent night's sleep since."

Matt interrupted, "Let me guess. Ryder's pissed 'cause we've had some rain, and the job's taking longer than we figured on. You know what, that's tough. Ryder thinks 'cause he played for the NFL thirty years ago, he shouldn't have to put himself out to do anything but sign autographs. Barry was the only one who knew how to talk to him, but if you want me to, I'll give him a call myself when I get a chance."

"Hold on, let me finish. You need to hear this. Other day, I'm over at the Ryder place with the electrical inspector when Jack Ryder comes out all bent out of shape. I heard about the marble countertop fiasco, so I figure that's the problem, but he starts pitching a fit about my men taking too many breaks. Says he's seen a couple of 'em hanging out by the truck sneaking beers. I told him my guys don't take any more breaks than normal, but as far as drinking on the job, that's not okay, and if I see any of it, I'll kick some ass. Didn't put it that way, but you get my drift. Anyway, Ryder's still fuming. He says something along the lines of, look, you'd be upset, too, if you'd just paid sixty-two thousand dollars for renovations on a carriage house that, from the looks of things, isn't even going to be finished in time for your son to move in when he gets back from Europe, assuming the kid *is* in Europe and not some out-of-state correctional facility or rehab, which is what I, personally, think."

Jonas ground out the cigar. He took a tube of breath mints out of his desk drawer, shook half a dozen into his hand, and popped them into his mouth. "So I raise my eyebrows and say, 'sixty-two thousand dollars, huh,' 'cause I think he's blowin' smoke out his ass, throwin' around a figure like that. Ryder gets even hotter then. He goes inside and brings out a contract, and you know what, he's right. He's damned fuckin' right. He wrote out a check for sixty-two thousand dollars to Anaheim Remodeling to do the same job my company's doing for forty thousand, except *I* haven't even seen a dime of that forty grand."

"What are you talking about, Jonas? That isn't possible."

"Hell it's not, I saw the contract. All I know is *we* didn't get that forty thousand. We haven't got squat. Now, I've known you a long time, and you've always been solid with me, so I didn't say anything to Jack Ryder. But till I know what's going on, my men aren't doing any more work over there. And I want some answers. More to the point, my guess is Jack Ryder may want some answers when he finds out he paid sixty-two thousand for a job my company put a bid in for forty."

"Christ, I don't fucking believe this! I don't know what the hell's going on, Jonas, but I'll get over to the office right now and find out."

"Yeah, Matt, you do that. But, look, don't leave me hangin' here. Call me as soon as you know anything." He picked up another cigar from the container on his desk and began to unwrap it, thoughtfully, carefully, as though not quite sure what was inside. "I know things get fucked up sometimes, Matt. The pressure gets on, the bills start to pile up, looks like there's no end in sight. I've been there, believe me. When I was just a kid, my sister got real sick. We didn't have insurance, so my old man 'liberated' a few thousand dollars from the hardware store he was working at into his checking account. Never told me about it until years later, when I was growed up. He was one damned lucky son of a bitch. He put it all back, never got caught. If you're involved in anything like this, I suggest you do the same."

"I'm no thief, Jonas. Whatever else you may think of me, I'm no fucking thief."

"Neither was my old man. But things happen, Matt. People get tempted."

Tempted.
Yeah, right. It wasn't like he didn't know about

temptation. The temptation to run away from his troubles, to hop into bed with the wrong woman—how many times had he given into *that* one?

But for Jonas to think he'd pull some kind of scam, bilking one of his clients. . . . For all his troubles in the past, *he* knew he was an honest man trying to live a decent life—problem was at this point he couldn't *prove* it.

Exceeding the speed limit by a margin that would have done credit to his former sister-in-law, he drove back to Chula Vista and let himself into the office. Phil wouldn't be getting in until late afternoon; most of the rest of his men were working at the Bledsoe-Tull job site. Turning on the computer, he keyed in a few strokes and pulled up the records for the Ryder renovation. He sat there scrolling through the numbers, studying what he saw, trying not to jump to conclusions.

According to this, a draw for fifteen thousand dollars had gone out to Jonas Grey Construction three weeks earlier, then another ten thousand had been paid at the start of this week. The final payment, minus overhead, would be paid upon completion of the project to Matt's and Jack Ryder's satisfaction. So far, so good. Except Jonas claimed he hadn't received any money.

Matt thumbed through the file cabinet, pulled out the Ryder folder, and went through it item by item. There were bids on bathroom fixtures, floor tiles, and cabinetwork. Four bids had come in for the roofing, electrical, and carpentry work that Jonas' company was doing. Lowest of the four was the bid made by Jonas, for forty thousand plus overhead. Highest was from Anaheim Remodeling, with a bid for sixty-two thousand plus overhead, along with a copy of a cashier's check from Jack Ryder made out to Engstrom Construction for the total amount.

Matt stared at the papers in his hand for several minutes, unable to believe what he was seeing. It couldn't be, yet it was—sixty-two thousand dollars paid to a subcontractor who hadn't even been awarded the job. Jonas' company was doing the work for two-thirds the price—the computer indicated that the money owed to Jonas had been drawn out of Engstrom Construction's account—but Jonas said he hadn't been paid. According to the paperwork, Jack Ryder had written a check for a bid that was never accepted, which meant sixty-two thousand dollars of Matt's and Jack Ryder's money was unaccounted for.

Meaning that, unless this was some kind of ungodly clerical error, someone in the office, either Barry or Phil or the two of them, had been scamming both Matt and Jack Ryder.

But if you're going to embezzle somebody, why the hell would you leave proof, Matt thought. The copy of the cashier's check from Jack Ryder, the bid from Anaheim Remodeling that had undoubtedly been presented to Ryder were right there in the files for anybody to find. Why make it so stupidly obvious?

To make it look like I did it, he realized. *So when this falls apart, as it would have to as soon as Jonas and Jack Ryder compared notes, when the police come with a warrant to search my office, they'll find all the proof they needed that I'm bilking my customers.*

So much was coming down on him at once, Matt felt the first twinge of panic in his gut—if Barry's murder and the missing funds were just an ungodly coincidence, that in itself was devastating. But what if the two events weren't a coincidence? What if Barry and Phil had been involved in some scheme together, something that backfired horribly and was about to take Matt down with them?

Hands shaking with a combination of fury and fear, he picked up the phone and called Phil. At this time of morning, Phil should have still been in bed, but if so, he wasn't answering his phone. Heart hammering, Matt locked up the office, jumped in his truck, and headed for Mission Bay.

Chapter Nine

Except for a visit to Sea World with Shawn a few months back, Matt hadn't spent any time in Mission Bay Park since the days when he and Calla would come here to windsurf and swim. Too crowded, he told himself, and too noisy, but what he realized now that he really meant was, too damned young. To judge from the looks of Mission Boulevard and West Mission Bay Drive, the population seemed to be aging in reverse. Kids zigzagging on skateboards, catching air with kamikaze abandon; packs of Rollerbladers that had to be exceeding the posted pedestrian speed limit of eight miles an hour. Long-legged teenage girls with skin like fine suede and miles of bright hair that floated out behind them as they bicycled and Rollerbladed and jogged.

He saw a dark-haired girl with fushcia lipstick who reminded him of Noel and forced himself not to stare. She caught the edge of his lingering gaze anyway and turned away, disdainful and mocking or maybe just stoned.

He checked Phil's address again and continued along West Mission Bay Drive toward the channel. Crisp, jaunty sailboats caught the breeze on Sail Bay. Gulls plunged and careened overhead.

He finally located Phil's building—a beige stucco duplex where two cats dozed in a bay window, surrounded by an array of cacti in large Mexican urns. Flower beds under the windows exploded with color—

profusions of zinnias and morning glories and other flowers he couldn't identify.

He took the stairs to Phil's second-floor apartment two at a time, whacking the door so hard with his fist that passersby on the sidewalk below gawked like they might be witnessing a drug bust in progress.

"Phil, open the door!"

Nothing.

He put his face to the window and peered inside through a space where the curtains were partially open. From what he could see, someone who didn't like Phil very much had been busy redecorating his living room—either that, or a troop of wild chimps had passed through recently. A disaster. He was about to break the glass to get in, when it occurred to him that whoever had trashed the place probably hadn't bothered to lock the front door when they left. He tried it and, sure enough, it swung open.

Gingerly he stepped inside, skirting overturned furniture and the shards of smashed bric-a-brac.

"Phil, you here?"

Judging from the destruction, Phil's vandal had an epicurean bent. Books had been flung onto the floor and then soaked in ketchup and cooking oil. Framed seascapes and mountainscapes with inspirational tags—INNOVATE, MOTIVATE, FACILITATE—had been smashed and then retitled—FUCK YOU, ASSHOLE—in what appeared to be mustard. Phil's prized autographed picture of Andre Vykos had been scissored into strips. Desk drawers pulled out, their contents dumped on the floor and soaked with booze. On top of the stereo sat a melting tub of Rocky Road ice cream that had congealed in dark rivulets on the beige carpet.

Stunned by the destruction, Matt proceeded to the bedroom, where the chaos took a more ominous turn—a knife had replaced condiments as the weapon of choice. Bedspread, pillows, and drapes, as well as Phil's clothes had been slashed into strips, the mattress stabbed so repeatedly it looked like curdled swiss cheese.

A bathroom adjoined the bedroom and connected to a second bedroom that Phil used as an office. Here the contents of the medicine cabinet had been emptied out and the mirror over the sink shattered. Pills and glass crunched under Matt's boots. Shards filled the basin and glittered on the seat of the toilet along with a few droplets of blood. More blood dappled the floor and led to the edge of the tub.

Fuck.

Spinning around, he yanked the shower curtain down with enough force to send rod and curtain crashing to the floor.

Phil's girlfriend Paula flung out her arms and screeched, "Don't hurt me! I didn't do anything!"

In her present state, Paula was hardly recognizable as the pretty girl Matt had met a couple of times. She cowered against the wall, cradling her hand, which dripped a thin line of blood onto the tile. The seductive voice that Matt had found alternately amusing and alluring was now a harsh moan. Her ash-blond hair, which normally hung in a single straight braid down her back, framed her face in snarled ringlets.

"What the hell's going on?" Matt demanded. "Where's Phil?"

"The slimy, cheating little bastard's run out on me."

Matt looked at her arm. "Jesus, what have you done? You cut yourself?"

She rolled her eyes, which were a washed-out blue, rimmed with red and globs of running mascara. "God, you think I tried to kill myself? You gotta be kidding. That jerk's not worth a paper cut. I hurt myself on the glass when I punched the mirror."

"Let's have a look."

She stepped out of the shower and held her hand under the tap while Matt rummaged around in the cabinet under the sink. He finally found a box of Band-Aids and taped Paula's hand while she sniffled and used her other hand to blot her eyes.

"What are *you* doing here, anyway?" she asked miserably.

"Same as you. You just beat me to it."

"You gonna call the cops?"

"What do you think?"

She sagged against the sink. "Please don't. I'll go to jail. I'll lose my job. What'll my parents think?"

He thought of the mustard, mayonnaise, and ketchup squirted around the living room and said, "You should've thought of that when you were getting Phil's sofa confused with a hotdog bun."

"Oh, Jesus, Matt." Fresh tears started to surge. "I'm such an idiot."

"Yeah, well, there's a lot of that going around these days. What the hell were you thinking, anyway?"

"I just wanted revenge."

"And you think there's anything here that's worth going to prison over? Believe me, honey, I know about prison. Nothing's worth that."

She shook her head miserably.

"Look, I tell you what. You and I are gonna wait here for Phil, and I'll let him decide whether to forgive and forget or have the cops haul your ass off to jail."

She looked at him with a mixture of disbelief and scorn. The expression aged her dramatically, making Matt wonder if he'd been as mistaken about her age as he had about her disposition. "Don't you get it? Phil's not coming back. He's fucking *gone*. And I'm so mad at myself, 'cause I *knew* he'd pull something like this eventually. I *knew* I couldn't trust the little sleaze, but I went along anyway, believing his bullshit about all the money he was making in the Market, about how he was gonna move to New York and get a job on Wall Street, how he wanted me to—to—oh, fuck, what an *idiot* I am."

She turned suddenly, walked out of the bathroom, and headed for the door.

Matt went after her, caught her arm. "Whoa, where are you going?"

She pulled free. "Well? You said you weren't gonna

call the cops. I figured I'd find the nearest liquor store, buy a fifth of something hundred proof, then go home and drink myself blind."

"Not so fast. I need to find Phil, too. So just sit down and tell me what the hell's going on."

"I *told* you. He's gone. Skipped. Taken off."

Matt steered her toward the kitchen, where he righted a couple of chairs and sat her down at the table. "Okay, where is he? How do you know he's not coming back? I mean, look around you, he left all his stuff. That means he's coming back, right?"

She shook her head. "You don't know Phil. He's got a safe in the back of the bedroom closet where he kept his cash, his passport, his fucking cubic zirconia cuff links and that piece-of-shit watch he claims is a Rolex. When I looked, he'd left it open and there was nothing inside. Cleaned out." She shivered and, leaning forward, murmured something so softly Matt had to ask her to repeat it.

"I said that bitch. When I realized he'd taken off, I played his messages back. Just like I figured, there was one from his Vegas whore."

"Who?"

"Cindee. Phil's other girlfriend. The one he always saw when he went to Vegas. Oh, at first he and I used to go together, but then when I started getting on him about how much he gambled, he started finding excuses to go by himself. So the next time he and I were out together and he called home to check his messages, I watched and memorized the code, so I could check his messages, too. This Cindee would call to find out when he was coming out to Vegas. For a fucking cocktail waitress, she's got a Boston accent that makes the Kennedys sound like country hicks, but then Phil's a sucker for crap like that. She's probably convinced him she's an heiress with an MBA from Vassar."

"So you think Phil's in Vegas?"

"I *know* it. He *comes* for that town. Just wait till I get some real money together, he'd say, I'll triple it in a weekend. He liked to talk like he was James Bond raking it in at blackjack or something. The truth is he doesn't even know how to play blackjack or craps. He plays the fucking poker slots. Poker slots, like the old geezers they bus in from the retirement homes, for God's sake. He's got all these theories, too. Like he always plays the machines closest to the door because he thinks they're loose."

"I knew Phil liked to gamble. But I thought it was just recreational, you know, a hobby."

Paula laughed. "Don't kid yourself. He'd sell his grandmother's kidneys to an organ ring if he thought it'd improve his odds. He's a fucking addict. I tried to tell him that, but he'd just get mad. Plus—" She started to cry again. "Oh, I am such a fool. God, I hate him. I hate myself."

"Don't, Paula." He rubbed a hand between her shoulder blades. "Whatever you did, it was the best you could do at the time."

"I lent him money, that lying little con man. I'd saved it to start my own decorating business. It was before I realized he had a problem, and we were talking about getting married. He convinced me he knew some stock he could make a fortune with. I know he gambled it away. And now I know I'll never get it back. He fucked me over and he got away with it."

"I know the feeling," Matt said grimly. "Jesus, I guess I ought to call the police."

Paula looked up, alarmed. "Wait a minute. You said you—"

"No, no, I don't mean about you. I mean—" He tried to imagine calling the police to report the embezzlement of sixty-two thousand dollars. Trouble was, there was no proof Phil had stolen the money. From the cops' point of view, it could just as easily have been Matt who'd been cheating his client and subcontractor both. In fact, the more he thought about it, the more he realized that was how it *did* look—like he was ripping off everybody. And if that was the case and if Barry had found out about it and confronted him, then there was the murder motive the cops were looking for. Even if a case could be made that Phil, with his gambling habit, looked equally suspicious, Matt had no doubt that it was *his* ass that Uhlen-kamp wanted.

What had probably *really* happened, he thought, was that Barry had caught on to what Phil was doing, confronted him, and then called Matt to tell him they had something "urgent" to discuss. Phil could have found out about the meeting at the Rose simply by looking at Matt's appointment calendar. Then either Phil or someone working with him waylaid Barry on the way to the Rose and killed him.

Matt figured the latter scenario was more likely. Whatever else Phil was capable of doing, he couldn't see the fastidious, physically slight accountant slashing Barry's throat with a razor and then dumping the much heavier man in the back of his pickup truck.

"Night before last, I called the office a little after nine," he said to Paula. "Phil answered, and I heard your voice in the background. He said he was showing you something on the computer."

"Well, we were in the office, but I don't know how much got done on the computer. More like the floor."

"This is important, Paula, so don't lie. How long were you and Phil at the office? From when to when?"

"I don't know. A couple of hours. Before that, I met him at Rafferty's for dinner. Why?"

"So you were with him all evening?"

"That's right."

"And there were witnesses who could verify you were at Rafferty's?"

"Sure, Phil goes there all the time. The waitresses, the bartenders, they all saw us."

"You spent the night with him?"

"Yeah."

"You're absolutely *sure* about that?"

"Yes."

Misreading the expression on his face, Paula said, "What is it? Did *you* lend him money, too?"

"In a manner of speaking. It's important that I find him right away. This Cindee, do you know where she works?"

"The Luxor. Phil always stays there when he goes to Vegas—when I went through his wallet last time, I found the receipts."

"But suppose, let's just say Phil came into some money recently—would he just take off for Vegas to gamble it away? I mean, he was always following the stock market, wouldn't he invest it or something?"

In spite of her distress, Paula laughed tearfully and wiped at her eyes. "That investing in the market stuff was bullshit. Phil never had enough money left over from gambling to invest in anything, but some more rolls of quarters. You want to find Phil, he'll have one hand on the one-armed bandit and the other inside this bitch's pants. Count on it."

After his talk with Paula, Matt drove home, threw some things into an overnight bag, and phoned Maria to see if she could spend the next couple of nights with Shawn. There followed an awkward exchange where Maria tried to explain she had a family emergency involving her father, while Matt could hear a woman saying in the background, "Not at *that man's* house, you're not baby-sitting. It'll end up another Brentwood, you'll see."

He phoned Trina, who didn't answer, and then Howie. The maid picked up and said Mr. DeGrove and his daughter were out for the rest of the day. With some reluctance, he then rang Coop's cell phone over at the job site. He remembered the alcohol he'd smelled on the man the day before, but today Coop sounded okay. He said he'd swing by Matt's house first thing after work and bring Shawn home to spend the night with him and Eloise.

"You can tell Shawn the truth about where I'm going, but anybody else asks where I am, tell them I've checked into a motel to avoid the press and you can't give out the phone number. I'll call in for my messages." He hesitated, weighing the risks of another matter that had been on his mind since talking to Paula. "Coop, there is one other thing, but I kind of hate to ask."

"What is it, Matt?"

"You know I can't legally own a gun."

"One of the perks of being a convicted felon."

"Yeah, well, I know you bend that rule a little. Didn't you get Eloise a shotgun and a couple of semi-automatics over the years?"

"Sure, she's got a nice little collection. All in her name, of course."

"I'd like to borrow one. Just for protection."

There was a pause. Then Coop said, "Stop by my house on your way out of town. I'll call Eloise now and tell her to expect you. She'll fix you up."

"Thanks."

He hung up the phone feeling guilty as hell. Leaving town even overnight was a violation of the conditions of his bond. Not to mention the fact that he was getting ready to arm himself with a pistol. But he didn't know what was waiting for him in Vegas and, even if he found Phil, it was unlikely his former employee was going to come back to San Diego willingly.

Lastly, he wrote a check for twelve thousand dollars out of his personal account and put it in the mail to Jonas Grey as partial payment for his work at the Ryder place. He didn't have enough cash to reimburse Jack Ryder's sixty-two thousand, but he figured he'd worry about repaying that later.

Hell, he thought, *maybe I'll get lucky in Vegas.*

The phone rang as he was going out the door, stopping him cold. For a few seconds, he did one of those little comedy routine numbers—started back to answer it, changed his mind, went out the door, changed his mind again, went back, hesitated like the phone was something that might rip off a finger if given a chance, then picked it up.

"Matt?"

It was *her*.

"Noel? Noel, please don't hang up on me again, okay? That isn't fair. It's made me crazy ever since you called."

"I'm sorry, Matt. You're right. It isn't fair."

At least she wasn't drunk or high this time. Her voice sounded resigned and flat, but steady, measured out in thimblefuls.

"I had the news on last night, and I heard about you getting arrested for killing Barry. Jesus, Matt, what happened? Did you do it?"

"Noel, I *didn't* kill anybody. How could you even think that?"

"You've got a temper, Matt. You told me what you went to prison for."

"That was an accident, I explained that to you."

"And you've got enemies."

"What enemies?"

"I mean—"

"*What* enemies, Noel?"

"Don't raise your voice, Matt. Or I swear I'll hang up. When I called the other night, I lost my nerve. But I need to talk to you. I've got something I've got to tell you."

He felt himself losing patience. "Then *tell me*, for God's sake. I can't stand this. Stop playing games."

"I'll tell you. And if you hate me, I don't blame you, but you need to know the truth. I saw a doctor a few weeks ago. I hadn't been feeling right, so I had some blood drawn. What she found was that, well, Matt, you need to know I'm positive."

He heard her words, knew what she meant, yet couldn't let himself know it altogether. Not now, not *this*.

He waited and when she said nothing else, he asked her, "Positive of what, Noel?"

She laughed then, a high, loopy, hysterical laugh. "Oh, God, you're so funny. What do you *think*? For AIDS, Matt. I tested positive for AIDS."

Chapter Ten

A little after one in the afternoon, Howie landed the Cessna on a narrow strip of tarmac simmering under the summer sun on the outskirts of Cottonwood, Arizona. As unpretentious as its name, Cottonwood was a small, heat-blasted, workingman's town, dotted with scrub oak and sagebrush, about a half hour's drive from the New Age mecca of Sedona to the northeast and an hour and a half from the more conservative, cowboy-oriented culture of Prescott to the southwest. From the air, Trina had thought the town appeared drab and brown and dusty, its nondescriptness unrelieved by the stands of cottonwood flanking a narrow, winding stream. Now that they were on the ground, she thought the place looked even more desolate and arid.

"*This* is what you got me all excited about? This is what we flew all this way for?"

"It's not Rio, I admit," said Howie gruffly, "but not every place worth seeing has to have a carnival with marimba bands and floats and samba dancers."

Trina reached into her purse for a small tube of sunscreen, squeezed a dab into her palm, and began spreading it over her nose and cheekbones. "Can you at least get a martini here?" she said sullenly.

"A cold beer might be more in line with local custom."

She rolled her eyes. "Oh, Daddy, you do bring me to the world's meccas of sophistication, don't you?

Paris, Rome, Cottonwood—where next, Podunk, Arkansas?"

She thought he was ignoring her, but a minute later, as he brought the plane to a halt, he surprised her by saying, "Is there such a place?"

"What?"

"Podunk, Arkansas. Is there any such place, or did you make it up?"

She raised an eyebrow. "Oh, Daddy, I invented it. You know how Trina loves to invent things to make her life more interesting."

"As if your life weren't interesting enough!"

Climbing out of the plane, the heat thudded over their heads like hurled bricks. They trudged across the tarmac, through the tiny airport, and outside the main door, where Howie stopped at the car rental counter, flashed a Gold membership card, and was handed the keys to a white Saab that waited for him outside in the shade.

"Some surprise destination," Trina said, looking around the bleak landscape as they headed north. "All we need now is a cow skull by the side of the road and a few circling vultures."

"Bear with me, Trina."

"Wait a minute—I know!" She brightened suddenly. "I'll bet there's an antique car dealership in town, and they've got some fabulous vintage car you know I can't live without. That's it, isn't it? You brought me here to look at a car?"

Howie's mood seemed to have soured during the time that they'd been in the air—the effects of his exertions in the sea that morning catching up with him. "For once, Trina, can you not think of yourself and of material acquisition? Did I really raise you to be this superficial?" He squinted behind his sunglasses at the dry, brittle-looking landscape they were passing. Stunted trees and brown grasses, distant hills that looked dull and smudged, like faded fingerprints, against a bleached-out sky.

"Sorry, Daddy." Chastised, she crossed her legs and

stared listlessly out the window while they cruised slowly through the town, passing a small strip mall with an Albertson's, Drug Fair, and half a dozen small stores, a retirement community, and a trailer park, fire department, and elementary school. Finally Howie pulled up in front of a diner on the town's northern-most fringe.

Trina unhooked her seat belt and was getting out of the car before she realized Howie hadn't budged. He let the air conditioner blow full force in his face and stared at the place with its shiny faux-fifties exterior, its fake palm trees and plastic flamingos, its glaring chrome and glass trim.

"What's wrong, Daddy? Are we going to eat here or what?"

"So this is what they built here," Howie said softly, almost to himself. "There was a motel here a long time ago, where your grandmother and I stayed. I bought it years ago and had it torn down. Then I sold the land to developers. I never knew what they did with it until now."

"When were you and grandmother here, Daddy?"

"Years ago. I was a little boy. Your grandmother was— oh, c'mon, let's go inside. My blood sugar's dropping. That's why I'm cranky. I need red meat."

"Is that your way of saying you're sorry you snapped at me?"

"I'm sorry, okay? And I'm also starving. I had an unusually tough swim this morning. I guess I didn't realize how much it took out of me."

They went inside and sat at a Naugahyde booth with a jukebox belting out Elvis. Howie had chili fries and a cheeseburger and a chocolate shake. Trina had a hamburger—hold the bun—and a Coke and a small dinner salad. She picked at her food while Howie wolfed his down. When they'd eaten and Howie had paid for the meal, they went back outside. Coming from the diner's air-conditioned interior, the heat now felt even more brutal.

"Come on," said Howie. "I've put this trip off fifty fucking years. I want to get it over with."

They drove north into the hills toward Jerome, an old mining town turned tourist destination that clung to the steep cliffs overlooking Cottonwood. Howie stopped the car twice to get out and peer down into the valley, pacing and murmuring to himself like a man in the grip of some acute, private fever.

On the edge of Jerome, he pulled over again and tromped down a dusty, rock-strewn embankment to a tiny graveyard enclosed by a slanted, weatherworn fence. Trina, hurrying to keep up, stubbed her toe on a rock and would have gone sprawling had Howie not whirled around in time to break her spill. Embarrassed, she sputtered and cursed and shook the red dust from her hair.

"My God, what a hellhole you've brought me to. You could have at least warned me. I thought we were coming someplace *nice*."

"Hush," said Howie. He bent down and started clearing away the weeds from some of the headstones. "Hang in here with me another minute or two. That's all I ask."

Trina stared at the sky. The heat flayed her face, stung her back. "It's your mother, isn't it? She's buried here."

"Yes."

"Why *here*? Couldn't her body have been taken back east? She had family, didn't she?"

"A few relatives, but there wasn't any money," Howie said. "Besides, back then, having a child outside of marriage was scandalous enough, but not knowing who the father was—that was sheer disgrace. So there wasn't really any family who hadn't disowned Mother, except for my Aunt Gloria. And she didn't have a pot to piss in, poor soul, but she took me in anyway."

"And this is the first time you've been back here since—?"

"—since she died."

"Jesus," muttered Trina, wiping sweat onto her sleeve, "you could just leave somebody out in the sun here, they'd be cremated in no time."

Howie glanced up sharply. "What did you say?"

"Nothing, Daddy."

He nudged some weeds aside with his toe. "*Here*. Here it is. Come here, Trina. Look at this."

Behind the darkly tinted sunglasses, Trina rolled her eyes, but she obliged him, trudging dutifully to the grave. Her grandmother's full name, Yvonne Katrina DeGrove, and her birth and death dates were engraved on the small headstone. Howie knelt and tenderly caressed the slab, hands moving over the letters like a blind man reading braille.

"She was only a couple of years older than you are now when she was killed."

"A car accident," said Trina. "You told me it was on the way to California, that she was hoping to start a movie career, but you never said exactly how it happened or where. Were you with her?"

"Yes."

"How old were you?"

"Ten, eleven. I'm not sure. It's all kind of a blur."

"What made her think she could make a go of it in California?"

Howie exhaled a long breath. "Ever since she was a teenager, people had been telling her she looked like Vivian Leigh. Mysterious, beguiling, but sweet, too. Innocent-looking. And her laugh—it was like wind chimes. Just hearing her laugh was enough to make you love her."

"*You* certainly loved her." If there was bitterness in Trina's voice, it was lost on Howie.

"Everywhere we went, men looked at her. Followed her with their eyes. She was that beautiful. I asked her once if it didn't make her nervous, but she said I was being silly, that no one looked at her. But she was lying, of course. I always knew when she was lying. Her voice changed. It would get so soft and low,

as though she thought that if she whispered, it
wouldn't be a lie."

"You do that, too, you know."

"I *do*?"

Trina laughed. Too loudly, almost a bray, making
her laugh intentionally harsh and grating.

"No, Daddy, I'm just yanking your chain. You're
much too good a liar for anyone to catch you at it."

Howie sighed. "Why are you always angry at me?
What have I done?"

"I'm not angry with you."

"Since Calla died, it seems to me you're always
angry."

"Because you loved her more than me and because
you obviously loved your mother more than me and
because—just because it hurts to feel like I'm in com-
petition with the dead. The dead are always perfect.
They never make mistakes. They never fuck up."

"The way the living do?"

She shrugged. "I don't mean to give you a hard
time, Daddy. You can't help it if you're obsessed with
two dead women. But if I stand out here in the heat
much longer, it's going to be three." She started walking toward the car, calling back over her shoulder,
"Toss me the car keys, will you?"

"Trina, wait. Please. This isn't going the way I'd
hoped it would. I need to tell you something."

She strode a few more paces and stopped. Waited
for him to catch up.

"I lied to you about how she died."

For a second, Trina's legs went wobbly and no
longer felt connected to the ground. She bit her lip
and whispered, "Calla?"

"No, no, of course not. I'm talking about your
grandmother Yvonne. There wasn't any car accident.
She was murdered."

"My God, Daddy. Why did you lie? Why the bullshit story about Yvonne getting sleepy and running
off the side of the road?"

Howie combed his fingers through sweat-plastered

hair. "Maybe I thought if I explained your grandmother's death as an accident, I'd start to believe it myself. You think I'm tough, Trina, but I'm not. Far from it. I'm actually weak."

"No, Daddy, I don't believe that. You're the strongest man I've ever known. A lot of guys are all strutting and ego and noise, but it's all show. They run like rabbits in a crunch. Believe me, I know. You're not like that. You're quiet, but you make sure things happen. That's the only kind of strength that counts—when people know that if they cross you they're fucked."

Howie seemed to consider that for a moment. Then he said, "Come on. If you can stand the heat a bit longer, let's walk back to the grave."

She shrugged, rubbed at a red place on her heel that was starting to blister, but followed him back to the plot of cracked, weed-infested stones. A pot of desiccated flowers that had blown onto its side distracted her. She bent to right it, but the second the hot breeze struck the dried blooms, they disintegrated and blew away like so much bright dust.

"I was just thinking," mused Trina, "that Shawn was even younger when Calla died than you were when you lost your mother. Two losses like that in the same family. Sad stuff, huh? What are the odds?"

"I know," said Howie, "I've thought about that. In my darker moments, I've asked myself if this family is cursed."

"You mean like voodoo? Black magic?"

"Of course I don't give credence to any of that nonsense. But I know people who believe in karma, and they say that we come here to learn certain lessons. And if the lessons aren't learned, then they get tougher and tougher, until finally we're *forced* to learn. I start wondering if Calla was murdered—maybe because I didn't save my own mother and so I was given a chance to save my daughter, but I failed at that, too? And does that mean I'll have to go through something this awful *again*? I worked so hard to build a fortune, in part, because I knew that money is power, and money can keep people safe from all kinds of terrible things, but I found out it's a double-edged sword. As much as wealth has the power to protect, it also attracts danger. I know you thought I was insane when I hired bodyguards for you after that rash of kidnappings a few years back, but I tell you, girl, I couldn't stand to lose either you or Shawn. It would kill me."

"Don't be ridiculous." The wind blew grit into Trina's eyes. She dipped her head and swiped at the tears. "Nothing's going to happen to me or Shawn. And as for whatever happened to your mother, you were just a little boy. And when Calla died—how could you have prevented it? You weren't even there. Nobody knows what happened to her, if the killer was somebody she knew or a complete stranger who just picked her at random. We'll probably never know."

Howie sighed. "The only one who knows the truth about a murder is someone who was there when it took place."

"You mean—the killer?"

"Not necessarily," Howie said. "I was there when my mother was murdered. I saw it all."

"Oh, God."

"We were staying at the motel in Cottonwood, the one I had torn down. It was so god-awful hot—today's balmy by comparison. We had the windows open, but there wasn't any breeze. Mother went out to get ice. I remember I told her to hurry up—I wanted that ice to rub on my face—and she just smiled and said, 'Howie, you're so impatient, you have to learn how to *savor* life.' I was a self-centered little bastard, when I look back on it—all I ever wanted was to be the center of her attention.

"She'd been gone just a few minutes—I was half asleep—when the door opened and these two men came in. Scruffy-looking, smelling like they hadn't bathed in a week. They weren't old really, but they *looked* old—hard, lined faces like they'd been working

in fields or on a chain gang. I should've realized right
away what was happening but—"

"You didn't yell out for help?"

"There was a window open not six feet away. If I
could tell you how many times in my dreams, in my
imagination, I've dived out that window and run to
get help—Jesus God, every day of my life, Trina, I
jump out that window, and I run to get help screaming
at the top of my lungs, but I didn't, no, I—"

"You were too shocked probably," Trina put in.

He shook his head. "I stared at them, and they
stared at me—they hadn't known there was a kid in
the room—and then my mother came in with the
bucket of ice, and they grabbed her. I remember the
bucket flying out of her hands and chunks of ice
bouncing off the floor like broken teeth. She started
screaming and the bigger one, the fat, redheaded one,
slammed her onto the bed and put a pillow over her
face. I jumped on his back, and the other pulled me
off and smacked my head into the wall—again and
again. Everything went bright red. The whole room—
I'll never forget it—the room cracked right down the
center like the wall was made out of eggshells, and
the cracks filled up with black until there was nothing
but black.

"When I came to, they were both on the bed with
her, and there was all this blood. Her blood was all
over the bed, all over them. I don't know if she was
still alive then, but they'd both raped her, and they
were—doing things to her—with the knife. Seeing how
far they could get the blade—inside her. It went on
and on, and I couldn't move, my legs wouldn't work.
The only reason they didn't stab me, too, I think they
thought I was already dead.

"But the worst part, the part that haunts me to this
day is the fact that I didn't cry out, I didn't go out the
window and run for help when I know I had time to."

"You were young, you were scared."

"No, that wasn't it. What shames me to this day is,
well, you have to understand my mother loved men.

All kinds of men. They were her hobby, you might say. And sometimes they were her source of income. She had already said we might not be able to get any more motels—we might have to sleep in our car for a while, we were that low on money. When the two men came in, my first thought was, I thought she'd invited them. I thought she was going to come in any second all smiling and ask me to go wait outside while she and her new friends had some drinks. She'd done it before. I thought that was what was going on, and I was so angry at her—at that moment I wanted her dead. And in just a few minutes, she was."

"God, Daddy, you couldn't have known."

"If only I hadn't been so quick to judge her. To assume the worst."

"It sounds like she was pretty wild. You couldn't help but think she might have invited those guys to party." She paused, kicked at a stone. "Do you suppose I take after her, Daddy?"

He put his arm around her. "She had a lot of wonderful qualities, your grandmother. If anything, she was just born in the wrong era. Today her lifestyle wouldn't draw the kind of condemnation it did then. She could have had all the lovers she wanted and never married, and no one would have questioned her right to do that."

"The men—did they ever catch them?"

"Oh, the town got all excited for a few days—you didn't get too many rape-murders in Cottonwood—but the two men weren't local, and the sheriff figured they were hobos who took off as soon as they killed my mother. I used to fantasize about tracking them down, torturing them and killing them, but—where would I have begun to look after so many years? The best I could do—after DeGrove Hotels started to take off and I had some money, I sent someone to buy the motel she was killed in and had it torn down. That was the best I could do.

"So, there you have it, Trina, my secret. Not my

darkest secret perhaps and not my only one, but surely the most painful."

She looked at the ground. "I have secrets, too, Daddy. But I'm afraid that if I told you what they were, you wouldn't love me anymore."

"That's impossible, Trina. Nothing you could do could be so terrible it would make me not love you."

"Don't be so sure."

"I *am* sure. Believe that."

They walked back to the car holding hands. Along the way, Howie said, "I've always been thankful for one thing. At least the men who killed your grandmother were strangers to her. Men she'd never met or had any dealings with."

"Why?" said Trina glumly. "What difference does it make? Dead's dead."

"True," said Howie, "but the worst thing I can imagine is for someone to be murdered by one of their own friends or family, to look up into the face of a loved one who's wielding an axe or a gun or a club and that's the last face you see, the face of the person who's killing you and the face of the person you love."

"Jesus, Daddy." Trina hunched her shoulders and drew a sharp breath. "What a goddamn morbid thing to say! Whether she knew the men who murdered her or not, it's not like she's any less dead for it."

"I'm sorry, honey. I didn't mean to upset you. I only meant—at least she didn't have to die feeling she'd been betrayed."

They walked a little farther before Howie said, "There's something else I've wanted to talk to you about for a long time now. It's about Calla. How she died."

Trina blew at a lock of damp hair straggling into her eyes. "We'll never know what happened to Calla. Not unless someone comes forward and confesses, which isn't likely."

"No, I agree with you. The detectives say the case is still open, but people get murdered every day, and there're only so many investigators to go around. How much can they do? And I don't want or expect Calla's death to get special treatment just because her father has money."

"Commendable of you," said Trina.

She staggered suddenly, sagged against him. Started to sob.

"Trina, what is it?"

Now the sobs came uncontrollably. "It's *Calla*, you're obsessed with her! Even after she's dead, you *still* only care about Calla. It's like I'm invisible. It's like I don't count."

"No, no, that's not true."

He tried to comfort her, and she shoved him away with a furious strength, tear-filled eyes wild and blazing. "I swear to you, Daddy, if I could change places with Calla, if whatever happened to her that night could happen to me and she could be alive, I'd make the trade. Then at least you could be happy. At least you'd have your precious Calla back."

"You're so wrong. If you only knew—"

But she was running now, back toward the car, her arms flailing. She was still talking to him, but Howie couldn't hear. Watching her go, it was as if the ocean closed over his head for the second time in one day, and he was adrift and helpless.

When he reached the car and slid into the driver's seat next to her, she was calm again and said quietly, "Daddy, I want to go home. Can we *please* leave this place now?"

"Yes, Trina, we don't have to talk about Calla again. We can go home now."

The flight west, even with strong tail winds pushing them on, seemed twice as long as the one going east. Howie flew with the fortitude and grim determination of a fighter pilot on a doomed mission, responding to Trina's comments with monosyllabic grunts until, tired of being rebuffed, she, too, fell silent.

For Howie, though, the exhaustion had as much to do with disappointment as the physical exertions of the day. He'd come all this way and still, like some

benighted pilgrim who aborts the journey just short of
the shrine, had somehow failed. Had not told Trina
the whole truth.

But what if she was too mentally fragile to *bear* the
truth? And what if she hated him for telling her?

He flew southwest, chasing the sun, and when it
finally escaped him, sliding below the sleek rim of the
Pacific, it was with a bitter relief that he aimed the
Cessna back home, into the darkness.

Chapter Eleven

Under different circumstances, Matt would have enjoyed the drive through the desert to Vegas. Twilight, languid and hazy, hovered over a seemingly endless expanse of pale ocher, sagebrush-strewn sand. Except for the occasional truck rumbling past, there was little traffic.

As it was, though, he was driving like those road-raging idiots he liked to curse—too fast and too careless, like his mind was exceeding its own safe speed limit by about thirty miles per synapse.

Which it was.

Noel had said he had enemies. That idea lodged in his mind like a sliver of glass.

I'll get you, you fucking murderer! You may get out of prison, but you'll never have a minute's peace. I'll see to that!

Harold Petrovsky's brother Zeke had screamed those words at Matt's sentencing. Was that nightmare from Matt's past somehow connected to the nightmare ensnaring him now?

Harold Petrovsky. Stalker and nutcase and world-class degenerate or maybe just a sick, sad man whose demons killed him long before he and Matt ever met. Before Petrovsky ever laid eyes on Calla.

"He's harmless. Just a guy who comes into the bookstore," Calla had said when Petrovsky first called their apartment in Pacific Beach. Shawn had just turned three then. Matt had quit his job as construction foreman a year earlier to go into business for himself. They were struggling to get by, neither one of them wanting Howie's help, and Calla had taken a part-time job at a bookstore up the street. Harold Petrovsky worked at an accounting firm nearby and stopped in almost every day on his lunch hour.

"He's into catastrophic weather and natural disasters," Calla said. "Hurricanes, tidal waves, earthquakes. He knows the names and dates of all the major storms the way some men know football stats."

Matt had grunted something to the effect that, unless this character was calling to warn them of an earthquake fault directly under their house, she should tell him to fuck off.

"I already did," Calla said, "and I reminded him that I'm married." She shrugged. "I think he's got a little crush on me."

It turned out to be more than that. Petrovsky kept calling on one pretext or another, ignoring first Calla's and then Matt's demands that he cut it out. They started screening their calls. Calla wanted to get an unlisted number, but Matt refused, saying to do so would be "giving in to this flake."

Then he started to leave gifts at their front door— an arrangement of orchids, an expensive coffee-table book of erotic art, a basket of imported paté and jams. Apparently Petrovsky considered himself a connoisseur of more than just weather patterns. The anonymous gifts were always pricey and sophisticated, in impeccable taste, and if paté wasn't exactly to Matt's liking and too rich for Calla, then Shawn enjoyed eating the gray paste on Ritz crackers, and Matt and Calla both derived creative inspiration from the book of erotic art.

The attention stopped being even marginally funny, though, the day Matt came home to find a police car outside the house. "He broke in while I was at work," Calla told him tearfully. "It had to be him. He left a book of erotic poetry on the bed. And he took some of my underwear and a garter belt."

But since there was no proof that Petrovsky was the actual intruder, there was nothing the police could do except suggest to Calla that she hide her spare key in a different spot and get an unlisted phone number. Matt was furious. The next time Petrovsky called, he grabbed the phone from Calla and enumerated in graphic detail what would happen if he ever bothered them again.

"I don't blame you for being upset," came the restrained reply. "I love Calla, and I'm going to take her away from you. It's just a matter of time." And before Matt could respond to that, he hung up.

They got an unlisted number and put new locks on the doors. When Petrovsky started pestering Calla at work and following her when she went to buy groceries, when she dropped Shawn off at day care, they went to court and got a restraining order, which, a lawyer friend of Matt's informed them cheerfully, was useful only in restraining sane, law-abiding people who didn't become stalkers in the first place.

They debated whether or not to call Howie, but neither of them wanted to get him involved. Matt, because he felt he should be able to protect his own wife and son. Calla, because she knew at the very least her father would want to hire round-the-clock bodyguards.

For Matt, the final straw came when a neighbor told Calla she'd caught a glimpse of a man standing on their front porch masturbating, and Matt and Calla found suspicious-looking stains dribbled across the welcome mat.

"Oh, Jesus," Calla said, "you think he *really*?— God, that's so disgusting!"

"I'll take care of it," Matt said. "He's never going to bother us again. I promise."

It was a promise that—to his everlasting regret— he kept.

He already knew where Petrovsky lived—he'd done a little stalking of his own, following Petrovsky's late model BMW one day when he left the accounting firm where he worked. His home was on the curve of a cul-de-sac in an upper middle-class neighborhood, a trim blue stucco house with a kidney-shaped pool out back and a mailbox decorated with painted-on ivy. All it lacked was a white picket fence and a swing set in the backyard to give a pristine bourgeois impression.

Matt remembered the night he'd visited Petrovsky with the black icy clarity of a near-death experience that leads not to heaven but hell. Only a little more than a week before Christmas, all the other houses on the cul-de-sac were decked out with an extravagance of bells, baubles, and lights. Petrovsky's house sat in darkness, immaculately kept but somehow sad and stark in its complete lack of adornment. The door to the garage was open, the black BMW parked inside. Matt rang the bell, then rapped on the door with his fist. No sound came from inside, no sign of Petrovsky.

He tried the door, found it unlocked. Decided to invite himself inside. It was without doubt, he later reflected, the stupidest, most ill-conceived impulse of his life. But if Petrovsky was inside, he wanted to find him. If he wasn't, then he wanted to pay him back for breaking into their house, wanted to make him feel that sense of violation that comes from knowing a stranger has been in your house, pawed through your wife's things, jerked off on your front porch, for God's sake.

He let himself into the dimly lit entryway, where an old-fashioned hat rack threw weird shadows across the ornate arabesques of an Oriental rug. He remembered pausing to call out for Petrovsky, then proceeding a little deeper into the house.

Stacks of books loomed everywhere. They overflowed bookcases, cascaded off tables, and cluttered the floor. On the mantel, a pair of onyx gargoyles was losing the battle to contain Petrovsky's collection of pornographic comics. More pornography—this time Japanese—overflowed from a desktop. Draped across this display, like some sort of obscene trophy, lay a pink-and-black lace garter belt that Matt would have sworn was Calla's.

He reached to pick the garment up, feeling a fresh surge of rage as he touched it and then let it fall to the floor with a grunt of disgust. Petrovsky had made good use of it—the fabric was so stiff it could have stood up on its own.

Behind him, a voice said, "Do you realize no jury in the land would convict a man of shooting an intruder who breaks into his house and then threatens his life?"

Matt whirled around, saw Petrovsky descending the shadowy staircase at the front of the living room. Matt couldn't see him clearly, but there was no mistaking the gun in his hand, which he raised slowly and aimed at Matt's head.

"Give me one good reason why I shouldn't kill you right now."

"You're too smart for that, Petrovsky. You'll never get away with it, you'll end up spending the rest of your life in prison." He lifted both hands, miming surrender and began to back up. Petrovsky took a step toward him and worked his thumb in a trigger-cocking gesture.

"I told you I'd take Calla away from you, but I had to make her a widow first. If I shoot you dead right here, it's all legal, because you broke in."

"Bullshit, the front door was open."

"You assaulted me. I've got the bruises to prove it."

Slowly, theatrically, Petrovsky descended the staircase. His face was round, smooth, and almost unlined, at once youthful and yet oddly more menacing for its veneer of boyishness.

Before Matt could move to try to close the distance between them, he lifted the gun and struck himself violently across the mouth with the handle. Blood spurted out between his teeth.

He spat out blood and bits of tooth and said, "I knew it would just be a matter of time before you came slinking over here, trying to defend your wife's honor. I'll tell the police you beat me up and threatened to kill me. I had no choice but to shoot you."

The phone rang. Petrovsky's head jerked to the side for just an instant, long enough for Matt to grab one of the gargoyle bookends off the mantel and hurl it at his head. He'd been a pitcher on the baseball team in high school. Even after all these years, his arm and his aim were still good. Too good. The bookend slammed the man between the eyes. He fell straight back with skull-cracking impact when his head hit the edge of the stairs. He didn't move. Matt rushed over to him and saw that the gun was still in his hand. When he lifted Petrovsky's wrist to feel for a pulse, the weapon fell to the floor. Matt stared at it, feeling a terror more acute and soul-sickening than any he had ever felt before—it was a well-crafted, authentic-looking toy.

At the trial, the prosecution had argued that Matt had smashed Petrovsky's mouth, that in desperation, Petrovsky had tried to frighten him with the toy gun, only to be beaten to death. He had learned a lot about Harold Petrovsky—that his only criminal record was a domestic violence conviction in a prior marriage ten years earlier, that since then he'd lived alone and had, as far as anyone knew, no real relationships. Coworkers and family described him in all the glowing terms reserved for the departed. No one could *prove* he'd broken into Matt's and Calla's home, no one could *prove* he'd masturbated on their porch. Nor could anyone prove definitively that the female underwear found in his possessions was actually Calla's. Matt was portrayed as a hotheaded bully who'd beaten to death a much smaller, weaker man—a man whose only crime had been to become infatuated with his wife.

Matt didn't remember all the details of the prosecution's and defense's arguments. What he did remember was that members of the large Petrovsky clan appeared in court every day, especially the brother Zeke, a florid-faced man with hooded eyes so deeply shadowed that they looked ringed in purple.

Was it possible Zeke Petrovsky had nursed a grudge all these years and concocted a Machiavellian scheme of revenge? That somehow he'd enlisted Phil's aid in an embezzlement plot that set Matt up to look like the culprit? Was Zeke Petrovsky capable of murdering Barry or having him murdered, if he thought he posed a threat?

Matt didn't know. And Noel's disease—a final, perverse twist of the knife on the part of a universe that didn't think he'd suffered enough already for his mistakes?

I've got to get tested, he thought, a litany that had been going through his brain now ever since Noel called. *I've got to find out.* And now a second thought came to him, one he relished even less. *I've got to talk to Zeke Petrovsky.*

A highway patrol car overtook him. A glance at the speedometer told him he'd been driving in excess of the speed limit by a good fifteen mph. The patrol car rode his bumper for a quarter mile or so, then sped up and passed.

A close one, he thought.

Up ahead the lights of Vegas pulsed against the desert sky like a neon-lit Oz. Fear thrummed in his veins, and he hated it, tried to tell himself it was just an adrenalin surge triggered by going alone into an unknown situation. But it wasn't anything outside himself he was afraid of, and he knew it. It was thinking of what might be inside him even now, cells spawning in his bloodstream, dooming him to a death his mind protested he was way too young for, wasn't ready for. Knowing that a simple test could tell him yes or no and knowing, at the same time, that he couldn't do it. That he was too afraid to find out.

Every time he visited Vegas, it took Matt about half a day to remember why he hated the place. His first reaction was always wonderment and a surge of expectation. Towering, garishly lit neon palaces, the mad crush of vehicular and pedestrian traffic that suggested

an urgency of purpose and surfeit of pleasure. Those
first few hours, Matt was as much a mark for it all
as a tipsy conventioneer on his first trip outside his
hometown. But then, after a few hours, disappointment—and exhaustion—always set in. The blitzkrieg
of noise inside the casinos, the chaos of lights, and the
subliminal stench of greed oozing from the pores of
too many alcohol-addled gamblers started making
him queasy.

Usually it took him a few hours, though, to get to
that stage. Tonight it required about twenty minutes.
He'd missed the exit for the Luxor off I15 and ended
up getting onto the strip further north, finding himself
caught in a half mile of gridlock. Cabs blared their
horns. A white limo about as long as the stage of a
Broadway musical cut him off across from the MGM
Grand, and a light-heavyweight championship fight
taking place at Caesar's had the major intersections
tied up in every direction.

Up ahead to the right, he saw the looming gold
facade of the new Mandalay Bay Hotel. In front of it
rose the black obelisk of the Luxor, presided over by
a gigantic, neon-bathed sphinx, which viewed in profile
appeared to be gazing up balefully at the towering
Mandalay. Behind the sphinx, liquid lights flowed
from the brightly lit apex of the pyramid, quicksilver
dribbling and trickling up and down the ebony sides.
It was beautiful, garish, dramatic, and tawdry all at
the same time—Ramses and Tutankhamen must be
spinning in their sarcophagi.

Resisting the temptation to use the valet parking—
bad idea, if he needed to make a fast getaway—he followed the directions of an attendant and parked in a
multilevel garage overlooking the pool. Then he hoofed
it back to the hotel, a distance that, in the hothouse
swelter of the Vegas night, seemed only a little less
than a couple of football fields.

Inside the Luxor's gigantic casino, he felt disoriented, overwhelmed. Judging from the decibel level of
the slot machines' gonging and flashing, several jack-

pots had been hit simultaneously. Bells clanged, lights strobed. A slat-thin, café au lait–colored woman with a cone of hair as sleekly coiffed as a slab of obsidian jumped up and down, clapping her hands. Rounding a corner, Matt passed a red Lamborghini rotating majestically on a turntable above a bank of Fastest Cash and Jackpot Jewels slot machines. He stopped a girl taking drink orders from the slot players to ask directions to the lobby. She answered in a twangy southwestern drawl that reminded him of a TV honky-tonk princess, telling him to pass Pai Gow Poker and mini-baccarat and hang a left at the Pyramid Café.

More from luck and perseverance than her instructions, he located the lobby, a huge, high-vaulted area of black-and-beige marble floors, soaring palms, and mammoth, faux sandstone statues of the pharaohs. The reception area backed up to floor-to-ceiling murals of life on the Nile, nubile maidens assisting Nefertiti with her toilette, studly slaves hoisting a pharaoh in a sedan chair on their shoulders.

Several tour groups—one German, one Italian, one apparently a Midwestern high school girls' basketball team—appeared to be checking in simultaneously. The lines of people and luggage fanning out behind the various check-in desks made navigation difficult for those trying to get to the elevators with luggage carts. Maybe it was the acoustics, Matt thought, but people seemed incapable of talking at a normal volume; they were all shouting, jabbering, gesticulating in a frenzy of excitement and a babble of different languages, inebriated by the tang of money, sex, and alcohol.

After standing in line half an hour, he finally reached a plump blond receptionist wearing a fashionable, but decidedly un-Egyptian-like red jacket, black skirt, and white blouse and checked in under the name Edward Mattson, paying cash for the room.

"A friend of mine, Phil Rollins, is staying here," he told the girl, whose lacquered nails were studded with tiny diamonds and stars. "I wonder if you could see if he's checked in."

She struck a series of computer keys, frowned, shook her head. "No one by that name is staying here, sir."

She handed him his "key," a piece of plastic about the size of a credit card, and directed him to the nearest "inclinator."

"The what?" Matt said.

"It's an elevator on a slant. There're four of them, one in each corner of the lobby." She lifted a plump, gold-bangled arm and pointed. "Your room's on twenty-two, so you need to follow the left wall until you pass the King Tut Camera Shop. It's right across from the Lamborghini that's grand prize for keno. And have your key out to show Security, because otherwise you won't be allowed up."

Matt thanked her and set out on his mission, which turned out to be more daunting than he'd imagined, especially since he first went looking not for the inclinator, but for the bank of "loose" slot machines near the door that Paula had described to him as the likeliest place to find Phil. Trouble was, the Luxor casino was designed, he decided, to maximize the odds of anyone stumbling into its sprawl never finding their way out again. At least while they had a quarter left to their name.

It was after eleven now. The craps and blackjack tables had players and kibitzers three feet deep. Every slot machine was in use. Periodically bells rang and whistles blew, and the clang of coins could be heard regurgitating out of some slot machine's metallic belly.

He had no luck spotting Phil, although he checked the Nefertiti Lounge and Pyramid Café and took the elevator up to the tonier Isis and Sacred Seas Restaurants, nor did any of the cocktail waitresses he buttonholed know of anyone working there named Cindee. He wanted a cigarette for his nerves, but the air was already so thick with smoke, you could cut it, and he was getting a nicotine headache.

Passing a mens' room, he went in, took a piss, then stood at a sink rinsing his hands. The guy next to him, broad-shouldered and blessed with abundant black locks that curled over the edge of an expensive-looking sport coat, seemed to be taking an uncommonly long time at the mirror. So long, in fact, that although he generally wasn't in the habit of checking out guys, Matt couldn't help but take note of him. He might have been handsome once, this guy, but something had happened over his forty-some years, and now he was coarse-featured, the skin dimpled from old acne and pulpy around the nose, like orange rind. Just as the guy was prying himself away from the mirror, he paused, brushed at his shoulders, and glared at Matt as though looking to assign blame. In a tone of haughty exasperation, he said, "*Lint!* Fuck!I can't believe I have lint on this jacket."

Shit happens, Matt thought, and shook his head, wishing lint were the worst of his problems.

Chapter Twelve

Before it was time to take the inclinator down to the Luxor Casino, BuddyLee Baines stood in the bathroom of his hotel room and drew a razor blade lightly over his heavily scarred forehead. He was careful not to break the skin, although a part of him itched to do so, but simply practiced the gesture, scowling and grimacing as he imagined the way the blood would course down the furrows and rivulets of his face in a grotesque mask.

Even unbloodied, BuddyLee Baines's round, fleshy face was about as aesthetically pleasing as roadkill. A number of pugilistic misadventures had reshaped his ears, genes from a father who'd given him little besides second-rate chromosomes caused him to squint myopically, and a string of car crashes and drunken falls had placed his nose and teeth at imaginative angles.

Then there were the tattoos, everything from crude jailhouse doodlings on his forearms to the elaborate multicolor designs that proliferated over his three-hundred-plus frame. Before he'd discovered the subtler pleasures of the razor blade, BuddyLee had decorated his massive body the way an interior designer on psychedelics might furnish a living room. He liked traffic-stopping colors and lurid designs, particularly ones involving half-human, half-animal females with exuberant breasts and sloping, reptilian eyes.

Because of that penchant for the decadently exotic,

his hotel room here at the Luxor pleased BuddyLee. Darkly-lined Cleopatra-style eyes stared at him from the bureau and lamp shades. Exotic ebony bodies undulated across the bedspread—portents, he hoped, of sensual indulgences to come. And by the door, an alligator briefcase.

He'd peeked inside, of course. He'd even touched it. The sight and smell of all that money had given him a rush almost as intense as when he sliced his forehead. Things were looking up, all right.

Reluctantly he set aside the razor and began to dress, stuffing his arms into a short-sleeved shirt patterned with black and red flowers while he watched a hotel-sponsored infomercial on TV about how to win thousands at keno. Then it was time to go. He gave the alligator briefcase a pat, picked it up, and headed downstairs for the lobby, marveling at the gullibility of the little dweeb who actually thought he was going to walk away with all this money.

Even in a place as bustling with keno-playing customers as the Pyramid Café, Cindee spotted the guy Phil had described to her right away—how could you miss him? He looked big and bulky, about as easy to budge as a soft-drink machine. He was hunched over the red Formica table, frowning down at a keno card the way some people read the fine print on a car rental agreement. A cocktail waitress in black pants and a salmon-pink blouse bent toward him for a drink order, scribbled something on a pad, strutted away.

Show time. Cindee put a hand to her neck and fingered the raised surface of Phil's lucky Chinese medallion. Piece of crap made in Taiwan, but he'd gotten all sentimental and insisted she wear it, although now that she'd seen the guy she was to rendezvous with, she wondered if a cattle prod and a can of Mace wouldn't have been more practical.

She did a mental check of her facial muscles, her limbs. No twitching, no tics, no visible signs that her

nerves were frayed as old shoestrings. Good. Now, of
all times, she couldn't afford to flip out.

Okay, here goes, she thought grimly, sweeping past
the black hostess in her tasteful turquoise jacket and
sliding into the seat opposite the man she had come
to meet.

"You BuddyLee?"

The floppy-haired lug in the flowered sport shirt and
khaki shorts glanced up from his keno card, grunted,
and gave her a chest-to-crotch once-over. He frowned,
an expression that caused his soft Kewpie-doll features
to bunch together in the center of a face that seemed
inappropriately large for its miserly mouth and slitted
gray eyes. He wasn't a happy man, Mr. Baines. He
didn't like what he saw.

Well, not exactly—he sure as hell liked the way her
small, pointy tits showed underneath the low-cut, long-
sleeved emerald blouse. He liked the ripe, bitable-
looking lips and round, wide-set blue eyes with their
fixed, frazzled stare. All in all, the chick looked pretty
frayed around the edges, like despite the careful
makeup and sexy outfit, she'd been ridden hard and
put away wet. Like she was jonesing big time. Not that
Baines cared—sometimes the desperate ones were the
wildest fucks. What he *didn't* like was the fact that
this was all wrong, all screwed up. He was supposed
to be meeting that little creep Rollins.

"Who the hell are you?"

"So you *are* Baines?"

"I might be."

Impatient, she summoned a server with a crisp flick
of her fingers, ordered a vodka tonic, then turned her
attention back to Baines, pinning him with a rude
stare. She wore heavy makeup, dark olive-green eye-
liner, fake lashes, and flame bright crimson lip liner.
A tattoo of a flamingo, its feathers an intricate master-
work of ornate scrollwork, graced the back of one
wrist.

Baines picked up a black crayon, began marking

off numbers on the keno card. "You ain't Rollins," he said.

"I'm here in his place."

"Fucking great. How do I know you're not just pulling a scam?"

"How would I know your name or what you've got for Phil and me if he hadn't told me?"

"Oh. So now it's Phil and me?" He marked a couple more numbers, changed his mind, scratched one out, raised a fist to his chin in a gesture that seemed intended to mime deep thought. "Give me a number."

"What?"

"You got a number? A lucky number? What is it?"

"Jesus, I don't know. Thirty-one."

He checked it off using the crayon. "That your age? Your birthday?"

"No. It just came to mind."

The server brought Baines's drink and Cindee's and collected the card. She had a nice ass, and Baines ogled it with slit-eyed fascination before turning back to Cindee. "So Rollins don't want to be seen with me in public, is that it? He's an asshole."

"Funny, he feels the same way about you."

Baines grunted and marked a number on a new card.

"So we've established you two probably won't be going down the aisle together," Cindee said. "Now why don't you give me what you've got?"

"Honey, I'd *love* to. You'd love it, too."

"Fuck you."

He had to give it to this chick—she had balls, but he'd thought the same thing about any number of people who later on screamed and pleaded for mercy. He took hold of her wrist in his thick, nicotine-stained fingers, turned it around in his hand, and scrutinized her tattoo. "Be nice now. Let's see this. Where'd you get it done?"

"What difference does it make?"

"I *said* be nice, and this will go smoother."

"Here in town," she said grudgingly.

"Let me guess. Eddie Munschnick. Am I right?"

"No."

"Wait, don't tell me. I'll get it. I know all the top guys. Maynard, right? BusStop Maynard? Got busted for smack, did some time in San Quentin a few years ago."

"Maynard MacDougal. Yeah, this is his."

"Nice. Nice work." When she tried to pull her wrist back, he held on. "Want to know how I knew it was BusStop? It's the scrollwork on the feathers gives it away. I got one of BusStop's myself, but if I was to show it to you, we might attract the wrong kind of attention."

"Or maybe no one would notice. Can we get down to business now?"

Baines studied her, weighing his chances of ever getting a dish like this into bed. Salerno, now if Salerno was here, it'd be different. Way chicks opened their legs for Salerno, you'd think he was a fuckin' gynecologist. Absently, without thinking what he was doing, he used his free hand to brush back the unruly brown hair flopping over his forehead. Too late. He saw her eyes shift, her face change. Big mistake. She'd got a look at his forehead, which was crisscrossed with thick ridges of scar tissue, a bizarre, waxen stitchery extending well up into his hairline. Her big eyes got even bigger, round and blue and unblinking, like somebody'd stuck a ten-inch dildo up her ass. Made him feel like a freak, a weirdo.

"What the hell are *you* looking at?" he snarled at her.

"Nothing." She averted her gaze, grabbed her drink, and drained half of it. "Look, I'm in a hurry. Will you please let go of my wrist?"

"When I'm ready." He was angry now, wanting to pay her back for the way she'd minimized him with her stare. Gripping her wrist even tighter, he started unbuttoning the cuff of her blouse with his other hand.

"What are you—?"

"Take it easy, sweetie, I'm just lookin' for more tattoos. By the way, do you happen to know who I am?"

"Sure I do. A goon who's too stupid to know keno is the worst possible game to play in Vegas."

"Ha, ha. Very funny. What, they pay smack whores to do stand-up comedy these days?"

He rolled the sleeve of the blouse up to her elbow, took a peek, then rolled the fabric back down and buttoned it for her. "No wonder you're in such a hurry. How many hours it been since you had a needle in your arm? You're jonesing."

He saw her eyes track to the side and then past him. Looking for her chickenshit boyfriend, no doubt. Her voice was shaky when she started to speak, but she steadied it. "Look, I know who you're working for. If you renege on the deal, Phil calls the cops, tells them everything. So just give me the fucking money, you grotesque thug, and let me get out of here."

Spittle flew out between her teeth. Her face reminded Baines of those hate-filled faces he saw in his dreams—furious, mocking, drooling contempt, the kind of faces you'd expect to find in some snake-pit mental asylum, brimming over with insanity, nastiness, bile. He started to rise, then remembered where he was, sat back down again. Took a deep breath and got himself under control.

"Take the damned thing." He reached down by his feet and picked up a gray snakeskin briefcase, which he shoved across the tabletop into her hands.

She looked surprised. "It's all in here?"

"You were expecting a fucking backpack? Twenty thousand dollars fits in there real good. It's all there, okay?"

She checked. Saw he was right, snapped the case shut, slid out of the booth, and stood up. Smiled or, at any rate, attempted to arrange the muscles of her face in a pleasant expression. "Nice doing business with you."

Now that the business part of the transaction was ended, Baines felt compelled to try for something more. "Hey, sit down, will you? At least let me buy you a drink," he said, feeling expansive. "I'll bet if you think real hard, you can figure out where you've seen me before."

"Sorry, I don't watch *America's Most Wanted*."

Clutching the briefcase in her fist, she undulated away, groin-achingly juicy-looking, a strung-out Red Riding Hood wending her way through a forest of slot machines and Big Bad Wolves holding cupfuls of quarters.

Without thinking, he reached up and touched the scar tissue ridging his forehead. It felt hard and slick, like the carapace of an insect. Then he wet his lips, thinking of Cindee's satiny flesh and what, with just a little bit of luck, could still be accomplished tonight.

Chapter Thirteen

Phil Rollins took his eyes off Cindee, the briefcase, and the larded-up mass of meat she was talking to for less than ten seconds—just time enough to hit four of a kind on the Midas Touch poker slot machine he was playing. When he looked up again, all three of them—his girlfriend, the goon, and the money—were gone.

Shit! What now? His palms went clammy and the pads of his fingers felt hot and prickly. In defiance of the best anti-perspirant on the market, sweat snaked down his temples and formed large semicircles under the arms of his navy blue sport shirt. Even under the best of circumstances, Phil's personality tended toward paranoid. Ever since Barry'd been murdered, he'd been looking over his shoulder, wondering what else could go wrong. That was why he'd bribed Cindee to pick up the cash for him. But now what if she'd split?

Shit, why should I trust her? he thought, hating himself for having succumbed to the urge to try and win a few more lousy bucks when a fucking fortune might be sashaying out the door. Maybe she and Lard-Ass had hit it off during their brief meeting. Maybe the guy was carrying and had offered Cindee more and better quality dope than what Phil had upstairs. Hell, you never knew about addicts—maybe she'd just gotten greedy and decided to take off on her own.

He stood up, trying to spot either Cindee or the thick-bodied thug she'd been talking to, but the casino was packed, every slot machine in frenzied use, a sea of arms pumping the one-armed bandits with an enthusiasm Phil hadn't seen since he engaged in a group jerk off with his fraternity brothers. Near the exit, an outlandishly frumpy bride was cursing a photographer while a swarm of distracted bridesmaids milled around, looking embarrassed. No groom in sight, small wonder. No sign of Cindee, either.

He was about to go look for her when, glancing down, he noticed that a red-lit message at the bottom of the slot machine was inquiring if he'd be interested in DOUBLE OR NOTHING. Tempting offer. He was already up over three thousand dollars, and he'd only been gambling since yesterday morning, with maybe six hours deducted for sleep, food, and bathroom activities. Oh, yeah, and sex with Cindee, if you could call it that; what with her so twitchy from wanting a fix, it was all he could do to hang on for dear life when he rode her.

DOUBLE OR NOTHING? Sure. He punched a button that dealt him a new hand, four cards turned down, one card—a ten of clubs—faceup. Shit, the seven of clubs. He could beat *that*. He tapped a card on the screen with his finger. Jack of spades. *All right.*

DOUBLE OR NOTHING? blinked the screen.

No, no. He punched NO, but then hit BET MAXIMUM and dealt himself a new hand. Four hearts and a diamond came up.

In spite of the urgency he felt with regard to Cindee's whereabouts, *because* of that very urgency, he suddenly became convinced—*knew*, in fact—that this was the "Big One." Fate was toying with him, tempting him with seemingly logical reasons to leave a golden machine just when it was about to pay off.

He dumped the single diamond, held onto the other four cards, then hit the PLAY button, which turned over another electronic card, the five of spades.

Shit! Fuck! Piss!

"What I want to know is, who'd you have to kill to make the kind of money that's in this briefcase?"

He looked up Cindee's endless legs to the succulent

jut of her boobs, and then to her eyes, which were flat, cold, and lusterless as the coins in the paper cup at his elbow. For a beautiful woman, she didn't look so beautiful anymore.

"Where the hell did you *go* just now? I was looking for you."

"No, you weren't. I was right over there while that Neanderthal asshole just about twisted my wrist out of joint. You were too focused on your fucking game to notice you'd started watching the wrong table. *Here*." She thrust the briefcase at him. "So what is it, you blackmailing that guy? You scared of him? Is that why you wanted me to pick this up for you?"

"Remember that old saying, payback's a bitch? Well, I helped a guy get some payback, that's all. I don't trust the guy who's paying me, though. I *especially* don't trust anybody who has friends like that BuddyLee character." He opened the briefcase, glanced inside, shut it quickly.

"It's all there just like he gave it to me," Cindee said, "except the grand I took out to reimburse me for my trouble."

"Dammit, who told you you could—" But he stopped, reminding himself that he could win the extra thousand she'd awarded herself in a few hours' play. Sure, gambling was for suckers, but if you were smart *and* lucky, like *he* was . . .

"All right, fine," he said sullenly. "I guess you earned it."

"Are you going to tell me where the stuff is?"

"In the room, where do you think?" He handed her a slip of paper with some numbers scribbled on it. "I put it in the safe."

"The room safe? The fucking room safe?"

"Why not? That's what they're there for, right—to stash jewelry, cash, drugs? Oh, come on, Cindee, chill out. Go up to the room, get comfortable. I'll gamble some more and come up later. We'll do some drugs, have sex, do some more drugs. It'll make you feel good. Like old times."

"Come up or not, I don't care. Just don't disappoint me about what's inside that safe."

He shook his head. "Jesus, Cindee, one a' these days, we gotta get you into rehab."

"That's sweet of you, Phil. And I'll do that, too, just as soon as you check in with me to get some help for that little problem you got with gambling."

That shut him up. She dug the room key out of her purse and took off past the "Wheel of Fortune" in the direction of the inclinator, looking back over her shoulder once, like a woman who knows something is pursuing her, unseen and terrible and gaining on her steadily.

Watching the jittery-looking blonde talking to Phil, then striding away as though she couldn't get away fast enough, Matt couldn't believe his good luck. Paula was right. The embezzling little son of a bitch was right here, feeding Jack Ryder's sixty-two thousand dollars to the slot machines a quarter at a time.

He'd found a seat on a Naugahyde-covered stool at the base of the Lamborghini turntable and was putting coins in just often enough to give the impression he was actually paying attention to the machine and not the woman with the briefcase.

When the woman—the infamous Cindee, he presumed—shoved the briefcase into Phil's hand and left, he didn't take time to form a plan, but let his fury propel him forward. He came up behind Phil and slammed a hand down at the juncture between his shoulder and neck, exerting painful pressure while he said, "Paula told me you'd be here, you embezzling little piece of shit, but I couldn't believe you'd be that stupid or that predictable."

"Matt?" Phil tried to turn around, but was prevented from doing so by the hand gripping the side of his neck.

"Who the hell else *would* it be? C'mon, Phil, did you really think you could get away with it?"

"I don't know what you're talking about," Phil said

evenly, "but if you don't mind, Matt, take your god-damn hands off me before I have you arrested for assault. I've got a bad neck from an old ice hockey injury. You could really fuck up my neck."

"You're gonna have a lot more than a bad neck."

"What the hell are you doing here anyway?" He tried to twist around again, but Matt put his left hand on the man's other shoulder, like he was giving him a massage, and he stayed still.

"What am I doing here? I'm looking for my book-keeper, for starters, and to find out how Jack Ryder paid out sixty-two thousand dollars to Anaheim Remodeling for a job we gave to Jonas Grey's company for forty. Any ideas?"

A gaunt man in a blue Izod shirt with a profile like an Indian arrowhead was playing the machine next to Phil's. From time to time, he glanced over warily, like he was trying to decide the likelihood of any violence that might break out spilling over onto him. Not wanting to attract attention, Matt let up the pressure on Phil's shoulder. At once, like something mechanical had been activated, Phil's right hand started working the machine again. Punch a button, pause, punch another button, punch, punch, punch. Spewing out words at a furious rush all the while. "I don't know what you're talking about, Matt. I was shook up over Barry getting murdered, and I needed some time away, to get my head straight, not that you deserve any explanation."

"Nice of you to let me know you were leaving."

"Yeah, like it was nice of you to let me know you're the prime suspect. How does that work anyway? A dead body turns up in the back of your truck. The cops arrest you. Fuck me for not knowing the criminal justice system, but aren't you supposed to be in jail?"

"But I'm not in jail, am I, Phil? I'm right here. And I'm not leaving your side until we get back to San Diego and talk to the cops."

"You're dreaming, Matt. I got every right to be here. You don't like it, then I quit the damn job. Everything's coming down on my head at once, it feels like, Barry getting murdered, Paula and me breaking up."

"Broke up is a good description of your apartment right now."

"My apartment? What, you went to my place, too?" He punched more buttons, discarding cards. Leaned on the lever again. Angry now. Discarding a perfectly good ace. Not paying attention. "You think that was appropriate?"

"I think right now it would be very fucking appropriate if I rammed your face onto that lever so hard your teeth came out your ass."

The man with the arrowhead face swiveled around in alarm, collected his quarters in a plastic bucket, and moved to another machine while muttering something about lowlifes polluting a classy place like the Luxor.

"We're attracting attention," said Matt, sliding onto the vacated seat. "I don't like that. So rather than force me to beat the shit out of you and get blood all over that nice shiny money you're making, why don't you tell me just what's going on? Did Barry catch onto the fact that you were embezzling from the company? Or were you and Barry in this together and something went wrong, so you made a few calls, got in touch with somebody, maybe you only intended to have him roughed up, but it got out of hand? I know *you* didn't kill him, Phil, that's the main thing. I talked to you at the office that night, and Paula backs up your story of where you were and what you were doing."

There was a metallic clanging. Lights flashed, sirens keened. Some sort of minor-league jackpot. "Hey, I *won*!" hollered Phil. He punched the COLLECT button, and a cascade of quarters erupted from the entrails of the machine. Grabbing a plastic bucket to position under the flow, he started catching the torrent of coins.

At that point it was obvious to Matt that he could've had a .45 rammed in Phil's ear, or for that matter, up his ass, and it wouldn't have made an impression. Phil was lost in the land of Big Winners.

"Look at me when I'm talking to you, you little fuck!" He grabbed Phil by the shoulders again and spun him around so fast that the accountant's hand, still balancing the container, tipped it sideways over the lip of the machine. Quarters rained down, pattered onto the lime-colored carpet, rolled in every direction. An immensely overweight woman in a forest-green pullover and black skirt, with a dark jaw-length haircut that made her resemble an obese Betty Page, saw the spilling coins and dropped to the floor with a speed suggesting someone had just fired a bullet over her head.

"Hey, that's my money!" Phil shouted.

The woman didn't look up, but her chubby fingers scurried frantically across the floors, pushing the quarters into a plastic container of her own.

"Fucking thief! What'd you do, lady, gamble away the kids' milk money?"

"Hey, keep it down, will you?" hissed Matt. "Forget the damn quarters. You're coming with me."

Phil shook free of Matt's grip, grabbed the bucket holding what was left of his money, and charged toward the inclinator, leaving the fat woman on her hands and knees shoveling coins. Matt followed, seized him by the arm, and slammed him into the wall under a frieze of Egyptian gods—Thoth, Anubis, and Set in stiff-legged profile, divided by vertical bands of hieroglyphics. Jammed a forearm across the diminutive accountant's windpipe. Phil started wheezing, his face turning red, when a voice behind Matt announced, "Security. You better leave."

The slightly nasal baritone was unaccountably familiar, but then, when Matt turned around, so was the faint dusting of lint on the impeccably tailored sports coat.

"My friend here spilled his money is all," said Matt, determined, for the moment, to keep the matter between himself and Phil. "He got a little excited. Don't worry, I'll keep an eye on him."

The square, queerly expressionless face that Matt had first seen admiring himself in the mirror of the mens' room remained impassive. The man was wearing an expensively tailored suit of the type he had seen on some of the security guards discreetly patrolling the area. Unlike them, however, he wore no identifying name badge. "Sorry, asshole, this isn't a request. You have to leave. Now."

Something about this didn't feel right. "How do I know you're Security? Let's see some ID."

The Lint Man smiled stiffly, showing pointy incisors. His face was scarred, not just by acne, Matt could see now, but with the short, irregular cuts around the eyes like those a boxer gets. Painful and bloody, slow to heal. "I'll show you all the identification you need—once we're outside."

"If you can't show me some ID, I'm not going anywhere. In fact, I might just want to talk to the police."

At that last threat, which Matt had no intention of carrying out, Phil bolted, zigzagging like a linebacker through an obstacle course of slot machines. Matt took off after him. He'd gone only a few strides, though, when the Lint Man's hand reached out to enclose his. A smooth, fluid movement, like an Olympic runner passing a baton to the next man in a relay race. A lightning-fast interlacing of fingers and then pain, white-hot and knee bucklingly brutal, shot from Matt's palm into his fingers and burned its way upward as though his forearm had been sloshed with acid.

"I said *outside*." Lint Man's obsidian black eyes bored into him. Matt brought his other hand around in an attempt to pry himself free, but was stopped by an increase in pressure on his captured fingers. It took all his will not to scream. Far away, he could see Phil dodging around the crowd at the roulette wheel, disappearing into a blurry sea of slot machines. The noise from the slots had become overpowering, somehow increasing along with the agony in his hand, which felt like it was being crushed and reshaped into some hideous bonsai tree created from fingers and flesh.

"Walk with me nice and calm-like. Don't fight or try anything, and it won't hurt as bad."

He felt himself start to shuffle forward. Leaning some of his weight on his captor, because the carpet was starting to writhe now, things moving and tilting beneath it, a rippling green and gold eddying around his ankles, making him think he was sloshing through puke.

"A little more pressure and your wrist and three middle fingers will dislocate," the Lint Man said in a pleasantly affable tone. "You don't want me to do that, I don't think. That would *hurt*."

They passed the prize Lamborghini whirling like a wheeled dervish on its turntable, the craps tables, the Pyramid Café and the ramp and bank of elevators leading up to the second floor. Matt half staggered, trying to get his mind to function. He tried to grab something to slug the son of a bitch with, yell out to a *real* security guard, anything but let himself be carted outside while Phil got away.

He could do nothing, though. All his will and energy focused on enduring the pain. There were moments, in fact, when he thought he'd blacked out on his feet— a blink of time that he couldn't account for and then a slightly different scene, a fake palm tree or curio store that hadn't been there a second ago—but he kept moving, impelled by the merciless grip on his fingers and hand. He thought of the Ruger he'd borrowed from Coop in the truck's glove compartment . . . a lot of good it was doing him now.

They went up a short flight of stairs and through an ornate glass door held open by a uniformed young doorman who rolled his eyes when he thought Matt wasn't looking. Just another drunk gambler getting 86'd on a Saturday night.

Hot, stagnant night air added its dampness to the sweat glossing Matt's forehead as his captor steered him past the huge, oblong swimming pools. He got a glance upward and saw the lights of the pyramid, liquid globs of shimmering silver, cascading along the structure's ebony edges. In his mind, it darkened into blood, cold blood pulsing from some metallic artery.

They approached a row of cabanas set up beyond the chaise lounges. He got a shove from behind and toppled forward, catching himself with his good arm on one of the chairs.

"Don't fuck around here any more or next time it'll be worse."

Lint Man's voice was low and surprisingly mellow, a Northeasterner, from the accent. He made a hand-washing gesture, like he was trying to rid himself of something unpleasant, and stalked back toward the hotel.

Matt stumbled out of the cabana and leaned against the fake sandstone wall, watching his assailant leave, feeling too limp and shaky to try to stop him. The guy turned when he was almost past the pool and glared, then disappeared through the doors into the hotel, brushing lint off his shoulder as he did so.

Chapter Fourteen

Phil Rollins was outside, racing down the stairs, past the towering statues of Ramses that presided over the hotel, the briefcase full of cash swinging at his side, when his free hand went to his neck.

Fuck! He'd let Cindee wear his medallion for her rendezvous with Baines and had forgotten to get it back when he took the briefcase from her. Now he had to leave the medallion behind or go back to the room to get it.

Forget it, he told himself, and went on a few steps. Got as far as the valet parking when a second voice preempted the first, reminding him of the money he'd won when wearing the medallion. He'd lost money, too, of course, but how much worse might it have been without the lucky piece?

He let the voices fight it out, until he couldn't stand it anymore—it was like being a small child between two battling parents—and gave in to the louder and more threatening of the voices, the one that said, go back, go back at any cost.

Fuck this, he said, shoving his way past a trio of overweight male conventioneers, boisterous, cheerful, and obviously plastered, as he headed back into the hotel lobby.

As the door of the inclinator that went up to fourteen whispered shut behind him, he started getting mad again, thinking about all those quarters—*his* quarters, for God's sake—being scooped up by that obese, greedy bitch in the unspeakable clothes and vowed to win the money back tonight. Not here in the Luxor, of course. He'd go to one of the casinos off the strip. No need to get a room, he'd play all night, leave town tomorrow morning, maybe head east to Colorado. Hole up in one of those little gambling towns up in the Rockies, Central City, Blackhawk, Cripple Creek. Keep a low profile for a while, stay away from the strip until something could be done about Matt.

Stepping out of the uncomfortably crowded inclinator, he felt calmer, more in control. There was no way Matt could find his room, even assuming his former boss was still capable of walking and talking once the other goon had finished with him, and Cindee, even if she realized he was taking off without her, would be too high by now to object.

He strode rapidly along the carpeted walkway, glancing nervously around the corner and into the alcove containing the soft drink and ice machines, knowing it was foolish to expect Matt to jump out at him, but unable to stop himself. He passed a dozen doors, two dozen, three. The Luxor's cavernous interior was daunting under the best of circumstances, labyrinthine if you were in a panicked hurry to get in and out. Every now and then he stopped and looked over the railing to check out the action on the bustling mezzanine below. This wasn't the casino, but something resembling a small theme park with a number of restaurants and specialty shops. Lines had formed for the IMAX show, *King Tut's Tomb*, and the nightclub Luxor Live.

Peering over the side, he tried to spot Matt somewhere in the crowd below, but there were too many people swarming around. No one had followed him up from the casino level, either, although what did he expect anyway—for Matt to pop out of one of the inclinators with a coterie of cops? There was no proof he'd fucked with the books. Matt was just as likely the embezzler as he was.

His mind was churning so fast that he passed the

room and was three doors beyond it before he realized his mistake, came back, and unlocked the door.

"Cindee?"

The room was in total blackness. He fumbled for the light.

"Cindee, you in here or what?"

He found the light, flipped it on. Saw a fist the size of a bowling ball hurtling toward his face. Saw something else, too—more horrifying—a dazzling after-image that lingered on his retina for a split second after the fist connected and his mind began a slow, zigzaggy down spiral into unconsciousness.

"Vykos," Matt said, trying hard to be patient with the desk clerk. "Andre Vykos. That's spelled—" He tried to remember the signature of the Russian ice hockey star from the photo on Phil's wall. It was a long shot, but at the moment, it was all Matt could think of.

The desk clerk, an exotic-looking girl with burnished skin and deep-lidded, heavily mascara'd eyes, gave him a slitty-eyed stare that might have been boredom, irritation, or blatant sexual interest. Her voice was thick and slow, as though he'd wakened her from deep slumber. "Is that *V-i-c-k* or—?"

"No, *V-y-k*, I think. *V-y-k-o-s.*" He hoped she wasn't an ice hockey fan, or she'd think he was a pushy fan, but her lynx eyes gave no hint that the name meant anything.

"I see." She typed that into the computer. "Actually there is a Mr. Andre Vykos who checked in yesterday, but I can't give out his room number. It's against our policy."

Matt wanted to say fuck policy, but figured that would probably only get him kicked out for the second time that night.

The girl smiled vacuously. "Is there anything else I can help you with?"

"I understand your policy, but—look, Andy Vykos and I went to college together. We haven't seen each other in twenty years. I know it sounds corny, but I wanted to surprise him. Show up at his door unannounced."

She stared at him as though he were slow-witted or crazy or both. "Sir, do you have any idea how often I've heard that story. Now if you—"

As she talked, he pulled out his wallet, took out a hundred-dollar bill, and slid it across the counter, covering most of it with his palm. "It'd mean the world to me, it really would. I'd be very grateful."

One corner of her mouth tilted up, giving her face, for a moment, a pleasing asymmetry.

"*How* grateful?"

He added another hundred, thinking the cost of bribery, like everything else, had skyrocketed in recent years.

She sighed, slid her long, tapered fingers under his and retrieved the money. "Room 1433. And don't look so miffed. This is Vegas. You got a bargain."

The mirrored inclinator he rode up in was packed with people in various stages of elation or despondency, depending, he supposed, on how their luck was going. He felt relieved when he was the only one who stepped off on fourteen. Idly, for no reason he could think of, it occurred to him that the fourteenth floor of most hotels and office buildings was actually the thirteenth. Maybe the ill luck associated with the number thirteen wasn't in effect if everyone thought they were on a different floor, but he had a feeling that, if there actually were malevolent forces afoot in the universe, they probably weren't suckered by superstitious misnumbering.

Then he took a second glance at the numbers over the elevator doors and realized there *was* a thirteenth floor at the Luxor, and he decided some gamblers probably thought *it* was the lucky one.

Although as far as his own luck went, he'd decided to go back to basics—he'd returned to the truck and gotten Coop's gun out of the locked glove compartment. The revolver made a heavy, satisfying weight inside his black denim jacket.

Outside 1433, he thought he heard movement inside the room. Matt stood there, waiting silently, hoping to hear the sound repeated, but it didn't come. Finally deciding whatever he'd heard had come from one of the adjacent rooms, he knocked, waited, knocked again. Nobody answered.

Alone in the hallway, Matt contemplated the door. Solid steel—not the kind of door guys kicked in with ease in the movies. Still, he was thinking about using some skills he'd picked up in prison to try to open the door with a credit card when a couple of middle-aged women got off the inclinator. The one in the brocade jacket must have lost big—in a distressed voice, she was asking her friend if she couldn't lend her some money so someone named Bill wouldn't have to find out. The other woman seemed sympathetic, but not enough to help out with cash. Matt pretended to be fumbling around for his room key until they went by.

When the hall was empty again, he was just about to try his Visa card on the lock when he realized he was being watched through the peephole.

"Phil?" he said, banging on the door with his fist.

A voice, timorous, muffled, croaked out, "Who's there?"

"Who the hell do you think it is? Open the door!"

"Matt?"

"Yes, Matt!"

"Are you alone?"

"Christ, yes, I'm alone!"

A beat of silence, then some kind of scuffling around, the metallic purr of a chain being eased back. The door opened on utter darkness. Aware that Lint Man could easily be waiting for him in there, Matt slid a hand into his jacket. "Step back from the door slowly, and turn on the light."

"I don't know what you're afraid of, Matt. I'm alone."

"Then, back away from the door and get some lights on in there."

With his hand on the gun, he fought down the urge to rush into the room. He drew a breath and stepped over the threshold. And knew instantly that something was terribly wrong.

He reached out with his left hand, groped along the wall till he encountered a light switch, and flicked it.

"Dammit, Matt, did you have to do that?" Phil's voice sounded at once strident and borderline hysterical, like an elderly vamp caught dentureless. He did a weird little shuffling step backward into the room—maybe limping from an injury, maybe disoriented or trying to seem that way, but not before Matt saw the raised welt under one eye.

"What happened to you?"

"What? Nothing." He brought a hand up to his face, touched it, winced, then looked down at the blood on his fingers in disbelief. Panicky, not quite able to comprehend he'd been punched that hard.

"Who else is in here?"

"Nobody."

"If you play poker as bad as you lie, Phil, I'd say your future as a professional gambler is pretty limited." He pulled the gun out of his jacket and proceeded into the room, Phil backing up wildly now, flailing his arms like some gawky bird attempting flight as the fox advances.

"A gun! You brought a gun in here?"

There was a closet to Matt's immediate right. He yanked the door open, glanced inside, saw it was empty. Turned back to Phil, whose eyes ticked to the left, toward the honey-colored armoire with its black trim and inlaid hieroglyphics. Misreading the cue, Matt grabbed the door handle with his left hand and yanked the armoire open as he aimed the revolver at whoever might be hiding inside.

What came out first, though—with stunning effect—was the odor, pungent and sickeningly sharp. Then the body of the woman he'd seen talking to Phil in the casino tumbled out and thudded onto the carpet at his feet, so that she was in some weird, feet-behind-her-head yoga-type position. Her clothes, balled up and wedged into the armoire with her, fell out after.

"God, what happened?"

He forced himself to look closer. There was so much blood—her throat had been cut, but other things had been done, too—the area around her forehead and hairline was so mutilated it looked like her killer had made an amateurish effort to scalp her. Deep, zigzagging wounds that, in some places, cut to the bone.

As he stared, horror-struck, at the body, the gun lowered at his side, the bathroom door at the rear of the room suddenly slammed outward, and a man—a *huge* man, not the phony security guard—charged him. The guy's enormous slab of a shoulder struck him broadside, slamming him into the wall like he'd been hit by a semi.

No pain, only impact. It was all happening too fast. The man loomed above him, lifting a huge booted foot to deliver a kick. Matt rolled, aimed the gun. "Don't fucking move!"

There was a beat of silence while the guy stared into the muzzle of the revolver. Then he muttered to Phil, "Fuck, you didn't tell me he'd have a gun!" and suddenly, with amazing agility for a man his size, leaped over Matt's legs and bolted out the door.

Phil, cringing against the wall, wailed, "He did it! He killed Cindee!"

Torn between the desire to stay with Phil and to go after the fleeing man, Matt shoved the gun inside his jacket and took off down the hall. Up ahead, he saw the guy turning the corner. He thought about going back for Phil, who could be easily subdued, but he also knew it wasn't Phil who had carved up that girl, and he was damned if he was going to be left with another dead body to try to explain.

At the end of the corridor, the guy hesitated in front of the inclinator, did a little two-footed dance as he waited for it to open, then realized this was taking too long and went dashing along the next section of corridor. Midway down, he yanked open a door marked emergency exit and hurled himself through it.

Matt followed, saw the guy clambering down the steel stairs two flights below, his mop of brown hair bouncing around his head as he took the stairs two and three at a time.

Six flights down, seven, eight. The big guy kept going, but he was starting to run out of steam. Trouble was, Matt wasn't in such great shape himself at the moment, his right hand still partially numb from whatever the Lint Man had done to it. He was only a flight of stairs behind the man now. He had the Ruger out, aimed at his back.

"Hold it! I'll shoot!"

The guy leaped the last four stairs to the next landing and another exit door. He yanked it open and ran through it into the crowd of Saturday-night revelers packing the mezzanine. Matt jammed the gun back into his jacket and continued his pursuit.

The fact that the guy was at least a head taller than almost anybody else meant at least Matt couldn't lose sight of him. The first of two nightclub shows at Luxor Live had just ended, creating a jam-up of people blocking a thirty-foot stretch around a central obelisk and two stone sphinxes and the food court, where people were queuing up to get into Little Caesars and a half dozen other fast-food joints. Even a man this big couldn't plow down a wall of people ten feet deep. He swerved, slowed. Matt caught up to him. He grabbed the guy by the belt and shoved the barrel of the Ruger into his kidney. "Don't say a word, just walk."

His fist gripping the belt caused the guy's T-shirt to ruck up. The top half of a felinelike face, part woman, part animal, glowered out at him. Matt saw a pair of slanted eyes whose pupils weren't pupils at all but tiny, tattooed flames, her hair was flame, her eyebrows curling wisps of smoke, and that was all he had a millisecond to take in before there was a loud noise—

like a burlap bag full of rice being smacked against stone—followed by a high, jagged scream ripped simultaneously from dozens of throats, as though everyone on the Luxor mezzanine had suddenly realized there was a murderer being held at gunpoint in their midst.

For no reason Matt could understand, the crowd surged and stampeded blindly, thrusting itself between him and the other man, driving them apart. He had no choice but to stuff the gun out of sight and watch helplessly as he was swept backward by a human tide, some of whom were screaming, crying, others gaping upward in horrified shock.

"Jesus, did you see it?"

"Fuck, was that for real?"

And a woman clasping two children to her, "Don't look! You don't want to see that!"

A pair of security guards, yelling at the crowd to make way, shoved through the crush of people surging toward the exits.

Matt caught a glimpse of the obelisk outside Luxor Live. Saw streaks of something dark and slick-looking glistening along the sides. He grabbed the arm of the man in front of him, shouted, "What the hell happened? What's going on?"

"Up there!" The man was clutching a woman by the elbow, herding her toward the stairs. "You didn't see it? A guy just jumped from one of the top floors! Christ, to do a thing like that—he must have lost a fucking fortune!"

Chapter Fifteen

Matt checked out of the Luxor and drove back from
Vegas that night, holding his breath when, twice, he
spotted a highway patrol car going in the opposite
direction. He was convinced the cops knew that he'd
left San Diego and put out an APB, probably already
linking him to Phil's death as well as Barry's.

Phil—he couldn't shake the mental image of his
broken body smashed to pulp against the Luxor's obelisk. A host of recriminations—if he'd stayed in the
hotel room instead of pursuing the man with the tattoo, if he hadn't confronted Phil in the casino, if he'd
never left San Diego in the first place?—ranted and
raved in his head like a chorus of sadists.

He tried to block out the mental tumult with sheer
noise, turning the radio up as loud as he could
stand it to a rock and roll station, but it was no use. Methodically, he began listing the events of the past few days:
first Barry's death and now Phil's, the phone call from
Noel alerting him to the fact that he just might have
a terminal illness, the fact that he'd been set up to
look like he was cheating his clients.

Noel's illness had to be fate, he figured. Lousy luck,
but not entirely unpredictable if you were sleeping
with a woman of Noel's personal proclivities without
benefit of protection. But the rest of it beggared belief
and suggested some sort of ominous connection.

You've got enemies, Noel had said.

Which made him wonder again how she knew. Had

someone contacted her, threatened her? Tried to use her as a pawn against him? Was she *afraid* to be with him? Was she hiding out?

Matt could think of only one person who might hate him enough to concoct a scheme to frame him for embezzlement and murder, utilizing Phil as a ploy. But if Zeke Petrovsky was that bent on revenge, why not just waylay Matt in a dark alley some night and blow his brains out? Was the man capable of nursing a grudge for so long and then putting the plan into action? Matt didn't know. All he knew was that, at least at the time of Harold's death, Zeke Petrovsky was manager of a 7-Eleven in Chula Vista. He remembered because the 7-Eleven was convenient enough to his office and home that he might reasonably have stopped in there on occasion. Under the circumstances, of course, he went out of his way never to do that.

At Matt's sentencing, Zeke Petrovsky had seemed sufficiently vindictive and out of control to be capable of anything. The more Matt remembered the man's outburst that day, the more convinced he became that Zeke might be involved in his present predicament.

The idea, turning in his brain over the course of the drive back to San Diego, wore a groove in his thinking. By the time he reached Chula Vista, exhausted, bruised, and unshaved, it seemed only logical to try to find Zeke Petrovsky.

"He doesn't work here anymore," said the gangly black youth who was refilling the sugar and cream dispensers next to the coffee machine in the 7-Eleven.

Of course not, thought Matt. Why would he have assumed the guy still worked here after nine years? He turned to go.

"He's manager over at the Imperial Avenue store now," the kid said. "You hurry, you can catch him before the end of his shift."

Matt reached the 7-Eleven on Imperial Avenue a few minutes before nine. When he told the big-hipped, beleaguered-looking girl behind the counter that he wanted to see Zeke, she looked skeptical, but said she'd check in back to see if he was still there.

A minute later she returned. "What's your name?" Matt told her.

"And you want to see him about what?"

"He'll know."

She was gone only seconds this time. "He's not here. He's left for the day."

"Why'd you need to know my name, then?"

She scowled so hard that deep furrows bisected her forehead. "It's policy. I had to ask." She turned to a guy waiting to buy a bagel and Coke and started ringing up the purchases.

Matt strolled to the back of the store and went through the door the cashier had come through moments earlier. He found himself in a storage area with a couple of doors marked EMPLOYEES ONLY. "Mr. Petrovsky?"

He was not unaware of a hideous déjà vu element to this scenario: walking through a door uninvited, calling out that same name. But this time, there was no one waiting in ambush. Zeke Petrovsky stepped out of a rest room, drying his hands on a paper towel. He hadn't changed much in the years since Matt had last seen him—the hair was still slick and ebony black, without a fleck of gray, the eyes still piercing, the complexion as florid as if he spent his days laying bricks under a baking sun instead of working in a convenience store. He wore tan slacks, a brown, short-sleeved shirt, and a belt with a hunk of mottled turquoise shaped like a shark's tooth.

When he saw Matt waiting for him, he halted as though he'd walked into a wall.

"You. You got some gall coming here."

"I wouldn't be here if it wasn't important."

Petrovsky wadded the paper towel he was drying his hands with and tossed it into an open trash bin. Matt got the impression he'd like to do the same thing with his head if he could. "Saw your name in the paper the other day and felt like I was having a flashback. Has to be a different Matt Engstrom, I said to myself. Then I read a little more, and the article mentioned Harold and said how you'd gotten manslaughter for killing him nine years ago. I thought, shit, if justice had been done when you killed Harold, then this Bischoff guy wouldn't be dead now."

"I could waste my breath telling you I didn't kill Barry Bischoff, but you've obviously made up your mind, Mr. Petrovsky."

"Oh, Zeke to you. I mean, in a sick, fucked-up way we're almost family, aren't we? All those days in the courtroom together. Watching each other. Me wondering if I should try to smuggle a gun past the courthouse metal detector and shoot you where you sat. You wondering if I was gonna do that."

"I didn't worry too much what you were gonna do. I had other things on my mind."

"I'll bet. So what'd you come here for? If you want a character witness for your next murder trial, I'd say keep looking."

The girl from behind the counter stuck her head in the door, told Zeke his wife was on the phone, then lingered as long as she could, even after Zeke snapped, "Tell her I'll call back."

Matt looked around. "Is there someplace we can talk in private?"

"This is as private as it gets. What'd'you want?"

"Just this: at my trial, you shouted that you'd get me someday no matter what. That was nine years ago. What I want to know is do you still feel that way? Do you still think I got off too easy? Is revenge still on your mind?"

"I don't get it. What the hell kind of questions are those?"

"Because if you wanted me punished beyond what the court gave me, then I'd say you should be jumping for joy. I'm a suspect in a murder case where I'm innocent. I was set up. And while I know there's no reason to think you'll tell me the truth, I'm gonna ask anyway. I want to know what you know about why someone would pick *my* truck to dump a body into.''

He could have gone on, but he'd already decided to keep it simple, leaving out the part about embezzlement and the two toughs who'd killed Phil and his girlfriend the night before.

Petrovsky leaned against a packing crate, eyed Matt up and down. There was no wariness in his face, only indifference and a slight bemusement. "So you're involved in another murder, and your first thought is to come ask me if I framed you? Well, I gotta admit you're about the last person I'd ever expect to drop by for a visit, but now that you're here, I'm glad you did."

"And why's that?"

" 'Cause when Harold was killed, they didn't have that victim impact shit or whatever they call it now, where the friends and relatives of the dead guy get to stand up and say what they got to say to the accused. And there were things I wanted to say to you that day in court, things I never did get to say."

"You got your point across," said Matt, remembering how Petrovsky had been hauled screaming and struggling out of the courtroom that day.

"No, no, I didn't. You only knew Harold as some creep who wanted to fuck your wife, who called on the phone, who scared you. And when you killed him, even if it *was* accidental, like you claim, you figured the world was still probably a better place, at least for you and your wife.

"What you didn't know, though, was the Harold that was somebody's brother and nephew and son. And he had problems, sure, but nothing he deserved to be *killed* for. People were always after Harold, for one reason or another, all his life. And I'd always protected him. It was my duty; I was the older brother. I was the tough one. Harold was geeky and bookwormy and shy. He carried a lunch box and wore these goofy wire-rimmed glasses so he looked like some kind'a little professor. The other kids picked on him. They called him four-eyes, stole his lunch money, beat him up. Till I got hold of 'em. Then they left him alone. So I took it real personal when he died, like I'd failed him. Even though he was grown up and responsible for his own jams, still I felt like I should'a got to you first before you got to *him*."

"If it makes you feel any better," said Matt, "that's how I felt when my wife was murdered. Like I should've been there, should've protected her. All I wanted in the world was to be able to go back and make it come out differently."

"Your wife was murdered?"

"Soon after I got out of prison, yeah."

"Jesus. I didn't know about that. They catch the guy?"

"No."

"Shit, I need a smoke." Zeke lit a cigarette and opened a back door that led into the alley behind the store. There were a few cars parked back there and a couple of young kids who looked like they were in the middle of a drug transaction. They took off when Matt and Zeke walked outside.

"I'm sorry about your wife. But maybe that was God's way of giving you back a taste of your own medicine."

"If that's true, fuck God."

"Yeah, well, before you go too far with that, you ought'a know that same God saved your ass."

"How's that?"

"Because I did think about killing you."

There was no one else in the alley. For a moment Matt wondered if he was walking into another trap. But Petrovsky said, "My wife changed my mind, though. Not about killing you—I never told her or anybody else that was my plan—but she must've guessed. She told me anybody who takes another human life is interfering with God's plan for that person. It's like grabbing the steering wheel and twisting it when you're not the one driving the car. It leads to a helluva wreck."

"Your wife sounds like a smart woman."

"Well, not so smart maybe for marryin' me, but smart enough. I figure if killing my brother was an accident, then you got punished enough. And if it wasn't, then God will think up something to do to you that's more just than anything I could come up with. And I can accept that. I never thought I'd live to say this, but I don't hate you anymore. I've found peace."

"I'm glad for you, then," said Matt, but he had to force the words out.

As he headed back to his truck, though, he figured one of two things: either Zeke Petrovsky had changed tremendously for the better over the intervening years or he'd become more accomplished an actor.

His cell phone rang as he was getting into his vehicle.

It was Trina, suggesting lunch. Reluctantly, he agreed to meet her at one o'clock. That would at least give him time to go home, shower, and shave. After the ordeal in Vegas, all he really wanted was to sleep for twelve hours, but something in his former sister-in-law's voice told him that saying, No, thanks. How about another day? wouldn't be well received.

Chapter Sixteen

The Bangkok Wok, a half mile from Matt's house in Chula Vista, occupied a narrow slot between Julio's Pawn and Gun Shop and the Center for Contemplative Living. One could conceivably buy a Saturday-night special at Julio's, hear a talk on the virtues of nonviolence at the Center, have a change of heart, and go back to Julio's to pawn the now unwanted weapon, all with time for a sinus-clearing meal of pad thai at the Wok in between.

Matt had been eating here at least once a week since he moved to Chula Vista. The menu was as familiar to him as the information on his birth certificate, and the day waitress, a Vietnamese girl with seductive eyes and makeup so thick she looked like she'd stepped out of a Saigon brothel, set a hazelnut latte in front of him as soon as he sat down.

When Trina had said she wanted to go to "that Thai joint you told me about that plays Elvis," Matt had at first suggested a couple of other places. Put charitably, the Bangkok Wok had a certain relaxed standard of cleanliness he'd thought Trina might find off-putting, but she quickly set him straight.

"What do you think, I only eat at places with crystal finger bowls and maître d's that make more than most lawyers?" she said, opening up a red plastic menu with stains on the front. "Besides, this is a nice change from my macrobiotic diet."

Matt looked up from his latte. "I didn't know you were on a macrobiotic diet."

"Oh, yeah. Big Macs, Chicken Mcnuggets, those great skinny fries. I'm a grease junkie, didn't you know?"

"It sure doesn't show." The day had turned hot, and Trina was wearing a black leotard top and wrap skirt, a Balinese print in purple and brown and a deep mustard-colored yellow. When she'd walked in, several minutes late with a light sheen of sweat on her forehead, he'd been able to make out her hipbones underneath the sheer material.

She accepted the compliment, then took in Matt's haggard appearance and said, "Rough night?"

"You could say so."

The waitress took their orders and returned in a few minutes with heaping platters of duck, chicken, and stir-fried rice. Trina took a few bites, then set her chopsticks aside.

"What's the matter?" asked Matt, "Is the food okay?"

"Oh, it's fine. But here I'm being all chitchatty with you, like we're out on a date or something, when really I'm mad as hell at you. Only I don't know how to show it except by doing something juvenile and stupid, like throwing a glass of water in your face."

"Actually, on a day like this, that might feel pretty good." He wrapped a hand protectively around his coffee mug. "Just don't grab the latte by mistake."

Trina leaned forward, picking up her chopsticks again and tapping them on the tablecloth for emphasis.

"Look, Matt, you're a good friend, and I've tried to be a good friend to you. But I called your house last night just as Shawn was getting ready to leave with Coop, and he let it slip where you were. Then Coop grabs the phone from him and starts pitching this bullshit about Shawn being confused, that you hadn't gone to Las Vegas, you'd checked into some motel called The Vegas to get away from the press.

How the hell could you do this to me? How could you just take off for Vegas when I put up seventy-five thousand dollars to guarantee you'd stay put? I know you think I'm rich, and for some reason I don't understand, people seem to think it's perfectly okay to rip off rich people—you should see some of the scams that've been tried on Daddy over the years—but I'm not *that* rich, and even if I was, it's the fucking principle."

Her eyes today were pale blue, like the ice chips floating in her tumbler of Perrier. And angry. Matt looked down at his food before meeting her gaze again.

"I wouldn't rip you off, Trina. Your money was safe. It wasn't like I wasn't planning to come back."

"Tell that to the bail bondsman."

"I'm sorry, Trina. But I'm back now, I've checked in with the cops and with my attorney like a good little suspect in a homicide, and no one's the wiser about me being gone."

"So you've told me where you were. How about telling me what happened?"

"You're sure you want to know, Trina? It can't go any farther than this table."

"Hey, if I trusted you with my seventy-five thousand dollars, you can trust me with a little information."

He had to admit she had a point. Briefly, he outlined the events of the night before. Trina listened quietly, only showing emotion when he told her about Phil's death.

"Jesus, what a way to go! And now that he's dead, there's no way you can prove your theory that he embezzled that money."

"It's more than a theory," said Matt, irritated. "I know *I* didn't steal that money. I don't think Barry did, either. Phil had the motive—he was a compulsive gambler—and plenty of opportunity working in my office. Plus he ran like a rabbit as soon as he found out Barry was dead."

"So you think he killed Barry?"

Matt shook his head.

"That might explain why he killed himself, though," Trina went on. "If he *did* murder Barry and the guilt was catching up to him?"

"He had an alibi that night. Besides, I don't think Phil's death was suicide any more than I believe Barry crawled into the back of my truck and cut his own throat."

Trina fidgeted with her chopsticks. "I don't understand. You told me you were chasing the guy you caught in Phil's room, the guy you figure murdered that woman Cindee, when Phil jumped to his death?"

"I think there was someone else—that phony security guard I told you about—hiding in the bathroom that night, keeping Phil under control while the other one got rid of me. As soon as the coast was clear, he probably whacked Phil on the head and dumped him over the balcony. A fall from that height, even if Phil was already dead when he was thrown over, you wouldn't be able to tell."

"Jesus, Matt, that's scary stuff. If you really believe that's what happened, why don't you go to the cops?"

"Well, aside from the fact that I don't have any proof, I'd have to admit I left town in violation of my bond, which gets me in more hot water. But more important, I'm positive Phil's death and Barry's are connected. Barry had something he needed to tell me—I'm sure now he'd discovered Phil was stealing from the company. Maybe he told Phil what he knew—hoping Phil would come clean or put the money back—"

"Or maybe give him a cut?"

"I don't like to think that of Barry, but yeah, I guess it's a possibility. Anyway, Phil sicced the two goons on Barry, the big dude and the dark-haired one who posed as a security guard, and then later they followed him to Vegas and killed him and his girlfriend at the hotel."

"Kind of a rough justice to it, huh?"

"What goes around, yeah."

"But why murder Phil and his girlfriend? What's that accomplish?"

"Maybe they were afraid Phil would get caught for embezzling and he'd plea bargain by telling the cops he knew who killed Barry. Or maybe Phil was blackmailing these guys with the *threat* of ratting them out. When it came to money, I'm beginning to think Phil went through it like water through a colander. He might have been squeezing them."

"Or maybe this all goes back to Phil's gambling habit?" said Trina. "Maybe he owed money to the wrong people. He didn't honor his debts and they off'ed him."

"That's possible, too. I picked up a copy of the *Union Tribune* this morning, on my way out of town, and there was a piece on Phil and the woman he was with—according to the article, the cops in Vegas said it looked like a murder-suicide. Apparently heroin was found in Phil's room, so it's beginning to look like some kind of drug deal that went sour and turned into a double homocide."

"You said there was a lot of blood—this Cindee woman, was she stabbed?"

"I didn't get a very good look—everything was happening so fast—but her face was mutilated. Like the guy slashed her with the edge of a blade. Maybe even a razor."

"A razor?" Trina shut her eyes, then covered her face with both hands. "Jesus, that's so gross, so disgusting when I try to imagine it."

"Then *don't*," said Matt sharply.

"I can't help it. I have an active imagination." She motioned the waitress over and ordered a beer. They changed the subject for a while, then Trina said, "So, bottom line, Matt, you're still a suspect in Barry's murder?"

"I'm afraid so. And if the police find out I was there when Phil did his swan dive, they'll try to nail that one on me, too."

"Have you talked to Alex?"

"Yesterday, before I left for Vegas I gave him a call. He says the evidence against me is pretty circumstantial at this point. Also the cops found hair fibers in Barry's clothing that didn't belong to me or to Barry, and there were footprints around the truck that don't match mine, so if it comes down to a trial, chances are I'll walk. I say chances are, because with a jury, you never know."

"And there's the little matter of the four years you did for manslaughter."

"That wouldn't be admissible in court. But it doesn't matter. If this goes to trial, even if I'm acquitted, I'm fucked. My life's over. It's that simple. My business will go under. And what this will do to Shawn, after everything else he's been through, I can't even imagine." He pulled a half-empty pack of Marlboro out of his shirt pocket, shook one out, and stared at it a moment, then put it back.

"Jesus, Trina, you know what gets me? Since I got out of prison, I've tried to be as decent a guy as I know how. I've walked away from I don't know how many fights, turned down bribes from crooked inspectors, even once refused an offer to fix a fucking parking ticket, for Christ's sake. And this is where it's got me. My life going down the toilet and a murder charge hanging over my head. Not to mention my—" He stopped, immediately wishing he hadn't got that line of conversation started.

"Not to mention what?"

"Just that on top of everything else, I've got some— I may have some medical problems."

"What is it, Matt? High blood pressure?" She looked at the outline of the Marlboro pack in his pocket. "Not emphysema or—?"

"Forget I said anything, Trina. Okay? My health's fine." He stabbed at his food with chopsticks, put them down, and picked up a fork. "Trying to eat with a couple of twigs. I never did get the hang of it."

"It's all in the wrist, babe," said Trina, demonstrating by picking up a bean sprout. "Seriously, though, if you're in such great shape, why don't you get into triathlons like Dad? Get it out physically. He won't talk about the things that eat his lunch, either. A couple of days ago—I mean this is so—so fucking *Daddy*—he gets this bug up his ass about his mother. So we hop in the plane and fly to some hick town in Arizona, because grandma's buried there, and he wants me to see the grave and tell me about how she really died. Can you imagine what that was like for him, not telling me the truth about my own grandmother all these years?"

Matt looked up from his meal. "What are you talking about? Wasn't your grandmother killed in a car wreck?"

"That's always been the official story, yeah. Now Dad says she was murdered."

"Jesus, Trina."

"But telling me the true story didn't seem to make Daddy feel any better. In fact, he's been in a blue funk ever since, so I've been spending more time at his house. Trying to keep an eye on him. If he'd just see a shrink, try some antidepressants. I try to tell him there's no shame in drugs. The only people who aren't on Prozac are the ones who've moved on to something stronger. But you know how men are—"

"No, Trina. How are they?"

"Suffering from testosterone-induced insanity, that's what. It's why Daddy has to go around proving himself all the time. Climb the highest mountain, swim the deepest ocean, that sort of bullshit. It's how boys are socialized—to be tough, macho, in control. Don't feel their feelings, act them out. Between you and me, I think he's disappointed the thing with that woman he was seeing didn't work out. Myriam or Millicent or whoever she was. I think for some reason he blames me that she walked out on him."

"And we both know you'd never do anything to interfere with one of your father's romances."

"Don't be snide." She laid a chopstick flat on the

table, twirled it. "If anything, I think Daddy's worried sick about Shawn and what he must be going through."

"He's not the only one, believe me."

Matt watched the waitress bring out two pink drinks in glasses the size of small goldfish bowls and set them in front of the couple in the next booth, heard them joking about needing a designated driver. Felt suddenly thirsty. Swallowed hard.

"About Shawn, Matt. Daddy just wanted you to know that, not that anything's going to happen to you, but if it does—"

"If I end up going to prison, you mean?"

"—you don't have to worry about Shawn, not ever. And while this is getting sorted out, he can stay with Daddy—or with me, too, for that matter—anytime."

"Thanks, Trina. I may take Howie up on that. The other day, there was a reporter skulking around, talking to neighbors, hoping one of them would say I'm obviously a psycho pervert with dead bodies stashed in the basement. I don't want Shawn exposed to that. If one of those vultures was to start harassing him, I'd strangle him with his damn camera strap."

Trina shook her head. "Spoken like a true DeGrove man—even if only by marriage. Daddy would be proud of you."

The waitress laid the check in the middle of the table, and they both grabbed for it. Matt won, but Trina snatched it away from him. After some discussion, they finally agreed to split it. They left the Bangkok Wok and walked outside into blast furnace heat. "You got to get back to work right away?" Trina asked.

"As soon as I can, yeah, but first I've got an errand I need to run."

"Well, I'm not doing anything this afternoon. How about if I tag along?"

"I'd love the company, Trina, but you'd be bored, trust me."

She took his arm. "Oh, I don't mind."

He cursed himself for not just lying to her in the

first place and saying he had to get right back to work. As it was, he'd finally made an appointment to get tested at the health clinic. And he wasn't about to let Trina or anybody else tag along for *that*.

"I want to be focused for this, Trina. I really need to be alone."

"I see." She looked rebuffed and let his arm go. "So whatever this 'errand' is, I guess I can assume you're not picking up dry cleaning or getting your nails buffed."

"I'd say that's safe to assume."

They walked a few more paces before Trina brightened and said, "Oh, I almost forgot, I want you to see something. Oh, I hope it's still here." They walked to the end of the block, past Matt's truck and Trina's convertible, turned the corner and went another half block before Trina exclaimed "There it is! Isn't it gorgeous!" She led Matt over to a sleek, metallic gray Cadillac Coupe de Ville.

"What do you think? Should I leave a note on the windshield, see if the owner might be interested in selling?"

"*Another* car, Trina? Won't you have to get a bigger garage?"

"Are you kidding? You hardly ever see the Coupes from '69 or '70 anymore. See, you can tell the year because the windshield wipers are hidden by the shrouding on the hood. And this one looks like it's in mint condition." She ran one lacquered nail across the hood and over the curve of the fender. To Matt, the way she touched the car looked like she was caressing something alive, something whose flesh might shiver under her touch. Without taking her hand off the car, she turned and directed a sultry stare back at him.

"You know why I like hard, fast, solidly built cars, Matt? They make me horny. It's a hell of an afternoon to be out in the sun. I left the AC on high at my place. Why don't you forget that stupid errand, whatever it is, and come back with me to cool off?"

Before he could answer, she stood up and took a

step forward, penetrating his personal space at the same time that her perfume, something faint but intense, musk with undertones of vanilla, reached him. In the bright light, the tinted contacts made her eyes look almost pearlescent, gray-blue with a bottomless sheen he found difficult to look into without putting his mouth on her lips.

"Trina, don't do this."

"Trina, don't do this," she mimicked softly, putting her arms around his neck. "What's the matter, Matt? You don't find me attractive anymore? It's only been a few years. I can't have aged *that* much."

He stepped back, extricating himself from her arms, aware of the hot tingling sensation her fingertips left on his neck. "You haven't aged at all, Trina, and you know it. But things were different then."

"We were both drunk."

"We were drunk, and what we did was a mistake. It's not something I'm proud of."

"Jesus, Matt, what a moralist sobriety's made of you. So you went to bed with your sister-in-law before you went off to prison. So what? Calla never found out. Who knows, if she had, she might have surprised you. She might have wanted to join in." She shook her head, the bright beads of her earrings clinking merrily against the sides of her face. "What is it, Matt? Are you scared of me? You think I'm such a promiscuous wench that it's not safe to have sex with me? So we'll use condoms."

He almost laughed at the irony of it—her thinking he might be leery of *her* sexual history.

"I'm going to be late." He turned and strode back toward his truck, knowing if he hesitated, he'd end up going home with her, making love to her in that big canopied bed with the black and white silk sheets that he still remembered as vividly as the sun beating down on his neck. Making love to her and, in the process, making his life more complicated than it already was.

"I'll talk to you later, Trina."

He heard the chime of her laughter, tinkly and high. "Have it your way, Matt. Just don't forget you owe me. If you skip town again, you may have to pay me in sexual favors."

Chapter Seventeen

It was midafternoon when Matt got to the job site, and he was furious with himself.

Following lunch with Trina, he'd driven straight to the clinic where he'd made the appointment to get tested. He had parked his truck a block away and strolled back, trying to pretend this was no big deal, but feeling as furtive and jittery as a married man rendezvousing with the town madam. The neighborhood wasn't exactly high end—he spotted two of those virtually windowless bars where hard-core alcoholics start lining up outside at ten a.m. for their first eye-openers and battled the voices in his head insisting that if he ever *needed* a drink, now was the time.

Well, he didn't take a drink, that was the good news. But he didn't get his blood drawn, either. He glanced inside the clinic, saw the room was packed, told himself he didn't have time to wait all afternoon in a room full of screaming kids coming down with the flu, and took off.

Then he headed for the Bledsoe-Tull project, getting madder and madder at himself along the way as the same mind that had insisted he couldn't cool his heels in a waiting room all afternoon now accused him of cowardice.

By the time he arrived at the job site, he was ready to bust somebody's balls—with himself at the top of the list.

Bledsoe-Tull was the first commercial project undertaken by Engstrom Construction, a turning point for Matt's business. It occupied a city block between East Tull Street and Bledsoe Avenue and employed a full-time crew of thirty-five men. A six-story, two-million-dollar office building with an underground parking garage and a central atrium, the finished complex would house a trio of law offices, an accounting firm, and an upscale fitness center. Completion date was set for early December. Until recent events had drastically altered his priorities, Matt's main preoccupation had been making sure the various phases of building were moving according to the projected timeline and budget.

Until Bledsoe-Tull, Matt's company had worked exclusively in residential construction and remodeling, but the money wasn't as good, and fastidious clients— Jack Ryder being a prime example—sometimes made him wish he were back pouring concrete on a labor crew instead of trying to satisfy the demands of rich people whose greatest problems in life seemed to revolve around kitchen counters and matching bathroom fixtures. For a long time, Matt had hoped to move into commercial work. The Bledsoe-Tull building had given him that opportunity, and he was damned if he was going to let the project fall behind schedule, no matter what else was going on in his life.

When Matt arrived on the job site this afternoon, heavy columns of red iron, the framework that constituted the building's support structure, were being hoisted into place on the fourth floor. A workman in the cab of a hydraulic crane was lifting a huge I-beam—the crosspieces that formed the building's skeletal structure. Other crewmen stood on the already erected I-beams to guide and secure the heavy beams into place. He parked the truck, got out, and walked around the Tull Street end of the project, where another crew was working on shoring that would temporarily support the west stairwell while it was being completed.

He reminded himself that he was the boss here, that

he was in charge, but he felt like he was trapped in one of those mortifying dreams where you suddenly find yourself stark naked in public. Like the men were all staring at him, looking for clues in his body language or demeanor to help them decide if he was just a regular joe or a psycho killer who'd murdered Barry Bischoff.

A few of the men, who he knew personally from previous jobs, nodded hello. Others seemed to get extra busy and focused on their work as he passed. And there were a number of faces that were unfamiliar to him, guys Coop had hired in recent days or who were replacing other men.

Barry's murder and the events surrounding it had played hell with Matt's usual schedule, which took him to every job site at least once a day and Bledsoe-Tull, often twice. Since he was last here, concrete had been poured for the walls of the garage and L-shaped sections of angle iron had been set in place to support a layer of bricks. Excess angle iron, or "off fall," littered the ground where workers had trimmed it. Matt looked around for Coop, didn't see him, and headed over to the trailer parked near the curb.

He passed a couple of crew who were pulling out spud wrenches and turnbuckles from one of the dozen or so gang boxes, the heavy, wheeled metal boxes the size of a large shopping cart where the mens' tools were locked up overnight. Next to the gang box stood the canisters of acetylene and compressed air that were used to power the welding equipment. The men rummaging in the gang box weren't being particularly orderly: bolts and flanges and bright orange rebar caps lay strewn on the ground. As Matt stepped over and around the contents of the gang box, his leg jostled an acetylene canister. It wobbled and started to fall. Matt reached down to steady it and saw that the safety chain that should have prevented the canister from falling over had been left open.

He fastened the safety chain, then turned his pent-up anger on the two crewmen. "Who the hell left this unclipped?"

They were young guys, new to him. One of them heavyset, with broad tattooed forearms, wearing dungarees. The other a fox-faced young kid, with a dark ponytail and a gold ring in his ear. Both of them muttering and stammering in only borderline coherent fashion, but what it came down to was they hadn't touched the canister, didn't know anything about it, no sir, no way, no how.

Their disavowal of any and all knowledge was possibly true, since anybody could have left the canister unsecured. These two guys just happened to be standing next to it when Matt walked by, but he took it out on them anyway. "Do you know what can happen if one of these things falls and the valve gets knocked off? They explode, they can take your head off, that's what can happen, you got that?"

They nodded grudgingly, clearly miffed at what they must see as an unjust tongue-lashing within hearing of the rest of the crew. When Matt turned away, the one in the dungarees muttered under his breath, "Fuck, I didn't touch the damn thing." Matt heard him and whirled around, eyes flashing. "You wanna work here or not?"

The guy was sweating profusely. He put his hands on his hips, a stance of offended exasperation that in so large a man was strangely effeminate, and gazed fixedly at the gang box as though he were addressing the spud wrenches inside. "Yeah, I wanna work here."

"Then, shut up and get back to work! And put these tools away like you found them. You've got shit laying all over the place."

Lying all over the place, Calla's voice whispered in his mind, which angered him even more—damn Howie for his obsessive fixation with grammar that he had passed on to Calla, who had succeeded not so much in cleaning up Matt's grammar as in making him eternally self-conscious about it. What he *didn't* need right now was to be thinking about Calla and transitive verbs.

"Hey, Matt, what can I do for you?" Coop came out of the trailer carrying a clipboard and pen, and strode toward him with a forced grin plastered across his face. He wore khaki trousers and a Hawaiian-style shirt whose flamboyant maroon and fuchsia blossoms almost disguised the sweat stains and grime streaks that went with them. He looked rough. The whites of his eyes were shot through with pink that clashed with the dark half-moons sagging beneath them.

"You had an acetylene canister over there that wasn't hooked in," said Matt. "You ever see one of those things explode?"

Coop looked blank for a second, then seemed to comprehend and said in his most conciliatory voice, "You're right, Matt, that shouldn't have happened. I'll mention it to Sam before we go home today."

"Sam's the job superintendent, he's got other things to worry about," Matt said. "You're the one I expect to stay on top of these guys, especially the new ones." He jerked his head in the direction of the men putting tools back into the gang box. "Those two, I haven't seen them before."

Coop nodded. "Yeah, Jarvis and Kiddman, they're new and so are a couple of others. Had 'em sent over from the union last week."

"What for?"

"Couple of guys quit, one called in sick, another two I had to let go for showin' up late or not at all. You know how it is, Matt."

"Yeah, too much work out there right now. Everybody figures they screw up on one job, they can have another one by the same afternoon," he said, still feeling lousy and wanting to take it out on somebody. "The new guys, they workin' out?"

"So far." Coop glanced up above to where a thin, wiry guy with dirty brown hair was standing on an I-beam, using an impact wrench to screw the bolts into the iron. Below him, a bare-chested guy with a mustache maneuvered the tag line, a rope attached to the cross beam that was being lowered into place by the crane.

"Those two, the union sent over this morning. Marshak up top and Dingler workin' the tag line. A little green. Marshak was fuckin' around last night with the halogen lights, movin' 'em to a new position, and caught me right in the eyes—'bout burned out my retinas."

Matt cupped his hands around his mouth and hollered at the guy holding the tag line above the noise of the crane, "Hey, buddy, if you're gonna work on my job, you wear a shirt and a hard hat." He turned back to Coop, "OSHA inspectors would have a field day with this—canisters unsecured, guys without hard hats."

"I know, Matt, I've told the men over and over that safety's the number one thing."

"Well, tell 'em *again*," snapped Matt.

He stalked off toward the trailer, well aware that some of the men were staring at him, that he was busting Coop's balls for infractions that, while genuinely dangerous, could still be found at one time or another on almost every job site. As Matt well knew, the construction business wasn't exactly pristine when it came to maintaining safety standards. It employed men of vastly different skill levels and varying degrees of responsibility and clearheadedness to do inherently dangerous jobs. During his adult life, Matt had done almost all of them—operated every kind of heavy equipment, poured concrete, hefted drywall, done framing—and at one time or another, if he were honest, he'd fucked up in just about every way that you could, either by being half in the bag on the job or just careless and stupid.

The good news was most of the time a fuckup didn't make a whole lot of difference. Only once in a while, if you were either really stupid or unlucky or both, it could prove fatal.

"Where's Shawn at today?" Coop said, eager to redirect Matt's attention, but Matt was still focused on the work going on overhead.

Finally, when Coop thought he either wasn't going to answer or had forgotten the question, he said, "His granddad picked him up this morning, and they went to the beach. Shawn's into boogie-boarding, whatever that is. He's gonna ride his bike over later and put in a couple of hours—Howie's place is just a little over a mile from here."

"How's he taking all this?" said Coop.

"About as well as can be expected. I'm letting him spend more time with Howie till it blows over."

"How about you, Matt? You doin' okay?"

"I'm a suspect in a murder, Coop. Does it *look* like I'm doing okay?"

Coop started to say something else, but Matt didn't feel like talking anymore. He went into the trailer, sat down at Coop's desk, and started looking over phone messages and scheduling. Coop came in and shut the door after him.

"I know you got a lot on your plate these days, Matt, but don't take it out on me."

"You work here, don't you?"

"Yeah."

"Then I expect you to measure up. You gotta ride these guys harder about safety, or somebody's gonna get hurt. And Sam should be doing the same thing. Where is Sam, by the way?"

"He's not coming in till the afternoon. Had to take his wife to a doctor's appointment."

"Fuckin' great," said Matt. He pulled a pad and pen out of his pocket and scribbled himself a note to give Sam a call that night. Find out exactly what kind of appointment this was and why his wife needed a chauffeur to get there.

"Eye trouble," said Coop, reading his mind. "Doctor told her she'd have to have somebody to drive her home."

"Yeah, Calla used to have problems like that, too—

especially on days when I was too hungover to make
it into work."

"I don't think that's the case with Sam. He never
hits the bars after work with the rest of us. I never
even seen him drink a beer."

"You might try following his example," said Matt.

"You think I got a problem with booze? No way!
Just 'cause a man enjoys a drink now and again don't
mean he's an alcoholic. And just 'cause he *don't* drink
don't mean he's some kind'a saint," he added pointedly.

*You don't think you have a problem, try looking in
the mirror,* Matt was starting to say when a series of
sounds—violently loud, discordant—exploded in quick
succession. Matt and Coop both rushed outside. The
bare-chested man on the tag line suddenly—for no
reason that Matt understood—let go of the line. No
longer under manual control, the I-beam being hoisted
by the crane swung around violently. Marshak, the
shaggy-haired guy doing the bolting, screamed and let
his wrench fall.

"What the fuck—?" Coop said.

"Jesus," breathed Matt.

Men came running. Dingler, the guy who'd let drop
the tag line, was babbling something about having
tripped on a turnbuckle, but nobody was paying attention. Up above, at the third-story level, Marshak continued to scream. His hand had been caught and
crushed between two of the I-beams. He was slug
white, swaying from shock, while standing on a beam
no wider than the length of his feet.

"Get that I-beam down *now*," Coop yelled to the
man operating the crane. "*You*," he yelled to Dingler.
"Get ready to go up and help him as soon as the
crane's free."

"We don't have time," Matt said. The other lifts
were already in use at different parts of the job site.
It would take too long to get them into position to
hoist up help. He grabbed Marshak's dropped wrench,
jammed it under the back of his belt, and wrapped his
hands around the column of red iron that intersected

with the beam Marshak was standing on. Then he started to climb, gripping the column with both hands while wedging first one boot and then the other into the corner of the iron.

It was a torturous climb, something he hadn't done in years and definitely wasn't in shape for. Thanks to cranes and forklifts, no one but muscular young hotshots with more brawn than brains who were hoping to impress short-skirted secretaries down below actually scaled red iron bare-handed. If he could still do it, though, now was definitely the time . . .

Before he was even halfway up the red iron, his arms and shoulders were aching with strain, and his thigh muscles burned from the effort of keeping his feet braced into the corners of the iron as he "walked" inch by inch up the column. He could hear Marshak yelling for help and, down below, Coop's voice amid the commotion of men trying to unload the crane so it could be sent back up empty.

Only a few feet to go now. He paused for a second to shake out his arms—slowly, carefully, one at a time—while his full body weight rested on the remaining arm and his legs, then hauled himself up the remaining span, hooked a leg over the cross beam, and pulled himself up into a sitting position on the beam. Something sticky on his hand. He glanced down and saw that both his hands were scraped and bleeding. Saw at almost the same time—for now he was standing up on the beam and moving toward where Marshak teetered, looking weak-kneed and ashen—that the man he'd climbed up here to rescue was bleeding, too.

Blood. Jesus Christ. For the first time the full import of it hit him. His blood was—might be—poison. In trying to save Marshak, he might be bringing him death.

"Hey, man, hang in there. Lift's on the way up. You're gonna be fine."

Through gritted teeth, Marshak hissed, "Just get me out'a here, for fuck's sake."

"We will." He went to work on the beam with the

wrench, using care not to let his hands come in contact with Marshak's, wiping his hands on his shirt when blood started to well up in the cuts. Everything was happening with maddening slowness—the beam yielding in agonized increments while below, the crane was unloaded and sent up again carrying Dingler and Coop.

Marshak was able to pull his hand free just as the crane reached the third-floor level. He was trembling from pain, white as linen. His knees buckled as Coop and Dingler helped him into the lift. Matt passed on getting into the lift with the three of them, saying Marshak needed room to sit down, that they could send the crane back up for him in a minute, and they bought that because mostly it was the truth, not suspecting the real reason: that he was afraid he might bleed on them. That what was in his veins could be more dangerous than any on-the-job calamity they could imagine.

He stood on the beam while he waited for the lift to be sent back up, not watching the activity on the ground—Marshak being lifted off the crane, someone running over with an emergency medical kit—but looking off toward the west, not bothered at all by the height or the fact that he was standing on a beam not much longer than his boots. With all the hubbub going on down below, he suddenly felt very alone. He wished he were a few floors higher up, so he could see Point Loma and imagine he were one of the aliens wading through the brown water, listening for birdcalls that issued from human throats, and he chided himself for entertaining such a stupid, romantic fantasy even as he envied them their surreptitious flight to a new life and a new kind of freedom.

How he wished he could flee, just fuck everything and run. Except there was no way to run from what frightened him most.

The beam he was standing on seemed suddenly narrower than when he first stepped on to it. Reaching for the vertical I-beam, he steadied himself with one hand and watched the blood seeping out of his scraped fingers.

I gotta get the damn test, he told himself. *I gotta find out the truth before I go fuckin' crazy.*

Chapter Eighteen

Steve Salerno paced around the pool of the Holiday Inn just outside Barstow, California, a small town almost equidistant between Vegas and L.A. He was talking on his cell phone. Actually there wasn't much talking on his part. Mostly listening. The Boss was furious about the way things had gone down in Vegas, but Salerno put the blame on BuddyLee. If BuddyLee hadn't decided to follow the girlfriend up to Rollins's room and do her before Rollins got back, things wouldn't have got so fucked up. Not to mention the fact that if some idiot do-gooder hadn't paid Engstrom's bail, he would never have showed up in Vegas in the first place.

Only good thing about the phone call was that he and BuddyLee now had more work, which clearly they'd be well paid for.

Salerno hung up and was about to go back upstairs to the room and interrupt BuddyLee's tryst with one of Whores-R-Us' finest, when something stopped him. He saw *her*, playing by the side of the pool, and got seriously distracted.

"Nice sunglasses, sweetie."

"You like them?"

"Yeah, a lot."

She was obviously starved for attention. One word from a strange man, and she came trotting over, long black hair flying behind her, beads of water rolling off her gleaming skin.

He stared at her. Was tempted to stare at himself, too, reflected in the lenses of the flamingo pink, rhinestone-festooned sunglasses she was wearing.

Before he could become absorbed in one of those Hallmark moments of intense self-infatuation, however, vanity lost out to lust, and he wanted only to look at *her*. He already believed, of course, that he was a beautiful man. Jet-black hair that fell to his collarbones, soaring cheekbones that were a gift of some Native American ancestor a few generations back, lips made just a bit fuller by judicious injections of collagen, and a physique muscular enough to enable him to get away with such frippery. In short, he considered himself a hunk any female would die for. Even the one standing here now, who had begun prattling the moment she walked over and was telling him that she'd just turned eight years old.

The little girl turned briefly to check on her mom's location at the rim of the Holiday Inn pool, then continued to chatter, "My mom and me are on our way to Vegas. She's gonna play poker, and I'm gonna see the white tigers. You ever see the white tigers, mister?"

"Yeah, I've seen the tigers," said Salerno, but what he saw in his mind was Rollins's body flipping over the railing at the Luxor like a sack of wet towels. Did the shock of falling snap him back to consciousness, Salerno wondered. In the milliseconds before he landed ass-first on the obelisk, did he *know*?

So maybe Rollins wasn't supposed to die quite so dramatically and maybe his girlfriend wasn't supposed to die at all, but then nobody'd figured on Engstrom showing up at the Luxor. At least Rollins's "suicide" had provided a distraction. He and BuddyLee had gotten lost in the crowds, slipping past security before anybody could question them, and gotten the hell out of Dodge. They'd been holed up at a Holiday Inn on the outskirts of Barstow ever since, BuddyLee amusing himself with TV and hookers, Salerno . . . well, Salerno amusing himself.

He turned his attention back to the girl. "So you like tigers, huh?"

"Yeah, the white ones. I like the striped ones, too, but the white ones, they're better. They're *special.*"

He reached out, brushed the dark bangs from her eyes. "Well, you know what, I think you're special. You have such pretty hair. I don't think I ever saw hair this long."

She squinted at him from behind the colored shades with their plastic flamingoes. "You didn't? Really?"

"No, never. I sure do like long hair."

"My mom doesn't like it. She said it's too hard to take care of. She says I'd be cooler in the summer if I let her whack it all off."

Salerno wanted to say, *Listen up, kiddo, your mom's a fat old bat pro'bly jealous of you already and totally full of shit.* Instead he said, "Would you let me braid it?"

"Ummmm . . . I don't know."

"C'mon. It would look good. I do really nice braids. You know why, 'cause I used to braid my own hair when it was longer. With yours, I'd clip the braids up on top of your head so you'd look. like a model."

She giggled, a long, uneven sound that seemed to incorporate the chirps and warblings of several different kinds of wild birds.

Salerno asked, "Is your hair long enough so's you can sit on it?"

"No, it's not *that* long."

"I'll bet it is, too. Turn around."

She did a quick pirouette, dark hair fanning out thickly. "See?"

"No, slower. You turned too fast. All I saw was a blur."

She gave a theatrical sigh. Like: *You are so stupid, mister,* but he could tell that she craved the attention, that she was lapping it up. "Okay."

She turned again. Slowly, this time. Moving her hips, he thought, a little bit more than necessary. They knew so much, little girls nowadays. Knew stuff with-

out even knowing that they knew it. Must be TV, he
thought, or watching older sisters—or maybe it was
just instinct, the way animals know how to do certain
things without anyone ever explaining it. This one, he
thought, give her a couple more years and she'd be
one helluva hot little cocktease.

"You *can so* sit on it," he said. "I can tell. It brushes
up to the crack in your ass."

"Isabel?" The child's mother ambled over to the
edge of the pool. She was a ripe, swaying tub of a
woman. Big breasts and belly squeezed into a bulging
black tank suit, a scary foreshadowing of what her
nimble young daughter might look like thirty years
hence.

"You'd better be careful. Isabel will talk you to
death if you give her a chance. She's a regular little
chatterbox."

"I don't mind," said Salerno. He leaned back, squinting through his Ray-Bans to get a better look at Big
Mama. Decided the broad, buxom woman would look
good on her hands and knees in a harness, oinking
like a pig and getting it up the ass. For a second this
vision transfixed him, and a silly, smitten look that the
woman might have interpreted God only knows how
played on his features. Then he said, "I love kids.
Looking forward to the day when I have a bunch of
my own."

"Don't make it a big bunch," laughed Mama.
"They're a pain sometimes."

"Yeah, but they're worth it."

"Maybe. So, look, could I ask you a favor?"

"Shoot."

"I need to run up to my room for a few minutes.
Would you keep an eye on her?"

"Glad to," said Salerno, favoring Big Mama with
his most lascivious smile. Got her so discombobulated
that she almost walked off into the deep end of the
pool. Where was Pop in this picture, he wondered.
He'd have to find out. Maybe Big Mama wasn't all

that repulsive—not when you looked at the overall
picture.

"You gonna swim some more, mister?" asked the
little girl.

"Naw, I'm tired. I already swum fifty laps. I thought
what I'd do now is lay down and soak up some sun.
Then how 'bout you let me braid that long hair?"

She giggled and covered her face, peeking at him
through spread fingers. A cute gesture that made him
smile. Her hair, long and black and straight as a Cher-
okee princess, really did hang down to her ass. Past
her ass really. She had big wide-set eyes the color of
two Hershey's kisses, and the burnished gold skin
tones he associated with exotic Asian cities known for
perverse sex practices.

They went over to the chaise where Salerno had spread
out a couple of white bath towels. On the table next to
the chaise sat a bottle of suntan lotion and a highball
glass that held the slushy remains of a drink. He pulled
up another chair for Isabel, got a fresh towel off the
pile next to the rest rooms, and spread it out for her.

"What's your mom's name, Isabel?"

"Jewel."

"Hmmmm. Pretty name."

"You were out here swimming before I got up. It
was almost still dark." She grinned at him, mirthful
and sly. "I know a secret."

"You do? Well, if it's a secret, then you probably
shouldn't tell."

"Oh, it's okay."

He nodded. "If you say so, then."

"My mom, she was at the window. She was looking
at you."

"She was, was she? Naw, I think you're wrong."

"Uh-unh. I saw her. She was watching you swim."

"No sh—I mean, no kidding?"

"No shit," she said.

He'd been out doing laps at daybreak, when the sun
looked like a flat fried egg sizzling on the surface of
the horizon. Vegas long out of sight. The desert silent

and still, like something embalmed, nothing moving but the harsh hot breeze skimming over the bug-dappled water of the motel pool. He liked getting up early, being alone when the world had the flat, painted-looking quality of a stage set and it felt like he was the only one in it. This morning, however, he'd gotten up only to escape the disgusting noises coming from the connecting room that Baines was sharing with a couple of hookers. Salerno prided himself on the fact that he didn't use whores—not the kind you had to pay, anyway.

He picked up the bottle of suntan oil. "You want some of this?"

"No, Mom already put some stuff on me."

"Yeah, but you been in the pool. It's probably washed off by now. Here, just a little bit to make sure you don't burn."

He squirted a glob of white lotion into one palm, began massaging it into the girl's arms and hands. Her skin felt like satin. Not a crease, not a wrinkle, not a visible vein. He was discreet when he did her legs, stopping well short of the edges of her purple bikini bottom. Careful, careful. He didn't do her belly at all. When he got to her back, she held her hair up off her shoulders. The sheer heft of its glossy tumble took his breath away. She was perfection, exquisite, a diminutive doll. *Oh, Big Mama, what is your phone number?*

When he got through, he handed the tanning oil to Isabel and said, "Now, you do me."

"*Every*where?"

His head snapped around. *What the* . . . But she was just a kid, didn't know what she'd said. "Just my shoulders," he told her, drifting in and out of fantasy images: first the mother with her low-slung, melonous tits rolling around on his sheets like a great, wet mound of dough, then Little Miss Lolita-Rapunzel with that long hair, obscene hair, done up in glossy black braids. You could do a lot with braids. Stuff hairdressers never dreamed of. Salerno had almost become a hairdresser once. Right after college, when the pro football teams weren't exactly beating down his door, he'd actually thought about it. Why not? Alcoholics got jobs working in liquor stores, dirty old men coached Little League and volunteered with the Boy Scouts, candy addicts could surely be found stirring the vats of chocolate in Hershey, Pennsylvania. If he wasn't going to be making big bucks on the gridiron, no reason he couldn't spend his days plunging his hands into the sweet tresses of women's long flowing hair.

That fantasy, of course, had lasted only about as long as it took him to find out what beauticians actually made for a living. *No, thank you, I don't think so.*

Then other opportunities had come along, more lucrative, to say the least, and well, Salerno thought, the rest was history.

He gazed down at the kidney-shaped pool with its lolling sunbathers. Kids splashing in the shallow end, playing Marco Polo, moms and older sisters of varying degrees of pulchritude spread out like smears of luscious paté, oiled and gleaming, on the chaises. If he kept his focus on the pool and replaced the surrounding desertscape with the fantasy of a tropical oasis, he could almost imagine he was in Asia. In Thailand, to be exact, luxuriating in the scents and sounds and various lush sweetnesses of the beaches of Phuket or the sexual Shangri-la of Bangkok.

Some men fell in love with movie actresses. Others obsessed about some woman they glimpsed for an instant in a subway car or sitting in the vehicle beside theirs at a red light—the curve of a thigh, the slant of an eye, the dewy, promise-laden sheen of a pair of painted lips. Salerno conceived erotic fixations on places, cities, on far-off mountains and legendary lagoons. He'd researched Thailand: a certain kind of research, anyway, that had little to do with the country's history or spiritual practices or culinary delights. As he understood it, Thailand was the capital of concupiscence, the answer of the modern world to Sodom and Gomorrah that made Vegas, by comparison, look like the cartoonish wet dream of a callow teenage boy.

And there were some women, Salerno had discovered, who looked like they belonged in a Bangkok brothel, even if they'd never traveled out of state. Who looked used and debased and exquisitely soiled even if they were virgins.

He twisted his head around to smile at Isabel, who was squeezing more suntan oil onto her palm, when suddenly her big dark eyes grew wide. She gasped, "What was that?"

For a moment Salerno didn't respond. He was lost in a dream of his own: tiny Isabel, underage and unattainable. He was floating on her thin, boyish body and drowning in the lush waves of her hair. Then he heard it himself, a woman screaming from one of the rooms on the second floor. It wasn't Big Mama—she was waddling around the corner of the pool, wearing a white T-shirt over her bathing suit and an absurd, floppy-brimmed hat. She, too, turned in the direction of the commotion.

Fuck. Salerno didn't like this a bit.

" 'Scuse me a minute, sweetie. Be right back." He jumped up and hotfooted it around the side of the pool and up the stairs to the second-floor walkway. A door slammed and the hooker who'd been entertaining BuddyLee came clomping out, looking disheveled and agitated.

Salerno said, "Hold on. Something the matter?"

"Look at me! Look at me!" She held up her hands. There was blood on her palms, on her wrists. "Fucking psycho john."

She elbowed past him, muttering. He contemplated— and decided against—slamming her up against the stucco wall so hard her gold fillings popped loose.

Fuck. Now what?

He used his key to unlock the door. BuddyLee was nowhere to be seen, but he smelled something—an odor that was subtle, but still stomach-turning.

"Baines!"

He tried the bathroom door, found it locked, banged on it with his fist.

"If you're doing what I think you're doing, so help me, I'll—" He took a few steps back, preparing to assault the door with a hinge-popping karate kick, when suddenly Baines opened it. He took in Salerno's ready-to-charge stance, snickered, and said, "What you gonna do? Bust down the door?" before he turned back to the mirror.

Salerno walked into the bathroom, glowering at what he saw: a fucking, filthy *mess*. Blood in the sink, on the tiles, ruby droplets spattering the toilet seat. Baines's face was a gory mask. Like a man undecided whether to shave or slit his own throat and so doing something somewhere in between, he leaned into the mirror while maneuvering a razor blade across his forehead.

"Jesus," hissed Salerno. "You dickhead, you want to bleed, I'll make you bleed. How do you expect me to use this fucking bathroom? It's contaminated. It's a fucking Chernobol of bacteria, for Christ's sake."

Baines said, "I gotta get the pressure off. The fucking bitch took off before I got to come. You know this is the only way I can come without a woman!"

"Bullshit! She had blood on her when she left the room. You could'a fucked her and you were doin' this instead."

Baines shivered with pleasure, and the tattoos on his biceps twitched. "All right, I fucked her first, but it wasn't enough. Her pussy didn't get the job done, know what I mean?"

"I *told* you you were gettin' hooked on that cuttin' shit," said Salerno. "I *knew* it. Now you're *addicted* to the slicin' and dicin'. You can't fuckin' stop!"

"Well, what'd you expect me to do? Not come?"

"Jerk off like everybody else on the fuckin' planet!"

"I tried. It don't work for me no more. I need to cut." Baines put the razor down, looked up dreamily. "I remember the first time I cut myself. I did it 'cause I had to. Blade, Tully told me, or lose your job. And

I hated it. Got so sick to my stomach, I almost threw up. But now when I bleed, it's like more than just blood comes out. Bad shit comes out, too. Negative shit, evil karma. I feel so light, it's like I can fly."

"I'll make you fly," said Salerno, balling his fist.

Baines whirled around and gave him the full force of his "scary" stare, the one he practiced in front of the mirror, where the cords of his neck bunched up like broccoli stalks and his eyes bulged out like hard-boiled eggs. Salerno had seen scarier faces made on the playground by fifth-grade bullies. He smirked and turned away, hoping Baines would take a shot at him, so he could retaliate. But not even Baines was that stupid.

"Aw, fuck you," said Baines, backing down.

"Christ, look how you're bleeding! If you gotta do that, dammit, you make a cut, a clean cut, you don't try to do fucking brain surgery."

Baines ducked his head back into the stream of water. "I kind'a liked that chick I was with."

"Then why the fuck did you scare her off, asshole?"

Baines straightened up, toweling his face. He appeared to be thinking deeply. "I didn't think she'd barge right in on me like she did."

He straightened up, flexing his biceps for the mirror as he finished toweling the blood off his face. "Fuck, it feels good to bleed. Lets all the pressure out. Like takin' a handful of ludes."

"You sick fuck."

"Hey, Salerno, why can't we hang out here another night? Lay out by the pool. Call some more girls." He wadded the bloody towel and tossed it into the tub. "We stay here another night, I want a black chick this time."

"You forgetting we gotta be in L.A. by tomorrow afternoon? Besides," Salerno added, "I didn't tell you the good news. I just talked to the Boss, and he's got more work for us. Just as soon as we finish up in L.A., we're gonna get to do more than just fuck a girl. We're gonna get to kill one."

Chapter Nineteen

"Where you going, Dad?"

Feeling guilty, like he'd been caught at something, Matt aborted his rush out the front door and came back into the living room. Shawn and his buddy Ryan, who lived five doors down, were watching a TV show that featured a couple of bulked-up guys and a freakishly muscular woman whose brick-hard buttocks were showcased by the thinnest of thong bikinis, all of them screaming at each other. The boys' skateboards were leaned up against the sofa. Both were wearing loose tops and baggy jeans worn as low on their hips as decency would allow and baseball caps turned backward on their closely cropped heads. The fact that his son and his buddies all dressed like wannabe gangbangers still bothered Matt from time to time, but he remembered some of the fads of his own youth and tried to accept it.

"Just gotta run a few errands," Matt said. It wasn't an out and out lie, but still far enough from the real truth that he felt uncomfortable.

"What time you gonna be back?"

"Couple of hours."

"There's a Championship Pro Wrestling show on PPV tonight," Shawn said. "It's gonna be *sick*."

"I believe it," said Matt, glancing at the screen in time to see a guy with face paint giving the finger to a jeering audience. Nice. "They can do that on TV these days? They can flip somebody the bird?"

"Sure," said Shawn. "They do it all the time."

"We thought you might like to watch the PPV with us," said Ryan, doing an excellent, if unintentional, imitation of Eddie Haskell.

"It's at eight-thirty," said Shawn, picking up where Ryan left off. "It's gonna be cool. The Embalmer's coming back from the dead tonight."

"Hey, sick!" exclaimed Ryan. "Did you see him pour embalming fluid on that jobber last week?"

"You mean four-eyes?" said Shawn. "The juice-junkie?"

"That was *so* cool. It went down four-eyes' trunks and everything. Plus the blood—"

Shawn, seeming to remember the subject at hand, said, "So, Dad, if you get home in time, you want to watch it with us?"

"Sorry, guys," said Matt. "Not really my thing."

Shawn and Ryan exchanged looks.

"Dad, well, then, how about can we watch it?"

The conversation was getting depressingly familiar. Matt sighed. "How much does it cost?"

"Only thirty-two dollars," said Shawn.

"For a pay-per-view wrestling match? You gotta be kidding. For that kinda money I'd want Mike Tyson at the least. Or one of those Ultimate Fight guys. The ones who fight for real, not just playact."

Shawn smiled. "You mean like that shoot-fighter we saw last year? Lars Shamrock?"

"Yeah," said Matt, taking the bait, "like him. A real fighter, there's somebody I'd pay money to see, not a bunch of stuntmen."

"Lars Shamrock's on the show," said Shawn, clearly delighted.

"He joined Championship Wrestling last year when his fight contract ran out," said Ryan.

"So now it's not just the failed football players and washed-up weight lifters, but legitimate fighters who're becoming pro wrestlers? Good Lord, what's the world coming to?"

"So can we watch it?" said Shawn.

"Are you paying for it out of your allowance?"

"Aw, Dad, you know I'm saving for amps."

"Sorry." He started toward the door.

"Dad, can we go out for pizza when you get back?"

"Actually, what I was thinking—I may be pretty tired when I get home and want to go right to bed. How would you feel about spending the night over at Ryan's? If it's okay with your folks, of course, Ryan?"

"Sure, Dad."

"Yeah, that'd be cool, Mr. Engstrom. My mom's making lasagna."

"Good. It's settled, then. And, Shawn, I know you like to sleep in on Sundays, but be back here by eleven, okay. We'll go to Mass."

Matt wasn't waiting for Mass the next morning to do his praying, however. He was already asking God to give him the courage to do what he had to do as he walked out the door.

Although he didn't believe in Hell, Matt was convinced that, if such a place existed, it would be a gigantic, under air-conditioned waiting room full of magazines more than a year old, with at least one wailing child and a couple of adults competing to see who could get lung cancer the quickest by hyperventilating through cigarettes at a lung-blackening rate. The fact that, in this case, he was one of the smokers—the other being a heavyset African American woman whose wire-rimmed glasses kept sliding down her nose and who'd gone through four Camels since she sat down with her toddler half an hour ago—didn't diminish his impatience in the least.

He stared down at a page of *Field and Stream*. The same damn page he'd been looking at for what felt like hours. He kept reading about fly-fishing and then thinking about something else, getting sidetracked by the kid screeching or the woman's hacking cough as she pushed the glasses back up on her nose, coughed them down again, pushed them up. He read the same paragraph over and over.

"Mr. Engstrom?"

The nurse summoned him. He went to the desk, and she handed him a pen and about ten pages of paperwork to complete.

Have you ever been treated for a mental illness? Have you ever had a sexually transmitted disease? Name and address of next of kin.

He found himself unable to concentrate on even the simplest questions. His mind wandered and back-tracked and then spiraled down in long, depressing loops.

So is this my punishment, he thought. *Is this happening to me because of what I did to Harold Petrovsky? But didn't I serve my time for that? Haven't I been punished enough?*

On the one hand, he didn't believe in a punishing God sitting on high, meting out earthquakes and fires and flood, selecting the victims of drive-by shootings and convenience store holdups by totaling up a dunning score on some weird cosmic abacus. At least the grown man that he was didn't, but the little boy in him—the boy who'd gone to confession every week until he reached his teens, the boy who still worried God knew about the time he stole MaryJean Longaker's blue silk underpants out of her mom's laundry hamper and took them home to commit unspeakable acts on them—that little boy wasn't nearly so sure.

The nurse came to the doorway and yelled out a name. The black woman lumbered to her feet. He caught the nurse's eye. "The doctor going to be very much longer?"

She flashed a saccharine smile that must have been pretty when she was younger and more idealistic. "We'll be getting to you shortly, Mr. Engstrom."

He sat back with his *Field and Stream*, lit a cigarette, then realized he already had an unfinished one smoldering in the gray ceramic ashtray.

Sweet Jesus, he thought. *I can't afford to have a terminal illness. Can't afford it financially, can't afford it emotionally, can't afford it as a father.*

That would be the worst part if it came to that. Telling Shawn.

He shut his eyes, wondering why in hell he'd thought protection wasn't necessary after Noel told him she was on birth control. Had he really been dumb enough to believe only gays and IV drug users got AIDS? But whoever said Noel never used IV drugs? Why wouldn't she? She'd done everything else. And why was he so arrogant as to think the virus couldn't have come from *him*?

He had wanted Noel the first time he saw her—at a Home Builders Show where Engstrom Construction had rented a booth. She was buying a hamburger at the snack bar, and he had struck up a conversation. She told him she'd been hired by a local real estate firm to hand out flyers, but the job had fallen through, leaving her with no work and the rent coming due.

She didn't tell him about her work as a stripper until later—if she had, he might have wondered why a woman who took in three hundred dollars on a slow night was upset over losing a minimum wage gig peddling flyers. As it was, by the time he found out about her real career, they were already lovers and he didn't give much thought to the incongruity of their initial meeting.

Right from the start, though, she'd been trouble. One of those people with lives in such a constant state of disarray and chaos that the daytime soaps seem tame by comparison, she left behind her a trail of bounced checks, irate landlords, and lost jobs. She wasn't even thirty yet, but already there were a couple of ex-husbands in the picture and God only knew how many former boyfriends trying to find her, either to win her back or exact revenge.

What made Matt angriest at himself was that he'd *known* all this. She hadn't hidden it from him. On the contrary, her disfunctionality was like her body—on display for all the world to see.

The helluvit was, in spite of turmoil that swirled around Noel like dust around the feet of the roadrun-

ner in a cartoon, he was still crazy for her. Her unbridled love of sex delighted and revitalized him. Her
unpredictability shook him loose from ruts he hadn't
even realized he'd been entrenched in. She got along
well with Shawn—liked the same movies, the same
fast food. That her tastes were at the same level of
sophistication as his ten-year-old son alone should
have told him *something* right there.

But, face it, on a certain level, he *liked* helping her
out of scrapes. *Enabling*, as it was called in twelve-step
parlance. Paying her court costs, lending her money to
have her car repaired after she got high and ran it into
a ditch, calling up dance club managers to say she was
sick, had made him feel important. Needed. So even
while he was bitching to himself about how much she
cost him in terms of time, money, and self-respect, her
neediness was providing him with ego strokes.

When she failed to show up for their last date, he
went to her apartment and found a note scribbled on
the back of a grocery receipt: *Matt, it's time for me to
move on. I'm sorry if I hurt you. I do love you, but it
was wrong to tell you so. I'm really sorry about everything. Noel.*

And that was it. Poof, she was gone. Like Calla. Poof,
gone. Into the ether, into thin air. He felt like a magi-
cian whose tricks have gone out of control. Women
disappearing on him so fast it felt like sorcery and he
had no way to undo the deed.

Until the phone call that had brought her back into
his life with all the subtlety of the Loch Ness monster
coming up under a tourist boat.

The black woman had another coughing fit. Her
glasses slid down again. She didn't bother to push them
back this time, but stared dully ahead, exhaling puffs
of smoke each time she coughed. The glasses kept
catching Matt's attention, and he realized they reminded him of the ones Harold Petrovsky had worn,
that had ended up on the blood-spattered stairs after
Matt hit him.

I always tried to protect my brother, Zeke Petrovsky

had said. *The other kids were cruel to him. They called him four-eyes.*

Four-eyes. Matt turned that over in his mind, trying to make the connection that was struggling to come through. *Four-eyes. A cruel term for a person wearing glasses. Or could it just as easily mean something else?*

He went to the receptionist's desk and asked to use the phone, dialed his home number, and waited, growing ever more impatient until finally Shawn picked up the phone. "Shawn, that pay-per-view you were talking about—"

"It's okay, Dad. We decided to rent a video instead."

"There was a wrestler you mentioned that you called four-eyes. Did you call him that because he wears glasses?"

Shawn laughed. "A wrestler wearing glasses? No, Dad. We call him that 'cause he's got these freaky eyes tattooed across his back."

The nurse said, "Mr. Engstrom? The doctor will see you now."

But Matt was already out the door.

A few miles from the clinic, he called Shawn again on his cell phone and was relieved when the boy picked up the phone on the fourth ring.

"We were just headed over to Ryan's house, Dad. What's up?"

He debated, then decided there were enough things he couldn't tell Shawn. No need to keep him in the dark about this, too. "Can you keep a secret?"

"Sure!"

"You can't tell anyone. Not Ryan, not even Aunt Trina. Especially not Aunt Trina. Understand?"

"Yeah, Dad."

"I'm driving up to L.A. to take in that wrestling show you and Ryan talked about. I think there's a guy I met in Vegas who may be there. He and I've got some business to discuss."

There was a pause before Shawn said, "So the rea-

son you're going there alone, even if you knew somebody else who really wanted to go, is that it's
business, right?"

"Right," said Matt, appreciating Shawn's careful
wording for Ryan's benefit. "Otherwise, I'd take that
someone with me."

"I gotcha, Dad. Be careful."

"I will. And thanks, Shawn, you may have helped
me more than you know."

Chapter Twenty

The traffic north into L.A. on this rainy Saturday night was so bad Matt wondered if there was some disaster approaching San Diego that he didn't know about—an earthquake or a tsunami about to wash away everything from La Jolla down to Point Loma. He took the wrong exit for the Coliseum and spent twenty minutes finding his way back to the freeway so he could take the off-ramp two exits farther north. The line of cars snaking into the parking areas amazed him. When he finally found a spot to park the truck, it was in a muddy, unpaved lot that the steady drizzle was turning to the color and consistency of wet cement. He fumbled with the antitheft device, an iron rod that screwed onto the steering column, then decided to hell with it, no one in their right mind would try to steal the dilapidated vehicle and shoved the device back under the front seat.

The rain pelted his shoulders and head as he loped toward the stadium. He bought the best seat still available and an overpriced program, which he scanned briefly once he got to his seat. There were photos of wrestlers who apparently were the top stars, but no one with any visible tattoos. One guy sported bizarre red, black, and green face paint, but his build was much slighter than the monster who'd nailed Matt in the room at the Luxor.

After sitting through a couple of lackluster matches, replete with missed spots and crowd chants of "Bor-

ing," he wasn't any closer to seeing anybody with
dragon's eyes tattooed on their back than before, but
he'd figured out wrestling had changed quite a bit
since the days when he was a kid sitting glued to the
set, watching the matches coming out of Atlanta. In
those days, he recalled, the good guys wore white
trunks and shouted, and the bad guys wore black
trunks and shouted even louder, and the only time a
woman got into the picture was when Fabulous Moola
defended her title against some pretty blond Texas
girl, and he hadn't even seen all of that because his
mother had walked through the room, scowled at the
set, and snapped it off, saying something about not
having her boy watch "catfights."

Well, "catfighting" was the least of it these days.
There was the Amazon with biceps the likes of which
men join gyms to develop that he'd already seen on
TV—he figured she must have enough testosterone in
her bloodstream to power the Dallas Cowboys—and
another with breasts that had passed merely volup-
tuous several cup sizes back and now verged on ana-
tomically impossible. At any moment Matt expected
her to tip over and fall on her face. Apparently, she
was well-known to the crowd, who waved signs saying,
"Marry Me, Misty" and "Misty, 42DDD!"

It wasn't easy to tell the baby faces from the heels
anymore, either. One guy came out giving everyone
the finger, but the crowd cheered him wildly. His opponent, a lanky kid with deranged-looking eyes, carried a Bible and quoted Scripture—the crowd jeered
him lustily, hurling epithets disparaging what they apparently believed to be his sexual orientation.

The only tattoos Matt saw so far were the ones on
the biceps and back of the Amazon.

Leaving his seat, he made his way as close as he
could to ringside. A dozen or so burly men wearing
bright yellow shirts marked "Security" stood between
the fans and the action, although occasionally the latter spilled over into the audience when the wrestlers
took their act into the aisles.

Matt joined a crowd that had gathered over by the barricades to get a better look at the wrestlers as they ran to and from the ring. If he leaned over and craned his neck, he could see a few milling around backstage, but not one of them had any visible tattoos.

Turning to the fan beside him, a college-age kid wearing a T-shirt with the face of a sneering grappler on the front, he said, "How about the big guy with eyes tattooed on his back? What's his name?"

The guy shrugged. "Don't know. I'm here to see how much bigger Misty's tits are than the last time she wrestled. Her doctor must be getting rich. They get just humongouser and humongouser every time I see her."

"Hey!"

Whirling around, Matt glared at the fat, screeching girl on his right who was waving a placard and spewing obscenities. She had just tromped on his foot. She ignored both his query about a tattooed wrestler and the possibility that she'd broken his toe, but before he could say anything else, a voice behind him muttered, "You're kidding? You spent fifty bucks to come see a jobber?"

"A what?" Matt turned around, making room for the skinny black teenager with a Jamaican accent to stand nearer the barricade.

"You know. Jobber. Guy who do jobs."

"Guess I don't know," said Matt.

"Jobber acts like a bad ass, but then he lose to the guys gettin' the push, make them look good. The guy with the tattoos—that's all he is, man. A jobber. He big, but he misses spots all the time. Last time I seen him, guy he be rasslin' holds out his hand for an arm bar and BuddyLee, he fall flat on his face."

"That's his name?"

"BuddyLee Baines, yeah," the kid answered, "but he ain't worth watchin'. He just *job*, man."

"Well, we all gotta start somewhere," said Matt, elbowing his way over toward the gap between the barricade and the wall, where a half-dozen high-school-age girls, apparently dressed up as hookers, had stationed themselves. The full-lipped Asian-American security guard was ignoring the girls and appeared to be in the grip of boredom-induced catatonia, but when Matt tried to slide between him and the barricade, the man jerked to attention as though he'd been goosed.

"Where you think you're going?"

"Just wanted to get an autograph for my son."

The guard looked affronted. "You gotta be kidding. You can't go back there."

"What about all those young girls?"

"Yeah, what about 'em? Go back to your seat."

Matt moved back a bit, but continued to hang with the group that was crowding the barricade. The match in the ring had just ended in some sort of complicated debacle involving several more wrestlers than had been there at the start, a turn of events that had the entire Coliseum on its feet, roaring approval or outrage. The wrestlers, exiting the ring, ran a gauntlet of desperately reaching arms and screaming faces. A guy in a tuxedo came out and announced an intermission. People started trooping to the rest rooms and concession stands.

Beside Matt, a softly musical female voice purred. "You wanna get in where you ain't supposed to, huh?"

He looked down at a petite, olive-skinned girl who flashed him a bright, naughty smile. Her sultry voice was ripe with innuendo. She wore a tight black skirt, chunky gold clogs, and a clingy red tube top that accentuated her breasts better than any Wonder Bra ever made. Her eyes were outlined in Cleopatra-kohl, her fingernails painted a plush shade of purple that matched her lips. Matt figured she must be all of fourteen.

"That depends," he said cautiously.

She laughed. "Like backstage?"

"How would I do that?"

"You can't. There's too much security."

"Can you get back there?"

She looked at him like he was brain-damaged. "Yeah, well, not to burst your bubble, honey, but I got an advantage. The boys—most of them, at least— like what I've got a lot more than what you've got." Her black, almond-shaped eyes traveled to his crotch and lingered there before slowly ascending. "Although what you've got ain't bad."

He forced himself not to stare at her body with equal frankness and turned away.

She elbowed her way after him. "So you wanna chance to hang out with the boys or not?"

"Sorry, I don't look good in drag."

"I know most of them personally."

"How about BuddyLee Baines? You know him?"

She shrugged. "I been with him, but only because he parties with his manager Salerno and some of the top guys. Salerno's *hot*, but BuddyLee's weird, you know what I mean? Creeps me out."

"My kid wants his autograph."

"No shit? Maybe your kid should see a therapist."

"It's all the violence he watches on TV. So the autograph, think you could help me get it?"

"I might be. Depends." She gave a languid, cat-licking-cream-off-its-face smile and let her lids droop almost shut, achieving an expression of such blatant sensuousness that Matt revised his opinion and decided—hoped—she had to be at least eighteen. "Guess I could ask Salerno to get it for me," she said, drawing out the syllables of the name like an erotic mantra. "Now Salerno, he himself don't give autographs. But, honey, if you got what he likes, then he gives everything else."

Her name was Astra (or so she said), she'd be sixteen in two weeks, and would Matt like to buy her one of those "Bite Me!" T-shirts and matching cap on sale at the concession stand? That, in addition to the hot dog and Coke he'd already bought her, might motivate her to exert some influence in his behalf.

In the meantime, she regaled him with information

about "the boys," much of which he could have definitely done without. Evidently she had slept with most of the guys that were on tonight's card. Her two girlfriends, also here tonight, had similar sexual predilections. They kept score, compared notes as to size, technique, and personal quirks. It sounded like the sexual version of trading baseball cards.

"Now, Big John, he's got a ten-inch dick, but you can tell just from talkin' to him, that's where most of his brains are at. I don't want that. I want somebody I can talk to after. Someone with a mind."

"That's important," Matt said.

"Although a body's important, too."

"Can't live without one."

"You're makin' fun of me."

"I'm sorry," Matt said. "I know it's none of my business, but you seem a little young to be—to be—"

"A ring rat?" Astra chewed the last of her hot dog, blinked fat, mascara-thickened lashes. "It's fun hanging out with the boys. It's exciting." She gave a quick, appraising stare. "You know what it's like to be with a whole room full of people at one time? Men and women both? All of 'em sweaty and turned on like crazy? One of 'em somebody you might even be in love with, a few people you've had sex with before, most of 'em strangers? Naw," she said, answering her own question, "I can tell you've never been into that scene. You don't look the type."

"Looks can be deceiving."

One thinly plucked eyebrow arched doubtfully. "Go on! You mean you've done group sex?"

"Not lately," said Matt, remembering the days when he was young and crazed with lust on a regular basis and nobody had ever heard of AIDS. "Not in a really long time."

He bought Astra the T-shirt and made her promise to help him get backstage. *No problemo*, she assured him. A security guard at the west exit was hot for her. If she flashed her tits, he'd probably pass out, and Matt could go back easy.

"So when do we go?"

"After the Battle Royal starts, when everyone's distracted." She reached down and tugged at her tube top, adjusting it for maximum cleavage. "I'm not gonna settle for just giving no blow job tonight—I want Salerno to take me back to his hotel room." She stuck out her chest and wiggled around for Matt's benefit. "Well, what do you think?"

What he thought was that if this girl had parents, they ought to be horsewhipped, but he kept that opinion to himself and told Astra that she looked very pretty. Besides, the Battle Royal was underway, the crowd surging back to their seats.

The idea behind a Battle Royal was, apparently, to fit as many wrestlers as possible into the ring and see who fell/jumped/got thrown out first, then continue the process until only the one stalwart soul sufficiently beloved by the promoter, to be given a push remained. Right away a short swarthy guy with oiled pecs and fringe on his red wrestling boots got pitched over the top rope. He was followed by a blond kid with jiggly love handles who looked like the only reps he practiced were done with a fork. Then a third guy seemed to lose interest and just called it quits, sliding out under the ropes on his own—when he left the ring, Matt saw there was blood on his chest and part of a bloody footprint at the ring apron.

With so many arms and legs flailing, it was hard to see what was going on. He climbed up on an empty seat, ignoring the shouts of protest from the people behind him. He could see now where the blood was coming from. A big, shaggy-haired guy who'd been knocked down early on and was now struggling back up to his feet. Blood fountained from a cut over his eyebrow. It spattered other wrestlers, ran down his face, and speckled his broad chest.

Several others ganged up on the bleeder and hurled him over the top rope like they were hefting a sack of garbage. Even if he hadn't had a good view of the guy's back, the fans provided all the information Matt needed. "Four-eyes sucks, four-eyes sucks!" they chanted derisively, hurling paper cups and cigarette butts and other trash at the guy as he stalked out of the arena.

Chapter Twenty-one

"That's him!" Matt said to Astra, but the spot where she'd been standing was now occupied by someone else. Looking around, he saw her chatting with a blotchy-faced security guard whose gaze never got above chest level. Astra didn't seem to mind. She stood on tiptoe to give the guy a quick kiss, then trotted merrily backstage without so much as glancing in Matt's direction.

"Hey! You!" Matt had to shout to be heard above the din of the crowd. He ran over and got in the guard's face. "What the hell you think you're doing with my daughter?"

"Your daughter?"

Matt grabbed him by the collar. "My thirteen-year-old daughter, you sick fuck! She says you let her go backstage if she lets you feel her breasts."

"Hey, man, I don't know what you're talking about."

"That's it," said Matt. "I'm calling the cops. You're a fucking statutory rapist's what you are."

"Wait, no, hold on, now!" The guard's Adam's apple bobbed furiously, like an elevator out of control. "Take your hands off me. She told me she was eighteen, swear to God."

Matt let go of the guy's jacket. "I'm going back there and get her, take her home."

"Now wait—"

"What, you gonna try and stop me getting my little

girl?" He grabbed the pimply-faced youth again and backed him against the wall.

"No, no. Go ahead. Go get your kid, get out of here."

Matt hurried backstage. There were more people than he'd figured on—photographers with laminated ID cards around their necks, gofers rushing about with the urgent air of those on vital errands, a Japanese camera crew filming an interview with the guy whose face was on the T-shirts being hawked at the concessions. A couple of wrestlers who'd appeared in earlier matches came out a side door and passed Matt without a glance. They wore street clothes and carried their gear in shiny silver suitcases. Another wrestler, apparently just ousted from the Battle Royal, jogged past. He muttered, "Fucking clusterfuck," to no one in particular, and barged through a door into what looked like a dressing room.

Now that he knew he wasn't going to be summarily ejected, Matt tried to assume an air of confidence. He checked out a couple of dressing areas, found one empty, the other occupied by a group of wrestlers who had gathered around a TelePrompTer to watch the finish of the Battle Royal. BuddyLee Baines wasn't among them, so he shut the door again and continued down the corridor.

To his left, a door opened, and a couple of wild-haired young guys in tights and face paint bolted out, glancing back over their shoulders, sniggering. The smaller one, who probably weighed only about two hundred fifty pounds, said to Matt, "If you're the guy from *Wrestling Review*, I wouldn't go in there yet. Tully's reaming somebody's ass."

"Not to mention there's blood all over the floor," said the other one.

"I can wait," Matt said, but he cringed inwardly at the reference to blood. He lit a cigarette and loitered near the door. He didn't have to stand very close. The voice inside, raised in furious agitation, carried all the way up the corridor.

"Fucking asshole, you got any idea what the network's gonna do to us! Good family entertainment, we tell them! Nothing too violent, nothing too gross, we say. No blood, no ethnic shit, no beatin' up on women—and what do we give them? You sawing your head open like you're cuttin' logs, bleedin' all over the first three rows, you fuckin' moron!"

A second voice, softer, but laced with loathing, protested, "What about the show last week at the Cow Palace? There was so much juice, guys were slidin' out of the ring?"

"That was a fuckin' house show, you jackass. Not national televised pay-per-view. And it was booked that way! Did I book it this way tonight? Did I say to juice? Did I say any fucking body was supposed to juice?"

"No, Tully, but—"

"You're outta here! You're fuckin' out! You got three months left on your contract—far as I'm concerned, you can sit home with your thumb up your ass till the time runs out."

"What about Salerno? I walk, Salerno walks, too."

"Fuck Salerno! And fuck you! I'll can both your asses!"

Something crashed to the floor, a table or some other heavy object being upended. "Hey, keep away from me, dickhead!" the one named Tully yelled.

Another crash. Then, before Matt could move fast enough to conceal his eavesdropping, the door slammed outward. A short, balding blond man charged out into the hallway, huffing for air. He was built like a fireplug, thighs so thick they must have chafed together when he walked, upper torso so disproportionately broad he resembled a malformed troll. He glared at Matt. "Hey, no smoking in here."

"Sorry." Matt dropped the cigarette, crushed it out.

"Who the fuck are you anyway?"

"I'm from *Wrestling Revue*. You've heard of us, right?" He intended the question to be innocuous, but from Tully's reaction, it was anything but.

"Yeah, believe I have. You're the dirt sheet printed that poll said I was the 'most pathetic excuse for a booker in the business and number one person for the promotion to get rid of if they wanted to succeed in the coming year.' " He gave a smile so twisted Matt all but expected sarcasm to drip from his teeth. "That would be you?"

Matt held his palms up. "Maybe you're not the person I want to talk to."

"Oh, but you're wrong, asshole, 'cause I want to talk to *you*." The gnome threw a punch. Matt blocked it, sidestepped, threw a left with all his weight behind it. Not enough to fell the gnome—it would have taken a backhoe for that—but landing as it did full force on his ear, the blow probably imploded an eardrum.

BuddyLee Baines poked his broad, bloody face out the doorway. His eyes locked on Matt and on Tully, who was backpedaling, clutching the side of his head. Confusion registered first on Baines's features, then cruel mirth when he realized Tully'd been hurt. Then his small, squinty eyes flashed back to Matt, and recognition dawned.

"Security!" Tully screamed. "Get fucking security!"

Matt didn't feel like hanging around to see if the cops would believe Rumpelstiltskin had thrown the first punch, and he sure as hell couldn't risk an assault charge with murder one hanging over his head. He bolted, sprinting half the length of the hallway as a security guard rounded the far corner and trotted toward him. A second corridor veered to the left. He took it, shoving his way past a couple of startled-looking maintenance men and part of the Japanese camera crew, who had finished interviewing the star and were passing a joint back and forth.

To his left, a door marked *men's room* opened into an anteroom filled with soda, candy, and cigarette machines, folding chairs, and several ashtrays so overflowing that they resembled miniature versions of Mount St. Helens. Except for a guy with cameras around his neck who was feeding a bill into the cigarette machine, that room was unoccupied. A second door, next to a condom dispenser, led into the rest room. Matt dashed in, shut himself inside a stall, and crouched with his feet braced on either side of the commode. The minute his body stopped running, however, his mind seemed to speed up to compensate, a thousand thoughts skirmishing madly for his attention. He was sure BuddyLee Baines was the one he'd chased out of the Luxor hotel room. He was equally sure the guy had probably killed Barry. Should he go to the cops? What proof did he have? No one knew yet about the scam Phil had pulled. No one other than himself had reason to believe there was a connection between Barry's murder and Phil's so-called suicide. The minute the LAPD realized he was a suspect in a San Diego murder investigation violating conditions of bond, he'd be back in the slammer, and this time not any amount of money Trina could come up with would bail him out.

On the other hand, if Baines and his height-challenged blond buddy caught up to him, the cops might be the least of his worries.

While he was debating the next course of action, the bathroom door swung open, and two people came in. One of them was wearing black wrestling boots, the other—a female—wore clogs that made a clip-clop carriage horse sound on the tile floor.

"Anybody here?" The voice didn't belong to either Tully or Baines. The security guard maybe, making a halfhearted check? He heard a zipper come down. "Oh, yeah, baby, yeah," a male voice said.

He peeked underneath the door of the stall and realized he was looking at Astra's towering gold clogs, the soles of which were facing him as she knelt on the tile floor.

"Suck it, you little bitch," said the man, followed by the sounds of saliva-slick, juicy, face-fucking.

Astra's partner, Salerno-who-doesn't-give-autographs, Matt assumed, liked to talk and kept up a steady stream of verbal abuse—*little whore, bitch, cocksuck-*

ing little slut—that became more and more repulsive.
By the time the two finished, Matt wanted to pour
disinfectant into his ears.

The boyfriend wasn't leaving just yet, though. He
had to soap up and wash himself off, then bitched
about the quality of the paper towels he was drying
his dick with.

"Are you guys staying at Hojo's tonight?" asked
Astra.

The man grunted.

"You know what room you're in, I could come over
later. Spend the night."

"I don't think so."

Astra, pouting now: "But I never get to sleep with
you. This is always it. Blowjobs in a bathroom or a
locker room. When do we get to spend time together?"

"We don't."

"Why not?"

"Because I fucking say so, that's why not."

"Is it because of that fucking girlfriend of yours?
That tired old whore?"

The man gave a chuckle that was so coldly evil Matt
felt it as a repellent touch along the knobs of his spine.
"Sweetheart, that 'tired old whore' knows tricks you
never dreamed about. In five years, when you're just a
fat, knocked-up little spic in line for food stamps, I'll
still be fucking her brains out, assuming she's got any
brains left to fuck, which is debatable. So go watch
the rest of the card. We're done here."

Silence followed. Then a zipper being closed and a
scuffling of shoes. The clip-clop of Astra's clogs.

What happened next, exactly, Matt was never really
sure. All he knew was that Astra uttered a cry unlike
any he had ever heard come from the lips of a woman.
In prison, he'd heard something like it a few times—
when a man, pushed to the absolute limit, became
possessed by wild rage that transported him beyond
any fear of injury, reprisal, or death. In such a state,
a person could be capable of anything.

Astra gave that wild shriek of anguish and rage. Matt heard the crack of a hand against flesh, the man growling in shock and surprise, then Astra squealing and whimpering.

"You fucking hit me? I don't believe you, you fucking bitch."

"No, please, stop. I'm sorry. Please don't, please."

"I'll break every bone in your fucking hand."

"I said I'm *sorry.*"

"Who do you think you are anyway? Just some fat spic trash with her brains in her tits. You're fucking lucky I'm willing to put my dick in that sewer you call a mouth."

"You're *breaking* my hand! Let *go!*"

"Hey! Let her go!" As Matt slammed the stall door open, it cracked Astra's assailant on the point of the elbow, knocking him momentarily off balance. Which was lucky, because the second Matt saw his face, he recognized him as the guy who'd just about twisted his arm off and handed it to him that night in the Luxor Casino. With someone this dangerous, playing fair would be suicidal. Matt kicked him squarely in his freshly scrubbed nuts, watched as his deeply tanned face acquired an unpleasing pallor, then grabbed Astra's hand and hauled ass outside into the maze of corridors.

"*That's* Salerno?" he asked as they rounded a corner in the Coliseum's labyrinthine underground, took some stairs to a second level, and made it outside into a rear parking lot. A light, chilly rain was still falling. People hoping to escape a traffic jam by leaving early were beginning to trickle out. A couple of limos had pulled up, their engines idling. Matt felt relatively safe. If he and Astra were going to be roughed up, it probably wouldn't be in front of a few dozen witnesses.

"He doesn't wrestle much," said Astra. "He mostly comes to the ring as BuddyLee's heel manager and whacks other guys when the ref isn't looking." She was rubbing her wrist, which was bruised and starting to swell. "His name's Steve Salerno, but he won't let anyone call him Steve. God, I hate him. I hate him and I hope he *dies*, the son of a bitch."

She shook rain out of her hair and adjusted her tube top in a gesture more self-conscious than seductive. She looked less like a baby hooker now, more like a child for whom bad behavior is no longer fun. Hair mussed, makeup streaming, eyes brimming with tears. The rain was soaking her clothes. Matt offered her his jacket, but she refused.

"You can press charges against that guy, you know. He attacked you. Plus the fact that you're underage."

She shivered and shook her head. "I can't fuck with Salerno. I do that and none of the others will ever talk to me again. I'll be poison."

"Jesus," Matt breathed, "after all this—you still want to hang out with those creeps?"

She sighed, swiped at her tears with her good hand. "You don't understand. I mean, I know he's a creep, but he's important—he's gonna be getting a push real soon, he'll be a star—and when I have sex with him, it makes *me* feel important, too. It makes me feel alive. Like I'm important. You just don't understand."

"No," Matt said, "I guess I don't."

He offered to give her a ride, but she said she was going back to try to hook up with one of her girlfriends at the exit where they'd planned to linger to watch the wrestlers depart after the show. Then he asked her for directions to the Hojo's where the wrestlers partied after the matches. When he left her, he almost turned back to ask if he'd be seeing her at the motel later on. Then he realized he didn't want to know.

The show was still going on, the roar of the crowd a distant but still audible buzz as Matt slogged back across the paved parking area to the unpaved lot where he'd left his truck. He unlocked the door and had just started to step up into the cab when a voice behind him said, "Your little girlfriend, the ring rat—she said if I hurried I could catch up to you, that your kid wants my autograph."

Matt tried to turn, but a heavy forearm clamped over his windpipe. Pain lanced around his throat like barbed wire. A weird high-pitched buzzing, as though a horsefly had been turned loose in his skull, filled his ears. He braced his feet against the runner of the truck and pushed backward as hard as he could. Baines swayed for a second, then lost his balance and toppled backward, pulling Matt with him. The force of the landing loosened Baines's hold and allowed Matt to snap his head back into the bigger man's face. There was the audible crunch of cartilage crumpling, and Baines clutched his nose.

Matt reached under the front seat of the truck and grabbed the antitheft club.

"You fucker," wheezed Baines, "you *bloke* it, you bloke my fucking nose."

"It could only be an improvement." He sidestepped as Baines came at him again and brought the head of the club up into the man's gut, aiming high for the solar plexus. The blow made Baines double over, but as Matt moved in, he suddenly pivoted and aimed a kick that struck Matt's wrist and sent the club skidding away in the mud.

Both men dove after the weapon, but Baines reached it first and brought it around in a whooshing arc aimed at Matt's knees. Matt hurled himself toward the truck. The weapon missed him by inches and crashed down on the hood. Baines raised it again. Brought it down. This time the truck's windshield took the brunt of the blow, exploding inward in a shower of glass.

Matt tried to sidestep the next blow, but the mud was his opponent as much as Baines. His foot went out from under him, delaying the dodge a fraction too long. The club glanced off the knob of the elbow. An excruciating pain zigzagged from his wrist to his biceps.

Baines snorted blood and raised the weapon again. Matt ducked inside the arc of the descending blow and, with his good arm, landed a left hook to Baines's broken nose. He followed with a right, but it cost him—his injured elbow compressed sickeningly as his knuckles slammed the other man's jaw. Baines took the punches with the grunting stoicism of a man who doesn't give a damn how hard he's hit as long as he hits back harder. He swung the club again. Matt flung himself clear of the blow, but lost his footing in the mud and went sprawling. There was no place to go. Baines had the weapon raised again, ready to smash it down like an ax. Matt did the only thing he could think of—he rolled underneath the truck.

"Where are you, you fucker!"

The huge boots tromped furiously around the truck, splattering muddy water. Matt wiped the dirt from his eyes, squinting to see. For whatever reason, it appeared Baines was unwilling to crawl under the vehicle after him. He wished now he'd brought Coop's pistol with him. His right foot had gone numb from the ankle down, and he didn't know if he'd be able to stand on it, let alone fight or run, and his arm was anything but numb—the pain felt like bone chips from his right elbow were embedded in the bone all the way down to his thumb.

Baines had stopped circling the truck. Twisting around as far as he could, Matt tried to spot the man's feet. All he could see was the rain coming down like a solid sheet of gray nails and the pockmarks it made splatting into the mud.

A minute passed. Then another.

He began to think Baines had tired of the game and left. Then again, he might well be biding his time, waiting for Matt to conclude just that. Gingerly he twisted his ankle, trying to get some of the feeling back. The results weren't encouraging.

While he was weighing his options, he felt the truck creak overtop. The tires started to turn, spraying water and mud.

Jesus, Baines was pushing the truck.

Which meant he must have laid the antitheft club on the ground.

Hands grasping for the weapon, Matt rolled out from
under the truck and scrambled to his feet. Bellowing,
Baines came at him. Matt sidestepped and kicked his
feet out from under him, sending him on a wild skid,
legs up, limbs akimbo, into the cab of the truck.

Baines bounced off it with no sign of injury, but his
forehead was a bloody mess. The self-inflicted cut he'd
made during the Battle Royal had reopened. Blood was
streaming into his eyes, blinding him long enough for
Matt to stagger him with a right uppercut. The big
man wavered, but didn't go down. He swiped at the
blood in his eyes, then was blinded again—by the high
beams of the mud-splattered white Thunderbird that
came roaring toward them and squealed to a stop next
to Matt's truck.

A woman's voice commanded: "Hurry! Move it!
Get in the goddamned car!"

Trina?

She leaned over and flung open the passenger door.
Matt hurled himself in, slammed the door, heard her
hit the automatic lock button. Baines not moving now,
just standing there, blinking stupidly as though he
couldn't believe what he saw.

Trina gunned the engine, went from zero to forty
backing up between rows of parked cars, then shifted
into drive and zoomed out the Coliseum exit.

Matt slumped in his seat. "Jesus, what the hell are
you doing here? How'd you know I was here?"

Trina swerved over a double yellow line and
speeded up to pass. "I called your house, and some
other kid answered. It turned out Shawn had for-
warded his calls over to his friend's. When I spoke to
him, he let it slip that you were headed to the L.A.
Coliseum. I figured I stood a better chance of finding
your vehicle in the lot and waiting than searching for
you inside with ten thousand screaming yahoos."

"Shawn told you where I was?"

"Relax, Matt, I wheedled it out of him. You know
how good I am at getting my own way."

"Hey, watch it, you're in the wrong lane!"

Trina's driving had gone from merely erratic to out-right suicidal. With no more cars to pass, she was still driving on the wrong side of the double yellow line.

"Take it easy, will you!"

She swerved right. "So what the hell were you doing here? And what'd you do to piss off Godzilla?"

"It's a long story."

"Jesus, look at you! You're covered in mud. What do I have to do to keep you in town, Matt? I'd offer you my body, but maybe you'd rather get dressed up in feathers and face paint and go for two out of three falls."

"The way I feel right now, you'd probably win." He bent forward, clutching his elbow. His forearm felt like it was being amputated an inch at a time by a mad surgeon using a buzz saw. The pain made his stomach turn cartwheels.

Trina glanced over at him. "Jesus, you're hurt, aren't you? Do you want to go to the hospital?"

"No, forget it. No hospitals."

"Okay, look, I'll take you to my place. That way, if you wake up black-and-blue tomorrow, you'll have time to think up something to tell Shawn."

"Shawn wasn't supposed to tell anyone where I was."

"Oh, don't be mad at him, Matt. He's just a kid. You know kids can't keep secrets."

He started to say something, but talking seemed like too much effort. By the time Trina turned onto the freeway, he had shut his eyes, glad that—for the moment—someone else was in the driver's seat.

Chapter Twenty-two

At two in the morning, the rain had stopped, and the steep winding streets above Balboa Park were silent and hemmed in by fog. Ashy tendrils clung to the trees and shrouded the street signs, giving a smudged, spectral cast to the rows of imposing old Victorian homes.

Trina turned onto Kalmia Street and pulled up in front of her mammoth garage. She flicked a button, and the door silently rose on a line of sparkling, vintage automobiles. Despite the pain he was in, Matt couldn't help but be impressed. He'd seen a couple of Trina's cars and heard her speak of buying or trading various vehicles, but not even when Calla was alive had he ever visited the inner sanctum of her automotive wonderland.

"Like 'em?" she said, looking pleased as she read his expression. "The Jag I was telling you about is last one on the left."

"Impressive," said Matt.

"And this one, the Corvette, is the one Daddy bought me for my birthday last spring. Like it?"

"Like it? I've seen a 'Vette like this maybe two or three other times in my life. It's gorgeous."

She took his arm. "Be a good boy, and you can take me for a spin in one tomorrow morning. Just in case you don't realize what an honor that is, Trina never lets anyone but Trina drive her cars."

If he hadn't been so exhausted, Matt would have

told her how annoying it was when she spoke of herself in the third person, but he merely followed her into the house. The narrow hallways and innumerable small rooms were even more cluttered than he remembered from the few times that he and Calla had stopped by with Shawn for the occasional visit. Shelves overflowed with bric-a-brac, antique vases shared shelf space with kitschy beer clocks, an entire bookcase was devoted to commemorative souvenirs of celebrities as diverse as Mike Tyson and Princess Di.

Along the wall of the upstairs hallway, she'd mounted an elaborate collage of photographs, most of them of herself and her friends—mostly male—Trina riding a dirt bike at Borrego Springs, Trina windsurfing, waving from the bow of a sailboat, Trina with her arms around a man and a woman, all three of them nude. There were even a few of Howie—straight ones, incongruous among all this salaciousness: Howie holding a highball glass, looking stiff and ill at ease as he faced the camera on the porch at the Coronado Hotel, Howie putting on the golf course, jogging on the beach.

"Don't worry, there's nothing of you there. I *do* have a picture of you, but not here. That night we slept together, I snapped it while you were asleep."

"I assume you're kidding."

"I'm perfectly serious."

"Why the hell would you have done *that*?"

She giggled and shrugged. "Don't look so shocked. In case you never came back to my bed again—which you *didn't*, you rat—I wanted something to remember you by."

"Jesus, Trina, I—"

Something caught his eye, a photo of Trina and Calla outside the Old Globe Theater at Balboa Park. Trina squinting, sun in her eyes, Calla eating a strawberry popsicle, the two of them holding hands like little girls. Twenty-five going on twelve.

"When was this taken?"

She gave the photo a quick glance. "Five years ago. Just before you got out of prison."

"Who took it?"

"I don't remember, but you can have it if you want. I look like somebody squirted grapefruit juice in my eyes, but it's great of Calla. She was always photogenic. Come on, let's get you to bed."

With a brief stop at the linen closet for towels, Trina showed him to one of the guest bedrooms. He was grateful it wasn't the one with the silk-canopied bed, the bed he still remembered so vividly.

"How's the arm?"

He bent it gingerly. Winced. "It's not broken, but my bowling league will probably have to do without me for a while."

"I'd offer to scrub your back, but the way your mind works, you'd probably think I was coming onto you."

"Who, Trina, not *you*?"

She grinned and shoved the towels at him.

The hot water on his sore body felt wonderful. By the time he'd dried off and put on the robe Trina left for him, all he wanted was to sleep for about forty-eight hours.

Trina knocked on the door, came in carrying a glass of water and a couple of tablets. "Thought you might want something for the pain. These are muscle relaxants my dentist gave me when I had a tooth out. They don't eliminate the pain, but they dull it enough so you can sleep."

"Thanks." He swallowed one of the pills and handed the other one back to her. "One's enough. I don't want to oversleep. I told Shawn we'd go to Mass tomorrow morning."

"What a good daddy you are," she said, smiling, half mocking. "Shawn's a lucky boy." She reached up and slid the robe off his shoulders. "Why don't you let me give you that massage? Don't worry, I'll be gentle."

"If it's all the same to you, Trina, I'm tired. I think I'll just go to bed."

"You may be tired, honey, but Trina's not." She cocked an eyebrow and gave a low chuckle that somehow managed to convey sweetness and utter depravity at the same time. "You just lie there and relax. I promise I'll do all the work. You'll be surprised what you find yourself capable of doing with the right stimulation."

"I'm sorry, Trina, I mean it."

He could see the start of serious anger flaming behind her eyes, but she doused it out with a sardonic little laugh.

"Suit yourself, sweetie, but don't say I didn't offer."

After she closed the door, he lay there staring at the ceiling, running the events of the evening through his mind, thinking he'd never be able to sleep with his arm throbbing and his head full of would-haves and could-haves and should-haves. Whatever was in that pill that she'd given him must have been potent as hell, because sleep dropped down on him more quickly than he'd expected, heavy and gray and inundating. It descended over him like the fog outside: blue-gray tendrils that flooded the bedroom, his body, his consciousness.

He dreamed that Calla floated toward him in the fog, parting it with her hands the same way she parted her long hair when it fell in a tangled mass across her face, covered her eyes. Calla peeking out at him from behind that lush, extravagantly obsidian hair. Ripe mouth parted, dark eyes fringed with jet lashes. *Matt, Matt.* He wanted to freeze the dream at that exact moment, never wake up from it, never let it fade. Just lie there, with Calla hovering over him, so close, so exquisitely touchably close.

He murmured something. Calla's fingers went across his lips. *Shhh, shhh.* Soothing cool soft fingers. Then it was her mouth he felt, her kisses on his neck, his nipples, while her hand moved downward, rumpling the hair across his chest and belly. He tried to open

his eyes or tried, at least, to want to open them. His
cock was hard now. She took it in her mouth, enveloping him in tight, warm wetness. One hand curled
around the base and followed her mouth up and down
in a swirling barber-pole motion. The pleasure was
inebriating. He couldn't talk, didn't want to ever end
that moment. Except that—

Oh, God, oh God, oh God!

His head snapped up off the pillow, eyes staring
into the dark. Gulping down air as though sleep had
smothered him. He was alone. The dream, so vivid a
few moments ago that he could have sworn he was
engulfed in Calla's warm depths, quickly dissolved.
Leaving him chilled inside and out, his skin damp and
goose pimpled.

And the woman screaming, had he dreamed that,
too?

"No, don't!"

This time there was no mistaking it. The voice was
tiny and distant and seemed to come from below,
drifting up through the old house's heating ducts. Instantly he was wide awake. He switched on the bedside lamp, put on the jeans that Trina had laundered
and left for him there by the bed, and went out into
the hall. The house was pitch-black. He groped for a
light switch, couldn't find one, then started feeling his
way down the hall. At the top of the stairs, he could
see a light on below in the living room.

"Oh, no, no, noooooo!"

The voice now was louder, more anguished. He felt
disoriented, unsteady, whether from the beating he'd
taken or something in the pill that he'd swallowed, he
wasn't sure. All he knew was that someone—Trina?
it *had* to be Trina, didn't it?—was in trouble. He
pressed on.

The first floor, from what Matt could deduce, must
have been laid out like a maze or a medieval cata-
combs. There seemed to be a multitude of oddly
shaped rooms, not to mention closets, half baths and
pantries and narrow, meandering hallways that ended

up back where they began. Trying to find his way
around the warren-like house in the dark was a nightmare of dead ends and miscalculations. It took him
several minutes to even locate a stairway that descended into the basement.

"Please don't. Oh, no, no, nooooo."

He took the steps two at a time. Found himself in
a room full of discarded furniture, boxes, and shelves
of paperback books. The cries sounded like they were
coming from the other side of the wall.

He went out into a hallway, tried the knob of the
door next to the room he'd been in, and twisted it
slowly. The door swung inward. He blinked and
caught his breath. At one end of the room, a bound,
naked woman was being flogged by a blonde in high
heels and a black leather corset. The victim twisted and
pleaded and screamed, her skin glistening with sweat
and drops of blood—real-looking—that appeared to
ooze from the cuts on her back.

Trina, curled up on a leather recliner facing the TV
screen, twisted around to stare at him with big, innocent
eyes. She wore a thin pink camisole held up by the
thinnest of spaghetti straps and black boxer trunks.
Her long legs glistened like they'd been oiled.

"What'sa matter, sweetie? Can't sleep?"

He was suddenly furious. "What are you doing
down here? What is this?"

She cupped her ear. "Sorry, hon, I can't hear you."
She gestured toward the screen. "These porn flics are
so *loud*."

"Dammit, Trina!" He blundered into the room,
groping for the volume control on the VCR. When
his fingers missed it in the dark, and when Trina didn't
appear disposed to help, he gave in to impulse and
backhanded the machine onto the floor. There was
the clatter of metal, and the TV screen went dark.
Then silence.

Galvanized, Trina sprang to her feet. "What the
fuck do you think you're doing? Or do I need your

permission to watch a video in the privacy of my own home?"

"I woke up and heard someone screaming. I thought you were—I thought maybe—Jesus, it sounded so real. It scared the hell out of me."

"What? You thought it was me down here? And you came to the rescue? That's sweet, Matt. I'm sorry if I'm not grateful. First you turn me down on the idea of sex. Next you won't even let me get off in the privacy of my own home. Tell you what, next time I see you about to get the shit beat out of you by some goon, I think I'll just keep driving."

"I'm sorry, Trina."

"Oh, sorry my ass. You're just like every other guy I know—everything's fine and dandy as long as you get your way, but God help us all if something happens to tweak your fragile male vanity! I only *came* down here to watch a movie, because I thought if I played the TV in my bedroom, it might disturb you. And I wouldn't be *watching* a trashy S/M porn flick in the first place, if you hadn't cast yourself as the star of your own private fucking morality play, with you the noble fucking hero and me the slut. And as far as what you *do* have to offer in the sack, when you finally get around to offering it, all I can say is you must've saved the *really* good stuff for Calla, because the one fucking shot you gave it, I sure as shit wasn't impressed."

Her eyes, uncamouflaged by any of her colored contact lenses, gleamed with an eerie luridness of their own. Sweat streamed from her armpits, plastered the camisole to her belly and breasts. There was no sound in the room, but her breathing.

Matt said, "Sorry if I didn't *impress* you during our one-night stand, Trina, but that just gives me one more reason to get the hell out of here."

He turned to go. Had no sooner taken his eyes off her than he felt her nails clamp into his back and her voice, completely different now, small, meek, little girlish, began to plead, "No, wait, Matt, please, I'm sorry. I just lost it there for a minute, because you pissed me off." She pressed herself against him, ground the soft mound of her crotch against his ass. "Trina's sorry she snapped at you, honey. It's just that you get her so hot. Just looking at you—I always wanted you, Matt. All the time you and Calla were married. You know I was always hot for you. C'mon, let's fuck and make up."

"Forget it, Trina, you already said I was a disappointment."

"I was *angry*. Jesus, Matt, how many men do you think turn me down?"

"I don't know. I guess it depends on how many hundreds you proposition."

Her nails stabbed at his arm, then she let go of him and marched over to a door directly behind the leather love seat that he had assumed was a closet. Pulled a key out of her pocket, held it up. Her expression daring him to do something to stop her.

"You think all I collect is cars? I collect guns, too, did you know that? Daddy keeps his hidden away in his library—in these cutesy little hollow books that are supposed to fool burglars. You think you're getting ready to read a self-help book, and you open it up, and there's all the fucking self-help anybody'd ever need in six little hollow points. That's Daddy's style, not mine. Me, I've got a whole fucking room full of firepower. I can unlock this door and blow your head off before you can stop me."

He weighed the likelihood of her statement being true, decided it was pure bluff. "You know what's saddest about this, Trina? I *like* you. I've *always* liked you. You're Shawn's *aunt,* for Christ's sake. It hurts me to see you degrade yourself this way. Acting like a spoiled brat who's going to shock everybody if she doesn't get her way."

He could see her fingers gripping the key like it was a tiny revolver aimed at his heart. "You *really* ought to take a look at what I've got in here before you dismiss me so quickly. Who knows, you might be surprised."

"I think I'll pass. I'm going back to bed. Unless, of course, you're kicking me out for bad behavior."

She took a deep breath, bit her lip. "No, hon, Trina's willing to turn the other cheek—*this* time. Go on to bed." She reached up and plucked aside the straps of the camisole. It slithered to her waist in pink folds. Her breasts, the nipples brown and urgently erect, held his gaze like a second pair of eyes. "Sweet dreams, Matt."

He looked at her a second longer—Christ, she looked *good*—then he turned and made his way back up the stairs.

He woke up well before daylight, stiff and sore, feeling like his body had been through a trash compactor, but otherwise ambulatory. Right away his mind clicked into gear, worrying about how he was going to get the truck back down from L.A. Decided he'd pull Coop and one of the other men off the Bledsoe-Tull job and get them to run up there for it. The last thing he wanted to do was see Trina again, so he decided to leave quietly and grab a cab home.

He dressed quickly. Then, feeling like somebody's philandering husband skulking home at the crack of dawn, crept out of the bedroom, boots in hand. In the hallway, though, he succumbed to the urge to take just one more look at the photo collage. He told himself it was merely good old prurient curiosity, but it was really the desire to look for more photos of Calla. The dawn light, filtering in the window at the top of the stairs, stripped away some of the provocativeness of the photos, made the expressions of Trina and her playmates look posed and tawdry. There were more shots of Trina and her buddies frolicking in the nude than he'd realized. Even one of Howie, caught getting out of a hot tub, trying to cover himself with a towel, but not being quite quick enough to beat the camera. Looking embarrassed and angry. *Goddammit, Trina, what now?* he could almost hear the old man bellowing.

A door opened up farther along the hall, and Trina stepped out, modest for once in a long crimson and turquoise silk robe embossed with butterflies and birds that might have been swallows. The shiny fabric flowed over her body like water. He reflected ruefully that somehow, while remaining completely covered, she managed to look more naked than she had the night before.

"Ah, I thought you might decide to sneak off without thanking your hostess. Really, Matt, where are your manners?"

He kept his eyes determinedly on her face. "After last night, I figured you'd be glad to get rid of me."

"Awww, you're sulking because I didn't slip into your room in the night and wrap my mouth around your cock. A lot of men enjoy waking up that way. It gets their juices flowing."

"I'll see you later, Trina. I gotta get going."

"In what? You don't have a car."

"I'll catch a cab."

"I can give you a ride."

"No need to."

"How are you feeling anyway?"

"No worse than if I'd been run over by a truck. Which, come to think of it, I almost was."

She pouted. "I didn't mean about the fight, I meant about last night. You. Me. What almost happened, what could have happened, what *didn't* happen because you were an idiot."

"It would've been wrong, Trina. You know that."

"Why, Matt? Forgive me, if I don't fucking share your moral scruples. Calla's *dead*, have you figured that out yet? I'm *alive*. Regardless of which of us you'd *rather* be fucking, that sort of limits your options."

"Trina, I'm not in the mood for this shit."

"You mean we can't be fuckbuddies?"

He started to move past her, but she blocked him.

Looked at the display of photos covering the wall and seemed to suppress a laugh. Her prelude, he had learned by now, to saying something naughty.

"At this point, most of my lovers look at my collage, figure out that these must all be people I've slept with, and ask me if I'm boinking Daddy."

He sighed, bent down, and started tugging on his boots. "Aren't you a little old to still be saying things just for shock value, Trina? It gets tiresome. What you and Howie do or don't do, I really don't give a shit, but knowing Howie, my guess is you'd have a better shot at screwing the Pope."

"Yeah, you're right. As far as Daddy's concerned, incest ranks right in there with bestiality and necrophilia. Not that I haven't thought about it, though—I'll bet he's a stud once he gets going. Unfortunately, he's also so straight he thinks oral sex means talking dirty. Although I'd *love* a chance to explain the difference to him."

"Enough," said Matt, raising his hands. "Trina, if I thought you meant even half the things you say seriously, then I swear—" He stopped as one of the photos caught his attention.

"God, Matt, you're no fun at all."

"What's this? When was this taken?"

The photo showed Trina, Howie, and a young woman posing next to the vintage Corvette he'd seen in Trina's garage the night before. The picture, taken with a wide-angle lens, framed the words JULIAN'S CLASSIC CARS on a sign above their heads. The girl standing between Trina and Howie had thick, shoulder-length black hair, huge, fawn-caught-in-the-headlights eyes, and a spectacular chest.

Trina glanced at the photo. "Oh, my birthday car, the one you saw in the garage. Daddy bought it for me this year. That was taken at the dealership in Ramona just before I drove it home."

"This girl—I know her."

"Now, why doesn't that surprise me?"

"Her name's Noel. How do you and Howie know her?"

"We *don't*. She was just this pushy little bimbo who happened to be at the dealership that day."

"Doing what?"

"She said she'd stopped in to say hi to her brother. He's the one who took the picture."

"Her brother?"

"He works at the dealership. When she found out Daddy was buying me the car, she came on strong, acted like she wanted him to fuck her brains out right there on the hood. I know she gave him her phone number, but I don't know if he kept it. I doubt it. One thing about Daddy, he's got sense enough to weed out floozies." She came up behind Matt, ran her hands across his chest. "Come on, Matt, Trina's going to get a complex if you keep staring at that picture when you could be looking at *her*."

"I'm sorry, Trina." He unhinged her fingers, disengaged, "I've got to go."

She came after him. "I don't understand, Matt. What's wrong with you? Why don't you want to fuck me? I know what it is—you're mad because we didn't have sex last night. You got up to your room alone, realized what a jackass you'd been, and—"

He looked at her then, really *looked* at her. Hard and long, not like a man looking at a woman, but one human being seeing another—maybe for the very first time. "What are you talking about? Do you even *hear* yourself? You're living in your own world, Trina. I feel sorry for you. I feel sorry for your father."

"Fuck my father."

He kept going.

"Hey, don't walk out on me." She grabbed his arm, the injured one, and twisted it around. The pain rekindled all the pent-up fear and fury that seeing a picture of Noel had revived. He shoved her against the wall, freed his arm and drew it back, then stopped himself in time.

Jesus, what am I doing?

"Go on, Matt," she sneered. "Do it. Hit me. You want to hit me, I know you do. Go on and do it."

He stared at her.

Her voice rose. "What's wrong with you, dammit! What kind of man are you? What are you, afraid? Hit me, dammit, do it!"

"Trina, stop it!"

"Fucking coward! You think you'd be the first? Go on, do it!"

She tried to punch him, but he caught her arms and pinned them to her sides. Stared into her eyes. She wasn't wearing colored contacts this morning, either. These were her real eyes he looked into. This was *her*.

"Christ, what the fuck is *wrong* with you?" he said, and let her go.

As he was heading down the stairs, she caught up and grabbed him again. Raw hate blazed in her face, "Aren't you forgetting something, Matt? Aren't you forgetting that you owe me?"

"The seventy-five thousand dollars bail—no, I haven't forgotten, I—"

"Fuck the fucking seventy-five thousand dollars! I'm talking about something worth a lot more—the *alibi*. The night Calla died, I told the cops you were with me, remember? Or have you forgotten that, too, just like you forgot where the hell you *really* were the night that she was murdered?"

Chapter Twenty-three

When it came to knowing where to strike, Trina had the instincts of a viper. Matt left her house feeling stunned and furious, hating what she'd said and, most of all, hating that it was true. He *did* owe Trina. By providing him an alibi for the night that Calla died, she'd saved his neck, and they both knew it. Still, his frustration was so great that, if his right arm hadn't already felt like there was a drill bit embedded in the bone, he'd have been looking for someone to punch.

Even if he'd had a vehicle, it was too early to go pick up Shawn at Ryan's, and he didn't want to go back to his empty house, so he watched the sun come up from the parking lot of a 7-Eleven, drinking black coffee and feeling a hundred years old, then called a cab to take him over to the Bledsoe-Tull job site. He figured he'd spend a few hours doing office work in the trailer, then drive one of the company trucks over to pick up Shawn.

He hadn't been to the Bledsoe-Tull job site since the day of the accident. Now the red iron was completed up to the fourth story, and a second crane had been brought in to speed up the process on the higher floors.

He paid the cabbie, got out, and walked through the empty skeleton of the parking garage, his mind automatically doing a mental inspection of the work to this point. Without even looking hard, he found things that were wrong—a whole section of rebars stood up uncapped, waiting to impale the first person who tripped, and a halogen light big enough to illuminate a football field had been left turned on.

On top of that, somebody had left a four-hundred-dollar nail gun lying on the ground. Even though it wasn't one of Matt's tools, the sight of it lying there pissed him off. What the hell were these guys thinking anyway? Grown men with families to feed, and some of them were less responsible than Shawn when it came to leaving shit lying all over.

He picked up the nail gun and headed over to the trailer, thinking he could call home and check his messages before he got down to work. Not that he was expecting to hear from Noel again now that she'd dropped her bombshell, but you never knew. He thought about the photo he'd seen at Trina's house. Was it a coincidence that Noel and Trina had met? Knowing Trina's sexual predilections, was it reasonable to assume she and a woman of Noel's equally strong sexual appetites were just "acquaintances"?

At least now, he thought, he had an idea where to look for Noel. Maybe he'd get some answers.

Are you really that stupid? he asked himself. *Don't you have enough on your plate as it is?*

But he already knew that the only thing preventing him from heading up to Ramona right then was the fact that he'd told Shawn they'd go to Mass together that morning.

Carrying the nail gun in one hand, he unlocked the door to the trailer and walked in. Sunlight slanted in behind him, illuminating a metal desk, file cabinet, and couch. A body was sprawled motionless on the floor beside the desk.

"Jesus!"

"Huh, wha'?" Coop rolled over, coughing and shielding his eyes. "That you, Matt?"

"Coop, what the—?" He bent down. The reek of Scotch assaulted his nostrils. He drew back, furious and disgusted.

Coop scraped himself together and sat up. His gray

hair was matted and disheveled, his eyes red-rimmed
and puffy. Slowly, as though his body might break
apart if subjected to sudden movement, he eased himself up onto the couch and looked around. From his
expression, it looked like he was waking up on Mars.

"What time is it?"

"Almost eight."

Coop blinked. "In the morning?"

"In the morning."

"Sunday?"

"Sunday."

"Shit, I fucked up, didn't I?"

"What the hell happened, Coop?"

"I'm sorry, Matt." He put a hand up to his jaw,
worked it back and forth as though testing to see if it
was broken. "Guess I tied one on pretty good last
night. Got in a scuffle with some asshole over at the
Dark Horse. Kicked the guy's ass, but when I got
home, I couldn't get in the house. Eloise'd had the
goddamned locks changed." He shook his head.
"Fuckin' women. My own home and she wouldn't let
me in."

"So you came here to sleep it off."

"I guess so. I mean, I don't remember coming here.
Guess I was in a blackout. Last thing I remember is
banging on the goddamned door and Eloise sticking
her head out the upstairs window, saying she's gonna
call the cops." He touched his jaw again, winced.
"Fuckin' women. Shit. What am I gonna do now?"

"I don't know, Coop, and I don't really give a shit.
Just get the hell out of here."

Coop got to his feet, swaying slightly. He steadied
himself on the desk and looked Matt up and down.
Grinned. "Hell, you seen yourself in a mirror lately?
You don't look no better'n me. What the hell *you*
been up to, anyway?"

Not the kind of question Matt was really eager to
hear. "Did you hear what I just said? Did you hear
me tell you to leave?"

"Now look'a here, Matt—"

"*Did* you?"

The tone of Matt's voice, the expression on his face, had a sobering effect. Coop's grin vanished. He stared down at his feet. "Fine. I'll see you tomorrow."

"That's not what I meant."

"What the hell did you mean, then?"

"Don't bother coming back. You're fired."

"Shit, how can you—? Just because I had a few too many one time, you gonna let me go? Shit, I thought we was friends."

"Jesus, Coop, what'd'you expect me to do? You think I think this is the first time you've slept it off here? It's the first time I *caught* you, that's all. Half the time I'm around you, you smell like a fuckin' distillery. You come to work hung over, you sneak beers on breaks, you think I don't know? I've offered to take you to A.A. meetings. I tried to get you to see you need some help."

"I need this job, Matt."

"And I need a foreman who isn't a lush."

"I thought we were buddies? All we been through together, that don't count for nothin'?"

"Jesus, that has nothing to do with it. This is the *real* world, Coop. It's not prison. Besides, it's not fair to you or me or the rest of the crew to keep you on if you're gonna be half in the bag all the time. You can't do your job right, and you can't do it safely."

"I've never *once* been drunk on the job. Ask anybody. I might've had a few beers, but that's different. I can handle it."

Matt waved his hand. "Oh, Christ, save that bullshit for somebody who hasn't heard it all before. Who do you think you're talking to anyway? *I'm* a drunk, too, Coop, are you forgetting that? The only difference between you and me is I'm a drunk who doesn't drink anymore. So don't try conning a con man, 'cause it won't work."

"You're serious, aren't you?"

"Yeah."

"Fuck. Then I guess I'll stop by end of the week get my back pay."

"Do that."

He turned back. "What're you gonna tell Shawn? About what happened?"

"The truth. What'd you expect me to tell him?"

"I was thinkin' maybe you could make up somethin', I got another job or I moved away or—aw, shit, I don't know. Forget it. I just like the kid. I hate him to think bad about ol' Coop."

"I don't know, man. I don't know what to tell Shawn but the truth."

"The truth is, Matt, I ain't no alcoholic. You caught me overindulging a time or two and because of that you jump to some conclusion about—"

"That's enough, Coop! I've heard all that bullshit before. Sometimes I've heard it coming out of my own mouth. You haven't got the balls to admit you got a problem and get help for it, fine, but don't expect to work for me."

Coop shrugged. "Whatever you say, Matt."

Watching Coop cross the street and get into his pickup, Matt remembered he needed a ride, but dismissed the idea of going after Coop. Damned if he'd ask for a favor from a guy he'd just let go. He found the spare key to a beat-up 4Runner that was parked over next to a backhoe. The last company truck that was available to commandeer—so far, his track record in that department was pretty lousy. Matt figured he'd better make sure nothing happened to this vehicle as he got in and headed toward Chula Vista.

On the way, his words to Coop—*you don't have the balls to admit you got a problem*—echoed in his head. He stopped at a pay phone, dialed the free clinic, and got a recording that said the clinic opened at noon on Sundays. *Okay,* he said to himself, *no matter how long I have to wait, today it is.*

Just making the decision made him feel freer. He was thinking about whether he might make a day of it and go to confession as well—it had been *years*—

when his cell phone rang and Howie's voice boomed,
"Good to hear your voice, Matt. You haven't been
returning my calls, and when I phoned your house just
now, nobody answered. I was starting to be concerned."

"To tell you the truth, under the circumstances, it's
not easy knowing what to say to you, Howie."

"Well, look, I can help you out if you'll let me.
With Shawn, that is. Why not let him come stay with
me till school starts? Or however long it takes for you
to get this situation resolved." There was a pause.
Then: "It would just be the two of us, you know. The
lady I'd been seeing, she gave me my walking papers
the other day. Guess she decided she had bigger fish
to fry."

"Sorry to hear that, Howie."

"Oh, hell, I'm probably better off staying a bache-
lor. At my age, it's too hard to change."

"You'll find the right one, Howie. You're a good
man."

"Well, the ladies don't always seem to think so, but
who knows? Anyway, I know this has got to be hell
what you're going through. Have the police come up
with any leads?"

"Not yet."

"Damn. What about a private investigator, Matt? I
know some people in the field."

"I can't afford that, Howie."

"I can."

"Thanks, but let's wait and see what the police
come up with. I didn't kill Barry, and they can't prove
I did. If they thought they could, they'd have me in
jail by now. But about Shawn—"

"I was thinking about flying down to Baja next
week for a few days," said Howie. "See how the
swordfish are running. Helluva long time since I've
done any deep-sea fishing. You think Shawn would
like that?"

"You kidding? He'd love it."

"Is he there with you now?"

"No, I'm on my way home. Shawn's staying with a buddy of his. I'm gonna pick him up in a little bit and take him to Mass."

"Well, if he's up for spending some time with his granddad, then bring him by the house afterward. He doesn't even need to pack. I've been promising to take him shopping for some new clothes. This'll give me an excuse."

"He'd like that, Howie. Just don't go to too much trouble. He's already got more stuff than he needs."

Howie chuckled. "C'mon, I'm his grandfather. An old man. Buying things for my grandson, this is one of the few pleasures I get in life."

"Somehow I doubt that, Howie."

"I'll see you and Shawn later today then?"

"Yeah, we'll stop by."

Around ten, after a quick stop at home to shower and change clothes, Matt picked Shawn up at Ryan's house and they drove toward St. John's Cathedral on Coronado Island for the eleven o'clock Mass. When Shawn asked what was wrong with Matt's arm, after he'd seen him wince a couple of times while turning the wheel, Matt explained that he'd taken a spill in a muddy parking lot the night before and banged up his elbow.

Other than that, Shawn's questions all centered around the wrestling matches Matt had seen, the various wrestling personalities and how the more popular story lines were being played out. Matt tried to answer honestly, but avoided mention of any altercations that hadn't taken place inside the ring.

When they pulled up in the parking lot of the cathedral and Matt started to get out of the truck, Shawn looked surprised. "You're going to church, too? I thought you were just dropping me off. Gee, Dad, you never go to Mass."

"Well, maybe it's time I started," said Matt, feeling contrite. "Maybe I should have been attending Mass a lot more over the years. Thing is, I was always so busy. Or I liked thinking I was anyway."

"Mom always wanted you to go to Mass."

"I know she did."

"And she wasn't even Catholic."

"Your mom had her own ideas about God. She believed in Him, but she wasn't big on organized religion. Got her fill of that as a little girl, I think."

"She did?" said Shawn, looking surprised. "Granddad's not religious?"

"No, I think your granddad's religion, if he has one, would be physical fitness. But your mom's mother was hard-core Southern Baptist. I think that was one of the problems she had being married to your granddad. He's always been pretty focused on the material side of things."

"Was that why she ran out on Mom and Aunt Trina when they were kids?"

"I don't know. Your mom didn't talk about it much, and Howie certainly doesn't."

They crossed the parking lot, threading their way through cars. Matt took Shawn's hand. As they went up the steps to the imposing white marble cathedral, designed after Paris's St. Sulpice, Shawn said, "Dad, you think it runs in families?"

Matt had no idea what he was talking about. "What?"

"What Mom's mom did to her and Aunt Trina? Running off like she did. You think it's some kind of family thing, like families where everybody's fat or they all drink too much or all have big ears?"

"I'm not sure I'm following you, son, but no—what your grandmother did was an aberration—something unusual, I mean. Mothers don't normally run off and abandon their kids, whatever the reason. It happens, but fortunately not often." They slowed as the crowd of people going into the church forced a bottleneck.

Shawn said, "What about fathers?"

So that's what this was about. Matt winced inwardly. "Are you worrying again that maybe I'm going to take off? Shawn, I told you I would never do that to you. Never. I promise."

"But—what if—" Shawn dropped his voice to a whisper. "What if you have to go back to prison? Ryan says they're gonna send you back whether you killed Barry or not because you're already an ex-con. He has a cousin who got sent up, and he says that's how the system works." They entered the foyer of the cathedral. Matt and Shawn both dipped their hands in the holy water before proceeding up the left aisle and taking seats. Matt asked God to deliver him from thoughts of grabbing Ryan by his big ears and ringing his scrawny neck.

The service, as usual, lasted longer than Matt would have liked, but he forced himself to pay attention to what the young priest had to say—a sermon about freedom and the lie implicit in the belief that freedom lay in excesses of drinking and drugs, in the worship of material things, and in addiction to sex. He hoped Shawn was taking it in. Prayed that Shawn could avoid some of the pitfalls that had made his life so much harder than it needed to have been.

Afterward, he asked Shawn to wait a few minutes while he went to confession. As soon as he knelt in the narrow little booth, a sense of claustrophobia—physical, spiritual, and emotional—overwhelmed him. He was suffocating in secrets, yet to divulge everything that ate at him felt like an annihilation akin to death. And if God *could* see into his very soul, then wasn't that enough?

He hemmed and hawed, owned up to a few minor transgressions, before finally getting around to what he knew he needed to say, "Four years ago, my wife was murdered. A friend provided an alibi and the police believed it, but the truth is, I was drunk the night she was killed. I don't know for absolutely certain *where* I was or what I did. From the bottom of my heart, I don't think I was capable of harming my wife—I loved her dearly—but we'd been fighting because she wanted a divorce, and I didn't. We'd just signed the papers a couple of days earlier. The fact that I have no memory of that night bedevils the hell out of me, and I needed to tell somebody. It's been four years, and I still wake up at night struggling to remember what happened. Wondering if I can't remember what happened because I was passed out drunk or if there's something there so terrible that my unconscious won't *allow* me to remember it."

To his vast relief, the priest who was hearing his confession expressed neither outrage nor shock. Merely heard him out, asked a few questions, offered some suggestions. Nothing changed really. Yet when he slid out of the booth, he somehow did feel lighter and less burdened. At least one person on this earth now knew what haunted him, without condemning or judging him. For whatever reason, that did seem to make a difference.

"Maybe if the police catch whoever killed Barry, you can drive down to Baja next week and meet up with me and Granddad," Shawn said. "We could do some fishing together. Or take a scuba diving class. That'd be great, wouldn't it? Granddad said he'd pay for me to get certified if it was okay with you."

Matt moved over into the right lane and took the exit for Coronado Island. "I think I'd rather you waited a couple more years on the diving. As far as me joining up with you guys, that'd be wonderful, but I wouldn't count on it. This kind of crime doesn't always get solved as fast as we'd like. And as long as I'm a suspect, I'm not allowed to leave town."

"But you *didn't* do anything wrong," Shawn protested. "Why can't they see that? Why can't they catch the guy who really killed Barry?"

"They will," Matt said. "Give 'em time. Just don't get your hopes up for me being able to join you in Mexico next week."

Shawn was silent for a while. Then he said, "They won't arrest you or anything, will they, while I'm away?"

Matt tried to sound more confident than he felt. "Of course not. I've got a good lawyer who's looking out for me. Nothing for you to worry about. I want you to have a good time down there in Baja. I want you to catch a swordfish. Bring back a picture of you standing next to the fish."

"And you'll be here when I get back, right, Dad?"

"Of course I will, Shawn. I'm not going anywhere without you. That's a promise. Understand?"

He took his right hand off the steering wheel, and they shook on it.

"I love you, Dad," Shawn said.

Matt swallowed hard. "I love you, too, son. So much."

They turned onto Mission Bay Drive and headed north along the waterfront toward the DeGrove Villa. Pop's place, as Calla used to call it. Or Granddad's beach house, as Shawn understatedly described it.

Whatever, even at a distance, it looked only a little more modest than your average Vegas casino and every bit as impressive as the hotels whose revenue had built it. One thing you could say about Howie, he wasn't shy about flaunting his money.

Whenever he visited his former father-in-law's palatial home, Matt remembered the first time he'd come here with Calla. Typical of her, she hadn't warned him what to expect. Maybe because she was self-conscious that she was one of *those* DeGroves, of the DeGrove Hotel chain, or maybe because she was genuinely indifferent to her family's vast wealth and never considered that those from a different background might find it intimidating, she never mentioned the fact that her father lived in a seventy-five-hundred-square-foot seaside mansion with a fifty-five-foot motor yacht docked at the nearby yacht club, or that he owned a private plane and a chain of upscale motels that extended into thirty-three states and fourteen foreign countries.

"Never underestimate the amount of misery that can be hidden under piles of money," Calla had said, and went on to regale him with the tale of how her mother ran off with another man when she and Trina were small, how her father had always waited for this woman to return, who, in Calla's opinion, was utterly unworthy of him.

Sometimes Matt almost wished Shawn had inherited his mother's cavalier, almost contemptuous attitude toward wealth. Because, make no mistake about it, when it came to the DeGrove side of the family, Shawn was impressed. Big time. Having a granddad who could fly his own plane to the Super Bowl or take off for a week of deep-sea fishing in Mexico was pretty heady stuff at any age, let alone for a ten-year-old boy.

And although Shawn was fiercely proud of the money he earned working on Matt's construction sites, how long would that ambition last, he wondered, when it finally dawned on the boy that, all things being equal, he stood to one day inherit a fortune.

"Granddad's going to buy me a new bike," Shawn said as they were approaching the house.

"That's fine, but don't pester him for a lot of other stuff," Matt said. "That's what birthdays and Christmas are for. And don't pick out the most expensive bike in the store."

"Aww, come on, Dad, Grandad can afford it. He could buy the whole store."

"That's not the point."

He was on the verge of starting his speech about money not being the most important thing in life when he realized that he and Shawn had had this conversation before, that it was more about his fear of losing his son's love to a higher bidder than any real concern for how much Howie spent on a bike. Howie could buy a dozen bikes, for heaven's sake. Or, in a few years when Shawn was old enough to get his driver's license, a dozen TransAms with a Maserati thrown in for good measure. The thought scared Matt sometimes. What if Shawn decided he wanted to spend every summer with Howie? All his vacations?

On the other hand, he was grateful that when Calla

died Howie had left the corporate world and never looked back. Deep-sea fishing, training for his next triathlon, spending time with his remaining daughter and grandson—these were the things Howie valued, and Matt respected him for that.

He caught Shawn looking at him, grinning. "How're you and Coop gonna get along without me on the job site? Think I can take some time off without everything falling apart?"

"Look, Shawn, I hate to have to tell you this, but I had to let Coop go. He's got a drinking problem he's just not dealing with."

Shawn looked thoughtful. "If he quits drinking, will you give him his job back?"

"I don't know. We'll have to see what happens."

They turned into Howie's driveway, which was flanked by royal palms and immaculately tended flower borders. When he saw Trina's cherry-red Corvette in the driveway, Matt's stomach knotted and he made a quick decision not to go in. Given the way last night had ended, he really didn't feel like seeing Trina for a while. And, with the enhanced clarity of morning-after thinking, he was wildly grateful not to have given in to the impulse to have sex with her. He'd be hating himself now, and he knew it.

After dropping Shawn off, he drove straight to the clinic. Amazingly, there was no line, and he got his blood drawn in twenty minutes. The same nurse he'd run out on before explained he'd have to come back in ten days to learn the results, but when Matt protested that for all he knew he might be in jail ten days from now, she finally relented—either through pity or fear that he was a dangerous criminal—and agreed to send the results to his house by registered mail.

One down, he thought, *one to go.* Sunday afternoon most of the traffic would be headed back into the city. With any luck, he figured he could make it up to Ramona and drop in on a certain luxury car dealership in a couple of hours. Rather than think about the blood test he'd just taken, he focused on what he regarded as the next task at hand—finding Noel.

Those were the thoughts percolating in his head, distracting him from what was happening in his peripheral vision, when he pulled up in front of his house. A black-and-white that had been stationed around the corner turned its light on and cruised slowly behind him, then pulled over with its motor idling. He got out of the car and approached the police car. A policewoman with soft gray eyes framed with crow's feet and frizzy hair tucked up under her cap got out of the driver's side and sauntered around the front of the car.

"Matt Engstrom?" she said.

He nodded. "What's this about?"

"I need to take you in for questioning."

"Am I under arrest?"

"Not yet, Mr. Engstrom, but you have to come with me. We got a tip that you were in Vegas the night an employee of yours fell off a balcony. The detectives down at the station need to talk to you."

Chapter Twenty-four

Twilight, the kitchen aromatic with the smells of saffron, oregano, and garlic, and the rich, nutty-sweet tang of piñon nuts. Trina had just finished chopping the carrots and onions, while Howie, over at the butchers-block table, was concocting what he referred to as his "mystery meat-loaf seasoning." She had a half-finished glass of Courvoisier at her elbow. He was drinking Perrier with lime.

"I still don't understand why Matt didn't come in the house this morning," Howie said, "why he just let Shawn out of the car and took off."

"He's probably ashamed to face you," Trina observed. "I mean, however much I want to believe he didn't kill that man, the body was found in Matt's truck. The police think he did it. And he *is* an ex-con who did time for manslaughter, even though he dressed it up in a pretty package to *sound* like it was an accident. I mean, let's be realistic, Calla didn't exactly pick a winner, did she?"

"Yes, but it sounds odd hearing that coming from *you*. You've always been such a supporter of Matt." He shook a pinch of nutmeg into the mixture and looked at her out of the corner of his eye. "Strange how Matt was able to come up with the money to bond out. I guess his construction business must be doing pretty well."

"Must be." She sliced into the onion with a series of rapid knife strokes, then glanced at her watch. "It's almost seven. What time did you tell Shawn to be home?"

"I told him no later than six-thirty, and that I'd given the cook the night off so you and I would fix dinner. But since the master chef and his assistant are running late themselves, I guess we can cut him a little slack."

Trina winked. "Aww, Daddy, you're much more than just my assistant." She selected another onion, peeled it, and started chopping it into quarters. "Shawn really loves his new bike. And the Nikes and the stereo and all the clothes. Quite a shopping spree you two had."

"Maybe help get his mind off other things," said Howie. "Besides, it gives me pleasure to buy him things."

"Then you should be on cloud nine," Trina said.

"In the vicinity, at any rate. I can't wait to get down to Baja and just kick back on the boat and do some fishing."

"Me, too, Daddy. And thanks for inviting me to tag along, too. I know this trip is a chance for you and Shawn to do some male bonding." She squinted, wiped at her eyes. "Damn these onions."

Howie said, "You could wear my swimming goggles."

"Very funny."

"No, I'm serious. I always wear them when I chop onions."

"You've got all the answers, don't you, Daddy?"

"Let's just say I'd like you to *think* I do."

"All right then, Mr. Answer Man. How about this one? What was really going on with you when we flew to Cottonwood the other day? I've never seen you so shaky."

"It was my mother's *grave*," Howie said, "and I was feeling a lot of shame and guilt over having concocted such a stupid self-serving lie about how she died and then sticking to it all these many years. You deserved better than that. You deserved to know the truth about your grandmother. So did Calla."

"Well, I forgive you, Daddy. I haven't been exactly truthful myself, you know."

"Maybe now would be the time."

"A minute ago you said Matt's business must be doing pretty well for him to be able to post bond. Well, I paid it."

"I thought as much." Howie emptied his Perrier out into the sink and refilled it with Courvoisier. "Well, it's your money. You do as you like."

"There's more, though. The other day in Cottonwood you wanted to talk about Calla, and I cut you off. I was a total bitch." She used the side of the knife to sweep the onions off the chopping board into a blue Pyrex bowl. "I guess I didn't realize how sensitive I still am about the subject."

"It's understandable."

"No, it's more than that. You aren't the only one who's been carrying around a lot of guilt. There's something I know. Something I probably should have gone to the cops with a long time ago."

Howie drained his drink and poured another one. He didn't look at Trina, but stared down at the mound of meat loaf he'd been kneading as though half expecting it to jump suddenly to life.

"Trina, before you go on—"

"What, Daddy?"

He hesitated. "No, no, you go first."

"The night Calla was murdered—remember I told the cops Matt stopped by my place? He'd been drinking, and we drank a little more, and then he was too drunk to drive home, so I let him sleep it off on my couch? That was Matt's alibi for where he was the night Calla was killed. Well, it wasn't the truth. I never saw Matt at all that night. I only made up that story, because I felt like he couldn't possibly have murdered Calla, and I knew how bad it would look to the cops if he said he was home alone drinking that night."

"The truth is you have no idea where Matt was that night."

"You aren't even surprised? I thought this was going to be a revelation."

"Oh, I figured out that you were lying to provide him with an alibi a long time ago—from the way Matt acted when I brought it up and things the cops said at the time. For what it's worth, they weren't all that convinced you were telling the truth, either. They just couldn't prove anything."

"And here I thought I'd fooled everyone."

"I'm not as old and oblivious as you think, Trina. I know—I've always known—you were in love with Matt. I expect you probably slept together, too—maybe even while Matt and Calla were married—although, if that's the case, for God's sake, I don't want to know. Just suspecting it may have happened is bad enough. It didn't surprise me that you bonded Matt out of jail, or that you lied to give him an alibi. What does surprise me is why you choose to tell me now?"

"Maybe because you told me the truth about my grandmother. And maybe because I'm beginning to think Matt isn't nearly as nice a man as I once believed."

"What you just said about Matt not being what you once thought—that's been my deepest fear, you know. That someday you'd reach that very same conclusion about me. I suppose there isn't a whole lot in this world that scares me, except the idea that you might think less of me—if you knew everything there is to know."

"Don't be ridiculous, Daddy. Everyone who's ever lived feels that way at one time or another." She came over, wrapped her arms around his waist, and snuggled her head into his shoulder. Taller than her father by several inches, she had to bend sharply at the waist in order to do so. "You'll always be the number one man in my life. The only *real* man. And for the record, I was never in love with Matt. He was like all the others—just a silly, sexual diversion."

If she felt her father wince at that disclosure, she ignored it. "Besides, nothing you could tell me is going to make me think less of you." She gave the lobe of his ear a fond nibble. "Come on, tell you what? I'll tell you another one of my secrets, if you tell me one of yours. The whole truth and nothing but. That way we're even. Fair enough? I'll go first."

"Trina, wait."

"What?"

"Is this going to have anything to do with your private life?"

"Private life. You mean, my sex life?"

"Because I don't want to know about that, understand. You've always been a very frank young woman, and I already know more about your—your personal habits—than I want to. I'm sorry if I sound like an old fuddy-duddy, but I'm your father and—some things just aren't appropriate for me to know."

"Fine, what you mean is, you don't give a shit what I do."

"I didn't say that, Trina. What I said was—"

The door off the patio slammed shut, and Shawn slumped into the kitchen. He didn't acknowledge either his grandfather or aunt, but went straight to the refrigerator, grabbed a Pepsi, and headed back toward the door.

"Whoa, hold on there," said Howie.

"*What*, Grandad?"

"Since when are you so snippy with me?"

Shawn shrugged, turned around. His eyes were teary and swollen, and the left one was blacking up in spectacular shades of fushia and red all the way out to his cheekbone. His San Diego Chargers T-shirt was ripped at the neck and stained with dribbles of blood. Howie gasped and rushed to his side.

"My God, what happened to you?"

Shawn tried to bite back the tears, but they erupted out anyway, racking his body with deep sobs. "Nothing, Granddad! I just want to go home. I want to call my dad and go home."

Howie, looking stricken, pulled the boy against his chest. "Shawn, you have to tell me what happened, understand? Whatever it is, no matter what, you can tell me."

"I just want to call Dad."

"You can do that later. Right now, you have to tell me what happened."

Slowly, in fits and starts punctuated by crying, Shawn got out his story. He'd been headed home, riding his new bike along Crosby Street about five-thirty when he was approached by three boys. Older boys, seventeen or eighteen, he said. One Hispanic, two white. "Get off the bike," said the heavier of the white kids.

Shawn had refused and tried to pedal away.

The Hispanic boy grabbed the handlebars. "Give us the damn bike, or we're taking it anyway."

And they did, but not before Shawn put up enough of a fight to get his eye blacked and his lip busted.

"You say that was five-thirty," Howie said. "But it's past seven now. What did you do all that time?"

Shawn shrugged. "I didn't know what to do. I was scared to come home. It was a brand-new bike. You just bought it for me. I called Dad, but he wasn't home, so I just wandered around."

Trina said, "I'll call the police."

"What good will they do?" snapped Howie.

"What else *can* we do?"

"All right, go ahead," he said grudgingly. He turned back to Shawn. "Come over here and sit down. We'll put some ice on that eye."

Thirty minutes later, two policemen stood in Howie's living room listening to Shawn's story and taking notes. Description of bike, description of kids, area where bike was stolen. They seemed sympathetic, but also resigned to being powerless in such matters.

"There's not a lot we can do about this except file a report," said the older cop, an Asian-American with a wispy black mustache and facial skin stretched so

glisteningly tight that the knobs of his cheekbones
looked in danger of popping through.

"You can go look for the little bastards," said
Howie. "You've got Shawn's description."

The cops exchanged haggard looks. They'd been
through this before. Stolen property, roughed-up kid,
outraged parents.

"We'll keep an eye out," said the younger cop, who
was fair-haired and burly, a gruff Viking type. "Don't
get your hopes up, though. This happens a lot."

"I understand. Just go do your jobs. Try not to get
that carpal tunnel syndrome from writing too many
parking tickets."

The younger cop started to say something, but the
older one tugged him along with a don't-start-any-
thing-it's-not-worth-it look. Howie smirked angrily
and slammed the door, then marched back into the
kitchen. Trina was trying to coax Shawn into eating
some dinner, but the boy was having none of it.

"You're going to sulk now, are you?"

The boy looked up, surprised at the rebuke. "What
am I supposed to do, Granddad? The bike's gone. The
cops as good as said they won't be able to get it back."

"Maybe not," said Howie, "but we're not going to
sit here and mope. We've done the so-called 'right'
thing; we've called the police, and look how much
good it's done us. Bunch of sniveling bureaucratic
wimps, the lot of 'em. Now we're going to do what
we should've done in the first place—go out and find
those creeps and show them what it feels like to be
bullied and beat up on."

Trina looked alarmed. "You're not thinking of
going after them?"

"Don't see any other choice. You'll know them if
you see them, won't you, Shawn?"

For the first time Shawn showed some enthusiasm.
"Sure, Granddad."

"Daddy, this is ridiculous," said Trina. "You can't
go out there searching for three young toughs who're
probably long gone by now. You aren't going to find

them. Worse, what if you do find them? What are you going to do? Take on all three of them? Can't you just buy Shawn another bike?"

"No. I can't." Howie took her by the arm, hustled her outside onto the patio. "Of course, I can buy the boy another bike. That's not the goddamn point. Replacing the stolen bike won't repair the damage to his spirit, his pride. We probably won't find the kids who did it. What's important is, we're going to take action, not just sit around feeling like goddamn victims, expecting help from a couple of cops who'd given up before they ever walked through the door. I'm not going to stand by and watch my grandson become a victim. And if he and I have to drive around all night and all day tomorrow, too, then by God, we'll do it. And if we do find those scumbags—"

"—if you find them, they may kill you, Daddy. I don't care how great shape you're in, guys like that carry guns, knives. And there're *three* of them." She took a breath, lowered her voice, and laid her hand across Howie's. "If you must do something, you can *hire* people to take care of situations like this, Daddy. God knows, I don't have to tell you that. Look up those guys you had bodyguarding me after that coffee heiress got kidnapped and murdered the summer after Shawn was born."

"I could do that, you're right, but it would take time, which I don't have right now. Furthermore, I don't want Shawn exposed to that element of people."

Trina gave a short, mocking laugh. "Oh, you mean that element of people that was good enough to be following me around night and day, sleeping in my guest bedroom, escorting me on dates, is that the element of people we're talking about?"

"You're a grown woman, Trina. It's different. Besides, it's not up for debate. Shawn and I are going out and find these bastards. Now do you want to come with us or not?"

"Gosh, Daddy, I hate to miss out on another of

Howie DeGrove's Stirring Adventures, but I think I'll pass this time."

"Suit yourself."

"Do me a favor, though, will you? Take an Uzi. A few hand grenades. This probably isn't guys from the cast of *West Side Story* you're dealing with."

"I can take care of myself, Trina. And Shawn, too. You can wager your life on that."

"I know, Daddy." She shut her eyes for a moment. Took his hands. "I love you so much. I just wish I could be like you, Daddy, but I'm not. Not because I'm a woman, but because there's just something missing in me. Something God wasn't handing out on the day I got born. I'm not brave and I'm not noble and I don't risk myself. Sometimes I don't think I'm much of anything."

He patted her hand. "That's not true, Trina. You're fine, just fine. You're beautiful, intelligent, and God help the man who crosses you. You're everything I want you to be. Everything I could dream of in a daughter and—"

"Oh, stop it, stop patronizing me! That's total lying bullshit. That kind of lying's *my* department. It's unworthy of you. It's total bullshit!"

To Howie's amazement, she whirled and stalked away from him, darting into the shadows surrounding the patio, then breaking into a run as she went around the side of the house toward her car.

Chapter Twenty-five

Noel screeched to a stop in front of the bungalow, turned on the overhead light, and stared at herself in the rearview mirror. What she saw made her want to cry. Her hair was a matted mess, the ends clumped together in places with disgusting white goop, the rest of the hair corkscrewing wildly around her face. Mascara was smeared below her eyes, and a red bite mark marred the corner of her mouth.

Still, in spite of all she'd been through, she knew she'd gotten off lucky this time. It could have been worse.

But what was she supposed to do? Brandon wouldn't lend her any money, and no one had delivered any packages for her to his house. She had to work to support herself and pay her medical bills, didn't she? Right now that meant doing private dances for clients at a motel on the outskirts of Ramona where the desk clerk, a former dancer, was a friend.

The woman had called a few hours earlier, said there was a guy asking for a date with a woman he'd heard about who danced with snakes. He was willing to pay five hundred dollars for a private show, with more negotiable if other activities were agreed upon later.

Noel had agreed to the date and then arrived at the motel early, parking where she could watch the guy arrive and make sure it wasn't Matt.

Upon arrival, the date had looked harmless enough,

attractive even, but the encounter had turned into a nightmare. The guy was some kind of weirdo, a freak. Didn't care for her snakes, but wanted to plunge his hands into her long hair, braid it, and then choke her with her own hair until she was barely able to remember where she was. He'd said he was going to fuck her after she was dead and talked about it in detail. How long it would take to kill her, what he'd do to her body afterward, how and where he'd dispose of it.

She'd been almost sick with fear and had tried to persuade him to have unprotected sex with her, figuring that if he really did kill her, she'd have a shot at her own brand of revenge. That had made her remember what she'd done to Matt, and she'd started sobbing. Her "date," meanwhile, had laughingly produced a condom and insisted on using it before he finally pulled it off at the last minute and did his nasty business in her hair.

The threats to kill her had terrified Noel, but the other stuff, the constant stream of sick shit babble coming out of his mouth the whole time they fucked, had made her want to puke. Verbal diarrhea. *Daddy-this* and *Daddy-that* and *how's my little girl like it best, in the face or on the tits?*

What a night she thought, *what a lousy rotten night.*

She got out of the Fiat, came around to the passenger side, and lugged Monique in her heavy cage up onto the porch. Once inside the house, she checked on the rest of her reptiles, then spent half an hour in the shower soaping and shampooing herself over and over, trying to get clean. After toweling off and putting on fresh clothes, she realized she was hungry. Flicked the TV on to keep her company and checked the contents of the refrigerator. Pickings were slim. She'd forgotten to shop, so she called up a pizza joint in Ramona and ordered a medium pepperoni and pineapple and a large Coke. Settled back on the sofa with a joint and a *TV Guide*. *Scarface*, one of her favorites, was on HBO at one, so she switched to that channel and waited for dinner to arrive.

When the doorbell rang, she took the pizza from the delivery boy with one hand and gave him a twenty with the other. She carried the pizza back into the living room and returned with a couple of ones for the tip.

It was when she went back to the door that she noticed the parcel beside the porch steps. The way it was positioned, there was no way she could have missed it when she came up the steps earlier.

"Did you see anybody leave that," she asked the delivery boy, hoping for a description of Brandon.

He shook his head. "Sure didn't."

She bent down and retrieved the parcel, which was small and light, with airholes punched in the cardboard and the words LIVE ANIMAL printed on the sides. As much as she wanted to believe the money was inside, she felt wary. The money was supposed to have been delivered to Brandon's address, not hers. Had they found out where she lived? Brandon wouldn't have told anyone, would he? Or maybe the box *had* been delivered to Brandon's house, and he, knowing a live snake would need to be cared for and not being overly fond of reptiles himself, had dropped it off here? If that was the case, though, why hadn't he at least rung the bell or left a note?

She lifted the box in her arms and carried it inside, where she set it down next to her on the sofa and studied it in the light. No return address, but then she hadn't expected one, of course. Very carefully, working slowly so as to protect her freshly manicured nails, she peeled back the masking tape along the top and opened the cardboard flaps.

And her heart sank. There was no money inside. At least none she could see. The box was filled with wood shavings. Fucking wood shavings!

Then she noticed the edge of something white sticking up along the side and pulled out an envelope with her name printed on the front. She opened it up and found printed on the plain white card inside, *Found you at last! All is forgiven. I still love you. Matt.*

*   *   *

How do you dress to go to war?, thought Howie, as
he looked at himself in the mirror. Loose-fitting jeans
hugged a firm, almost completely flat waist. A black
T-shirt with a denim jacket added breadth if not
height to his already stocky torso. Stiff-toed boots replaced the soft loafers he habitually wore.

He was glad Trina had elected to leave. She was
too observant, too clever, too judgmental. She'd have
seen right through his show of righteous indignation
and grandfatherly wrath to the dark thrill with which
he greeted this opportunity to test himself yet again.
An old man wanting to take on three young thugs,
risking serious injury over as trifling a thing as a boy's
stolen bike.

But there were different kinds of pain, Howie reflected. There was guilt and dread and recrimination,
which shriveled the heart and leeched all joy out of
life. There was corrosive, soul-lancing shame, and
there was the interior numbness the mind created to
defend against it. Compared to any of the above, physical pain was at worst an inconvenience, at best a
much-needed distraction.

Already his willingness to expose himself to danger
was paying off, for he felt the way he did right before
the start of a triathlon—alive, razor-sharp, and galvanized. And, though he did not acknowledge it gladly,
afraid. If he and Shawn actually found the bastards—
which was unlikely, he reminded himself, they were
probably long gone—he would be overmatched and
outnumbered. He might get his ass kicked in front of
his grandson. He might wind up in the hospital. Or
the morgue.

So why was it then that as he started downstairs, he
realized, to his consternation, that he was carrying
along something not Miranda, not many of his former
lady friends had ever seen upon his person—a full-
blown, purple-headed, kick-ass erection? He wasn't
terribly surprised—the adrenaline jolt of potential
danger had had that effect on him before—only thank-

ful for the generous cut of the senior-citizen-style
jeans he had on as he rounded up his grandson and
headed out on his mission of justice.

He took the least showy of his several vehicles—a
late model dark blue Olds Cutlass—and cruised the
area where Shawn told him the bullies had struck. In
the passenger seat, Shawn stared out the window, trying to spot their quarry. They checked out the CD
shops and the 7-Elevens, the video stores and fast-
food joints, and the Great Guns Pawnshop, where a
pack of kids hung out in front performing tricks on
their skateboards, a couple of whom Shawn knew
from school. But he didn't see the boys who had attacked him.

After about an hour, they widened the net and
began checking the area as far north as Old Town and
as far south as the Convention Center, but still had
no luck.

By ten o'clock, they drove west again, cruising the
territory where they'd started out. By this time, Shawn
was yawning, getting bored with the game. He started
fiddling with the radio dial, turning the volume too
loud. Howie snapped at him, "Pay attention! Do you
want to find these little creeps or not?" Shawn re-
coiled, looking chastised and hurt. Howie felt a pluck
of shame. Clearly if they didn't find the boys tonight,
his disappointment would be keener than his grandson's. He spun the wheel around the corner, heading
back south, when suddenly Shawn yelled, "There they
are, Granddad! Over there!"

"You're sure?"

"Yeah, yeah, Granddad, it's them! All three of
'em!"

Howie continued to look straight ahead, but his eyes
ticked to the left, checking them out. Not exactly NFL
material maybe, but a long way from being easy
prey, either.

They were stationed outside a liquor store—sidewalk lounge lizards wreathed in attitude and Marlboro
haze. They wore jeans, T-shirts, and high-top sneakers,

and veneers of belligerence so identical Howie
thought they must have practiced together in front
of a mirror. It worked, too. They looked tough. Not
athletically tough or especially fit, like running-back
material, but in-your-face, kick-ass hoodlum tough.
One of them, short and bullnecked, seemed to be taking excessive interest in a red Chevrolet parked at the
corner. The other two hung back in the shadowy area
between the liquor store and the laundromat next to
it.

Howie circled the block and pulled up in front of a
grungy-looking appliance store where a steel grate
over the windows protected the booty inside.

"Okay, this is it," he said solemnly.

"What are you gonna do, Granddad? Call the
cops?"

Howie almost snapped at the boy, but silenced himself before the words had a chance to erupt and do
their damage. It wasn't Shawn's fault that Matt was
raising him to be weak, he reminded himself. That the
boy's idea of fighting back, of dealing with adversity,
meant letting the goddamn police handle it. That
wasn't the way the real world worked. Howie knew
that, and Matt *ought* to. It was time Shawn did, too.

"We already called the cops, and you see how much
good it did. Now I'm going to show you how real men
handle a situation like this. We're going to make those
young lowlifes wish they'd never seen Shawn Engstrom or laid a hand on his property."

Shawn looked nervously back and forth from his
grandfather to the trio on the corner. "Look, Granddad, maybe this isn't a good idea. Maybe we should
just forget about the bike. I appreciate you wanting
to help, but you could get hurt. I mean, there's *three*
of them there, and they're bigger than us and—"

Howie nailed him with a glare. "I thought this was
what you *wanted* to do? I thought you wanted to go
get the bastards."

Shawn looked forlorn. "It was what I wanted, and

I did, sort of, but—but I guess I didn't think we'd really find them."

There it was, thought Howie. The real truth, in all its pathetic ugliness.

"Are you scared, Shawn?"

The boy didn't answer at first, but squirmed in his seat. Then, finally, he managed, "Granddad, there're *three* of them. And they're *big*."

"There's no shame in being afraid, Shawn. Only fools don't feel any fear, but there *is* shame in not facing it down. In not defending yourself, your loved ones, your property. There's shame in that, because that's being a coward."

"But, Granddad, it's only a bike."

"Only a bike, huh? It didn't seem that way earlier this evening when you were bawling your eyes out over it."

"Okay, I know that, but—"

"It's much *more* than just a bike, Shawn. It's pride and honor and self-respect. Self-respect, you lose that, boy, you don't ever get it back. Not *ever*. You understand?"

The boy nodded, but without conviction. He cleared his throat and seemed to have great difficulty choosing his words. "Listen to me, Granddad. Dad says if he hadn't gone after that guy who was stalking Mom, that Petrovsky guy, that he would never have went to prison."

Howie's eyes flashed with rage. "*Gone*, Shawn. Not went. He never would have *gone* to prison. Good Lord, boy, what do you go to school for?"

"*Gone*, then. Whatever. He wouldn't've *gone* to prison. The point is what he did was stupid, because of what happened to him, and—"

Howie cut him off. "That was a different situation. Matt was stupid. Stupid to walk into that man's house and beat him up—"

"Wait a minute, Dad didn't beat him up! The guy was crazy, Dad testified that he punched *himself* with a fake gun and—"

"—and Matt was even more stupid to call the cops when there weren't any witnesses, nothing could've been proved, Calla could've provided him with an alibi for where he was at the time. But it's too late for discussion now. We're men, and we're committed to this. And it's time to take action."

Shawn hunkered down in the seat and crossed his arms in front of him.

Howie turned right again and guided the Cutlass up next to the curb. Cut the motor and lights. In the darkness he reached under the seat and slid something up the sleeve of his jacket. "You stay here," he commanded. "This part's up to me. Anything goes wrong, you lock the doors and stay put. But nothing's going to go wrong."

"Don't you want help?"

"Not this time. You stay here."

Then he was out of the car, a squat, wiry phantom with a shock of wild white hair, striding resolutely toward the trio on the corner.

Shawn locked the door behind him, and watched him go.

Chapter Twenty-six

Noel stared at the card signed *Matt* and then back at the box full of wood shavings. Was this somebody's idea of a joke? Matt had no way of knowing she was in Ramona. Only Brandon knew her address, and she trusted him not to give it out. She could have been followed from the motel, of course, but even if Matt had somehow found her, she knew he'd approach her directly. She couldn't see him leaving something at the door and just driving away. Unless, of course, he'd come by and dropped off the package while she was in the shower.

The fact that the note was printed argued against Matt's having written it, too. And while the signature *might* have been his, she couldn't honestly say whether she'd be able to recognize Matt's signature or not. She'd only seen it on the checks he'd signed when he lent her money—a messy scrawl she'd barely glanced at at the time.

On the other hand, how many people knew about Matt and the fact that receiving a package from him would mean something to her? Only one other person, as far as she knew; the one who was supposed to send her the money.

She held the note up, studying it in the light, and when she looked back at the box, the wood chips seemed oddly different somehow. As though a portion of them had settled slightly in the instant she looked away.

Lucy Taylor

Fuck, she thought, *there's got to be something in there.*

Impulsively, she plunged both hands elbow-deep into the shavings.

Felt, too late, as something deep within the pile thrashed to life and bit into the fleshy pad below her thumb. She squealed and pawed through the shavings, then smiled, despite her throbbing hand.

For there it was next to her wrist, small and brilliant black and orange. She'd never seen one like it before. Jewellike. So beautiful a creature that she thought Matt might have sent it to her, after all—until she felt the pain intensify and start branching up into her wrist and arm, traveling at a terrifying rate throughout her body, carrying its red agony straight toward her heart.

Watching from the car as his grandfather confronted the three toughs, Shawn realized he was much more frightened than he'd been when his bike was stolen. That had been bad. This was worse. His grandfather, who had always seemed immense to him, now looked so small and so old, and he could tell the boys weren't taking him seriously, but smirking, jeering, laughing in his face. The tallest one kept hitching up his pants and looking around like he expected to see a camera crew getting this down on film. *World's Wildest Videos* or some such thing.

Shawn felt sick to his stomach. He tried to think what his father would want him to do—*stay in the car*—but he also knew his grandfather was about to get his ass kicked, and he had to do *something*.

He reached for the door handle and was getting out of the car just as he saw Howie lunge for the taller of the white boys, bringing his right arm around in an arc. The way the boy dropped—like a cement block had hit him on the head—Shawn thought at first his grandfather had delivered an uppercut in the class with Mike Tyson's. Then he saw the tire iron in Howie's fist and realized his grandfather must have concealed it up his sleeve before he left the car.

Shawn screamed, "Watch out, Granddad!" and Howie whirled as the other two came at him from behind. He took a glancing punch off the side of his head and clanged the tire iron across the Hispanic's forearm. There was the splinter and crunch of bone shattering, followed by a high, desperate scream as the boy collapsed clutching his arm.

The third one tried to run, but Howie drove the iron into the small of his back, then lobbed a kick to his head as he pitched forward.

The one with the splintered arm was getting groaningly to his feet. Howie advanced on him. "Not so tough now, are you?"

He lifted the bar.

Shawn sprinted forward and grabbed Howie's arm from behind, yanked it downward.

"No, stop it! Don't, Granddad, don't!"

Furious, Howie shook him off. "Didn't I tell you to stay in the car?"

Shawn stared at the carnage on the sidewalk with huge, stricken eyes. "That's enough, Granddad! Leave them alone."

The Hispanic lurched to his feet. Shawn, still holding onto his grandfather's arm, shouted at him, "Run! Go on, get out of here!" and the boy sprinted into the alleyway, clutching his arm to his chest.

Shawn pulled at Howie. "Come on, Granddad. Let's go before the police come."

"The police—?" He stared down at Shawn, at the metal bar gripped in his fist, the blood speckling his pants. "What police? What are you talking about?"

"Someone will call the police, Granddad. We have to go. We have to go *now*."

To his horror, Howie thrust the metal bar at him and nodded toward the boy still on the ground. "Here, take it! Hit him!"

"No, Granddad!"

"Take it!"

He took a step backward, aware that his fingers

seemed to twitch with unknown capabilities and a terrible eagerness. "I can't!"

"Of course you can! Do as I tell you!"

Shawn grabbed the weapon and stepped back, then flung it as far away into the alley as he could. It crashed to the pavement with a great reverberating clang that didn't seem nearly so loud as the pounding of his own heart as he realized that, with that one gesture, he might have lost his grandfather's love.

His dad would have been proud, though. He knew that and held onto that idea to keep himself from bursting into sobs.

He risked a glance at his grandfather. Howie couldn't have looked more stunned if the tire iron had whacked him between the eyes.

"Shawn, what—?"

"I don't care if you hate me! I can't do it!" He bolted back toward the car with Howie right behind him, pain etched across the old man's features as he cried out, "Good God, Shawn, I don't hate you. I love you with all my heart. I did it for *you*, boy, don't you understand? I did it for you."

Chapter Twenty-seven

When he woke up in his own bed the next morning, Matt thanked God. Another day of freedom. Another day he wasn't behind bars.

How many of those did he have left, he wondered.

He'd been taken down to police headquarters and grilled for a couple of hours about the night Phil ended up decorating the obelisk on the Luxor's mezzanine. At least they were calling it murder now, following up on the anonymous tip Matt had phoned in. Trouble was, he wasn't the only person phoning in tips. He hated to think Trina was capable of betraying him to the cops, but after the way they'd parted company the day before, he figured this might have been her way of getting back at him.

They'd questioned him for a couple of hours, Uhlenkamp and Mulholland. Wanting to know where he'd been the night Phil died, who, if anyone, he'd been with, and wasn't it just too fucking coincidental that he couldn't come up with an alibi?

Matt stuck to his story. Saying he'd been wiped out, exhausted that night. Had come home, taken the phone off the hook, popped a couple of sleeping pills, and passed out for twelve hours. He'd let his son spend the night with his foreman, because he didn't want to have to deal with the kid's questions. End of story. Take it or leave it, he'd thought, praying that Coop didn't mention anything about the trip to Vegas or the gun that he'd borrowed when the detectives inevitably called to question him about Matt's statements.

But whether Coop gave him up or not—and lying to the cops to protect an ex-boss might not be high on his list of priorities—it was just a matter of time, Matt figured, before the cops found him out and hauled his ass back to jail. And when that happened, not even all the money in Howie's bank account could get him out.

Today, though, he had today.

Which, he reminded himself as he showered and dressed, was all he or anybody else ever had anyway.

Grabbing a cup of instant coffee only a little worse than what he'd gotten used to in prison, he headed out the back door to the shed where he kept the Harley.

Just seeing the shiny black bike lifted his spirits. Next to sex, nothing felt as good as riding the Harley on a red-hot scorcher of a day with the sun blasting down, wringing the sweat from his skin as fast as the wind could dry it, the engine rumbling and vibrating like some primitive beast under his legs. Noel, he knew, would have agreed. Might even have rated riding the bike a notch or two above lovemaking.

Before he took off for the hills east of the city and the tourist town of Ramona, he spent a few minutes with a screwdriver attaching the sissy bar to the back of the bike. A narrow padded backrest between two curved metal bars, the sissy bar provided support for a passenger and a sturdier handhold than clutching onto the waist of the driver. When he and Noel were together, he'd always kept the sissy bar on the bike, but he'd removed it after she disappeared. Without a passenger, he felt it marred the clean lines of the Harley, not to mention emphasizing the emptiness of the passenger seat.

Now, with an optimism he recognized as completely unwarranted, he was reattaching the sissy bar. He could imagine finding Noel, offering her a ride on the bike, and she—for he had never known her to refuse such an offer—climbing aboard, holding onto his waist while they roared down the highway, her long hair flying, unencumbered by a helmet, eyes wide and bright with excitement.

A half hour later, with the mid-morning sun blazing overhead, he took off, stopping at a local diner for a Coke and a hoagie, after which he went outside to top off his meal with a cigarette. He'd stripped down to a white undershirt and jeans; sun and smoke burned him, inside and out. His leather jacket, chaps, gloves, and helmet were all affixed to the back of the sissy bar with bungy cords.

A couple of young guys going into the diner stopped to admire the bike, and Matt chatted with them for a few minutes: Harley styles and prices and the bike rallies in general being the main themes. One guy had been up to the big rally in Sturgis the year before. The other, younger fellow didn't own a bike yet, but was saving for one.

The conversation left Matt feeling wistful. Oh, to be twenty again and have everything to look forward to. To have freedom and choices and possibilities and an unbridled optimism about the future.

Before the feeling could spiral downward into a funk, he jumped back on the bike and roared up the curvy, two-lane highway toward Ramona. He hadn't been to the popular spa town and resort in years, but the little hamlet seemed just about the way he remembered it: spotless pastel Victorian houses laden with gingerbread and all kinds of froufrou that Matt thought excessive, but the tourists apparently loved—flouncy window shades and cutesy mailboxes, a sign out front advertising the place as a bed-and-breakfast or a tea shop or pastry shop. A store that sold nothing but teddy bears and another specializing only in Christmas ornaments.

He cruised around for a few minutes until he located Julian's Classic Cars on the east side of town, next door to a real estate office and an art gallery. Parking the bike, he strolled inside the dealership. No doubt about it, the cars on display were breathtaking vehicles. No wonder Trina and Howie had bought a car here. Matt ogled a gold Mazerati and a metallic burgundy Corvette until a balding salesman in a meticulously fitted suit and black Gucci loafers ambled over.

He nodded toward Matt's bike parked outside.

"Nice Harley you got there. I'll bet you'd ride it all the time, but now you need a car for rainy days and girlfriends who'd rather wear silk skirts than leather chaps."

"Not exactly," said Matt, "but you do have some beautiful cars. If I win the lottery, this is the first place I'll come." The salesman looked visibly disappointed, so he added, "Actually, I wanted to talk to one of your salesmen. His name is Brandon."

"Brandon Keating? He doesn't work here anymore."

"He doesn't, huh? Sorry to hear that."

"You a friend?"

"Yeah, but we've kind of lost touch."

"He was one of our top people. We hated to lose him. Especially so all of a sudden."

"Mind if I ask what happened?"

With no customers on the lot, the salesman seemed bored and chatty. "Well, he didn't get fired, nothing like that. Like I said, he was one of our best. Conscientious, knowledgeable, efficient. Seemed like he was good for the job, but the job wasn't good for him."

"I'm not sure I follow you."

"Just look around at these cars. Guy—or gal—who comes in and can afford one of these is likely to be pretty demanding, kind'a spoiled. I think Brandon loved the commissions, but he hated selling fancy toys to rich people. Last week it seemed like he just snapped. Said to hell with it. Picked a helluva time to quit, though. He'd almost closed a deal on a Jag for an older couple. Brandon showed them some cars, and they picked out the ones they wanted to buy—two Jaguars, mind you, his and hers, and then he just kind of—well, went to pieces, I guess you could say. Said he was tired of wasting his life stroking the inflated egos of rich assholes. Then he backhanded everything

off his deck and walked out, and we haven't heard
from him since."

"The take-this-job-and-shove-it exit."

"You got it." The man ran a hand through thinning
blond strands. "You got any idea how much money
Brandon was making here? People liked to buy cars
from him. He looked—oh, a little bit like that movie
actor Brad Pitt—young, but sophisticated, cultured,
like he'd been around the block—in a good way, I
mean."

"His sister, Noel, did you ever meet her?"

"His sister?" The man looked puzzled. "Oh, you got
that wrong, I think. I did meet Noel a couple of times
when she stopped by to see Brandon, but she wasn't
his sister. She was his fiancée."

Matt tried to process this information without letting the shock register on his face. Fiancée? Sister?
Trina had said the young woman who tried to pick up
Howie was the sister of the guy who sold them the car.
Could Noel have posed as this guy Brandon's sister in
order to appear available to Howie? Was having a
fiancée just another little item she'd somehow forgotten to mention while she and Matt were sleeping together every chance they could? Would she *do* that
to him?

Hell, yeah, she'd do it, he thought bitterly. Would
do it and probably had.

Still, the idea left him reeling. "Oh, right, his fiancée. Guess I got it confused."

"Beautiful young lady. Said she was a dancer with
the San Diego ballet."

"She did, huh?" An image blazed behind his retinas: Noel, nude, slick with sweat, breasts bouncing,
her glistening skin seething with serpent coils. Not exactly *Swan Lake* or *The Nutcracker*. "Yeah, ballet,"
he said, "something like that. Look, I really need to
talk to Brandon. Does he live around here?"

"He's got a house up in the hills. I don't know if
he's still there, though."

Matt said, "That's too bad. I really hoped to get in touch with him."

"Well, look, if it's a car you're interested in, I could—"

He shook his head. "It'd be nice, but they're a little out of my price range."

The salesman shrugged. "Hell, personally, between the two of us, I'd rather be riding a Hogg, but my wife, she thinks the only people ride motorcycles are Hell's Angels and their old ladies. I tell her, hey, it's a yuppie thing nowadays, but I don't think I've quite convinced her."

Matt forced a smile. "Not exactly the Hell's Angels anymore, huh?"

He turned to leave. "Say, this wouldn't be about Brandon owing you a pot, would it?"

"Huh?" For a second, Matt thought he was being asked if he and Noel's brother/fiancé were involved in some kind of dope deal, and his expression must have showed it, because the salesman quickly added, "You know what I mean, pottery. Lot of the weekenders coming up here are into that kind of thing. I never saw any of Brandon's stuff myself, but I know he got his picture in the local weekly once for winning some kind of art contest. Helluva dumb caption on the photo, something like From Porsches to Pottery. Anyway, I got the impression that was his true love, pottery. Lots of art galleries around here. You're looking to find him, you might check them out."

Chapter Twenty-eight

The Ramona yellow pages listed several art galleries, two art supply shops, and something called The Pottery Barn. Matt went down the list, pretending to have ordered pottery from Brandon Keating, but misplaced his address and phone number. The fourth call, to an art gallery called The Painted Lady got him the information that Brandon's phone had been disconnected, but that he had a home on Thunderbird Drive.

He stopped in a convenience store, bought a street map, and located Thunderbird Drive, a quarter mile up a two-lane road that wound through cool, shady stands of juniper and oaks. When the road turned to gravel, he parked the bike and hiked up a steep rise to a small stone house, elaborately landscaped with flower beds, hedges, and shrubs.

He could hear music—the eerie, atonal type he associated with peculiar Oriental instruments and long-haired guys who drove expensive cars and called themselves Maharishi. On the doorstep a gray cat sat posing next to a small stone Buddha. Of the two, the cat's stillness and composure seemed the more absolute.

Matt knocked on the door. Except for the ear-grating music, he heard nothing, so he called hello and knocked again. When still no one responded, he decided to do a little snooping and followed a cobblestone walkway around the side of the house to the backyard.

An open U-Haul was parked in the drive next to a

forest-green Blazer. Judging from the suitcases and duffles he could see through the windows, the Blazer was already packed and ready to roll, and the U-Haul was getting there, full of large boxes that had been labeled and sealed with masking tape, and a large oven-like object Matt took to be a kiln. More boxes were stacked on the steps, presided over by a white cat identical in its composure to the gray one he'd seen on the porch. A potter's wheel and several bags of clay sat waiting to be loaded.

He peeked into a box on the steps that was still unsealed, pushing aside some wrapping paper to uncover the rim of a large, extravagantly painted pot. Carefully he lifted it out of the box and turned it in his hands. A striking piece decorated with brilliant turquoise and black slashes, like tribal markings, that appeared random, but whose placement had surely been calculated to give just that effect. The sort of fiery, almost savage, color that Calla would have liked.

Behind him a man's voice said, "If you're thinking of buying that, it's forty dollars. If you like it so much you're thinking of stealing it, consider it a gift."

Matt spun around to see the slender, bearded young man descend the steps carrying a ficus tree in a brown and yellow pot. He wore a loose-fitting long-sleeved T-shirt and, over that, a bulky plaid shirt. At the foot of the steps, he set the tree down, rubbed some dirt from his palms, and said, "So what *are* you doing rummaging around in my things? Are you harmless or do I need to pull out the recently purchased .357 Colt I'm wearing in a holster under my clothing." He flashed a smile that was slightly devilish. "I'm actually itching for the opportunity. I never brandished a firearm at anyone before."

"Hate to disappoint you, but no need to do any brandishing," said Matt, who was amused by the man's choice of words and figured he was joking. "I'm actually harmless—most of the time, anyway." He replaced the pot in its nest of newspapers and said, "That pot's beautiful. Did you make it?"

"Yeah, I did. The design's West African."

"Then you're Brandon?"

"That be me."

He held out his hand, "Matt Engstrom. I'm a friend of Noel's. I don't know if she ever mentioned me, but—"

A host of conflicting emotions seemed to play on the man's thin face—surprise and concern and, unaccountably, a flicker of fear—before he shook Matt's hand. The handshake was brief, but solid. "Matt Engstrom, you say? Who gave you my address? Not Noel, surely?"

"One of the art galleries in town. I told them I was a great admirer of your work."

"I see. So it's safe to say you're not an art collector." His right hand slid underneath the plaid shirt. "You think I'm bluffing about the gun. I'm not."

"Look, I don't know what you're scared of, but all I want to do is to talk to Noel. Do you know where I can find her?"

"Maybe she doesn't want to be *found*. Maybe she's got good reason. For all I know, you're some kind of stalker who's watched her dance and started having fantasies. It happens, you know."

"I'm sure it does. Noel's very beautiful."

"Too beautiful for her own good."

"She also may be in trouble."

"And you want to help her?"

"If I can."

"Oh, really?"

The sarcastic tone grated on Matt, but he tried to be patient. "Look, if you don't want to give me Noel's phone number, why don't you go inside and call her yourself. Tell her I'm here, and I want to talk to her."

"I don't think so."

"I told you, she's in trouble."

"She's *always* in trouble, it's a lifestyle with her. So what is it? Does she owe you money?"

"It's personal," said Matt. "I can't tell you anything specific, just that I need to find her."

"Sorry, can't help you." He turned back toward the U-Haul. "Now, unless you want to help me load this truck, you're really going to have to leave. I want to be out of here by tonight."

Fighting to suppress his anger, Matt tried a different tack. "So this move of yours, at the dealership they made it sound like it was kind of sudden. Where're you going anyway? Out of town, out of state?"

"Out of country. Mexico." He caught the reaction on Matt's face and said, "Something funny about that?"

"No, no. My son and his grandfather are headed down to Baja next week, as a matter of fact. But I live right next to the border in San Diego. People are always sneaking across in the night, trying to get in. But for every Mexican that makes it out of the country, there's a gringo somewhere moving south. You got a particular place in mind down there?"

"San Miguel de Allende. Ever hear of it?"

"Been there actually. It's an art center, isn't it?"

"That it is. Popular with ex-pats and alcoholics. An art center with world-class ambience at Third World prices, elegance and charm with just a touch of sensuousness to keep it from getting boring." He nodded toward the white cat, who was gliding through the tall grass stalking an insect. "Plus, the cats enjoy the scrumptious variety of bug life."

"I traveled some in Mexico when I was younger," said Matt. "I remember San Miguel. There was a place that served the best damn margaritas I ever had."

Brandan offered a crooked, thinly contemptuous smile. "Out of everything you could remember, you picked the margaritas. Now, why doesn't that surprise me?"

"You said it was popular with drunks."

"Of which you're one?"

"Used to be."

"But not anymore?"

"Retired."

"Good for you. Look, I'm sorry I can't help you,

but I've really got to get back to my packing now."
He picked up a box, hoisted it into the back of the
U-Haul. "I wasn't kidding about the pot, though. If
you like it, you can take it with you."

"Thanks," said Matt, "but I don't have a way to
carry it. I came here on my motorcycle."

"That figures," said Brandon. "Noel loves Harleys."

Matt stopped. "How'd you know it was a Harley, if
she never mentioned me? If she didn't tell you what
I drove?"

"The motor," he said quickly. "I could hear the
sound of it coming up the road."

"Let me get this straight? You mean I stood right
outside your house and banged on your front door
and you didn't hear me, but you heard the motor of
my bike well enough to tell it was a Harley even
though I parked a quarter mile down the road?" He
closed in on Brandon. "Don't play me for a fool, pal.
You knew it was a Harley, because Noel told you
that's what I ride."

"Hey, I don't need this," said Brandon, holding up
his hands. "You're pissed, because she never mentioned you, that's not my problem. Now, I think you
better get back on your bike and leave."

"A minute ago you were offering me a free pot and
talking about the good life south of the border. Now
you'd like to kick my ass if you weren't scared to try.
What's the problem? What have you got to hide?"
He took a step forward. If his intention was to intimi-
date, then he accomplished that and more. Brandon
backed up rapidly, looking panicky.

"Get away from me. You're another one of them,
aren't you? Another of the scumbags Noel hangs out
with." His hand went to his waist, fingers fumbling
clumsily over the apparently unfamiliar action of un-
holstering a revolver. When he finally pulled it out,
his hands were shaking.

"Whoa, take it easy," said Matt. "Another one of
'them'? What are you talking about? Who is it you
think I am?"

"It was you and that other guy who came here last week and trashed my place, wasn't it?"

"What other guy? What do you mean? What did he look like?"

"About your height, but heavier. Black hair, shit-eating smile. Cocky bastard. He said he had a package for Noel and he wanted to know where he could find her to deliver it. I told him whatever it was, he could leave it here, but he said no, he had to see Noel in person."

"You didn't tell him where she's living?"

"No way. He looked like bad news."

"Thank God."

"But he found out anyway. A couple days later while I was out, he or somebody else came back and trashed my place. Tore things up, rifled through all the drawers, but didn't steal a thing. I know it was Noel's address that they wanted, and they found it— my address book was tossed out in the middle of the floor, like whoever did it wanted me to know they knew. That's when I bought the gun. As far as moving, I'd been planning to do that anyway ever since—I'd been planning to move, but this just speeded up the process."

"If this is who I think it is," Matt said, "you're right about him being bad news. You gotta tell me how I can find Noel or get in touch with her. I promise I'm not out to hassle her in any way, but this guy—his name's Salerno—I've seen him operate, and he'll hurt her if he has to. Or even if he doesn't."

Brandon took a deep breath, chewed his lip. "Fuck. *Fuck.* Jesus, Noel, what've you got yourself into now? Okay, it's true Noel did talk about you, but—"

"But *what,* Brandon?"

"It's over between you and her, fella."

"She must've said more than that. *Why* is it over?"

"I don't know. Honest, I don't. I think she liked you a lot, but you have to understand, Noel never liked *anybody* too much to use them any way she could. You may not want to believe it, but trust me, it's *done*."

"I'll accept that," said Matt, "when I hear it from her. Right now, I'm more concerned about that guy you say is looking for her. I *know* that son of a bitch, and I'm telling you, he's dangerous."

"And you're not?"

"Not to Noel."

Brandon reached inside his shirt, and Matt froze. Then he pulled out a pen and a scrap of paper, printed a phone number and an address on it. "Noel's gonna give me hell for this." He handed it to Matt. "Tell her to get her act together, will you? Life's too short."

"I'll do that," said Matt. He turned to go, stopped. "One more thing—I gotta ask, but at this point, whatever you say, I'm okay with it. Are you Noel's brother? Or was that just some scam she laid on me? Are you really her boyfriend?"

Brandon sighed and scratched the cat behind its ear. "Noel used to help me out when I needed a date for parties and such at work. My real partner's name was Edward. We're not together anymore. That's the reason I finally decided to 'follow my bliss' as they say, quit my job, and do what I really want to do, which is move to Mexico and make pots."

"Yeah, I guess sometimes a breakup leads to better things."

"It wasn't a breakup," said Brandon. "Eddie died five months ago. Of AIDS."

Chapter Twenty-nine

The sun had singed its way past the rim of the horizon half an hour ago, and it was getting hard to make out where the edge of the macadam merged into the gravel shoulder, but Salerno still had his Ray-Bans on as he drove south on Interstate 5 toward San Diego. Next to him, Baines sucked on a beer and grumbled about what he was going to do to Engstrom—the fucking s.o.b. asshole dickhead—when he got hold of him.

Baines finished the beer, crumpled the can, and pitched it into the backseat with the rest of the empties. He scowled at Salerno, who, given the clusterfuck at the Coliseum Saturday night, looked altogether too pleased with himself.

"How 'bout we stop for a real drink," he said, " 'fore we hit San Diego?"

Salerno's black eyes were riveted on the highway ahead, like a raven searching for roadkill. "No way, man. I been jonesing for this all fucking day. Been imagining how it's gonna go down—the look on her face when she sees us, what she'll say, what she'll do. Fuck, I hope she tries to run away or puts up a fight."

Baines said, "I don't believe you, man, you spent all day yesterday with a woman. What are you, some kind'a machine? The Bionic Dick?"

Salerno grinned broadly, showing an angular, off-white incisor flecked with a tiny crumb of the calzone he'd eaten for dinner. "Now, there's an angle! Salerno, the Bionic Dick. I could come to the ring dressed like a giant cock with a codpiece in my tights. Yeah, that'd drive the women crazy. I'll tell Tully that's my new angle."

"It was my idea!"

"I was kidding, you asshole."

Baines pouted a minute, then said, "Ain't nothin' wrong with my dick, y'know. I don't get no complaints."

Salerno gave a tight, nasty smile. "I think it's tough gettin' feedback, positive or otherwise, when your idea of sex is a razor blade in your right hand and your dick in your left. Just be careful you don't get fucked up some night and forget which hand's which." He hooted. "What would you call that, a do-it-yourself Lorena Bobbett?"

"I don't come that way *all* the time."

"I'm tellin' you, man, you got issues, serious issues. Guy who's gotta bleed to get off—that's an addiction, man. You're fuckin' hooked. You gotta go find yourself some kind of group, a Bleeders Anonymous meeting or something. Stand up and say, 'Hi, my name's Baines, and I *cut*.' "

"Wouldn'a ever started if Tully hadn't told me to," said Baines sourly.

"In the *ring*, dickhead, in the *ring*. To make the fuckin' vampires in the audience think they're gettin' their money's worth. Tully didn't say jack about juicin' for recreational purposes."

Baines swiveled the rearview mirror, looked at himself. "That asshole broke my nose."

"Serves you right. You should'a busted him up into little pieces before he got the chance."

"I would've," said Baines, "if that fucking bitch hadn't drove up and saved him."

Salerno laughed. "Talk about timin'! If I could'a seen your face when she drove up! Shit, I'd'a paid money for that!"

He speeded up to pass a semi, barely missed a collision with the black Miata that came racing out of the dusk in the opposite lane. Conceding defeat to the

fading light, he took off the Ray-Bans while Baines,
cursing, buckled his seat belt.

Baines was starting to feel weird and woozy, not all
of which was due to Salerno's nagging. A minor-grade
meltdown was going on in his head, crawly sensations
spreading under his scalp. He thought about the picture of a statue he'd seen once. A chick named Me-
dusa. Some Greek bitch who had snakes for hair. He
felt that way now, only the snakes weren't growing
out of his head, but seething around *inside* it. Slith-
ering and hissing and copulating in their nasty, reptilian way.

He turned to Salerno, seeking distraction, and said,
"I been thinking about somethin'. You ever done a
woman? I mean, with your bare hands?"

"What the fuck kind of question is that?"

"I been thinking about it, that's all—that broad
back in Vegas, the one was with Rollins. I been
thinkin' how she looked when I was doin' her. Her
eyes, man. Like when the razor blade went across her
throat, she just couldn't believe it. Like she was more
surprised than scared. And then she just kind of caved,
she gave up. She didn't fight me no more. And I was
wonderin', you think that was because she'd already
gone into that tunnel place with the light at the end that
I was reading about? Her eyes were lookin' at me,
but what she was really seein' was Jesus or God or
her dead daddy or whoever the fuck? You think she
was on her way to the other side while I was still
doin' her?"

"Ask a priest," said Salerno.

They drove in silence a few miles. Then Baines said,
"So have you?"

"Have I what?"

"Done a woman? With your bare hands, I mean?"

"Jesus," said Salerno, "not tonight. Not yet anyway."

Matt looked at the sad little stucco house with its
sagging screen door and peeling ocher paint, and was

surprised to realize he felt scared. Okay, he thought, this is it. *If she's here, what the hell do I say? If she's with a guy, what do I do then?*

It didn't matter, he decided. He'd come this far. He couldn't turn back. Maybe he could help her, give her money, a place to stay, a shoulder to cry on. And maybe she'd tell him to get the fuck out of her life. Or maybe she could help *him*. Offer him comfort from the nightmare around him, even if only for a few minutes.

Whatever, he knew he had to risk it. He had to see if Noel was inside.

As he neared the door, he could see the blue glow of a TV set flickering farther back in the house and hear the bray of a laugh track.

Stepping onto the front porch, he rang the bell and then knocked, but got no response. The screen door was locked, but there was a hole in the mesh big enough for him to put his fist through, so he did and lifted the latch.

"Noel? It's Matt. Are you here?"

A bulb burned in a hall leading off from the small, oblong living room. A pizza with one slice bitten into, pepperonis dried up to hard little disks, sat on the coffee table along with a large paper cup filled with what might have been Coke. On the sofa next to a pile of brown satin pillows, a *TV Guide* lay open with various TV shows circled in red.

For some reason, maybe to try to determine by the selection of shows if Noel had been the one doing the marking, he reached past the pillow to pick up the magazine.

Something slithered out from underneath the sofa cushion and flicked out its tongue. A small snake, coral-colored and gorgeous, it's lithe body banded in narrow strips of brilliant orange and mauve and black. Startled by its sudden appearance, he lurched backward, banging into the coffee table, almost upending it. The snake glided up onto the back of the sofa, then ran like a stream of colored water down the other side to the floor.

Matt stood watching it, his heart hammering absurdly fast, trying to recall where he'd seen such a snake before. It was certainly too small for Noel to use in her act, yet there was something familiar about it, something that made his flesh crawl. Made him want to put on heavy work gloves, not touch anything else in the house.

"Noel!" he yelled, although the house had an empty feel to it. He checked the kitchen and the two tiny bedrooms, which didn't take long. A few of the python cages were in the living room. The rest were housed in roomy aquariums along one wall of the kitchen. Well fed and drowsy, they snoozed in large piles in the threads of fading sunlight slanting in the kitchen window.

The refrigerator was open. When he went over to close it, he looked down and saw Noel's shoes. Pink, medium high heels, scuffed at the edges. He closed the refrigerator door, and there she was, wedged down on her side behind it. As though she'd been trying to open the door—to get to the pitcher of iced water inside maybe?—or was going toward the phone on the wall and grabbed onto the handle of the refrigerator for support as she collapsed.

He moaned softly, then lifted her gently, brushing the hair out of her face, thumbing her eyes shut. She felt incredibly heavy and yet utterly boneless, her legs sliding out akimbo on the linoleum floor, arms flapping and flopping, meaty and cold as something dead plucked from the sea, but there was no blood, no sign of injury that he could find. He wondered if maybe she'd taken something, committed suicide in despair over her illness. Or if maybe the virus was already so advanced that her heart had just given out, and she died on her feet without even knowing it.

"Oh, God, Noel, what did you *do*?" he heard himself cry. "Why didn't you call me back? I could've done something. I could've helped you." He cradled her body against him, rocking her, hiding his face in her hair. "Oh, Noel, I even brought the bike. We could've gone for a ride."

It was when he was raising one of her limp arms, trying to gather her together sufficiently to carry her into the living room, that he saw the tiny puncture wound on her left hand and the lurid, blotchy-purple area around it.

And he remembered the snake on the sofa.

Jesus God.

The snake. Banded snake. Colorful snake. Dangerous snake. *Coral* snake.

He'd seen one like it years ago when he took Shawn to the San Diego Zoo. Native to Florida. Deadly.

What the hell was she doing with a coral snake?

He laid Noel back down on the floor, found a long pair of stainless-steel tongs in a kitchen drawer, and began a meticulous, scrupulously careful search of the house, starting in the living room, where he found a small box marked LIVE ANIMAL that he presumed the snake or snakes—no reason to think there wasn't more than one—had come in. No return address, no warning that the contents could be deadly.

Suddenly the places where his skin was bare felt vulnerable and crawly. He was wearing cowboy boots, so his feet were safe, but his hands and wrists were exposed. Using the tongs, he poked around among the two armchairs and sofa, turning over pillows, easing cushions out onto the floor. The pythons in their cozy cages watched him with bright, baleful eyes.

He didn't see the brilliant little snake again, but when he was opening a desk drawer in the bedroom, he came across Noel's address book. Succumbing to morbid curiosity, he thumbed through it. Found his own name and phone numbers, of course—home, office, cell phone, and pager—along with those of any number of other men, including Brandon.

What he hadn't expected to find, however, was Howie DeGrove's name and number. Not just home, office, and cell phone, but the number Matt recognized as his private one—unlisted and zealously guarded. The number that, to the best of his knowledge, Howie reserved only for family members. What the hell would Noel be doing with it? And why would somebody be sending her a coral snake?

Barry, Phil, Noel—too many people around Matt were turning up dead. The only link, in fact, between the two men's deaths and now Noel's seemed to be Matt himself.

He thought about Shawn. He'd always believed the safest place the boy could be was at his grandfather's. But how could he be sure of that without knowing what the connection was between Noel and Howie? Or whether or not there was a reasonable explanation for the presence of a deadly snake in Noel's home?

Too many unanswered questions, Matt thought. To many things unexplained. Shawn would be disappointed, but the trip down to Baja would just have to wait.

He reached for his cell phone and dialed Howie's number. Tapping the tongs impatiently against the wall while he let it ring and ring and ring.

Chapter Thirty

Trina awoke from a fretful sleep to the sound of the basement door creaking inward. Like the rest of the windows and doors in the house, it was kept locked, and she tried to remember if she'd failed to secure it the last time she'd been down there, if the wind that was whipping the branches of the elm tree outside her window, might have made it swing open.

Her breathing quickened, and her heart began pumping out small bright bubbles of adrenaline that burst in her bloodstream like flares. The digital clock on the bedside table told her it was just after ten. Quietly she got up, slipped into a robe, and crept toward the door of her bedroom. Pausing and listening, holding her breath.

The house was achingly silent. Only the soft clack of the smaller tree branches scraping the panes and, far away in the street, music from the radio of a passing car that swelled briefly and then faded to nothingness. Still, she listened, muscles tensing as her pupils dilated to stare into the dark hallway, wondering . . .

A small frown creased her features. She turned back toward the bedroom, hesitated, then froze as a floorboard groaned somewhere on the first floor. Still, the noise might mean nothing. The house was old and often grumbled and growled like an underfed belly.

Lifting each foot carefully and placing it flat before committing her weight to it, she crept toward the stairs. An image came to her—so unbidden and sudden that it stopped her in her tracks for a second—her father somewhere observing this little tableau, his half-naked daughter skulking around in her grumbly old house, stalking an intruder who might or might not exist and might or might not be stalking her.

Quiet, quiet, she told herself.

She was at the top of the stairs now. If something or someone had entered the house, it was somewhere below her on the first floor or still in the basement. She thought of the locked door next to the video room where she'd told Matt she kept her gun collection, and a little tremor of excitement stole over her shoulders. She wet her lips and began to slink down the stairs.

She'd almost reached the living room when she heard the footsteps on the stairs coming up from the basement and realized there were two of them in the house. Her heart was pumping so furiously she began to feel sick. A queer, giddy kind of dizziness swept over her, and the floor seemed, momentarily, to ooze away into nothingness under her feet. Which way to go? Back upstairs toward the bedrooms, which offered places to hide, but no way of escape, down to the hall toward the front door, or through the kitchen and workout room to the back door, which led into a small fenced-in backyard and the alley behind it?

She opted for the back door, then changed her plan when she reached the short narrow hall that led to the kitchen and saw the broad back of the man blocking it. He was facing away from her, taking a step backward as he got ready to turn. He looked huge, monster-like. Her heart jittered and icy sweat streamed down her brow.

She whirled in the opposite direction and ran back toward the front of the house. Hand grasped the bannister, helping to pull herself up the steps two at a time. She reached the top of the stairs and was turning to run toward the warren of boxy, interconnecting rooms at the end of the hall when a hand went around her throat, shoving her face first into the wall, while the man's other hand delved inside her bathrobe, groping her breasts.

She smelled cologne, musky and laced with his sweat. When she arched and struggled against his immense strength, he put his mouth to her ear, but what he whispered—all vile threats and obscene suggestions—was eclipsed by the mad buzzing of the blood in her ears as he tightened his hold on her neck.

She didn't feel her legs when they failed to hold her, but she did know that she was starting to dream. A waking dream, in which she was swimming over a bridge made of water, her naked body warm and fizzy-feeling under a lush, moon-silvered lake, and she sensed that the man holding her controlled the pleasure and intensity of this dream by the degree to which he exerted pressure on her throat.

She gave herself up to it and began to follow the water bridge as it curved down and down, into a lake full of moonlight and stars, following the thunder of blood rushing away from her brain and into a galaxy of violent light that pulsed and blazed through her body.

In Noel's bathroom, Matt splashed cold water on his face, then dialed Howie's number for the third time. No point in calling the police. Noel was beyond help, and when the cops did arrive, he wanted to be sure he was back in San Diego—with an alibi this time. It occurred to him that Brandon had seemed in a hurry to get out of town. But if he'd had anything to do with Noel's death, then why would he have been so eager to tell Matt where he was going? Assuming, of course, he'd been telling the truth.

All he knew was that people were turning up dead with terrifying frequency, and all of them, one way or another, seemed to be connected to him—or to Howie.

Suddenly the line clicked, and Howie's voice boomed into the phone. "Hello?"

"Howie, it's Matt. Sorry to be calling so late, but—"

"What is it? Anything wrong?"

He decided to put off questioning Howie about his connection to Noel and said, "I know it's late, Howie, but I'm coming over now to get Shawn. I'll explain later."

"Well, you can't do that, Matt. I mean, this doesn't make sense. He's asleep."

"Wake him up, then."

"Why? What's going on?"

"I can't talk about it over the phone. I'm in Ramona, but I'm headed back to San Diego right now. I'll swing by in about an hour and pick him up."

Howie's voice grew strident. "Ramona? What the hell are you doing up there?"

"What difference does it make?"

"It's a violation of your bond, for one thing. Or is it of no concern to you that my daughter put up seventy-five thousand dollars of her own money so that you can be out there running around all over the state?"

Matt fought to keep his voice level. "I'm not skipping town, Howie. You aren't listening. I'm on my way *back* to town. I'm coming to get Shawn."

"Why? What can possibly be so important it can't wait till tomorrow?"

"I can't explain. But I want Shawn with me. There's some weird stuff going on."

"Weird stuff. Well, that certainly explains everything. Can you be a little more precise?"

"No, right now, I can't. But you know I wouldn't come and get Shawn if I didn't have a good reason."

There was a long pause before Howie said, "Tell me the truth, Matt, have you been drinking?"

"No, of course not. Do I sound drunk?"

"That's hard to say. All I know is you're not making any sense."

You wouldn't be making a lot of sense either if you'd just found your ex-girlfriend dead, he thought, *with your former father-in-law's private phone number in her address book.* "Be that as it may, Howie, I'm on my way to get Shawn. Have him ready."

"Hold on now, Matt. That isn't a good idea."

"Why not?"

"Because"—Howie sounded conciliatory now, embarrassed—"I'm afraid I wasn't exactly truthful with you just now, Matt. I lied to you. Shawn isn't here."

"But you just said—"

"Trina stopped by earlier. The two of them went to dinner, and she took him over to her house. When it got later, Shawn was tired, so she phoned and we agreed he'd spend the night over there."

"Dammit, Howie. What's he doing with Trina?"

"I just told you, they—is there a problem with Shawn's being with Trina?"

"No, no, I don't guess so. I'll call Trina and tell her to get Shawn ready, that I'm coming by."

"Well, all I can say is this is pretty damned inconsiderate of you, Matt. I thought we had an understanding that Shawn was going to Baja with me. It's all planned. We were going to take off tomorrow morning. Give the boy a break from all the chaos you've got going on right now."

"I understand, Howie, and I'm sorry I can't explain more. I just have a bad feeling about the way things are going, and I want Shawn with me."

"Matt, wait, I—"

"Sorry, Howie, I'll call you tomorrow. We've got a lot to talk about."

He hung up the phone and started to dial Trina's number.

Chapter Thirty-one

*Oh, Daddy, Daddy, you think you've got secrets! If
you could only see me now! If you could see your little
girl . . . if you could see . . .*

She emerged out of the slithery, star-spangled dark
in which her consciousness had been immersed, and
opened her eyes.

Checked out where she was and what had been
done to her.

Interesting.

She was spread-eagled and roped to a bed. Not the
one in her bedroom, but the mahogany one in the teal
bedroom, the one with the hand-carved Balinese posts
and the tasseled, pale saffron canopy. As she blinked
into the darkness, the shadows next to the bureau
parted and a man with very dark, almost blue-black
hair, stepped into view. He carried a very large knife,
which he placed at her throat.

"Hey, Salerno, let me cut her," said a voice from
outside in the hall.

"Shut the fuck up. It's me the bitch wants." He
drew the tip of the knife slowly along her lips and
chin and down between her breasts. "Don't you,
babydoll?"

"Who was that, Granddad?"

Howie acted as though he hadn't heard. He stood
out on the balcony, watching the waves crest and slope
onto black sand flecked with the sheen of a pale, pew-

ter moon. He wore shorts and a soft gray flannel work shirt that flapped in the breeze. When Shawn spoke to him a second time, he looked down at the cordless phone in his hand as though surprised to find he was still holding it.

"Granddad? You okay?"

"Yeah, sure. I thought you were sleeping."

"I wasn't sleepy. I was watching TV." He came out onto the balcony. "So who was on the phone? Was it Dad?"

"Your dad? Yes, actually it was."

When Howie didn't say anything else, Shawn blurted, "Something's wrong, isn't it? I mean, *really* wrong. I can tell."

Howie shrugged and turned away. His eyes were strange and vacant and very old, specks of wetness shimmering in the corners. He put his hand on Shawn's head. "I feel like a change of scenery would do me good. How would you like to fly down to Acapulco first thing tomorrow morning?"

"Acapulco? What about Baja?"

"We can go to Baja anytime. Baja's right next door. But Acapulco—now that would be an adventure. And after that, maybe to Rio. Trina *is* fond of Rio."

"Rio?" said Shawn. "Is that in Mexico?"

Howie laughed. "We'll do a tour of South America. Maybe learn a little geography on the way."

"That sounds like it'll take a long time. Did Dad say it was okay? Is that what you were talking about on the phone?"

"No, we weren't talking about Acapulco or Rio."

Dread crept quietly over the boy's face. He swallowed and said, "What *is* it, Granddad? Has something happened to Dad?"

"Your Dad's going through a very bad time. He says he needs to get away. So much is happening so fast. It would be bad enough for anyone, but with your dad's criminal record—"

"What, Granddad? What are you talking about?"

"Your dad thinks it would be best if he went up to

Canada for a while. I can't blame him really. It's only a matter of time before the police pin something on him that sticks. You understand, don't you, Shawn? You wouldn't want to see your father go back to prison. You'd rather know he's happy and safe somewhere in Canada."

Shawn's voice was a breathless gasp, the words tumbling out in a tumult. "What are you talking about? What are you saying? You're saying Dad ran away? You're saying he *left* me? You can't let him do that, Granddad! You gotta call him back. You gotta call him right now!"

"Now listen to me, Shawn. It'll be all right." Howie took the boy by the shoulders, but Shawn pushed him away and grabbed for the cordless.

"I don't believe you. Dad wouldn't do that to me. I'm gonna call him! I'm gonna talk to him!"

"He's not at home, Shawn. He was calling from a pay phone. I don't know where he was, just that he wasn't at home. He's gone, Shawn. I'm so sorry. He was already on the road."

Matt cut the motor on the Harley and nudged the rear wheel against the curb a few doors down from Trina's house. Across the street, a sprinkler outside a Tudor-style duplex hissed softly, casting a net of moonlit water across the lawn. A cat, silent, inquisitive, twitched its whiskers at him from the cover of some box bushes next door. At Trina's house, the porch light was on and another, paler light could be seen gleaming from behind white curtains on the third floor. Nothing else.

After a moment's debate, he opened one of the saddlebags on the side of the bike and took out the Ruger. Maybe it was ridiculous to be packing heat on the way to pick up his son, maybe he was being totally paranoid, but still, he decided, there were worse things than paranoia. Barry and Phil were dead. Noel was dead. Maybe her death and her connection to Howie could be explained, maybe he was dead wrong about that colorful little snake that looked so much like the one in the San Diego Zoo, but still there were too many coincidences, too many deaths. He wasn't going to take any more chances.

He rang the bell a few times, got no answer. Tried the front door. It was unlocked, which wasn't like Trina, who was well aware that break-ins and burglaries weren't unknown to Balboa Park and who had Howie to remind her of that fact, just in case she forgot. After their last meeting, he sure as hell wasn't anxious for Trina to catch him wandering around in her house uninvited, but he told himself all he wanted was to get Shawn and get out of there. If Shawn wasn't here, then he'd go over to Howie's. Why would Howie have said Shawn was asleep if he was with Trina? And if Shawn was really sleeping at his aunt's, then where the hell were they anyway?

Shawn probably talked her into taking him to a late movie, he told himself. Still, he couldn't get past the memory of his last evening in this house and Trina's late-night viewing habits in her basement movie room. Not that she'd expose Shawn to such things, but what if he wandered in, what if he heard the noises and got up out of bed the way Matt had done the other night . . . ?

The atmosphere in the house made the hair on the backs of his arms prickle. Silent, but not completely still, with that furtive sense of inhaled breath, of time being bided. He moved into the living room, acutely aware of his status as a trespasser in his former sister-in-law's house, and called Trina's name. Only silence, but still there was an undercurrent of—something—and he touched the revolver in his pocket, taking reassurance in its cool metal grip.

Although it was a warm night, the heater suddenly cut on, and the old house creaked and popped like a set of old bones. He smelled the citrusy tang of orange peels and a hint of gardenia perfume. Slowly, reminding himself to breathe, he ascended the stairs. Ahead of him stretched the broad, plushly carpeted hallway with Trina's photo collage on the wall. He

called Trina's name and then Shawn's. Got nothing
back but the heater's rattle and clunk.

In the first room he looked into, nothing moved but
some dust devils under a bed, disturbed by the air
displaced when he opened the door. A framed poster
from a Toulouse-Lautrec exhibit at the Met in 1995
showed a high-kicking Moulin Rouge vixen being eyed
by a black-hatted male. A mahogany dresser with a
stuffed bear, a trio of stiff-skirted collector-type dolls,
the kind that clearly no child ever played with, and a
framed photo of Princess Diana in her wedding gown.
The juxtaposition of the photo, the dolls, and the
teddy bear seemed to Matt odd—had he not known
who the blond woman in the elaborate wedding gown
was, he'd have assumed her to be a relative or a family friend.

He moved on down the hall, checked a bathroom
and a small linen closet before nudging open the next
door on the left. What he saw made the breath hitch
in his throat and his knees buckle. Trina, arms spread
over her head, roped to the bed, eyes huge and glazed,
giving no sign that she knew who he was or even that
she saw him. And the two men, Salerno with his fly
open, straddling her chest, Baines, fully clothed, playing the voyeur.

"Get away from her!" Matt yelled, but even as he
pulled out the gun, he was thinking that this didn't
make sense. He'd rung the bell, he'd called Trina's
name—they *had* to have heard him, yet here they
were, as unconcerned as if he'd walked in on the three
of them having tea. Arrogant bastards, they didn't
even look scared, but cocky, almost amused, and he
realized they must have been listening to his progress
through the house for at least a minute now, not even
bothering to interrupt what they were doing, but antic-
ipating his shock and horror when he walked in on
their little tableau.

"You, over by the wall," he ordered Baines. To
Salerno, he said, "And you, untie her. *Now!*"

"Ah, enter the hero," smirked Salerno, but he

folded himself back in his pants, zipped up, and began working the knots. When he finished freeing Trina's arms, she sat up slowly, whimpering and rubbing her wrists before bending forward to undo her ankles. She didn't look at Matt, but seemed to focus entirely on freeing herself, plucking at the ropes, pulling them loose with the graceful, measured movements of a seamstress working a loom.

Her almost dreamy slowness made Matt wonder if she was in shock. "Shawn, where is he?" he demanded. "Is he here?"

She looked confused. "No, of course not."

"Where is he?"

"At my father's."

"Howie said he was with you."

"I don't know why he would've said that. He's not here." She got to her feet unsteadily, reached for the silk robe with the swallows and butterflies that he'd seen her wearing the morning before, and put it on.

"Did they hurt you?" said Matt.

"I'm okay. Just shaken up."

"Fuck, she loved it," leered Salerno. "It's only a shame you had to interrupt when you did, Engstrom. I was getting ready to flip her over and fuck her in the ass. She especially loves that."

Baines snickered.

Trina hung her head.

"Shut the fuck up, or I swear I'll blow your dick out your asshole," Matt said, which quieted Salerno, but didn't completely erase the sick smile from his mouth.

"Go downstairs and call the police," he told Trina. "Tell them I'm holding these guys at gunpoint and give them a description, so they won't come in blasting away and shoot me by mistake. Then you wait outside till they get here." When she hesitated, he barked, "Get going! What are you waiting for?"

Clutching her arms around herself, she slunk out of the room.

Salerno said, "I wouldn't be so fucking confident if I were you, Engstrom."

"How do you know my name?"

"Oh, I know all about you, Matt. Why, at this point, I feel like we're practically brothers-in-law."

"You two killed Barry, didn't you? And that night at the Luxor, you threw Phil over the railing. Why? Was Phil into you or somebody you work for for gambling debts? Was that why he was embezzling money from my business? C'mon, answer me! This isn't one of your fucking wrestling angles, these were real people you killed!"

Baines twisted around. "It was my idea to dump Barry's body in your truck. Give you a little souvenir to take home."

"But why did you want to frame *me*? I wasn't any part of this, I was just—"

He saw Salerno's eyes track to the left and behind him. "Ah, Trina's back," said Salerno.

Without turning around, Matt said, "Trina? Trina, didn't I tell you to wait outside for the police?"

"I can't do that, Matt."

"What the fuck do you mean, you can't do it? You go now and you—"

"I'm so sorry, Matt. You shouldn't have come here. Daddy lied to you about Shawn."

A second too late, he heard the whoosh of air caused by a heavy object being swung—*fast*—toward the back of his head. There was a wild clanging as the room upended and swirled. His face crashed into the ceiling while the walls and the floor and the sides of his skull melted into a bottomless dark.

Chapter Thirty-two

He was dreaming. *Had* to be dreaming.

Or he was dead. But his wrists were bound behind him, and they hurt like a bitch. His ankles were bound, too, so tightly that one of his feet was starting to go numb.

But *Calla* was here. He could hear her talking. Her voice, just as casual and clear as if she were there next to him, asking did he want cream with his coffee. She always forgot that he took it black. Eight years together, and she never could remember how he liked his coffee.

Her voice was mock stern now, chastising someone lightly. "Jesus, put the camera away," she was saying. "You know how I feel about cameras. C'mon, I'm serious. Put it away."

He opened his eyes.

Shut them quickly. Unable to bear what he'd seen in just that brief blink. Then opened them again.

He was in Trina's basement movie room, stretched out on the leather love seat. Baines standing in the doorway, grinning. A tape was playing in the VCR, and Matt watched it, transfixed and disbelieving.

On the big screen a few feet away, images flashed. Burned themselves into his brain. Calla standing half naked in a tiny, brightly lit room. Manacles were attached to her wrists, and ropes threaded through the manacles were secured to a hook on the ceiling. She wore a white satin teddy with slits cut into it at the nipples and crotch and a thick, studded collar. A series of silver chains hung down from the collar and tumbled over her breasts. Slowly the camera panned down her body, lingering at her spread legs and the garters that stretched over her thighs, clipped to black nylons.

She glared briefly at the camera, then her expression changed as she focused on someone standing in front of her.

"Go ahead, if you want to." Her voice, low and sultry, oozed wetness. "But d'you have any idea what I paid for this outfit? You're gonna owe me. Big time."

A muscular male came into view. Salerno. His hair was longer and tied back in a ponytail. Ridges of muscle stood out along his shoulders and back. In his right hand, he carried a knife. Slowly he approached Calla, inserted the tip of the knife between the bra cups of the teddy and slit the flimsy garment down the center. Roughly he yanked it away, exposing her breasts.

"Wanna get fucked, little girl?"

Calla wriggled and thrust her hips. "Yeah, do it to me."

"You gonna beg me?"

"Yeah, I'll beg."

"Say it. Beg me to fuck you. Beg me to fuck you in the ass."

"Oh, please, yes, do it to me. Anyway you want. Just do it to me, *hard!*"

Then another close-up of her face, eyes half closed, lips curved in a drowsy, succulent smile, like she'd just inhaled some intoxicating drug. A look of pure lust, desire unbridled and carnal.

Blood was welling around Matt's wrists where he'd cut himself struggling against the ropes. He didn't feel it. Didn't feel his body at all anymore. The pain, excruciating, scream-wringing, centered in his chest and radiated out in great, numbing waves. He couldn't believe what he was seeing, what he was hearing. This couldn't be happening, yet it was, and now the camera zoomed in on two sets of genitals, a huge cock being pushed up between Calla's long, trembling legs. Hands on her naked hips, ramming her downward as Salerno thrust himself up. Impaling her, forcing out moans.

"Want more, little girl?"

Salerno reached up, unsnapped the collar, but left Calla's wrists tied. He closed his hand around her throat, and she appeared to swoon while Salerno supported part of her weight with an arm around the waist.

The camera zigzagged to the ceiling, caught Calla's half-shut, unfocused eyes, then moved downward to another pair of eyes: demonic, slanted, and ringed with small flames. Baines strode into view. Salerno had released Calla's neck. She was standing on her own now, but shaky-looking, dazed. Baines took Salerno's place, and penetrated her, while she whimpered and writhed and gave out long, shuddery sighs, an erotic vocalizing that, for Matt, was devastating in its familiarity. How many times had he heard those sounds issue from Calla? How many times had he watched her writhe and buck and wriggle exactly as she was doing now? Would the pain be any less, he wondered, if he believed that she was being raped? Or was it worse realizing full well the degree to which she was aroused and willing and enjoying this?

Baines said, "I'm going to do another line," and Salerno, off camera, could be heard saying, "Yeah, I want one, too. Let the bitch hang for a while and imagine what else we're gonna do to her."

Baines pulled free of Calla, who was watching him with rapt and avid eyes, like a shark who hasn't been fed. Moved out of range of the camera.

In the basement room, Baines, who was now standing next to Matt, licked his lips with a wet, smacking sound. "Here it comes," he said. "This is the best part. I could watch this over and over."

Then for a second, there was just a close-up shot of Calla's face: smeared lipstick, black smudges of mascara rimming her eyes, dark auburn hair wildly tangled around her shoulders. The camera was stationary now,

focused on a wide-angle shot that took in Calla's body
from the waist up.

A female voice, chirpy, mock little-girlish, hissed,
"Kiss me, cunt."

Matt froze. He felt like he'd been injected with a
fast-acting, paralysis-inducing poison.

Trina, naked, skin glistening with sweat, approached
Calla and said, "The boys have gone to suck each other
off. It's just you and me, big sister." She put her hands
on Calla's waist and rubbed against her, bestowed a lingering, openmouthed kiss. Smoothed the strands of wet
hair back from her face. "Enjoying this?" Suddenly she
drew back and slapped Calla resoundingly across the face.
The look of drowsy satiation left Calla's face. She looked
angry, then frightened.

"Trina, don't."

"Trina don't," she mimicked. "You liked that,
didn't you?"

"No."

"Didn't you?"

She hit her again.

Kissed her.

Hit her.

Kissed her again.

Blood on Calla's mouth, Trina's.

The camera, motionless, not wavering as Trina's
hands encircled Calla's throat. Playacting? Serious?
Calla's eyes went wide, then slitted down so she was
peering through the black, spidery fringe of her lashes.
The veins in the backs of Trina's hands began to
bulge. Her muscular wrists corded. Calla, hands still
tied above her head, began to arch her back and struggle. She thrashed wildly, trying to kick. And Trina
holding on, holding on, tighter and tighter, a look of
mad jubilation animating her face as she wrenched
Calla's head back and forth.

And Calla's movements growing less frenzied, di-
minishing, until finally she was still.

Someone came into the room, blocking the screen.
Shouting something.

The screen went dark. The film ended.

Baines whooped with glee.

"Wanna see it again? I'll rewind it. There's a bunch more tapes of us fucking and sucking. Trina wants you to see all of 'em, but I thought I'd let you see that one a few times more. Personally, it's my favorite. I never seen a snuff flick before, let alone a snuff flick where the snuffer and the snuffee were sisters. That must be one for the *Guiness Book of Records*."

Baines's words were babble. Matt could barely discern them as English. His head swarmed with static. Where his heart had been beating now lay a cold cavity in his chest.

"It's real, you know, 'case you had doubts," Baines went on. "Course Salerno and me, we just playact. Our rough stuff ain't real. We go easy on our opponents in bed just like we do in the ring. Trina, though, she don't understand playacting. She gets carried away." He laughed. "Not somebody you'd want to piss off."

"Calla," Matt heard himself murmur. "She murdered Calla."

"Oh, I don't think she meant to," said Baines, stepping into the room. "Afterward, she got upset. She was sorry. Hell, me or Salerno, we'd've stopped her if we'd've realized what she was doing. But, you know how it is, you do enough drugs, you get distracted, your mind wanders off . . . next thing you know, you come out of the bathroom and there's a dead body gotta be dealt with."

"So you just carried her out to a car and dropped her body off in Borrego Springs?" said Matt. "While for days, we didn't know—Howie and Shawn and I, none of us knew if she'd run away or been in an accident— we were all crazy with worry, praying we'd find her, and then the police called and said that some joggers—oh, you bastards, you fucking bastards."

"Hey, I didn't strangle her, all I did was fuck her," said Baines. "And a damn good fuck she was, too. Almost as good as her little sister. But then you'd know, wouldn't you? You've done Trina, too. Yeah, so don't act so fucking sanc—what's the word?—sanctimonious. She told us you and she got it on here one night. And the night your wife died, you were so drunk you couldn't even remember what happened—Trina had to provide you with an alibi." He hooted, smacked a hammy hand to his thigh. "That's a good one. The murderer providing an alibi for the guy who's not sure whether he could'a done it or not."

Matt drew his knees up and tried to reposition himself so he could see behind him. The effort of twisting his head brought a spasm of searing, excruciating incandescence behind his eyes and a blurring of vision, like somebody was roasting coals on his retinas. The love seat felt like it was floating on an uncertain sea or levitating up near the ceiling. When his head cleared again and he was able to open his eyes, he heard footsteps. Trina and Salerno stumbled into the room, clutching onto each other like adolescents getting off a ride at the fair. They were naked and smelled like a whorehouse.

"That was brave of you to try and save me from a fate worse than death," Trina said, "but some damsels like being in distress. These guys are old fuckbuddies of mine—ever since Daddy hired them ten years ago to be my bodyguards. They were okay as bodyguards, but I like them better as rapists who break into my house now and then and do unspeakable things to me. They've got—what would you call it?—a natural inclination."

"So it was all a sick game," said Matt. "Like what I saw on the tape."

"Did he watch the whole thing?" Trina asked Baines. When he nodded, she said, "Wind it back. Make him watch it again. Make him fucking memorize it. I want him to know every sound Calla makes, every word she whispers. He's just like Daddy—he loved Calla so fucking much, more than he could ever love me. I want him to carry the memory of how she died with him to his grave."

Chapter Thirty-three

•

Shawn crept down the back staircase of his grandfather's house like a burglar, planting each sneakered foot with care on the carpeted stairs, forcing himself to take the long, slow measured breaths that his dad had told him would quiet his heart and calm his nerves before a big test or a volleyball game. It wasn't that he feared being punished if he were caught taking off in the middle of the night. As far as he was concerned, there was nothing his grandfather could do to him that would matter at this point.

Except make him stay here.

He had to get out of this house, get out *now*, and for the first time in his young life, he wondered if he was feeling anything like what his dad must have felt when the cops hauled him off to prison and threw him into a cell. If it was anything like this—and he knew, of course, that it would have had to be much worse—then ironically it made it harder for him to hate his father. If, in fact, it was true what his grandfather had said—if his dad really had left for Canada. If he really had cut and run.

But Shawn didn't believe it. Wouldn't, couldn't believe his father capable of such treachery. Not now. Not after he promised.

The stairwell descended into a mahogany-paneled rec room with pool table, hot tub, and a couple of *Star Wars* and *Nintendo* video games that, Shawn knew, had been purchased primarily for his use. Beyond the wall, he could hear a TV going—CNN or ESPN from the sound of the announcer's measured baritone—and the low mechanical whir of a StairMaster in use. Granddad working out. For an instant, Shawn could imagine him vividly, dressed in sweats and cross-training Nikes, forearms corded and veined like thick vines had taken root under the flesh, sweat pearled on his temples, blue-gray eyes riveted on the digital readout that told how many miles climbed, calories burned, how much time elapsed since the start of the session. The thighs, thick as tree limbs under the sweats, working and straining, climbing Mt. Everest, scaling K-2, working, straining . . .

Then another image, as starkly etched in his mind as a white scar on darkly tanned flesh: his grandfather's fist gripping the tire iron, *Take it, for God's sake! Hit him!*

He started to cry. Silently, tears unfolding from the corners of his eyes and sliding quickly down the smooth planes of his cheeks. Why would his granddad lie to him about something so important? On the other hand, what if he *wasn't* lying, and his dad really *had* run away?

The StairMaster stopped. Shawn held his breath, then slipped past the pool table and through the French doors into an enclosed courtyard with a central fountain. On the rare occasions when his grandfather indulged in a Cuban cigar, it was here he came to smoke it. A faint tang of tobacco lingered under the fragrance of the perfumed water bubbling up and over a stair-step arrangement of smooth, layered stones. Scaling the low sandstone wall was no problem—he was up and over it, then dropped softly into the newly planted garden on the opposite side, the air around him suddenly moist and scented with the odors of turned earth and peonies and iris.

For just a second he allowed himself to think somewhat wistfully of the bike his granddad had bought him to replace the stolen one, but it was around the opposite side of the house, locked up in the garage, and would have to be forfeited. Besides, it was just a short distance between here and where he was going.

Wiping the damp earth off the soles of his sneakers onto the grass, he skirted the edge of the serpentine driveway, reached the broad, heavily trafficked boulevard outside, and began to jog slowly south, keeping his eyes peeled for a phone he could call his dad from.

Salerno zipped his pants and said, "How much money you keep in the house?"

"We just finished fucking our brains out, and that's all you can think about—money?" Trina kept her voice low as she wriggled into a pink T-shirt and snatched a pair of jeans from the closet.

"Why you whispering?" said Salerno. "What, you 'fraid Baines and your boyfriend can hear us down there in the basement? I don't think so, hon, I think that video's got both of 'em plenty distracted." He put his shirt on and started to button it. "Now, what about the money? I need some traveling cash."

"I've got maybe fifty dollars in my purse."

"Fifty fucking dollars! What the fuck's that? You're rich—you're supposed to have money."

"And where do you think I keep it, Steve—in a mattress? Maybe stuff a few grand in my makeup case or an empty tampon box?"

"Fucking fine, we'll go to an ATM."

She grabbed a pair of red thong sandals and bent to slide her feet into them. "Don't give me orders. I don't owe you anything."

He moved so fast she only saw a blur before his hands clamped onto her forearm and pinched, sending pain like a set of shark's teeth devouring its way through her biceps and shoulder.

She screamed and tried to twist away from the sensation of tendons being plucked away from the bone, but her legs turned to liquid and she sank to her knees, the red sandals scraping along the floor. He held her there a minute, looking down into her eyes so she could see the pleasure he took in what he did

to her, the hunger to do more. Then he let her go and
finished buttoning his shirt as he said conversationally,
"So which ATM was it that we're going to?"

A few minutes later Salerno stood outside the ATM
booth of a nearby bank with his back to the camera
while Trina punched in her code. There was a pause,
then the machine began spitting bills out into the
metal tray. She gathered them, came back outside.
Thrust the wad into his hand.

"Here."

He counted. Frowned. "You gotta be kidding! This
is all?"

"That's the limit for any twenty-four hour period.
You're lucky it's that much."

"What about savings?"

"That *was* savings."

"Fuck, you're *rich*."

"It doesn't matter if I'm Ivana Trump. It's a precau-
tion, so if somebody's holding a gun to my head—or
twisting my arm out of its socket—I can only get out
so much money at any one time."

"Yeah, did I hurt your arm?" He showed her the
butt of Matt's Ruger inside his jacket. "I ought'a
shove *this* in your fuckin' pussy, but you'd probably
get off."

"You think I'm lying about the limit? I'll give you
the fucking code, and you can see for yourself."

He debated whether or not she was conning him,
decided he didn't want to risk turning his face to the
camera in the corner of the ATM booth. "Fuck it, I
know your old man can get his hands on some serious
money. Wait till I talk to him and explain the situation—he'll be stuffing a suitcase full of it and begging
me to take more."

"Think so? Then you don't know my father."

They got back into Trina's Porsche, and Salerno
told her to take him back to her house. "What for?
Changed your mind about trying to extort money
from Daddy?"

"Not a chance. But I gotta check on Baines first. If

he's done what he was supposed to, by now he may be getting bored. You don't want Baines to get bored. Plus, I'm gettin' rid of that tape. I fuckin' don't know how I let you talk me into keepin' it in the first place."

Trina's eyes flashed to the right. She had on contacts that Salerno hadn't seen her wear before, pale green with all kinds of weird color flecks. Opal eyes, cloudy and cold, witchy eyes that, in spite of their creepiness—maybe because of it—made his dick twitch.

"I don't want those tapes destroyed," she said matter-of-factly. "They're all I have left of my sister."

Salerno chuckled darkly. "This sister you're referring to, would that be the same sister you choked to death?" He grabbed the dash and hissed, "Hey, watch the fuck out!" as Trina took a turn so sharply that the Porsche veered up on two wheels, bucked a curb, and bounced back down with an agonized screeching of undercarriage, like a metallic beast being skinned alive.

"Don't fuck with me, Steve. Remember what you are and always will be—an employee."

"And remember what I did to your arm. Want more of that, just keep on gabbing away."

She glared at him, but kept silent. He squelched a powerful, gut-deep urge to grab her behind the neck and bash her head into the steering wheel until her face turned to bright pulp. Crazy fucking psycho bitch. This was what you got when you consorted with nutcases. Salerno had long held that a female's prowess in bed was inversely proportional to her level of sanity, which probably explained how such wacko bitches stayed alive in the first place.

But in the case of men . . . his mind strayed back to Baines.

"He'll kill him, won't he?" Trina said. She was speaking almost to herself, but her voice broke into his thoughts so that his mind snapped back like a twanged rubber band.

"Naw, hon, I figure by now they're just startin' up a game of two-handed bridge."

"Because Matt may not seem like it, but he can be treacherous, devious. He's quiet as hell sometimes, but when he needs to, he can talk his way out of trouble."

"Don't matter what he says, Baines ain't listening," said Salerno. "Baines is tuned out. In his own world. That's the simplicity and the beauty of Baines."

Trina's slim fingers gripped the wheel so tightly that, in the darkness inside the car, the flesh had a luminous quality, like polished bone. She seemed to be talking to herself as much as to Salerno. "This is Matt's own fault. He didn't have to die like this. I know he didn't kill that guy Barry, but if the cops are so sure he did, then he and I could've run away together. Why the hell not?" She swung the car around another curve. Salerno gripped the door handle on the passenger side. "Matt can be so fucking stupid. He's got tunnel vision. He could have been fucking me, lying on a beach somewhere exotic and wonderful, sipping Mai Tais and living like a king."

"Yeah, I know that beach," said Salerno, smiling in spite of himself. "After tonight, that's where I'll be headed. Thailand."

Chapter Thirty-four

"Fuck, I love to watch sluts go at it!"

Baines squeezed his eyes shut in one of those sublime moments of masturbatory ecstasy, crooning to himself. His forehead looked a pitbull had been chewing on it. Blood streamed from a dozen slashes.

The man's hands were a flurry of motion, one pumping below the waist, the other—wielding the razor blade—sawing back and forth above. He looked like somebody showing off their coordination by attempting the world's most obscene party trick.

"You ever get that confused?" Matt said. "Slap yourself in the forehead and slice a notch in your dick?"

Baines growled and kept working.

Matt turned his head away. On the TV screen, unspeakable things were occurring. He could hear Calla's long, drowsy sigh. Not scared-sounding at all, but bone-deep, just-let-me-sleep weary, and he remembered how she'd sigh like that when he woke her up too early in the morning and roll over even as she snuggled against him, just-let-me-go-back-to-sleep, I'm-so-tired, please-Matt-leave-me-alone.

And Trina laughed, and the sound stabbed him all the way down to his soul. He felt stunned, overwhelmed, his mind wanting nothing more than to crash to a halt, like a car driven at a hundred miles an hour into a concrete wall.

Baines shuddered, put down the razor, and opened

his fist, swaying slightly as though the force of what
he'd just accomplished had dizzied him. Looked
around at the befouled room as though seeing it for
the first time.

"Fuck, Salerno's gonna be pissed when he gets
back. I better go clean up and then take care of business." He stood over Matt. "You ever heard of the
death of a thousand cuts? I read about that one time.
They used to do it in China to people who tried to
assassinate the king. Sounds like fun—I think I'll start
with your dick."

Matt didn't appear to be listening—the nerve of the
fucking son of a bitch. Baines booted him at the base
of the spine, a bone-jarring pain that rocketed breath-
takingly through Matt's back muscles. The cell phone
inside his shirt pocket flew out and skidded across the
carpet. Baines kicked it underneath the love seat.
"Just so you don't get any ideas about dialing 9-1-1
with your tongue," he snickered, walking out of the
room and aiming himself up the hall toward the
bathroom.

A second later, as though remembering Trina's final
admonition, he came back, grabbed the remote, and
rewound the tape so the segment with Trina and Calla
alone could play over again.

"So's you can watch your wife while you wait for
me," he said cheerfully.

Half blinded by the hot, numbing pain, Matt rolled
over on the blood-stippled carpet. His back was to the
TV, but he could hear a woman's soft, husky whimper.
Yeah, do me, do me, do me that way, do that again.
The voice was Calla's, and the pain of hearing it
throbbed through his body like a force that was slowly
pulverizing his bones. He rolled and bucked on the
coppery-smelling carpet, trying to use the voice to stir
in him some superhuman strength, but the ropes held.

Something slit into the meaty pad of his thumb. A
new kind of pain. Sharp and crystalline with the
bright, cold clarity of ice. The razor blade Baines had
been using, slippery with blood. He maneuvered it be-

tween the fingers of his left hand and began to saw at the rope. It seemed to take forever. Up the hall, he could hear water running. A toilet flushed. Then something that might have been a medicine cabinet slammed. Baines looking for first-aid ointment, maybe? Looking for drugs?

The top rope binding his wrists gave and broke. He commenced to saw at the second one.

The water in the bathroom started to run again.

Hands free, he bent forward and started working to untie his ankles.

Seconds later, Baines strolled back into the room, drying his hands on a towel. Instead of looking first to the right and down, to make sure Matt was where he was supposed to be, he glanced automatically up to the left, toward the obscene action on the TV screen. That was what Matt, flattened behind the door, had been counting on.

He sprang forward just as Baines, realizing his mistake, crouched and pivoted, a move that brought the fat folds of his neck into alignment with the crook of Matt's arm. Instinctively his hands came up to tear at the forearm across his windpipe. Matt swiped the razor blade left to right across his face. The blade slit open Baines's right eye, gouged a deep trench between the eyebrows, then sliced off part of the left eyelid.

Roaring, Baines clamped both hands to his face, and lurched into the room, Matt riding him, refusing to be dislodged. The razor blade was digging into his fingers, cutting him, making it almost impossible to hold. He swiped at Baines again, and the big man screeched and dropped to his knees.

"Did you like fucking my wife?"

Baines burbled something, blew blood out his nose.

"Did you like watching her die?"

He lifted the razor blade. For a second, raw hate—primal hate, as compelling and urgent as sex, as the desire to draw the next breath—gripped him, but when he put the blade down, Baines's neck was intact and he used the ropes that he'd cut through to tie the man up instead.

"I'm blind! I can't see! Get me to a hospital!" Baines wailed.

"If you're lucky," said Matt, "I'll find my kid at his grandfather's. *Then* I'll call the cops to get over here and send an ambulance for you. Till then, though, getting the cops involved would just slow me down. You'll have to wait."

Searching the room, he was unable to find the Ruger. Figured Salerno and Trina must have taken it with them.

From somewhere in the chaos of his thoughts, a memory nudged—something barely recollected, filed away as just so much more trivia at the time—the room Trina said held her gun collection. Visions of a private arsenal, of sawed-off shotguns and automatic weapons, enough firepower to overthrow a small Third World country filled his head. For once, one of Trina's crazy obsessions might do some good.

He hurled his weight against the locked door. It groaned and popped inward, admitting him into a tiny, triangular space, not much bigger than a jail cell, with a single overhead bulb connected to a chain. When he yanked it, a cool, lunar-like glow illuminated the cubicle and its contents, and for a stupefied second, he turned fruitlessly in a circle, with the look of disoriented consternation on his face of a man disembarked at the wrong subway station or airline terminal. Bewilderment and disbelief—then anger.

There were what some people might call weapons, all right, but it was a long way from high-caliber firepower. What it was, rather, was a dungeon. Nicely outfitted, too. High-quality leather whips and cat-o'-nine-tails hung from hooks on the walls. A preacher's bench and a heavy chair with leather restraints that looked like something you'd see on Death Row.

Not sure what good any of this stuff would do him, he nonetheless took a couple of items, and left by the back way. Trotting through the alley and back to his bike, he headed over to Howie's.

Trina stopped the car in front of her house. Said to Salerno, "After tonight, don't try to call me. Don't try to find me. I'll tell Daddy he's got to give you some travel money, but then you are *out of my life* forever. Understand?"

"Just like that?"

"Just like that. Daddy and Shawn and I will be somewhere in Mexico. I suggest you try that beach in Thailand. Just stay away from me. You got it?"

"Mexico, huh? When you coming back?"

"Maybe never. I may just keep going."

"You mean this ain't true love then, me and you?" smirked Salerno.

"It was fun, honey. You need stud references, Trina'll be glad to supply them."

The wrestler grinned, smacked his crotch. "I got all the references I'll ever need right here, sweetie. Enjoy Mexico. Try not to catch any crabs from the dinky dick wetbacks."

The sprinkler from the lawn across the street caught him as he was getting out of the car, wetting his pants cuff. He cursed and loped across the street as Trina pulled away from the curb. Headed to Daddy's as fast as all that horsepower could carry her. Crazy bitch. She might *think* she was going to Mexico tomorrow morning. Whole crazy fucking family of hers might think that. Didn't mean it was gonna happen, though. Unless the old man came up with enough cash to enable Salerno to live the good life in the tropical paradise of his choice, nobody was going anywhere except into the ground.

Baines must have turned off the VCR, or at least turned the volume way down, because the house was silent. Salerno didn't like that—silence, especially associated with anything Baines was involved in—didn't seem normal. He trotted down to the basement, saw the blood seeping out into the hall, figured Baines had got bored and carved up Engstrom. What he didn't expect to see was his partner hog-tied on the floor, skin white and waxy as he lapsed into shock, one eye cut through, the other one so full of blood it was impossible to tell if any sight remained.

No sign of Engstrom, but Trina's dungeon had been rifled, and the tape that had been left playing in the VCR was gone.

"Help me!" Baines moaned and thrashed on the floor, smearing blood into the carpet.

Salerno was reaching into his jacket when the phone rang.

He couldn't see it at first, but it was nearby, tinny and irritating and persistent. He listened.

Baines rolled from side to side, snorting blood and babbling about hospitals and getting help.

"Shut the fuck up!" yelled Salerno.

The phone kept ringing. He followed the sound to the love seat, got down on his hands and knees, groped about with one hand. Pulled out a brown cell phone in a slick plastic case. Looked at the object a minute, then punched talk.

"Dad? Dad, are you there?"

"Hello?"

"Dad? Who's this?"

"Uh, friend of your dad's."

"Where is he? Can you go get him?"

He tried to think quickly. "Uh, no, we were having a beer, and he stepped outside for a cigarette."

A gulp and a long pause. Had he said something wrong?

"Dad's drinking?"

Fucking great, thought Salerno, guy must be on the wagon or something. "Nonalcoholic beer," he said quickly. "That's what I meant."

"Oh."

"Look, where are you? Your dad's gonna be back any minute. I'll tell him where you are. He's worried about you."

"He is?"

"Sure he is. Where you at, he'll come get you."

"Well, I *was* over at Granddad's, but—I'm not there anymore."

"So where are you? How's your dad gonna find you if you won't say where you are?"

"Right now? I'm at a pay phone outside a 7-Eleven, but there's a cop pulling up, and I don't want to stay here. Tell my dad I'm headed over to the job site."

"What job site?"

"Bledsoe-Tull."

"Where's that?"

"Dad'll know."

"Right, but refresh my memory. Where's it at?"

"Mission Beach."

"Where—?"

The little shit hung up the phone.

Salerno dashed upstairs, found a phone book with a city map, and located the Bledsoe-Tull intersection, which turned out to be only a couple miles east of old man DeGrove's home.

Having found what he wanted, he quickly dialed Trina's cell phone. "Where you at, babe?"

"I'm at Daddy's. Just making the turn into the driveway."

"Well, looks like you got your wish. Engstrom's still alive, and the tape with little Trina's fun and games on it is gone. Three guesses where he's headed."

Trina's voice came back, hard and biting. "I'll take care of Matt. If he thinks he's going to show that tape to Daddy, he's fucking crazy. I'll kill him first."

" 'Atta girl," said Salerno, and hung up.

Having alerted Trina, Salerno trotted downstairs with the phone book in one hand, Matt's gun in the other. Judging from the amount of blood and other bodily fluids already on the carpet, he figured the mess in the TV room was already disgusting enough, so he jammed a pillow underneath Baines's head. Unable to see what was coming, Baines blearily thanked him for it—before Salerno fired a bullet up into the roof of his mouth and blew out the back of Baines's head.

Chapter Thirty-five

Matt was ready to break a window to get into the house when Howie finally unlocked the front door. He wore a terry cloth robe and sandals and, from the rate of his breathing and the amount of sweat on his forehead and upper lip, looked like a man who'd just completed a ferocious workout despite the hour.

His eyes bored into Matt with an intensity suggesting he were possessed of X-ray vision and was examining the contents of Matt's skull for brain damage.

"You've no right to come here, Matt."

"Howie, why did you lie to me? Shawn's not with Trina. Where is he?"

Howie's mouth twitched almost imperceptibly, but his eyes remained cold and unflinching, steel ball bearing in the deep pits of the eye sockets. "He's upstairs. Asleep."

"Can I believe you this time?"

"You have my word."

"There was a time when that would have been good enough. Now I'm sorry to say it's not. I want to see him."

"It's going to have to be good enough," Howie said, "because I won't let you see Shawn. Not in the condition you're in."

"What are you talking about?"

"You've obviously been in a fight. You're drunk

or—under the influence of something. You're not rational. Not making any sense."

"Shut up, Howie, and listen to me." He held up the tape. "If I'm not making sense, it's because I just got through watching *this*. I want you to watch it. The police will have to see this, but I want you to see it first."

Gingerly, like he wasn't sure whether the object in Matt's hand was a tape or a live grenade, Howie backed up from the door, let him in. "If you weren't the father of my grandson—" His voice trailed into an unintelligible muttering.

"Listen to me. Trina's going to go to prison. For a long time. Now, maybe, just maybe, you can hire F. Lee Bailey to figure out a way to get her treatment in a good hospital instead of locked away in some prison—that's up to you—but if you're going to be of any help to her, you'd better look at the fucking tape before I take it to the police!"

"Trina's in trouble? What are you talking about?"

"Watch the tape. But I warn you, it's a nasty, horrible thing. Once you've seen it, you can't unsee it, you understand? So if you'd rather not, if you'd rather I took it straight to the police—"

Howie sighed and shook his head in the short, jerky motion of a dog with a fish bone in its throat. "No, no, if Trina's in trouble, I want to help her. I can't do that by burying my head in the sand. Whatever I have to look at, I'll look."

Some of the anger seemed to have burned off. He looked older and, for all his bulk, somehow decrepit, as he padded across the floor in his slippers to the sunken living area off the entrance hall. "The VCR's over there," he said, indicating a TV set that occupied the central portion of a teakwood entertainment center covering most of one wall.

Matt popped the tape in, glanced around. "Where's the remote?"

"Is this what you're looking for, Matt?"

He whirled at the sound of Trina's voice, saw her

stand up from behind the other side of the sectional
sofa. A semi-automatic gleamed in her hand. "How
could you do that to me, Matt? How could you rape
me? I ought to blow your head off—but I think Daddy
wants to." She handed the gun to her father. "Thanks
for playing along with him, Daddy, while I got one of
your guns. He's all yours now."

Matt said, "You're making a big mistake, Howie. I
didn't do anything to her."

"You evil bastard," Howie said, "how *could* you?
On top of every other evil thing that you've done to
me, Matt, to this family—I swear to Christ if Shawn
weren't upstairs, I'd shoot you where you stand, and
I'd do it carefully—no major organs—so you could lie
there and bleed to death while you thought about the
vile things you've done."

"What the hell are you talking about?"

"I told him what you did to me," said Trina. "Told
him how you broke into my house tonight and raped
me. I told him how it wasn't the first time, either, that
you raped me before, years ago, but I didn't say anything because you were married to my sister. But tonight was the last straw, Matt. Tonight was the last
time you're going to terrorize me." She turned to
Howie. "Look at his hair, Daddy. He's got blood in
his hair from where I tried to fight him off." Her voice
broke. She wrapped her arms around her midsection
and swayed back and forth. "The things he did to me,
Daddy, the things he said, the things he made me
do—"

"She's lying," said Matt. "She's a monster. She and
her buddies, two goons she picked up at the wrestling
arena, tried to kill me. I left one of them tied up over
at her house. You don't believe me, Howie, look at
the tape. Just look at it. Then you still want to blow
my fucking head off, go right ahead!"

Howie glanced to the side. "Two goons? What's he
talking about?"

"I had a couple of friends over, that's all. Matt
scared them off with his psycho act before he attacked

me. He's a crazy man, Daddy. You were right all along. I should have believed you from the beginning. He murdered Calla because she wouldn't come back to him. He admitted it."

"I know, Trina," Howie said. "I've always known."

Matt exploded, "You can't believe that! She's brainwashed you. That tape on the table—watch the damn thing and you'll *see*. It's no mystery who killed Calla, she *taped* it, for God's sake! Taped herself murdering her own sister along with those two steroid freaks she's shacked up with."

"He's lying, Daddy," Trina said meekly, "but a little bit of it's true. The two goons—he means Baines and Salerno. After you hired them to be my bodyguards, I slept with them a couple of times. We still get together occasionally for old times' sake. That part's true. But I never pretended I was what you'd call a 'nice,' sweet virginal girl. I fuck around, and you know that, and it's not any big deal, but that doesn't mean I killed anybody."

"Of course it doesn't," Howie said. "He's a crazy man, and a coward, trying to put the blame on the very woman he defiled."

"So what are you going to do?" said Matt. "Shoot me in your own living room? With my son upstairs? You're not crazy enough to do that. Watch the tape. If it doesn't change your mind about me, call the cops. Have me arrested. Do what you have to."

Calmly, Howie leveled the gun. "Shut up, Matt. I will do what I have to do. I've *always* done exactly what I had to do. I know you murdered Calla. There was never any other explanation that made sense. After you got out of prison you were desperate to get her back, but she'd moved on. She wanted other men. You couldn't stand that, so you killed her. Trina told me she lied to provide you an alibi that night, that she had some kind of misguided crush on you, but I already knew that, too.

"If there's one thing in all the world I know how to do, it's wait. I didn't want Shawn to have to lose his father in such a terrible way right after he lost his mother. And I didn't want the criminal justice system to deal with you. Leave you to them, and you'd be back on the street in a couple of years. Crime of passion, that kind of lamebrain nonsensical bullshit. I wanted you for myself, I wanted to destroy you in bits and pieces, no matter how much time and patience and planning it took."

"And if destroying me meant having Barry and Phil murdered, then so be it, right?"

"I found out your little bookkeeper was a compulsive gambler who was desperate to pay off some debts. I offered to help him out in that department, plus a bonus, if he could do some tinkering with the company books so it would look like you'd been cheating your clients. Then Barry caught on—Phil had nothing to do with Barry's death, by the way, he only phoned me to let me know Barry knew what was going on and he was going to tell you—so I arranged to have Barry taken care of in a way that it would appear you were the killer. Then you showed up in Vegas, and things got out of hand. Phil wasn't supposed to die, but those two goons, as you quite aptly call them—they panicked."

"Noel?" Matt said, "What about Noel?"

Trina's head swiveled around. "Not that little bimbo we met at the car dealership?"

"Noel was the pièce de résistance," said Howie. "A true touch of genius, if I do say so myself, insurance that even if you don't get the death penalty from a judge, you already got it from dipping your cock in a poison well. But the last time she called, she told me she already gave you the sad news about that."

"Last time I saw her, she didn't say much of anything, Howie. She's dead."

"Oh." He winced slightly, shook his head. "Well, I'm genuinely regretful of that. A pretty girl, but greedy, very greedy. Always wanting more money. Something had to be done about her. Salerno wanted to kill the brother, too, but I told him, no, there'd already been too much death. I have a friend who deals in exotic reptiles, and I suggested to Salerno that he come up with something befitting Noel's lifestyle. I take it he accomplished that."

"You sick bastard," said Matt. "You had her killed."

"Only when it became obvious she wouldn't leave me alone. Otherwise, I'd have much preferred to let nature take its course. I saw her medical records. They weren't pretty."

"You're saying the thing I had going with Noel, it wasn't—I mean—" He was shocked at the surge of emotion that rose in him.

"That it wasn't love? I'm afraid not. Although I will tell you this, she did care for you. Claimed she did, anyway, that she was having all sorts of remorse over sleeping with you without protection. Didn't stop her from doing it, though, once I offered the right price. Been tested yet, by the way? I hear guys who are HIV positive have an especially hard time of it in prison."

Trina's eyes, round and huge, shone with pleasure, and she wriggled her hips with delight and admiration, like a pompon girl watching the quarterback go for a touchdown.

"Jesus, Daddy, I had no idea you could be so Machiavellian. I can't believe you came up with all this and never told me about it. But then you've always known I had a soft spot for Matt. If I'd known what was going on, especially if I was planning to fuck his brains out if I got the chance, I might have warned him what you were up to."

"Those wouldn't have been my words," Howie said, "but something along those lines. Putting up bail for him, that was generous, but misguided."

"You crazy sick bastard," Matt said, "to go to all this trouble to set me up for something I didn't do. I didn't kill Calla. All you have to do is watch this tape to see how your daughter died, and you're going to, whether you shoot me or not."

Ignoring the gun, he slammed the tape into the VCR and hit the rewind button on the machine.

"No!" Trina shrieked. "Don't look at it, Daddy! It's a trick! He's just stalling for time! Don't look at it, Daddy, please!"

She started across the room, but Howie grabbed her around the waist, yanking her backward. "What's wrong with you? Why *can't* I watch it?"

"The only reason he wants you to see it is to hurt me more than he already has," Trina said. "I can tell you what's on it—me and Calla having sex with Baines and Salerno. Doing dirty, filthy stuff. Talking trash. You're my father. It's not right for you to see something like this with your two little girls. The tape should have been destroyed a long time ago. It's one thing for you to see me like this, you know I'm a slut, but not Calla. Calla was the good girl. She wouldn't want you to see her like this."

"Calla's *dead*," Howie said, his words stone. "She's dead and her personal modesty is no longer of concern to me. Whatever she did, whatever you did, you're both my daughters and I love you. But I have to watch this thing, however much I may not want to, so I can judge for myself what Matt thinks is so goddamn important. If it offends my sensibilities, so be it."

Without relinquishing the gun, he hit the PLAY button on the VCR and sat down.

Chapter Thirty-six

Shawn was surprised at how different the Bledsoe-Tull job site looked in the darkness. With no men working, shouting, hanging out on a break, no trucks pulling up or leaving, no noise of cranes and forklifts in use, the structure loomed above him, a gaunt and deserted shell, beams stretching up six stories high into the starry silence. A backhoe and a hydraulic cherry picker were parked over near the west side. Up above, a tower crane swung out into the night sky like some kind of weird, skinny-necked dinosaur. He found himself getting a little freaked out, then chided himself for acting like a little kid. Everything was going to be fine. His dad wasn't running off to Canada. He would be here soon to pick him up.

The recent rain had turned the earth around the building into glutinous muck, a loblolly of mud, and Shawn crossed it gingerly, staying as much as possible on the two-by-fours the men had laid down at angles to one another to form a makeshift walkway. He stepped around a row of sawhorses where a sign posted read: DANGER. HARD HAT AREA. Skidded down a mud-slick embankment and cut through a corner of the underground parking garage, where his mud-caked sneakers slapped wetly against the foundation. Some mosquitoes decided his neck and ear made a perfect buffet, and he waved them away. He broke into a run and came up, breathing fast and shallow, at the opposite end of the underground parking, and made his way toward the trailer.

He retrieved the key from the little magnetized box stuck underneath the handrail, kicked off his sneakers so he wouldn't track mud inside, and let himself into the trailer. The cramped room reeked of cigarettes and sweat, so he left the door cracked and plopped down in the cracked, leather swivel chair behind the big desk, listening to the flutter of moths attracted by the light, beating their wings against the glass fixture. When the mosquitoes started bothering him again, he got up, thinking to close the door, and almost collided with a dark-haired, brawny-looking man who was coming up the steps to the door. The guy stood there, all muscle and attitude, blocking the light. Shawn noticed his eyes. They were dark slits, like he was either hungover or just pissed off and beat. Short scars, deep and ugly-looking, framed the outer edges of his eyes.

"Shawn?"

"Yeah." He knew this was the man with his father, the guy he'd talked to on the phone, but he felt weird about it. Something about the guy's face, something familiar. "Where's my dad?"

"He couldn't make it," the man said, pacing around the narrow interior of the trailer. He wasn't more than six feet tall, but something about the bulk of him, the width of his shoulders and the way the muscles of his chest bulged below the tight T-shirt he wore underneath the sport coat, made the trailer seem way too small for him, like a cage he might start to dismantle any minute.

Shawn retreated behind the desk, but stayed standing. "What'd you mean, he couldn't make it? Where's he at?"

"He stayed at the bar for a couple more drinks," said the man.

"My dad doesn't drink."

"Yeah, I figured that out. But he was sluggin' back those Shirley Temples."

"So when's he gonna be here?"

"He's not. We're gonna hang out here for a little bit, you and me, while I make a phone call or two, then we'll go meet him at the bar."

Shawn digested this information, found it bitter. "I'm going to call him."

"Hey!" The guy had been standing at the door, gazing out. Now he whirled and barked out the "hey" the way a dog owner might issue an order to a pet about to bolt out into the street. Absolutely authoritative, no nonsense. Shawn found himself backing up, intimidated by the commanding voice and powerful frame until those very qualities roused something in his memory. Slowly the expression of fearfulness on his face transformed until he was grinning ear to ear.

"Hey, I know you! You're Salerno, you're BuddlyLee Baines's manager!"

The man looked a little caught off balance by the remark, seemed to hesitate as though mentally checking to see if he was, indeed, who the boy claimed he was. Then he gave a short jerk of the head and said gruffly, "Yeah, yeah, that's me."

"I've seen you on TV. You're a friend of my dad's?"

"Yeah, we're old buddies."

"Really? You are? My dad never said anything about it."

"Well, maybe he don't tell you everything, you know what I mean?" He shut the trailer door, leaned up against it. "Your grandfather, he's a pretty rich guy, ain't he?"

Shawn shrugged, answered the way he thought Howie would have wanted him to. "He's got enough."

"Enough millions, you mean? So he won't be going on food stamps no time soon? Good, I'm happy for him." He grinned. "You know I stayed at one of his hotels one time. In Honolulu a few years back. Yessir, a DeGrove Hotel with TV monitors in the halls and a security guard on every floor. Felt like I was in fucking Attica. Didn't know whether I should check out at the front desk or tie bedsheets together and escape out

the shatterproof window. Your granddad, I think he'd
be better running prisons and insane asylums, where
the idea is to keep people in, than hotels where they're
s'posed to be free to come and go."

"My granddad wants the people who stay at his
hotels to be safe."

"Yeah, a sound sleep in a safe place," said Salerno,
parroting a line from one of the DeGrove-chain ads
in an in-flight magazine.

"He worries about his customers," said Shawn, feeling like he needed to defend Howie but not exactly
sure why.

"So this gramps of yours who's such a worrier, he
know where you are right now?"

Somewhat reluctantly, Shawn shook his head.

"If he was gonna come lookin' for you, would he
know to look here?"

"I don't think so," said Shawn. "He thinks I'm still
at his house, asleep."

"Why'd you run away?"

"He said some bad things about my dad." A mos-
quito hummed near his face, and he whacked it, leaving a small smear of blood on his hand. Then: "Hey,
can I ask you something?"

"Shoot."

"Well, I was just wondering—pro wrestling, I know
it's fake, but how much of it? I mean, do you ever hit
each other for real? And do you rehearse all the
moves in advance, or do you just kind of wing it as
you go along?"

"Oh, a smart mark," laughed Salerno, but there was
no mirth in his eyes. "Last smart-ass asked me questions like those, I punched out his lights."

"Sorry," said Shawn, wondering if this guy was
really an asshole or if he just got off pretending like
his super-tough, raging TV personality was the real
thing. Still, he couldn't meet Salerno's fiery eyes.

The wrestler pulled a cell phone out of his pocket.
"What's your granddad's phone number?"

"Why?"

" 'Cause we're gonna call him, that's fuckin' why."

"But I thought you were gonna call my dad. Grand-dad thinks I'm still at his house. He's gonna be pissed off."

"Oh, he'll be more than pissed off when I get through talking to him," said Salerno, and waggishly tilted one brow. "Now, give me the number."

Shawn tried to make sense of this—the wrestler he knew as Salerno not only being friends with his dad but now wanting to talk to his grandfather. Because he'd admitted to running away? But Salerno was going out of his way to act like his tough-ass TV character, so why turn into a do-gooder all of a sudden? Suddenly Shawn understood. Salerno knew his grandfather was rich. Maybe he thought that he'd get a reward—or he planned to demand one—for bringing him safely back to Howie's house. That rankled him—it seemed greedy and altogether unfair and not even in keeping with the kick-ass, rebellious character Salerno played in the ring. If Salerno wanted to help him, he ought to be calling his dad.

"Well?" The black eyes bored into his.

"I don't know his number. I forgot it."

"Like fuck you forgot it." Salerno moved toward him like a cat closing in on a pigeon. Then he seemed to catch himself, and a strained facsimile of a smile slithered across his lips. "Now, look, Shawn. I'm trying to help you, understand? So we can do this easy or we can do this hard, but I fuckin' well know you know your grandfather's phone number, so spit it out, kid, or pretty soon what you'll be spittin' out is teeth."

Shawn laughed nervously and hesitated, not totally sure if this was real or if Salerno was putting him on. Maybe because he'd dared to question wrestling's authenticity the guy was playing with him? Maybe Salerno was one of those wrestlers who took themselves and the sport real seriously, who needed to believe that the fans believed it was real.

He thought fast and concluded that Salerno couldn't possibly be threatening him for real, that this was just the kind of stunt a wrestler would play on a kid to see if he cracked under pressure and then laugh in his face when he did. A mean trick, to be sure, but then these were tough guys and probably ribbed each other mercilessly all the time.

So he took a deep breath and, making his voice as manly as he could—which wasn't very manly at all, since his voice hadn't changed yet and using the kind of grammar his grandfather would have described as execrable, but which seemed to go with the situation, said in a single breath, "I ain't scared of you, dick-head. My granddad's sixty-three years old, and he could whup your candy ass."

When the words were out, even Shawn was astonished he'd said them. Horrified really. What was he thinking? Making the kind of dumb-ass, I'm-gonna-kick-some-butt-around-here, hollow threat that TV tough guys tossed around all the time, but not something you said in real life. *Nobody* said that in real life. Not to somebody like Salerno at any rate.

And Salerno, with a fake sweet smile, said, "Sticks and stones, Shawn, sticks and stones," and moved in on him, eyes glimmering an arctic rage.

"Now that you got that out of your system, kid, we're gonna get down to business. How old are you anyway? Ten, eleven? You jerk off much? I bet you do. All kids do. How 'bout if I start this conversation by breaking all the fingers in your right hand?"

And the truth suddenly hit Shawn: *This is real.* "N-n-no." He stepped back until the knobs of his spine pressed the wall. Salerno advanced on him. "So you wanna know how much is real and how much is fake, asshole? Well, lemme tell you something, this here, right now, is fucking real. The noise of your finger bones crunching like Kellogg's Corn Flakes, that's gonna be real."

"Goddamn women, lock a man out of his own god-damned house, middle of the goddamned night, I ought'a—" a tipsy voice grumbled as the trailer door swung open. Shawn thought he'd pass out with relief.

Coop swayed there holding a pint bottle of Jim Beam in one hand. Wearing dungarees and a forest-green work shirt and an expression that went in an eyeblink from utterly bewildered to skulkingly guilty. His eyes flashed from Shawn to Salerno and back to Shawn without seeming to understand anything beyond the fact that he'd been caught sneaking into the trailer belonging to a company he no longer worked for.

"Hey, Shawn, I just stopped by to pick up some paperwork, didn't think anybody was here, I—" His gaze dropped to the floor. "Look, I'll be on my way. No need to say anything to your dad about this, right?" He started to back out the door, then stopped, squinted blearily at Salerno while holding on to the doorjamb like a man trying to keep his balance on the bow of a storm-tossed ship. "Now who the hell would you be?"

Salerno's hand slid to his hip.

Shawn shouted, "Coop, look out!"

But by this hour of the night, Coop's reflexes and synapses were soaked silly in a blood-bourbon cocktail. When the gun went off, he looked more like a man who'd just heard a very bad joke than somebody who'd just taken lead. The bullet seemed to lift him off his feet and muscle him back into the wall, where he stood for a second as though nailed there, while blood formed a dark, growing puddle on one side of the forest-green shirt.

Salerno looked at the gun as though disappointed in its performance. "I can't fuckin' waste any more bullets," he said, like a smoker lamenting the fact that he's almost out of cigarettes, and took two steps forward, raising the gun butt-first as he went, and smashed Coop across the side of the head.

Shawn screamed, and even to *his* ears it sounded high-pitched and birdlike. He realized he'd never been so scared in his life, never seen anybody dead before, and surely Coop had to be dead, the way the blood was soaking the front of the shirt, running down his whiskery cheeks and into the corner of his half-open mouth, where it gave the effect of ghastly red lipstick.

Salerno grabbed Shawn by the arm and said in the modulated, mellifluous tones of a department-store Santa, "Was that real enough for you, son? Or would you like to see more?"

"Please," whispered Shawn.

"Fuck," hissed Salerno, looking at Coop, "now I gotta get rid of him. But first, Grampa's phone number—let's have it."

Shawn gave it to him. "What are you going to do to me?"

"Put you someplace for safekeeping while I see how much your old fart of a granddad thinks you're worth." He grinned, the scar tissue around his eyes webbing. "And you better hope that it's *at least* as much as one of his hotels."

Chapter Thirty-seven

"Howie, give me the gun," Matt said. "There's no need for it now. We have to call the police."

But the old man wasn't listening. A few moments earlier, when the tape played out the final seconds of Calla's life, he seemed to fade away into a world of his own, a place of bottomless grief and devastation. When he finally managed to turn his head toward Trina, he seemed to look through her and past her, as though addressing someone who stood a few feet behind her.

"Dear God," he whispered. "You cold-blooded, evil girl. I loved you with my whole heart, loved you every bit as much as I loved your sister. And you killed her and were even perverse enough to tape yourself doing it. You didn't even kill her in a fit of rage. You did it on a whim, an impulse. Because something about doing such an evil thing must have *aroused* you."

He shook his head. "All the time and planning and care I put into my plans to destroy Matt—and it was you who murdered Calla—my own daughter. How? How did I raise such a monster?"

Trina curled bonelessly on the sofa, knees pressed into her chest. She whimpered, "What happened was an accident. It was a game that Calla enjoyed as much as I did, but it got out of hand. I never meant for her to *die*. When I realized she was dead, it was the worst moment of my life. I wanted to go to the police, but Salerno and BuddyLee wouldn't let me. They panicked. They insisted we had to get rid of the body, we had to dump her somewhere."

"So you just went along with it," said Howie. "You're saying you tortured and killed your own sister, but only because she wanted you to."

"You don't understand!" Trina shouted, real anguish in her voice. "Calla wasn't the little miss perfect you thought she was. She loved bondage games and group sex and sex with women—she loved all of it! She wanted to *do* all of it! Matt going away to prison gave her a chance to try stuff she'd never done before, so I introduced her to Salerno and BuddyLee, that's all. Then Matt got out and wanted to pick up where they left off, and Calla wasn't interested. She loved the life I'd shown her. She was only too happy to participate."

"This tape doesn't look like she's enjoying it," Howie said. "She wanted you to stop. She's *begging* you to stop. It's right there on the tape."

"It's a *game*," Trina said tearfully. "Calla was actually the one in control. We could only go as far as she wanted us to. I didn't know I was choking her for as long as I did. I'd done it before. I'd watched Salerno do it and had him do it to me. I had no idea it would *kill* her. I was scared to death when I realized she was dead."

"So scared that you saved the tape so you could watch it over and over?" Matt said. "So you could have *me* watch it. Even if you killed Calla accidentally— which I don't for a minute believe—you still *saved* the fucking tape so you and your buddies could get off on it."

"That's not true," said Trina.

"I think it is," Howie said. "I know what I saw on that tape, and what I saw was my daughter being murdered. And to think that all these years I was so sure that Matt killed Calla, because she wouldn't take him back when he got out of prison."

Matt's fists clenched as he turned toward Howie,

disgust rising in his throat like the remnants of a bad meal.

"And because you thought I murdered Calla, that made it perfectly justifiable to kill anyone else you had to in order to frame me," said Matt. "Jesus, Howie, what a waste of life. I understand now what's wrong with Trina. She's like you, she's exactly like you. The same disease has contaminated both of you— a complete disregard for anybody's life except your own. You're both sick and warped and pathetic."

"Shut up!" shouted Trina. She turned to Howie. "Make him shut up, Daddy! Shoot him! Shoot him now!"

Instead, Howie pivoted so that the gun was aimed at Trina. Their eyes locked. Trina, seeming to know what might be going to happen, stopped screaming and went very white. Her eyes ticked to the left.

"Expecting somebody?" said Matt.

"Salerno's going to be here any minute," Trina said. "He wants more money for all the work he's done for Daddy."

"He's going to get more than he bargained for if he shows up here," said Howie. "That two-bit buffoon doesn't scare me."

"Be scared," said Matt. "If not for yourself, then for Shawn. Remember he's sleeping upstairs."

"Shawn, yes," Howie said. "Poor Shawn. To be his age and to be exposed to such violence, that can scar a boy badly . . . the helplessness a boy feels at that age, it can turn him into something completely different from what he was destined to be."

Matt said, "This isn't the time for sad stories, Howie. I'm taking my son and getting out of here. Then I'm going to the police."

"Daddy, you can't let him do that!"

"And why not?"

"Because it's still not too late. You and me and Shawn, we can take your plane and fly to Mexico. We can go tonight. The police won't have anything on either of us if we just get rid of Matt."

Howie seemed to consider this. "I suppose that's one possibility. It would hurt Shawn, of course, to lose his father, but at this point, things have been set in motion that will hurt him terribly no matter what I do."

Trina swiped at her eyes and nodded. "Do it, Daddy. The two of us together can come up with a story for the police. You're a respected man in the community. Matt's an ex-con already suspected in Barry's murder. We can do it, Daddy. We can pull this off. All we need to do is get rid of Matt."

Appalled, Matt realized Howie might be desperate enough to believe her. "Jesus, Howie, whether you kill me or not, even if you fly to the end of the world, you won't get away with this. Even if Salerno and Baines don't cop a plea by fingering you—and they will, believe me—the police will figure it out. I wouldn't put so much faith in Trina here, either. Anybody cold-blooded enough to kill her own sister wouldn't hesitate to roll on her father."

"He's just trying to confuse you, Daddy," said Trina. "I'd never betray you."

"Yes, you would." Howie said calmly, "I have to agree with Matt on that. I think you'll do anything you have to, including betraying me or anybody else, if it means saving your own neck."

He shook his head and sat down heavily on the sofa. "I truly believed that, after what happened to my mother, nothing could ever really hurt me again. That if I survived watching her being brutalized, I could survive anything. But I was so wrong." He looked down at the gun, then at Trina. "I can't stand to look at you, but I still love you. And at the same time, a part of me knows you don't deserve to live."

Trina stood up quickly. "No, Daddy, you wouldn't hurt me."

"But I might—I might even kill you—so that doesn't leave me much choice, does it?" said Howie. He raised the gun. "We're both guilty of terrible things. You or me. Which one of us will it be?"

"Daddy, what are you talking about? You aren't going to shoot either of us. That's crazy!" She turned to Matt. "Stop him, Matt! Do something."

"Get out of here, Matt," said Howie calmly. "Go upstairs and get Shawn and take him out of here. Let Trina make up her mind."

"Matt, make him stop!"

"She's right, Howie, put the gun down."

"Your call, Trina. You or me?"

Trina's eyes brimmed with tears. "All right, Daddy, *me*! I'm the one who killed Calla, so kill *me*! All right? Is that what you want me to say? Kill *me!*"

Howie nodded. "Thank you. Thank you, Trina, for that much."

He put the gun to his head and pulled the trigger. Trina dropped to her knees with a wail. The sound of the gunshot reverberated through the house. Matt grabbed Trina, who put up no resistance as he folded her arms behind her back and cuffed her with the handcuffs he'd taken from the dungeon at her house.

Then he raced upstairs to get Shawn.

Moments later he came bolting back down the stairs to find Trina still on her knees beside Howie, weeping bitterly. "Shawn's not up there! Where the hell is he?"

She ignored him. He shook her till her head snapped back and forth and shouted in her face, "Where's Shawn?"

"He's *here*, I told you before."

"No, he isn't."

She shrugged. "I don't know. Maybe he got scared and ran off."

Matt grabbed the cordless phone to dial the police, but it rang in his hand before he could punch in 9-1-1. He answered it.

A voice, silky soft and reptilian said, "You know what's wrong with you, Engstrom, you're one of those fuckups don't finish what they start. You make a mess and leave it for somebody else to clean up."

"Salerno?"

"I can't say I'm too sorry about what you did to old Baines, but see, you left him alive, which was stupid. Never leave anybody alive, Engstrom. That's the mistake that we made with you."

"What the hell do you want?"

"I got your kid."

"What? How?"

"Don't matter how. Just don't call the cops, and you'll get him back in one piece."

Matt said, "I don't believe you. Let me talk to him."

Salerno said, "Put the old man on the phone. He's the one I wanna do business with."

Matt's mind raced. "I can't. He's not here. He went out looking for Shawn."

"And his psycho-bitch daughter?"

"She went with him."

"Well, go fuckin' find the old man. Tell him I want that plane of his, juiced up and ready to go for a long trip, and I want a pilot who knows what he's doing. I want a million dollars in cash. I'll have the boy with me the whole time. When we get where we're going, if nobody gives me any trouble, I'll let him go."

Matt said, "I think this is bullshit. I don't believe you have Shawn. Let me talk to him."

"You wanna talk to him?"

"Or you don't get a plane or a fuckin' dime."

"Hold on."

There was whispering, then Shawn came on the phone, sniffling and fighting back tears. "Dad, I'm sorry, Dad, I—"

His heart sank. He felt like somebody'd fired a bullet into his back. "Shawn, are you okay?"

"Uh, sort of, yeah. The plane he wants, can you get it?"

Matt swallowed hard, tried to keep his voice steady. "Your granddad can get one, sure."

"Dad, I'm—I'm so scared. I—"

"I know, Shawn, just—"

"—can you—"

"—hang in there and—"

"—find Uncle Coop at work? He's not drinking anymore. He could fly the plane."

"Uh, sure, yeah. Okay."

Then Salerno again. "That's enough fucking chit-chat, get the plane ready, get the money ready. I'll call you from where I'm at to make further arrangements."

He hung up.

Matt stared at the phone. *Uncle* Coop? Find him *at work*? Have Uncle Coop fly the plane?

"Trina, where does Howie keep his guns?"

She had slumped onto her side on the floor, one shoulder pressed into the spreading pool of Howie's blood, sobbing softly.

Matt grabbed her. "Listen to me! I need a gun. Where does Howie keep them?"

A trace of cunning came back into her eyes as she said, "There's a gun on the floor in front of you. Take it."

"Yeah, and put my fingerprints all over the gun Howie just used to shoot himself. I don't think so, Trina. You told me once that Howie keeps guns in his library. Where? Where exactly does he keep them?"

She shut her eyes.

He shook her again, almost screaming now. "Don't you get it! That was Salerno! He's got Shawn!"

She blinked stupidly. "How? Where? That's not possible."

"I think they're at the Bledsoe-Tull job site. But I can't go over there without a gun. You once said Howie hid his guns inside fake books—*which* books? Where does he keep them?"

"Give me a minute to think."

"Where?"

She spat in his face.

He flung her away from him and forced himself to stay calm while he rushed back upstairs and methodically tore apart Howie's library, sweeping whole shelves of books onto the floor. Thank God this was one thing Trina hadn't lied about—he found it on the fourth shelf of the cabinet behind the desk. A loaded black snub-nose .38 semiautomatic.

Howie had hidden it in a hollow facsimile of a motel room Gideon's Bible.

Chapter Thirty-eight

On the Harley, he made it to the job site in just ten minutes, cruised past once, then parked a couple of blocks away and approached on foot.

The hydraulic man-lift, a towering crane used to hoist the crew up the side of the building, was standing next to the west wall. He crouched behind it, scanning the densely overlapping shades of blackness for any sign of movement. To all appearances, the darkened construction site appeared deserted, but he knew that Salerno and Shawn could be anywhere—in the trailer or up on one of the partially completed floors. He started to pull out the .38, then realized that in the darkness, he could just as easily hit Shawn as Salerno, and he put the gun away. At least he had the advantage of surprise—Salerno couldn't know that Shawn had tipped him off to their location, unless of course, he'd already gotten jittery and decided to go elsewhere.

The logical place for Salerno to be holed up, of course—assuming you could expect logic from a homicidal sexual sadist—was inside the trailer, which sat kitty-corner to Tull Street on the north end of the block, and he set off in that general direction, then froze when his foot came down on—something; bolts or screws that the men had left lying around. He lifted his foot instantly, but in the surrounding silence the sound of metal rolling across concrete seemed like an explosion.

He tried to visualize the floor of the building, of the parking garage actually, as it had looked in daylight the last time he was here, but the hodgepodge of items scattered around, tools, piled lumber, angle iron, and God only knew what else, changed by the hour. Most of the tools were locked up in the gang boxes at night, but that didn't mean there wasn't a helluva lot of stuff left lying around on the ground to trip over, kick, or get snagged in.

His foot bumped something heavy. Reaching down, he found a forgotten spud wrench—sixteen inches of iron with a vicious spike at one end that was used for lining up holes in the I-beams—and he thanked God for somebody's irresponsibility.

After interminable minutes of picking his way around tools and equipment in the dark, he was able to make out the trailer a few dozen yards ahead, its boxy shape flanked by portable toilets and the weird, insectile silhouette of a crane looming overhead like a rendition of a preying mantis by some artist with a mechanical bent. To approach it from the open seemed foolhardy, but maybe if he came around behind the crane . . .

The shoring under the stairwell provided good cover, so he simply observed the trailer for a moment, looking for signs of anyone inside. No light on. No noise. If Shawn and Salerno were in there, they were holed up in darkness.

Time to get going. He crept from behind the shoring and had begun to move at an angle toward the crane when a noise halted him. Coming from the left, toward Tull Street. A scraping sound followed by the thud of something heavy being dropped into place. He peered from behind a beam and saw the outline of a man that, to judge from the breadth of the shoulders and narrowness of the hips had to be Salerno, standing in front of the looming dark rectangle of the halogen lights, looking down into the storm drain.

Normally, the drain was covered with a metal grid, but if guys had gone down there for some reason and were planning to return, they would have covered it with a lighter grid made out of wooden slats that was easier to remove. The drain was close to eight feet deep and, depending on how much rain had fallen, contained anywhere from a foot to five feet or more of water. A nasty, dangerous place. All Matt could think of was that Shawn might be down there.

Stuffing the spud wrench under his belt, he gripped the .38 with both hands. "Hold it right there! Hands up! Don't move!"

And for just the briefest of eye blinks, it looked like perhaps the command was going to be obeyed. Salerno froze, hands starting to go skyward, before he dropped, rolled, came up with the gun he'd taken from Matt earlier in his hand, and fired back. The bullet whined past, struck the column of red iron behind Matt and ricocheted off with a banshee-screech of metal on metal.

Then silence deeper than before as his deafened eardrums throbbed from the shock of the gunfire.

For a second he lost all track of Salerno. Then he heard footfalls clattering up the central stairway of what would be the building's atrium. Salerno, making no effort at stealth now, running up the stairs alone—unless he'd scooped up Shawn somewhere in the dark at the foot of the stairs and was carrying him, which seemed unlikely. What seemed more probable to Matt was that he'd dumped Shawn down the storm drain.

Instead of pursuing Salerno, he ran to the storm drain with its wooden covering, and began to pull it aside. "Shawn! Are you there?" No answer. He had almost removed the cover when a bullet struck the metal casing of the halogen lights to his left—Salerno, firing down at him from the stairs. If Shawn was in the storm drain, he could easily be hit.

Another bullet missed him, but struck the wood slats over the drain. He felt half a dozen sharp pricks as wood splinters pierced his shoulder and arm.

There was no time to investigate the drain. Whether Shawn was in there or not, the only way to save him was to take out Salerno first. Gun in hand, he ran toward the stairs, only to take an excruciating whack on the shin from what felt like an iron bar protruding up in the dark. Biting back a bellow of pain, he stuck his hand out and touched the top of the bar—found it was what he expected, an uncapped rebar sticking up out of the concrete. Gingerly he moved his hand to the left and found another one uncapped—and another. There was a whole row of them here underneath the stairwell. He made a mental note of the rebars' location. If he could surprise Salerno on the stairs and knock him backward, the uncapped rebars would do the rest.

Starting up the stairwell, he wanted to call out for Shawn, but that would expose his position and raise the odds on his getting hit. Then another bullet zipped past him, closer than the last, and he realized the odds were already too damn good as it was.

As he climbed, the sound of Salerno's footfalls on the metal stairs receded and stopped. A dull, cottony silence filled up the space the noise of the bullets had carved out in his head. He heard nothing as he continued on up.

The silence, however, was short-lived. Nails or screws were underfoot on the stairs. His feet hit them, and they rolled with a metallic clatter that seemed to boom through the night like a wrecking ball smacking steel.

He froze, waited for more gunfire. Then, when nothing happened, he continued to climb, past the first landing and on up to the second, where, looking up, he could just make out the square cab of the scissors hoist overlapping the top of the third-floor retaining wall.

He tried to concentrate, but his mind kept going back to the storm drain, imagining Shawn bound and gagged in water that, if he were injured or unconscious, would easily be deep enough to drown in. Maybe he should go back downstairs. Maybe . . .

Then came an explosion of noise, a violent clanging

and banging and the roar of something big and metallic *in motion* that assaulted his senses as the object hurtled out of the darkness above—one of the gang boxes pushed from above and crashing into the stairwell. It banged into the wall, then came screeching down the stairs *right at him.* He flung himself over the stair rail and clung there, sickened as he realized he'd dropped the .38, the impact of its fall to the concrete below drowned out by the roar of the gang box as it thundered past, caroming from wall to railing to wall. It finally stopped on the landing below, wedged on its side between the wall and the railing, upper wheels spinning.

He swung himself back onto the stairs, praying Salerno didn't realize he was unarmed now. The spud wrench was still under his belt where he'd stuck it earlier. He grabbed it and continued on up to the third floor, muscles tensed to dodge the next thing Salerno might find to push down the stairwell.

Then he was on the third floor, where he could see the outline of the scissors hoist more clearly, heard the scrape of feet on the concrete; he whirled and jumped to the side, but the bullet was faster and struck him with an impact like a linebacker coming full throttle up the field. He was powered backward with a *whoomp.* He staggered and fell into the cab of the hoist—he didn't feel like he'd been shot with a bullet, but with some kind of arrow, the shaft ripping the meat off his ribs—and then Salerno loomed over him, getting ready to fire an execution-style shot. But he wasn't expecting the spud wrench, which drove through the flesh under his collarbone with a wet thunk. At the impact, Salerno's arm came up automatically, dropping the gun, which flew over the side of the hoist into the dark. Matt yanked the wrench out and tried to bury the point in Salerno's gut, but pain didn't slow the guy down at all, and he kicked it aside. Then he was on Matt, not bothering with the sophisticated stuff he'd used in the Luxor, but doling out brute punishment with his fists and elbows and knees.

The blows came relentlessly; it was like being buried under an avalanche of bricks, and Matt remembered that the scissors hoist could only hold about two hundred fifty pounds—he and Salerno combined must weigh close to twice that.

He kicked against the side of the cab, pushing himself backward, rolling, wriggling, anything to get the two of them out into the hoist part of the machine. He was bleeding, and the blood made him slippery, harder to hold as Salerno's hands found his throat. Putting his weight on his elbows, Matt snapped the crown of his head forward. The blow smashed Salerno's nose sideways, stunning him for a second as Matt scuttled backward to the tip of the hoist. Salerno, blood fountaining out of his nose, continued to rain down blows, only a few of which Matt was able to block and fewer still to return.

He thought of the rebars underneath the stairwell and wondered if he'd be able to throw himself clear if the hoist went over. He wasn't sure, but at least if anybody got impaled, there was a fifty-fifty chance it'd be Salerno.

Under their thrashing bodies, the hoist groaned and started to lean. Matt threw all his weight to the back. The hoist shuddered, almost went over before righting itself. Salerno looked up, suddenly realizing what was happening—the big machine tilted again and tipped, then toppled like a felled tree toward the ground.

Matt waited till the last minute and jumped, clearing the rebars but landing so hard on the concrete floor that the blackness in the building was lit up with neon-edged stars. He tried to get up, but his left ankle wasn't working right, bones inside crunching and grinding. He crawled toward the wall, scrabbling with his hands for either of the dropped guns. He hobbled as far as the wall and sagged against it, blood pumping between his fingers as he clutched his side and looked around for Salerno, praying he'd fallen onto the rebars.

Instead what he heard were Salerno's boots on the

stairs up above him, realized the bastard must have managed to grab hold of the railing as the hoist fell and had pulled himself back to safety. Desperately, he looked around for a weapon. Saw the canisters of oxygen and acetylene a few feet away and crawled toward them.

Salerno was on the first-floor landing. Not hurrying now, but taking his time to look around and spot Matt on the floor by the canisters, talking as he approached, his voice velvet-covered steel as he said, "You and the kid are fucked, Engstrom. I know the old man offed himself. It didn't feel right when I called De-Grove's house, and you're all by yourself—the old man's not there, Trina's not there—so I called the house again five minutes later and, guess what, little Trina tells me you got her handcuffed—which she's loving, no doubt—but in spite of the fun and games, she still managed to get to the phone to give me the bad news about Daddy. Guess that means no airplane and no million bucks. Guess that means I grabbed a fucking kid who ain't worth squat."

"Where is he? What'd you do with him?"

"You'd a known where he was, you could'a touched him," laughed Salerno. "Probab'ly better you didn't, though."

"Trina and Baines will rat you out, you know that. They'll say you did it all." As he spoke, he quietly released the safety chain on the acetylene canister and turned it on its side. "Be better for you if you gave them up first and cut a deal." Groping now for something, anything, to use to smash the canister.

"Little Trina's probably on her way to some banana republic without an extradition treaty," Salerno said. "Her kind of money, she can buy herself respectability anywhere she goes. And Baines, he's been excess baggage for a long time now—whoops, what's this?"

He stopped, reached down, picked something up. When he straightened, he was holding the gun he'd dropped when Matt stabbed him with the spud wrench. "Well, look'a here what I found."

"The cops'll catch up to both of you," Matt said.

"I'll take my chances."

The floor was covered with debris. Matt found a piece of off-fall from the angle iron, an L-shaped hunk of steel just about the right size for his fist.

Salerno was only a few yards away now. "I'm pissed, Engstrom. I am so fucking pissed that I may not kill you with the first shot. Hell, I may not even shoot you. Maybe I'll beat you to death before I take care of the kid."

"Where is he? What've you done with him?"

"What'd you care? You're gonna be dead in a few minutes anyway."

Closer now, the boots clunking solidly into the concrete as Salerno approached.

Matt slammed the angle iron down on the valve of the canister. Nothing happened, but Salerno stopped, momentarily confused by the sound. He whacked the valve again, and this time it broke cleanly. Like a missile, the canister took off. It slammed into Salerno's chest, where it gouged a gaping hole before exiting through the back of his body, then took out a chunk of the concrete wall before imbedding itself in the metal shoring a few yards farther on. What was left of Salerno's body slithered to the floor.

Matt crawled to a squatting position and got to his feet. Waited till the wave of dizziness had passed and started hobbling in the direction of the storm drain.

He had barely covered half the distance to the drain, however, before he heard footsteps and the sound of someone breathing rapidly in the darkness up ahead. Sure that it was Shawn, he called out to him.

But it was Trina who answered. "You killed my father, Matt. You're responsible for his death." She was standing behind the stairwell, holding the gun he'd dropped in his fight with Salerno, the one Salerno had found and then dropped as well, when he died.

"Trina, how did you—"

"Those handcuffs you took from my house, they look like the real thing and they click shut like the

real thing, but they don't really lock. I had a locksmith
fix them so nobody could ever hold me against my
will." She gave a little giggle, high and loopy. "You
can't be too careful, you know. Sometimes rough sex
gets out of hand."

"So you're going to shoot me, Trina? What's that
going to solve?"

"If you hadn't meddled where you weren't supposed to, Daddy would still be alive."

"If it makes you feel better to believe that, Trina,
fine. Believe it. But put the gun away. Salerno's done
something to Shawn. We've got to find him."

"Shawn can wait."

"I think Salerno dumped him down the storm
drain." He turned and moved a couple of feet toward
her, gritting his teeth against what felt like barbed
wire rolling around inside his rib cage. She squeezed
off a shot directly over his head, and he stopped.

"I'm a pretty good shot, Matt, but don't test me.
Tests make me nervous."

"Trina, why are you doing this?"

"Because you killed Daddy."

"What the fuck are you talking about? He *shot*
himself."

Her voice was smooth and flat, lacking even the
slightest trace of irony. "If you hadn't showed him
that tape of me and Calla, he'd still be alive."

"And if you weren't a fucking psycho, Calla and
your dad would *both* still be alive, not to mention the
people your father destroyed in order to try to destroy
me. And if you care at all about Shawn, you'll put the
gun away and fucking help me find him."

"I'll look for Shawn later." She said it absently, like
she was adding *look for Shawn* on some mental To
Do list. Then, quickly, she added, "After I get rid
of you."

"Why'd you kill her, Trina? Why kill Calla?"

She gave a loud, exasperated sigh. "Oh, Christ,
you're so predictable. I knew you'd ask me that. I

knew if I didn't put a bullet down your throat the second I saw you, you'd be asking me that question."

"You were right."

"And you're expecting some convoluted tale of How Little Trina Got All Fucked Up, something with abuse and incest and perversion up the ass, but I don't think there *was* any. Unless you're like that shrink I heard one time talk about the violence of silence. Daddy was silent. He kept secrets. He kept everything inside. But that isn't why I killed Calla. I did it for the same reason some men do that kind of thing, Matt. To see what it would feel like and because I could."

She glanced in the direction of Salerno's body. "You know why I've got more balls than he did? Because he always fantasized about killing women, he *wanted* to, that was what the whole choking deal was about for him, but he never had the guts. Baines killed Cindee—he told me about it. And Baines followed your little girlfriend home from the motel and left the coral snake at her house. Salerno, his sex life was like his wrestling. The moves looked good and they looked real, and God knows half the time they *felt* real, but when you got right down to it, it was all a fucking act. All smoke and mirrors with a big dick thrown in for a bonus. Not Trina, though. When Trina did it, it was for real."

As she talked she took a couple of steps closer, then seemed to realize the jeopardy she put herself in by approaching him and halted. Gun steady as an extension of her hand.

"I'm sorry, Matt. I hate to do this, but it's your fault. All your fucking fault." She sighed again, more softly this time. "Baby, you should'a fucked me when you had the chance."

This time he knew she wasn't going to miss.

"Tough luck, Matt. I always—"

She winced as a blinding light flooded the building, illuminating everything with the garish, preternatural clarity of a hundred Fourth of July fireworks displays. He could see Trina clearly, like she was lit up in neon;

she couldn't see him because she was facing the light, but she fired anyway, and the bullet went wild, ricocheting off the beams of red iron over their heads.

Before she could shoot again, he had her on the ground, pinned underneath him, wrenching the gun out of her hand. Red splotches dotted her clothes, and he realized his blood was dripping onto her.

Then he saw Coop staggering from behind the big halogens, soaked to the skin, half his face covered in blood, his mouth mushy-looking where some teeth were missing.

"Jesus, Matt, I thought she had you for sure. When that bomb went off just now, I must'a come around then, and the grate was half off over the drain so I crawled up. Heard her talking. It's that crazy ex-sister-in-law of yours, ain't it?"

"Go to hell," Trina hissed.

"I expect to," Coop said evenly, "but I got a feeling you'll be there to meet me."

"Hang on to her," said Matt, "and shoot her if she moves. I've got to find Shawn."

They started yelling Shawn's name. Matt was just about to go call the cops from the trailer, when Coop said, "The master key to the gang boxes—it's not in my pocket."

"What master key?"

"Well, it wasn't exactly *the* master key, it was a copy I made after you fired me, 'case I forgot some of my tools and had to come back and get 'em. Now it's gone."

Matt looked toward the stairwell, where the gang box that had crashed still rested on its side. *Only a few inches away from you . . .* "Hurry up, help me open this." He grabbed a wrench and started prying off the lock.

When he opened the top, Shawn lay inside, bound and gagged. One leg was twisted awkwardly underneath him, and blood seeped from his scalp. He didn't move.

Chapter Thirty-nine

Matt stood at the edge of Resurrection Cemetery, hands in the pockets of his denim jacket, staring out over a broad, flawless green lawn dotted with gravestones. The day was cool and dazzlingly sunny, and he could smell the faint perfume of flowers. There were tears in his eyes.

Finally he began to walk down the slight slope toward the marble mausoleum that rose imposingly in one corner of the cemetery. He limped slightly, a condition that the doctors at Sisters of Mercy Hospital had told him was temporary. The shoulder wound would heal faster, they said, but might hurt a lot longer.

Just outside the mausoleum, he stopped. He could've gone inside to view the new vault, but couldn't bring himself to do so. Just being here at all was difficult enough. He'd tried not to be bitter about everything that had happened—he'd talked with a priest, read a couple of books that dealt with grief and acceptance, even seen a therapist a couple of times— but still a cold, inebriating anger sometimes overwhelmed him, made him feel like blood vessels in his head were going to explode. So much stupid waste, so many lives lost because of one old man's obsession, one young woman's psychosis.

At times he even hated Howie for being dead, because that robbed him of the possibility for vengeance.

"Dad, aren't you coming inside?" Shawn came outside, minus the arrangement of flowers he'd been carrying when he went in a few minutes earlier. His eyes were puffy, and he looked pale and exhausted. Not surprising, since he'd only been released from the hospital the day before. He'd been lucky, the doctor had said, as if Matt needed to be reminded. He'd suffered a concussion, contusions on his shoulder and leg, and a broken left wrist, but nothing nearly as serious as had originally been feared.

Remembering that, Matt felt his chest loosen up and the bitterness draining away. Funny how gratitude could do that.

"I don't think I'm up to going inside, son. I'd really rather stay out here. Get some air."

Shawn nodded. Both he and Matt had still been in the hospital when Howie was buried. Trina had been allowed to attend the funeral before being returned to jail to await her trial. The funeral had been very private and, Matt was told, rather sparsely attended. But once he was out of the hospital, Shawn had wanted to visit the vault where Howie's ashes were interred alongside Calla's.

"There're some fresh flowers at Mom's vault, too," Shawn said. "I guess Aunt Trina must'a brought 'em when she was here for Granddad's funeral."

"Maybe so," said Matt, although he knew the flowers were probably the ones he'd ordered sent out from the florist a couple of days before.

Shawn cleared his throat, then asked it again, the same question that kept coming up, that he couldn't seem to get past. "Do you think it's true, Dad, what the papers are saying about Aunt Trina? Did she really kill Mom?"

"I don't know, Shawn."

"You didn't really *see* her kill Mom on that tape, though, did you?"

"No, I just saw—bits and pieces of things—it's hard to tell what I saw."

"And they fake that stuff, you know. Like in the movies. Nobody really gets hurt."

"Yeah, sometimes it works like that."

He didn't want to outright lie to Shawn, but couldn't bear to tell him the full truth, either. Nor did he wish to remind him that faked violence doesn't produce real death. But Shawn kept asking the same questions, over and over. Had Howie really done all those terrible things? Was Aunt Trina really a murderer? Did violence run in families? Was craziness inherited?

They were horrible, heartbreaking questions that Matt didn't really know how to answer.

The papers had turned the whole tragedy into a three-ring circus, of course—multimillionaire hotel magnate kills himself, daughter charged with sister's slaying, the infamous "snuff" tape that was now in the hands of the police. He could only hope that by the time Shawn went back to school, the worst of the sensationalism would have died down.

Shawn sniffled and looked away, trying to be stoic. "I miss Granddad. I miss Aunt Trina, too, but at least she's not dead. And Granddad committed a mortal sin when he killed himself. Now he can't get into Heaven, can he?"

"I don't know, Shawn. Maybe God understands people like Granddad and forgives them. Maybe somewhere in time he'll get another chance. I just don't know how it works. I do know this, though, you need to forgive your granddad for what he did and Aunt Trina, too."

"But what if it's true, that she murdered Mom? How can I ever forgive *that*?"

Good question, thought Matt. But he remembered what Zeke Petrovsky had said to him that day in the alley behind the convenience store and told Shawn, "Whatever Howie did or Trina did, it's up to God to deal with them, and He will. Our job is to let go of it and leave it to God."

"I know," said Shawn. "You've told me that before. I'll try."

They started back toward where Matt had parked the truck. Matt holding Shawn's hand in one of his and with the other, feeling the envelope that he'd folded three ways and stuffed into his jacket pocket when it was delivered by registered mail that morning. The test results from the hospital. They'd finally come, but he hadn't been able to bring himself to open the letter.

Hard to say was the oh-so-precise and technical answer given by the doctor at the clinic when Matt had asked what the odds were that he'd contracted HIV from Noel. There were people who had unprotected sex with infected partners every day and never contracted the disease. And there were people who had sex one time and got it.

As soon as we get home, Matt thought. *I'll go out in the garage and open it, and I'll find out the truth. Whether it's good news or bad news, at least I'll know. But please, God, let it be good news.*

Unexpectedly, Shawn squeezed his hand. "It's gonna be okay, Dad, whatever happens. Even without Granddad and Aunt Trina. I know it is. It's gonna be okay."

ONYX

Tom Savage

"A thriller with heart...no one is safe."
—Lorenzo Carcaterra, author of *Sleepers*

VALENTINE

Now A Major Motion Picture

Jillian Talbot has it all: a beautiful home in New York's
Greenwich Village, a string of bestselling suspense novels, a handsome and
adoring lover.

She has something else, too. A silent stalker. A secret
admirer who sends her pink, heart-shaped messages—with an unmistakable
warning in blood-red letters.

A killer has invaded her privileged sanctuary. He will
imprison her in a nightmare more real than the fiction she creates. And, as the
price mounts ever higher for a crime that Jill had once committed but only her
nemesis can remember, he will meet her at last at the hour of his triumph.

Her judgment day.

❏ 0-451-40978-7 / $7.50